New York Times Bestseller
Indie Next Selection
Library Reads Selection
Great Group Reads Selection
Amazon Best of the Month Editors' Pick
Barnes and Noble Best New Fiction Recommendation

"See is one of those special writers capable of delivering both poetry and plot."

—*The New York Times Book Review*

"A lush tale infused with clear-eyed compassion, this novel will inspire reflection, discussion, and an overwhelming desire to drink rare Chinese tea."

—*The Washington Post*

"Lisa See is a confident, lyrical, smart, impeccably researched writer. . . . [*The Tea Girl of Hummingbird Lane* is] both unique and a universal story of motherhood."

—*Los Angeles Review of Books*

"Fans of the bestselling *Snow Flower and the Secret Fan* will find much to admire in *The Tea Girl of Hummingbird Lane*, as both books closely illuminate stories of women's struggles and solidarity in minority-ethnic and rural Chinese cultures. . . . In rendering the complex pain and joy of the mother-daughter bond, Lisa See makes this novel—dedicated to her own mother, author Carolyn See, who died last year—a deeply emotional and satisfying read."

—*USA Today*

"An alluring escape, a satisfying and vivid fable that uses an Akha belief to tap into our own longings for coincidence."

—*San Francisco Chronicle*

"Lisa See transports readers to the remote mountains of China. . . . Come for the heartwarming bonding between mother and daughter; stay for the insight into Akha culture and the fascinating (really) history of the tea trade."

—*Real Simple*

"With strong female characters, See deftly confronts the changing role of minority women, majority-minority relations, East-West adoption, and the economy of tea in modern China. Fans of See's *Snow Flower and the Secret Fan* will appreciate this novel."

—*Library Journal*

"With vivid and precise details about tea and life in rural China, Li-yan's gripping journey to find her daughter comes alive."

—*Publishers Weekly*

"A riveting exercise in fictional anthropology."

—*Kirkus Reviews*

BY LISA SEE

China Dolls
Dreams of Joy
Shanghai Girls
Peony in Love
Snow Flower and the Secret Fan
Dragon Bones
The Interior
Flower Net
On Gold Mountain

THE TEA GIRL OF HUMMINGBIRD LANE

A NOVEL

LISA SEE

SCRIBNER
New York London Toronto Sydney New Delhi

Scribner
An Imprint of Simon & Schuster, Inc.
1230 Avenue of the Americas
New York, NY 10020

This book is a work of fiction. Any references to historical events, real people, or real places are used fictitiously. Other names, characters, places, and events are products of the author's imagination, and any resemblance to actual events or places or persons, living or dead, is entirely coincidental.

First Scribner trade paperback edition April 2018

Manufactured in the United States of America

1 3 5 7 9 10 8 6 4 2

Library of Congress Cataloging-in-Publication Data is available.

ISBN 978-1-5011-5482-9
ISBN 978-1-5011-5483-6 (pbk)
ISBN 978-1-5011-5484-3 (ebook)

In memory of my mother,
Carolyn See

THE TEA GIRL OF HUMMINGBIRD LANE

AUTHOR'S NOTE

When the novel starts, in 1988, tea leaves picked in the mountains of Yunnan sold for 4 yuan a kilo (approximately 50 cents U.S. in today's money). The yearly income for tea farmers averaged 200 yuan (around $25 U.S.) a month.

Please note there are different spellings and pronunciations for the dark tea category known as *Pu'er*: *Pu'erh,* according to the Wades-Giles system of transliteration of Chinese devised by missionaries in the nineteenth century; *Puerh* in Taiwan; *Pu'er* in the People's Republic of China's pinyin system, which was officially adopted by the United Nations in 1986; and *Ponay* or *Bonay* in Cantonese.

When a son is born,
Let him sleep on the bed,
Clothe him with fine clothes,
And give him jade to play . . .
When a daughter is born,
Let her sleep on the ground,
Wrap her in common wrappings,
And give her broken tiles to play . . .

Book of Songs (1000–700 B.C.)

PART I

THE AKHA WAY

1988–1990

A DOG ON THE ROOF

"*No coincidence, no story,*" my a-ma recites, and that seems to settle everything, as it usually does, after First Brother finishes telling us about the dream he had last night. I don't know how many times my mother has used this praising aphorism during the ten years I've been on this earth. I also feel as though I've heard versions of First Brother's dream many times. A poor farmer carries freshly picked turnips to the market town to barter for salt. He takes a misstep and tumbles down a cliff. This could have ended in a "terrible death" far from home—the worst thing that can happen to an Akha person—but instead he lands in the camp of a wealthy salt seller. The salt seller brews tea, the two men start talking, and . . . The coincidence could have been anything: the salt seller will now marry the farmer's daughter or the farmer's fall protected him from being washed away in a flood. This time, the farmer was able to trade with the salt seller without having to walk all the way to the market town.

It was a good dream with no bad omens, which pleases everyone seated on the floor around the fire pit. As A-ma said, every story, every dream, every waking minute of our lives is filled with one fateful coincidence after another. People and animals and leaves and fire and rain—we whirl around each other like handfuls of dried rice kernels being tossed into the sky. A single kernel cannot change its direction. It cannot choose to fly to the right or to the left nor can it choose where it lands—balanced on a rock, and therefore salvageable, or bouncing off that same rock into the mud, becoming instantly useless and valueless. Where they alight is fate, and nothing—no *thing* anyway—can change their destinies.

Second Brother is next in line to tell his dream. It is ordinary. Third Brother recites his dream, which is worse than dull.

A-ba nudges me with his elbow. "Girl, tell us a dream you had last night."

"My dream?" The request surprises me, because neither of my parents has asked this of me before. I'm just a girl. Unimportant, as I've been told many times. Why A-ba has chosen this day to single me out, I don't know, but I hope to be worthy of the attention. "I was walking back to the village after picking tea. It was already dark. I could see smoke rising from household fires. The smell of the food should have made me hungry." (I'm always hungry.) "But my stomach, eyes, arms, and legs were all happy to know I was where I was supposed to be. Our ancestral home." I watch my family's faces. I want to be honest, but I can't alarm anyone with the truth.

"What else did you see?" A-ma asks. In our village, power and importance go in this order: the headman; the ruma—the spirit priest—who keeps harmony between spirits and humans; and the nima—the shaman—who has the ability to go into a trance, visit the trees God planted in the spirit world to represent each soul on earth, and then determine which incantations can be used to heal or enhance vitality. These men are followed next by all grandfathers, fathers, and males of any age. My mother is ranked first among women not only in our village but on the entire mountain. She is a midwife and so much more, treating men, women, and children as they pass through their lives. She's also known for her ability to interpret dreams. The silver balls that decorate her headdress tremble, catching the firelight, as she waits for my response. The others bend their heads over their bowls, nervous for me.

I force myself to speak. "I dreamed of a dog."

Everyone prickles at this revelation.

"We allow dogs to live among us for three reasons," A-ma says reassuringly, trying to settle the family. "They are essential for sacrifices, they alert us to bad omens, and they are good to eat. What kind was yours?"

I hesitate once again. The dog in my dream stood on our roof, alert, his snout pointed upward, his tail erect. To me, he looked as though he were guarding our village, and seeing him made me feel confident that I would make it home safely. But the Akha people believe . . .

A-ma gives me a stern look. "Dogs are not human, but they live in the human world. They are not of the spirit world, but they have the gift of seeing spirits. When you hear a dog howl or bark in the night, you know he has spotted a spirit and hopefully scared him away. Now answer me, Girl," she says, pushing her silver bracelets up her wrist. "What kind was yours?"

"The whole family was sitting outside when the dog began to bark," I say, when I know perfectly well that dreaming of a dog on the roof means that he hasn't done his job and that a spirit has sneaked past the protection of the village's spirit gate and is now roaming among us. "He frightened off an evil spirit. A-poe-mi-yeh rewarded him by giving everyone in our family a chicken to eat— "

"Our supreme god gave every man and woman his or her own chicken?" First Brother scoffs.

"And all the children too! Every single person had a whole chicken— "

"That's impossible! Meaningless! A fabrication!" First Brother looks at A-ba indignantly. "Make her stop— "

"So far I like her dream," A-ba says. "Go on, Girl."

The more pressure I feel to continue my story, the easier it becomes to lie. "I saw birds in a nest. The babies had just broken through their shells. The a-ma bird tapped each one gently with her beak. *Tap, tap, tap*."

A moment passes as my parents and brothers ponder this addition. As A-ma searches my face, I try to keep my expression as still as a bowl of soy milk left out overnight. Finally, she nods approvingly.

"Counting her babies. New lives. A protecting mother." She smiles. "All is good."

A-ba stands up, signaling that breakfast is done. I'm not sure what's more troublesome—that A-ma can't see everything inside my head as I always thought she could or that I've gotten away with my fabrications. I feel pretty terrible until I remind myself that I prevented my family from the worry my dream would have caused them. I lift my bowl to my lips and slurp down the last of my broth. A few bitter mountain leaves slip into my mouth along with the fiery liquid. Chili flakes burn their way to my stomach. For as long as that heat lasts, I'll feel full.

When we leave the house, stars still glitter above our heads. I carry a small basket on my back. My other family members have large baskets slung over their shoulders. Together we walk along the dirt lane that divides Spring Well Village, which has about forty households and nestles in one of the many saddles on Nannuo Mountain. Most of the homes are sheltered by old tea trees. The tea terraces and gardens where we work, however, are outside the village.

We join our neighbors, who live four houses away from us. The youngest daughter, Ci-teh, is my age. I could find my friend anywhere, because her cap is the most decorated of any girl's in Spring Well. In addition to tea, her family grows pumpkins, cabbages, sugarcane, and cotton. They also cultivate opium, which they sell to the spirit priest to use in ceremonies and to A-ma to use as a medicine for those suffering from the agony of broken bones, the torment of the wasting disease, or the mental anguish that comes from losing a loved one. The extra money Ci-teh's family earns means they can sacrifice more and larger animals for offerings, which in turn means that the customary shared cuts of meat that are given to everyone in the village are more and larger too. Ci-teh's family's wealth also means that her cap is decorated with lots of silver charms. Apart from these differences, Ci-teh and I are like sisters—maybe closer than sisters, because we spend so much time side by side.

As we continue toward our work, we leave the last house behind and proceed a little farther until we reach the spirit gate. Carved figures of a woman and a man are mounted on the posts. The woman has huge breasts. The man has a penis that is as thick as timber bamboo, longer than my entire height, and sticking straight out. Whittled birds of prey and vicious dogs hang from the crossbeam. *Be warned.* If someone doesn't pass through the gate properly—touching it perhaps—then something terrible can happen, like a death. We must all be mindful of the gate.

We begin to climb. Ci-teh and I chatter, catching up as though many weeks have passed instead of one night.

"I worked on my embroidery before bed," Ci-teh confides.

"I fell asleep before my a-ba had his pipe," I tell her.

"Hot water or tea with breakfast?"

"Tea."

"Dreams?"

I don't want to tell her any of that. We have a long way to go and the only other way to make the time pass quickly is through games and challenges.

"How many different parasites can you spot on the trees before we get to that boulder?" I hoot.

Nine, and I win.

"How are you doing with your weaving?" Ci-teh asks, knowing I haven't shown a talent for it.

"So boring!" I holler, and the men look back at me disapprovingly. "Let's see how many jumps it will take from this rock to that one way up there."

Seven, and I win again.

"Last night, Deh-ja"—that would be Ci-teh's sister-in-law—"said she wants to have a son."

"There's nothing new with that one." I point to a little rise. "Bet I can beat you to the top."

My feet know this route well, and I hop from rock to rock and jump over exposed roots. In places, the dirt is powdery between my toes. In other spots, pebbles poke at the soft underparts of my arches. Since it's still dark, I sense more than see the old tea, camphor, ginkgo, and cassia trees, as well as stands of bamboo, towering around me.

I win again, which nettles Ci-teh. But that happens between

sisters too. Ci-teh and I are close, but we compete against each other . . . constantly. I won our games today; she reminded me she's better at embroidery and weaving. Our teacher says I could prove I'm smart if I worked a little harder; he would never say that about Ci-teh.

"See you at the tea collection center," I say when Ci-teh follows her a-ma onto another path. I linger—watching them scramble up a steep stretch of mountain, their empty baskets bouncing on their backs—and then I skip ahead to catch up to A-ma.

After a half hour of walking, the black of night begins to fade and the sky turns pale. Clouds catch tints of pink and lavender. Then everything brightens when the sun crests the mountain. The cicadas waken and begin to trill. And still we climb. My a-ba and brothers maintain distance ahead of us so they can have their man talk. A-ma is as strong as any man, but she takes her time, looking about for herbs and mushrooms she can use in her potions. First Sister-in-law has stayed home with the children too young to pick tea and too big to be carried by their mothers, but my second and third sisters-in-law accompany us with their babies tied to their bosoms as they too forage, searching the moist forest floor for anything we might take home to put in our dinner soup.

We reach First Brother's tea terraces at last. I move slowly between the tightly packed rows of bushes, scanning the outermost branches for the bud and two, maybe three, leaves that begin to unfurl as the sun's rays warm them. I gently nip the tiny cluster between my thumbnail and the side of my forefinger above the first joint. My thumbnail is stained and the little pad of flesh callused. I'm already marked as a tea picker.

After two hours, A-ma comes to me. She runs her hands through my leaves, fluffing and inspecting them. "You're very good, Girl, at finding the choicest bud sets. Maybe too good." She glances in A-ba's direction a few terraces away, then leans down and whispers, "Pick a little faster. And you can take some of the older and tougher leaves. We need more leaves, not just ideal bud sets, from each bush."

I understand. More leaves means more money to be paid by the tea collection center. When my basket is full, I find First Brother, who transfers my pickings into a burlap sack, and the process begins again. We break for a lunch of rice balls rolled in dried moss, and then pick all through the afternoon. I stay close to my mother, who sings to keep us in the rhythm of picking and to remove our minds from the heat and humidity. Finally, A-ba calls, "Enough." We gather at the spot where First Brother has been consolidating our harvest. The last leaves are packed into burlap sacks. Then each sack is strung with ropes and a flat board. A-ma mounts the smallest one on my back, wraps the ropes over my shoulders, and secures the board on my forehead. All this is to help us carry the weight evenly, but the pull of the ropes on my shoulders and the press of the wood against my forehead are instantly painful.

Once the others have their sacks on their backs and our picking baskets have been bound together for us to retrieve on our way home, we begin the two-hour journey to the tea collection center. We're all aware we must hurry, but our pace can only be slow. One sure foot after another sure foot. We climb up and over more tea terraces, each one seemingly steeper than the last. And then we're back in the forest, which has engulfed forsaken tea tree groves and gardens. Vines wrap around the trunks, which have become homes to orchids, mushrooms, and parasites like crab's claw. How old are the trees? Five hundred years old? A thousand years old? I don't know the answers. What I do know is that selling leaves from them was abandoned long ago. Only families like ours use the leaves from trees like these for at-home drinking.

By the time we reach the tea collection center, I'm so tired I want to cry. We enter through big gates into a courtyard. My vision flits around the open space, looking for Ci-teh's distinctive cap. We Akha have our own style of dress. So too do the Dai, Lahu, Bulang, and the other tribes who live here with us. Everyone wears their work clothes, but every headdress, scarf, and cap is decorated, according to the traditions of that clan and the individual taste and style of each woman or girl. I don't spot Ci-teh. Her family must have come and gone already. They might even be home by now, eating their supper.

My stomach calls to me, aggravated yet entranced by the smells coming from the food vendor stalls. The perfume of skewered meat on an open flame fills my head. My mouth waters. One day I'll get to taste one of those. Maybe. Occasionally, we treat ourselves to scallion pancakes that an old Dai woman sells from a cart just to the left, inside the tea collection center courtyard. The aroma is enticing—not as rich as the grilled meat but cleanly fragrant with the smell of fresh eggs.

A-ma, my sisters-in-law, and I squat in the dirt as my a-ba and brothers take our bags through a set of double doors that lead to the weighing area. On the other side of the courtyard, I spot a boy about my age, lingering by a mountain of burlap bags filled with tea waiting to be transported to the big city of Menghai, where it'll be processed in a government-run factory. His hair is as black as my own. He too is barefoot. I don't recognize him from school. But I'm less interested in him as a person than I am in the steaming scallion pancake he holds in his tea-stained fingers. He looks around to make sure no one is watching—obviously missing me—before ducking out of sight behind the burlap mound. I get up, cross the courtyard, and peek around the corner of the wall of tea.

"What are you doing back there?" I ask.

He turns to me and grins. His cheeks are shiny with oil. Before he has a chance to speak, I hear A-ma calling.

"Girl! Girl! Stay near me."

I scurry back across the courtyard, reaching my mother just as A-ba and my brothers exit the weighing area. They don't look happy.

"We were too late," A-ba says. "They already bought their quota for the day."

I moan inwardly. We're a family of eight adults and many children. It's hard to live on what we earn during the ten days a year of prime tea picking, the two secondary picking times of another ten days each, plus what rice and vegetables we grow and what A-ba and my brothers provide through hunting. Now we'll have to take the leaves home, hope they stay fresh, and then tomorrow morning—early-early—climb back up here and sell them before rotating to Second Brother's tea garden to do our work for the day.

A-ma sighs. "Another double day tomorrow."

The sisters-in-law bite their lips. I'm not looking forward to walking here *twice* tomorrow either. But when my second and third brothers won't meet their wives' eyes, I realize even worse news is coming.

"No need," A-ba reveals. "I sold the leaves at half price."

That's only two yuan per kilo. The sound that comes from A-ma is not so much a groan as a whimper. *All that work at half price.* The two sisters-in-law slump off to a water spout to refill our earthenware jugs. The men drop to their haunches. My sisters-in-law return and give the water to the men. After that, the two women fold themselves down next to A-ma, adjust their babies in their swaddling, and give over their breasts for nursing. This is our rest before the more than two-hour walk downhill to Spring Well.

As the others relax, I wander back across the courtyard to the boy. "Are you going to tell me why you're hiding back here?" I ask as though no time has passed.

"I'm not hiding," he answers, although surely he is. "I'm eating my pancake. Do you want a bite?"

More than anything.

I glance over my shoulder to A-ma and the others. I'm not sure what's wrong with me, but whatever started with my lies at breakfast continues now. I step behind the wall of bags that smell of freshly harvested tea leaves. Once I'm back there, the boy doesn't seem sure of what should happen next. He doesn't break off a piece for me nor does he hold it out for me to take. But he offered me a bite, and I'm going to get it. I bend at the waist, sink my teeth into the softness of the pancake, and rip off a mouthful—like I'm a dog snatching a scrap from his master's hand.

"What's your name?" he asks.

"Li-yan," I answer, my mouth happily full. My given name is used only at school and for ceremonial purposes. In my village, people call me Daughter-of-Sha-li (my a-ba's daughter) or Daughter-of-So-sa (my a-ma's daughter). In my family, I am Girl.

"I'm called San-pa," he says. "I'm from Shelter Shadow Village.

My father is Lo-san. My grandfather was Bah-lo. My great-grandfather was Za-bah . . ."

Every Akha boy is trained to Recite the Lineage by naming his male ancestors back fifty generations—with the last syllable of one generation becoming the first syllable of the next generation. I think that's what's going to happen, when a woman's voice—angry—interrupts him. "Here you are, you little thief!"

I turn to see the old Dai woman who runs the pancake stand looming between us and the open courtyard. She grabs the cloth of my tunic. Then, with her other hand, she takes hold of San-pa's ear. He yowls as she drags us from our lair.

"Sun and Moon, look! Thieves!" Her voice cuts through the clatter of the courtyard. "Where are the parents of these two?"

A-ma looks in our direction and cocks her head in disbelief. Until today, I've never been a troublemaker. I never cross my legs around adults, I accept my parents' words as good medicine, and I always cover my mouth to hide my teeth when I smile or laugh. Maybe I colored my dream this morning, but I'm not a thief or a cheater in school. Unfortunately, the oily residue around my mouth shows that at the very least I ate some pancake, even if I didn't steal it from the Dai woman's cart.

A-ma and A-ba cross the courtyard. Seeing the confusion on their faces makes my cheeks burn red. I lower my eyes and focus on their callused feet as they talk to the vendor. Soon two other pairs of feet join us, taking spots on either side of San-pa: his parents.

"What is this all about?" A-ba's voice is polite and even. He can be gruff at home, but he's clearly trying to blow away the pancake seller's anger with his polite Akha ways.

"I've had trouble with this one before." The old woman gives San-pa's ear a yank. "As a thief, wherever he goes, may he be eaten by a tiger. If he passes by water, may he slip into its depths. When he walks under a tree, may it fall on him."

These are common, yet potent, curses, because they're hexing him to suffer a terrible death, but the boy beside me doesn't seem to care. He doesn't even cover his mouth to hide his grin.

The Dai woman regards my mother with sympathy. "Now it seems he's brought your daughter into his ring."

"Is this so, Girl?" A-ma asks. "Why would you do such a thing?"

I raise my eyes. "I didn't think I was doing anything wrong."

"Not wrong?" A-ma asks.

"He *gave* it to me. I didn't know it was stolen—"

Others crowd around us to see what's going on.

"Let's not allow this little girl to be blamed," the man I understand to be San-pa's a-ba says. "You've been in trouble in this very place before, Boy. Tell everyone the truth."

"I took it," San-pa admits, but it doesn't seem to cause him any pain. He's so matter-of-fact it's as though he's talking about rainfall or how many eggs the chickens laid last night.

"He offered me a bite," I chime in. "He wanted to share with me—"

But A-ma isn't interested in my excuses. "Now the world is out of balance for both children," she announces. "We follow Akha Law—"

"We adhere to Akha Law as well," San-pa's father states. "Every Akha on earth has a shared memory of what we can and cannot do—"

"Then we must perform cleansing ceremonies for these two children, our families, and our villages. The only question that remains is, will the ceremony be conducted with the children together or apart?" A-ma asks. A-ba is the head of our family, but A-ma, with her added status as midwife, conducts this negotiation. "The most propitious outcome would be if our two families could do it together." To strangers like these, her voice must sound as smooth and warm as my a-ba's during this confrontation—*this unpleasantness can be wiped away, and we can all be friends*—but I know her very well. What I hear is her disappointment in me and her concern for the situation. "May I ask on which day of the cycle your son was born?"

"San-pa was born on Tiger Day, the ninth day of the cycle," his mother answers, trying to be helpful.

My family members shift their weight from foot to foot in response to this regrettable information. We Akha follow a twelve-day week, with each day named for a different animal. I was born on Pig Day. The world knows that tigers and pigs should never marry, be friends, or farm together, because tigers like to eat pigs.

A-ma reveals the bad news. "This one was born on Pig Day. Separate purification ceremonies will be best." She courteously tips her head, causing the balls and coins on her headdress to jingle. Then she puts a hand on my shoulder. "Let us go home."

"Wait!" It's the pancake seller. "What about me? Who's going to pay me?"

San-pa's father reaches into an indigo satchel tied at his hip, but A-ba says, "A girl has only her reputation. As her father, I will pay the amount owed." He pulls out a couple of coins from the paltry sum we earned today and drops them into the Dai woman's hand.

I already felt bad. Now I feel awful. If Ci-teh had been here, I never would have gone behind that wall of tea, met San-pa, taken a bite of the pancake . . .

The Dai woman yanks San-pa's ear one more time. "Let me see you going but never coming back." It's another familiar, but haunting, curse that again hints at a terrible death. Fortunately, she does not say the same words to me. San-pa's parents begin to drag him away. He looks over his shoulder to give me one last grin. I can't help it. I smile right back.

That last spark of connection sustains me all the way home. My family is clearly irritated with my actions, and they say nothing to me in a very loud way. We stop only once—to pick up the baskets we left on First Brother's terraces. We arrive in Spring Well Village well past dark. The houses glow golden with open-hearth fires and oil lamps. When we step into our home, we're all hungry, and the smell of the steamed rice First Sister-in-law has made is almost painful to inhale. But we still don't get to eat. First Brother is sent outside to look for a chicken. Second Brother is given the job of pulling the ruma away from his evening pipe. Third Brother brushes a flat stone set into the hard-packed earth outside our door with the palm of his hand. A-ma sorts through her baskets, looking for herbs and roots, while First Sister-in-law stokes the fire. My young nieces and nephews gather around their a-mas' legs, peeping at me, their eyes wide.

Second Brother returns with the ruma, who wears his ceremonial cloak—which is heavily decorated with feathers, bones, and the tails of small animals—and carries a staff made from a dried stalk of tule root. He is our intermediary between the spirit world—whether inside spirits like our ancestors or outside spirits who bring malaria, steal the breath from newborns, or devour the hearts of beloved grandfathers—and the world of human beings in Spring Well. Tonight he's here for me.

My family gathers in the open area between the house and the newlywed huts, where my brothers sleep with their wives. First Brother holds the chicken by its legs. Its wings flap miserably, fruitlessly. The village elders—who lead us and care for us—step onto their verandas and descend the stairs. Soon other neighbors emerge from their homes and join us, because I'm not to be alone in my disgrace.

I see the blacksmith and his family, the best hunter and his family, Ci-teh and her parents, and Ci-teh's brother and his wife—Ci-do and Deh-ja—who sleep in the newlywed hut outside his parents' house. Ci-do has always been nice to me, and I like Deh-ja. The hair on Ci-do's face and scalp has grown long and unruly, because men must not shave or cut their hair once their wives are five months into their pregnancies. Our entire village is holding its collective breath—as it does every time a woman is pregnant—until Deh-ja's baby is born, when it can be determined whether it was a good birth, meaning a perfect baby boy or even a girl, and not a bad birth, marking the arrival of what we call a human reject.

The ruma's eyes bore into mine. He starts to shake, and the little pieces on his headdress and clothes rattle with him. My teeth chatter, I shiver, and I want to pee.

"A-ma Mata was the mother of humans and spirits," the ruma says in tones so quiet that we all must lean in to hear him. "*A-ma* means *mother* and *Mata* means *together*, and once upon a time man and spirits lived together in harmony. A-ma Mata had two breasts in front, where her human children could nurse. She had nine breasts on her back to nourish her spirit children. Humans always worked during the day, and spirits always worked at night. The water buffalo and the tiger, the chicken and the eagle, also lived together. But someone must always destroy paradise." He points to me with his staff. "What was the result?"

"Humans and spirits, water buffalo and tigers, and chickens and eagles needed to be separated," I recite nervously.

"Separated. Exactly," he says. "Since the decision to divide the universe happened during the day, men were first to pick in which realm they wanted to live. They chose the earth with its trees, mountains, fruit, and game. Spirits were given the sky, leaving them angry forever after. To this moment, they have retaliated by causing problems for humankind."

I've heard this story many times, but knowing that he's telling it on my behalf makes my heart hurt.

"In the wet season," he goes on, "spirits descend to earth with the rain, bringing with them disease and floods. In spring, as dry season begins, noise is made to encourage malevolent spirits to move on. But they don't always leave. They're especially active at night. That is their time, not ours."

My family and our neighbors listen intently. Here and there, people click their tongues to show disapproval for what I've done. I don't want to look at anyone too closely, because I don't want to be forced to acknowledge the shame they feel for me. Nevertheless, somehow my eyes find Ci-teh. She looks at me in pity. Nothing will hide the dishonor searing my flesh.

"We worship many gods, but none is greater than A-poe-mi-yeh, whose name means *ancestor of great power*. He created the world and this soul before me." The ruma takes a moment to make sure he has everyone's attention. "We have many taboos. Men must not smoke nor women chew betel nut when they walk through the spirit gate. A pregnant woman, like Deh-ja, must not go visiting to another village or she might miscarry there. A woman must never step over her husband's leg on his sleeping mat. We're always careful, and we always try to propitiate our wrongs, but please, our Li-yan did not hope to offend."

Is he saying nothing bad is going to happen to me?

Then he puts his forefinger under my chin and tilts my face up to him. What A-ma couldn't see in me, he sees. I know he does. Everything. But what he says to the others is very different.

"She is just a hungry little girl," he explains. "As the sun always comes up, as the earth is forever under our feet, as the rivers flow down the mountains and the trees grow into the sky, let us together put Li-yan back on the proper Akha path."

He stamps his staff on the ground three times. He sprinkles water over me and pats my head. He has shown me such mercy and forgiveness that I decide I'll never be afraid of him again. But when he turns away to perform the rite that will finish my purification, my stomach once again sinks. He takes the chicken from First Brother's fingers, presses its body to the stone that Third Brother cleaned earlier, and then cuts off its head. My family has so few chickens, which means very few eggs. Now I'm the cause of the loss of food in my family. My sisters-in-law glare at me. But then . . .

A-ma takes the chicken from the ruma and swiftly plucks the feathers from the twitching carcass. Then *whack, whack, whack.* The chicken pieces are thrown into the pot that dangles over the fire First Sister-in-law has been tending.

Twenty minutes later, A-ma ladles the soup into bowls. The men gather on one side of our family home; the women gather on the other side. We sit on our haunches to receive our bowls. The sounds of greedy slurping, sucking, and chewing are among the happiest I've heard in my life, yet frogs, mosquitoes, and night-calling birds alert me to how many sleep hours we've already missed. As I gnaw gristle from a bone, little sparks of ideas fly through my head. In my dream last night, the bad omen of seeing a dog on the roof told me I was going to get into trouble. And I did. But right now, in this second, each person in my family, as well as the ruma, has a piece of chicken to eat and rich broth to drink. That's just like in my dream too. My *fake* dream . . . The one I lied about . . . But in that dream we each had a *whole* chicken. Still . . .

No coincidence, no story.

A WATERFALL OF HEAVEN'S TEARS

We are a people who like to roam, traveling from place to place, using the traditional practice of slashing and burning forests to create fields to plant, and then moving on when the gifts of the earth have finished being used for crops. But during the last few generations, it's become hard to claim new land on Nannuo or on any of the tea mountains in Xishuangbanna prefecture, so we—and others—have stayed. Permanent, A-ba says, even though the idea is against our natures. Still, our home, like all structures in Spring Well Village, was built to be temporary. Before I was born, my father and grandfather went into the forest to gather the thatch that is our roof. They cut bamboo, tore off the leaves, and then tied the poles together with handwoven lashing to create the walls that would become the separate quarters for men and women. Our house is built on bamboo stilts, providing a protected area under our feet for our livestock, although we have no pigs, oxen, mules, or water buffalo, only a few molting chickens, a rooster, and two ducks. The main residence and our three newlywed huts compose the only home I've known, but something in my blood makes me long to leave it behind for a new and different location, where my kin can place our ancestor altar and build a new dwelling as loose and with as much air flowing through it as we have right here. This restless feeling heightens during monsoon season—the months when spirits hold sway.

Today, the women and girls in our household are gathered

around the fire pit on the women's side of the house to do needlework. The fire gives us light and warmth, while the choking smoke helps to ward off mosquitoes. First Sister-in-law and Second Sister-in-law have their heads bent together in private conversation. Puffy colored balls on the ends of wires wound with embroidery thread grow from First Sister-in-law's headdress like a meadow of wildflowers. Second Sister-in-law's headdress is fringed with a string of hollow silver balls about the size of peas that swish across her forehead like bangs. I fidget as Third Sister-in-law examines my needlework. Usually I have Ci-teh at my side for these inspections, but she hasn't been allowed to visit since my bad behavior cycles ago at the tea collection center.

The afternoon is interrupted when Deh-ja and her mother-in-law arrive, bringing A-ma a gift of peanuts. It's never too early to seal the bond with the woman who will bring your baby into the world. But poor Deh-ja. Usually you can barely tell when a woman is pregnant. Our clothes are sewn to be loose enough to be comfortable, while the many layers give added warmth, show family wealth, and have the clever ability to hide what's underneath. Beyond that, from childhood, girls like me are taught the proper behavior during pregnancy so we'll have a bone-deep understanding of our responsibilities when we go into marriage. When the time comes, we should be shy about our condition and stand at an angle so our stomachs will appear less prominent. We even have a courteous way of referring to a woman carrying a baby inside her as "one living under another," because she must obey her husband and never run away from him. It's hard to imagine Deh-ja under Ci-do or running away from him, though, because her belly is so huge with her first baby that she looks like a melon left too long on the vine, ready to burst.

"There must be a big son in there," A-ma says, as she lifts the kettle from the fire. "He wants to come out and give greetings to his a-ma and a-ba, and most especially to his a-ba's parents."

Deh-ja smiles happily. "Let it be a son. Let it be a son. Let it be a son."

She sure is reliable in her chanting, and I can see that her fealty pleases her mother-in-law, as do my a-ma's comments about the baby wanting to meet his grandparents. Pregnancy is a gift to the entire village. Even I know how to recognize when a woman has "come to a head," obvious from her morning sickness. A-ma has taught me to identify if the baby will be a boy or a girl by the way it sleeps in its mother's womb. If the baby is more on the right side, then it will come out a boy. If it's more on the left side, it will be a girl. I need to learn these things if I'm going to follow in A-ma's line by becoming a village midwife one day, as she wishes.

Not only is Deh-ja persistent with her chanting but she's also already memorized the rules for the introduction of her baby into Spring Well. She's been careful not to curse or eat on an uncovered porch—both of which would draw too much attention to herself. When she recites, "Ci-do and I will refrain from the intercourse for ten cycles after our son is born, as is proper," her mother-in-law beams proudly and comes back with the proper and happy response: "I bless you with an easy birth."

"It's good to see that Ci-do has also been doing his part," A-ma says as she pours tea for everyone. "He's avoided climbing trees, because the world knows that this might cause the baby to cry easily, which not one person in the village desires."

"And he engages solely in men's activities, especially hunting," Ci-do's a-ma boasts, "to make sure his firstborn comes out a son."

"Then all should be well," A-ma concludes, although I've overheard her express concern about Deh-ja's size to the sisters-in-law.

Third Sister-in-law has ignored this entire exchange. Her brow is furrowed in concentration as she counts my stitches for a second time—not a good sign. Her needlework is considered to be the most excellent in Spring Well. Her headdress is covered with embroidered and appliquéd designs of different creatures with special meanings: a frog and a monkey at play to show harmony; a bird with a worm in its mouth to signify her maternal love; and a butterfly whose head is embroidered to look like a lavender and yellow crab. Because she is so good at her handiwork, she can show off her expertise and creativity just for the fun of it.

She finally looks up from her examination and tosses the piece of cloth back in my lap. "You'll need to pull out every stitch and do them again." Third Sister-in-law is my favorite, but sometimes it feels like all she does is boss me around. She's the mother of a son and one day I'll marry out into my husband's home, which is why A-ma tolerates it. But then Third Sister-in-law goes too far by showing her sharp snout and critical tongue. "You'll never get a marriage proposal if you have to rely on your needlework."

A-ma shoots up a hand to keep her from uttering another word. Nothing so untoward should be spoken directly.

"Let her be," A-ma says in a manner designed to end all further conversation on this subject. "The girl will go to her marriage with a precious dowry. She will find someone willing to marry her, if only for that."

It's a small room, and surely A-ma sees the looks that pass between the three sisters-in-law and our neighbors. I have a dowry, true, but it's hardly precious. It's a remote tea grove high, high, high on the mountain and handed down by the women in her family. Its location is a secret because of tradition and because the grove itself is said to bring bad fortune to trespassers. Some might even call it cursed . . .

"Come sit with me, Girl," A-ma continues into the awkward silence. "I want to give you something."

Could it be her most prized and valuable possession—the silver bracelet with the two dragons facing each other nose to nose—which has been handed down by the women in her family? No, because she reaches up and lets her fingers dance lightly over her headdress. She's worked on it for years, adding beads, silver balls, bells, and beetle wings. Third Sister-in-law's headdress may have the finest needlework, but A-ma's is truly the most exquisite in our village, befitting her status as midwife. Her fingers find their destination. Using small scissors, she snips, then conceals the treasure in her hand. She repeats the process another two times before setting down the scissors. The silence in the room deepens as the others wait to see what she's going to do next.

"Now that I've passed the age of forty-five, when women should no longer be considering childbearing, it's time that I concentrate on my only daughter and the woman, wife, and mother she'll become. Give me your hand."

The others crane their necks like geese flying across the sky.

Without revealing what else she has hidden, A-ma drops one of the prizes into my outstretched palm. It's a silver coin decorated with foreign writing on one side and a miniature dreamworld of temples on the other.

"This coin is from Burma," she explains. "I do not know what it says."

I've seen Burma on the map at my school. It's the country closest to us, but I have no idea what the Burmese characters mean either.

"Next, here is a shell."

Across the room, First Sister-in-law hisses air through clenched teeth. She's complimented A-ma on this shell many times. I suspect she always thought it would come to her. Disappointment paints her face, but she and the other sisters-in-law should not be divvying up the charms on my mother's headdress just yet.

"This last is one of my favorites. It's a feather that caravanned on the Tea Horse Road from Tibet to our mountain. Think, Girl. These things have traveled over oceans and rivers, across mountain passes, and along trade routes. Soon you'll be able to attach them to the headdress you've been training to make, which will mark you as a girl of marriageable age."

My heart beats with tremendous joy, and yet I know that the only reason she did this was to swerve the conversation away from the unlucky land that is my dowry.

One week later, word passes through the village that Deh-ja has gone into labor. Her mother-in-law is attending to her, as she should in the early hours. A-ma spends the morning looking through her shelves, grabbing medicines and tools from various baskets and boxes, and placing them in her satchel so everything will be ready when Ci-do comes to fetch her. The cautious quiet is broken when someone runs up the stairs to the men's veranda. Even before Third Brother can knock on the wall that divides the two sides of the house, A-ma has risen and picked up her satchel. First Daughter-in-law waits at the door ready with A-ma's cape made from bark and leaves.

"Give it to Girl," A-ma says as she grabs another cape from a hook. Her eyes find me. "You'll come with me today. You're old enough. If you are to become a midwife, you must begin to learn now."

The three sisters-in-law regard me with a mixture of pride and fear. I feel the same way. The idea of wearing A-ma's cape makes my skin tingle with excitement, like I have ants running up and down my arms and legs, but helping her with a birth?

"Ready?" A-ma asks. Without waiting for an answer, she opens the door to the women's veranda. Ci-do has come around to our side of the house and stands in the muddy track that divides the village, rubbing his hands together with such urgency that I have to fight my desire to run back inside. A-ma must sense this, because she orders, "Come!"

The omens are particularly worrisome. It's the season of spirits. It's raining. And Deh-ja's baby is coming earlier than expected, even though her belly has been huge for many cycles now. The only propitious sign is that it's Rat Day, and rats live in fertile valleys, which should help Deh-ja in the hours to come.

As we near Ci-do's family home, I spot Ci-teh peeking out the door. Her brave smile momentarily boosts my confidence. A-ma and I continue on to the hut for newlyweds. Ci-do leaves us at the foot of the stairs. It's a Sun and Moon truth that if a husband sees his wife give birth, he might die from it. Once inside, Ci-do's elder aunt helps us out of our capes. A-ma shakes the wet from her head as she scans the room, which is even smokier from the fire than ours. Ci-do's mother squats on the birthing mat, her hands under Deh-ja, massaging.

"Move." A-ma has whittled her words down to almost nothing, having put away those parts of herself that are daughter, sister, wife, mother, and friend. She's here as the midwife.

In what feels like one movement—as three trees bending together in a storm—Ci-do's mother slides to her right and off the birthing mat and my a-ma drops down to it, pulling me along with her. I was curious about what Ci-do's mother was doing when we came in, so my eyes automatically go between Deh-ja's legs. Blood and mucus have pooled beneath her. *Waaa!* I wasn't expecting that! Blinking, I raise my eyes to Deh-ja's face. Her jaw is clenched in pain, her face red with effort, and her eyes squished tightly shut. When whatever has been happening seems to ebb, A-ma's hands move swiftly, first prodding between Deh-ja's legs and then moving up and over her belly in a series of squeezing motions.

"Your son is giving you a hard time," A-ma says.

I don't know if it's A-ma's words—*your son*—or the pleasant way she's spoken them, as though Deh-ja's situation is no different from that of any woman who gives birth on Nannuo Mountain, but Deh-ja responds with a smile.

A-ma spreads a piece of embroidered indigo cloth on the birthing mat. On this she places her knife, a length of string, and an egg.

"Deh-ja, I want you to try a different position," A-ma says. "Move onto your hands and knees. Yes, like that. This time when the pain comes, I want you to take a breath then let it out slowly. No pushing."

Three hours later, nothing much has happened. A-ma sits back on her haunches and twists the dragon bracelet on her wrist as she considers.

"I think we need to call the spirit priest and the shaman."

Ci-do's mother and aunt freeze like they're barking deer spotted in the forest.

"The ruma and the nima?" There's no mistaking the panic in Ci-do's mother's voice.

"Now. Please," A-ma orders.

Ten minutes later, Ci-do's a-ma returns with the two men. No time is wasted. The nima goes into a trance, but Deh-ja's pains not only don't ease, they intensify. Her eyes remain closed. I can't imagine what horrors she must be seeing on the backs of her eyelids. Red agony. Part of me is relieved to know that not every woman goes through this.

Finally, the nima returns to our plane. "Wrong cannot be hidden. An outside spirit is insulted because Deh-ja made a mistake in one of her ancestor offerings."

The nima doesn't specify the injustice, but it could have been anything. We make offerings to the mountains, rivers, dragons, heaven. We also make offerings every cycle to our ancestors. All of them involve food, so maybe an offering wasn't divided properly or a dog grabbed some of it and ate it under the house.

The ruma takes over. He asks for an egg—not the one on the birthing mat, but a new one. "Uncooked," he demands. The egg is brought, and he passes it over Deh-ja's body three times as he addresses the spirit. "Don't eat or drink in this house any longer. Go back to your own place." He puts the egg in his pocket, then speaks directly to Deh-ja. "You've been in labor so long, we're now on Buffalo Day. Buffalo help humans in their work. Now the spirit of the day will help you sweep the room clean of malevolence."

Deh-ja groans as her mother-in-law and A-ma help her to her feet. She cannot stand upright. Deh-ja is dragged across the room to the broom. I open my mouth, words of objection forming. A-ma catches sight of me and gives me such a stern look that my mouth snaps shut. I stand there helpless as the nima and the ruma make sure Deh-ja sweeps every corner. She's naked under her tunic, and bloody liquid snakes down her legs.

When the nima and ruma are satisfied the room is free from the bad spirit, they leave, taking gifts of money, rice, and the egg in the pocket. "Do you have the strength to squat?" A-ma asks as Deh-ja sinks to the birthing mat. Deh-ja whimpers as she gets into position. "Think of your baby slipping out of your body as wet and slick as a fish."

The sounds that come from Deh-ja are awful—like a dog being strangled. A-ma keeps encouraging her and massaging the opening where the baby will come out. Everything is too red for me, but I don't look away. I can't, not after already disappointing A-ma. She's given me this gift, and I must try to show her my worthiness. Deh-ja's entire body contracts, pushing hard. Then, just like A-ma said it would, the baby slides out and flops onto the mat. Deh-ja collapses on her side. The older women stare at the baby. It's a boy, but no one moves to touch or pick him up.

"*A baby is not truly born until it has cried three times,*" A-ma recites.

He's much smaller than I expected given how big Deh-ja was when he was inside her. We all count: ten toes, ten fingers; his limbs match—two legs, two arms, equal sizes; no harelip; no cleft palate. He's perfect. I've heard whispered what would happen if he were a human reject. Ci-do would have to . . .

Finally, the little thing cries. He sounds like a jungle bird.

"*The first cry is for blessing.*" A-ma speaks the ritual words.

He pulls air into his new lungs. This time his cry is even stronger.

"*The second cry is for the soul.*"

Then comes an ear-piercing wail.

"*The third cry is for his life span.*" A-ma smiles as she picks him up and hands him to his grandmother. A-ma ties the string around the baby's cord and cuts it with the knife. Deh-ja pushes a couple of times and what A-ma calls the friend-living-with-child—a gooey red blob—squeezes onto the birthing mat. This is put aside for Ci-do to bury under his parents' house right below the ancestor altar.

A-ma takes a breath—ready to give the baby his temporary name so that no bad spirits will claim him before he's awarded his proper name by his father—when Deh-ja suddenly moans. The expressions on the older women's faces tell me something is terribly wrong. Deh-ja draws her knees to her chest, curling into a ball. A-ma feels Deh-ja's stomach then quickly draws back her hands as though they've been scorched.

"*Tsaw caw,*" she utters. "Twins. Human rejects."

Ci-do's aunt covers her mouth in shock. Ci-do's a-ma drops the first baby on the floor. The way he sucks in the smoky air sounds frantic, and his little arms jab into space as though he's searching for his mother. And Deh-ja? She's in so much pain, she's unaware that the worst thing that could happen has happened. Ci-do's mother and aunt leave to give Ci-do the dreadful news. I shift on the mat, getting ready to bolt, but A-ma grabs my arm. "Stay!"

The firstborn baby lies alone, naked and unprotected. The second baby—a girl—comes out quickly. We don't touch her. We don't count her cries.

"Twins are the absolute worst taboo in our culture, for only animals, demons, and spirits give birth to litters," A-ma tells me. "Animal rejects are contrary to nature too. If a sow gives birth to one piglet, then both must be killed at once. If a dog gives birth to one puppy, then they too must be killed immediately. None of the meat can be eaten either. The birth of twins—which has never before happened in Spring Well—is a calamity not just for the mother, father, and relatives of the babies but for our entire village."

From outside, I begin to hear shouts and wails.

Ci-do enters the room. His tears mingle with the rain on his cheeks. He carries a bowl, his fingers kneading the contents in an awful rhythm.

"You know what you have to do," A-ma says sorrowfully.

Ci-do looks down at Deh-ja. His face is as pale as hers. She tries to swallow her sobs. It doesn't work. I can barely make out her words. "I'm sorry. I'm so sorry."

Ci-do kneels by the first baby.

"Close your eyes," A-ma instructs me. "You don't need to see this."

I've been shown mercy at last, but my eyelids refuse to shut.

Tears drip from Ci-do's cheeks onto the baby boy, who still squirms and cries in his strange hiccuping way. Deh-ja watches her husband with eyes that are pools of sorrow. I also stare, aghast, as he scoops a mixture of rice husks and ashes from the bowl and tenderly tucks it into his son's mouth and nostrils. The baby writhes for a few desperate seconds. My whole body rejects what I've seen. It *didn't* happen. It *couldn't* have happened.

Ci-do moves to the baby girl.

"No!" I sound small, tinny.

"Girl!" A-ma's voice is sharp.

"But, he can't—"

A-ma's open palm comes at me so swiftly and surprisingly that when it meets my face I'm nearly knocked to the ground. The stinging pain is shocking, but not as mind-numbing as the slap itself, because children are not beaten, kicked, or hit in our culture.

"We are Akha," she says harshly. "These are our rules. If you are to be a midwife, you must—*must*—follow our customs. Human rejects need to be sent to the great lake of boiling blood. This is how we protect the village from idiots, the malformed, or those so small they'll only prolong their own deaths. It is us—midwives—who keep our people pure and in alignment with the goodness of nature, because if human rejects are allowed to do the intercourse, over time an entire village might end up inhabited by only them."

Her words are directed at me, but they also give Ci-do courage. As he kneels by his baby girl, I hide my face in A-ma's skirt. Her hand on my shoulder feels like it weighs ten thousand kilos. The baby girl dies quicker than her brother, which doesn't make it any less horrifying. If every living thing has a soul, as I've been taught, then didn't Deh-ja's twins have souls? If God created a tree to represent each and every Akha, have two trees now toppled in the spirit world? Shouldn't we be hearing the echoing crashes, the sputtering of birds, the howling of startled monkeys? When A-ma finally lifts her hand, I feel so light that maybe I could float up to the ceiling, right through the thatch, and on to the stars.

She reaches into her basket, removes a length of cloth, and gives it to Ci-do. He silently spools out the cloth, places the infants side by side, and rolls them up. How does he know what to do? How has he known what to do for *any* of this?

"Ci-do, repair your face!" A-ma demands. "When you go outside, you must show our neighbors how angry—furious—you are at the spirits, who've allowed this hideous occurrence to curse you and your family. It is custom. Following it will help you."

He roughly wipes the tears from his cheeks with the backs of his hands. Then he nods to his wife, tucks the bundle under his arm, and leaves.

"Watch him," A-ma orders. When she adds, "Do it right," I know she's still disappointed in me for trying to stop Ci-do earlier. "Make sure someone meets him. He must be accompanied into the forest."

I hurry to the door. The rain sheets down—a waterfall of heaven's tears. Two elders stand in the mud at the bottom of the steps. Ci-do is not the same heartbroken man who was in the newlywed hut with us. He stomps down the stairs with his shoulders pulled back and his chest pushed out. When he reaches the men, he gestures angrily with his free hand. His words don't reach me through the rain. The elders take positions on either side of him and march him out of the village.

The room is so quiet now. Deh-ja silently weeps, her tears staining the birthing mat, but her suffering is not over. Blood escapes from the place where the babies exited her body. A-ma packs the area with a handful of leaves and dirt, but a moment later more red liquid seeps through. A-ma peers around the room until she finds me.

"Girl, run back to the house," she orders. "On the top shelf in the women's room, bring me the basket third from the left."

Outside, a deluge. The lane that divides the village has become a muddy river. I don't see a single person or animal.

My sisters-in-law turn their backs and shield their children's eyes when I enter the women's room. I grab what A-ma asked for and then trot back to the newlywed hut. Deh-ja's skin is even paler now, but she's stopped crying. A mound of blood-soaked leaves and dirt has grown on the floor next to her. Deh-ja may have brought human rejects into the world, but if she dies that will be an even greater triumph for bad spirits.

A-ma sifts through the basket.

"Pangolin shell," she says softly.

I'm not sure if she's speaking to me or to Deh-ja. Perhaps—and this idea scares me almost more than anything that's happened so far—she's addressing the spirits.

A-ma rubs the shell between her hands, seeming to warm it. Then she kneads it across Deh-ja's belly. "Do you see what I'm doing?" she asks me. "Take the shell. Keep sending it over the flesh in gentle circles to help contract her womb."

My hand quivers as I move the shell over and around Deh-ja's belly, which feels distressingly spongy under the smooth hardness of the shell. The blood is still coming out, pooling beneath her. I avert my eyes and see A-ma open a tiny box.

"I want you to watch exactly what I do," she says. She pulls out strands of hair that have been tied into a loop to keep them from tangling. "These were taken from a woman killed by lightning."

She places the oil lamp between us, then burns the hairs over the flame, making sure the ash falls into a cup of water. Once the concoction is finished, she hands the cup to Deh-ja.

"Drink it all," A-ma says. "When you're done, the bleeding will end, and you'll feel better."

The bleeding stops, but maybe Deh-ja didn't have any blood left in her. I wouldn't say she feels better either.

From her satchel, A-ma extracts a small piece of limestone polished flat and smooth, which she folds into Deh-ja's palm. "Nothing will completely take away the agony of your milk coming in with no child to suckle it away, but if you massage this on your breasts, the pain will be reduced." A-ma pauses. When she speaks again, it's as if she's delivering the worst news. "Soon you'll need to get up."

I'm confused, because every woman in our village gets up after childbirth. I've seen my sisters-in-law do it. A-ma helps them have their babies. They wait for the three-cry ceremony. And then they rise and go back to work. But Deh-ja gave birth not just to a baby missing a finger or ruined by blindness—who must also be smothered by their fathers—but to twins, the worst of all human rejects. I'm terrified of what's going to happen next.

"I suspect you'll continue to have pains and bleeding from here." A-ma gently touches Deh-ja's abdomen. Then she unwraps a bird's nest from a piece of cloth. Deh-ja watches with sunken eyes as A-ma breaks off a piece no larger than the tip of her finger. "This is from the nest of the great hornbill," she explains. "The great hornbill builds its home from mud and from the blood of its kills. Earth and blood help in cases like these. And last . . ." She picks up the egg that has been on the birthing mat this whole time. "You need to eat this heart-forget egg. It's supposed to help you forget the pain of childbirth. Maybe it will help you forget the pain of . . ."

There's no need to finish the sentence.

We sit with Deh-ja all through the night. During the long hours, A-ma's disappointment in me continues to radiate from her body like a low fire. Perhaps she could have overlooked my lapses as part of my learning, but my purposefully trying to stop Ci-do from his duty may be a miscarriage of Akha Law from which I'll never recover. I hate myself for failing A-ma, but I hate myself even more for not stopping Ci-do. Even considering those two ideas at the same time makes me a not very good Akha.

Roosters announce the morning, and light begins to filter through the bamboo walls. The spirit priest's voice calls through the insistent clatter of the rain.

"People of Spring Well Village, come!"

A-ma and I do as we're told, leaving Deh-ja alone. The spirit priest is positioned on his veranda, staff in hand, waiting for everyone to gather. Ci-do and the two elders stand a short distance away. Ci-do still looks angry, as A-ma told him to do.

The ruma raises his arms as he addresses the crowd. "A great power has sent an abnormal birth to our village. It's a terrible tragedy for Ci-do and Deh-ja. It's a terrible tragedy for all of us. Ci-do has completed his requirements. He has burned the rejects in the forest. Their spirits will not trouble us again. Ci-do is a good man from a good family, but we all know what has to happen next." *Clack, clack, clack* goes his staff on the floor of the veranda. "Our village will have ceremonial abstinence for one cycle. Everyone must be careful with their arms and legs." (Which is his way of saying no one can do the intercourse.) "Magic vine needs to be laid end to end to ring our village to protect us from more bad spirits. No school for the children. And . . ."

Ci-do's mother and Ci-teh weep into their hands. His father stares at the ground.

"The parents of the human rejects must be banished and their house destroyed," the ruma finishes.

Ci-do, the ruma, and the nima enter the newlywed hut. The rest of us wait. The wind picks up, driving rain into our faces. The ruma reemerges, holding up Ci-do's crossbow. Next, the nima displays Deh-ja's silver wedding bracelets for all to see. It's their right to choose whatever they want as payment for their services, but they've taken Ci-do and Deh-ja's most valuable possessions.

Ci-do steps outside. He doesn't wear his turban. He lugs a pack on his back, and his arms are loaded with as much as he can carry. Deh-ja appears behind him. The fact that she isn't wearing her headdress is one of the most shocking things I've seen yet.

The rain quickly soaks her hair, leaving it in strings that plaster themselves to her face and clothes. On her back, she carries her tea-picking basket—with the wood across her forehead to hold the straps that support the weight of her belongings packed inside. She takes a couple of steps and staggers. I want to help her, but A-ma holds me back.

As Ci-do and Deh-ja head for the spirit gate, the ruma calls after them. "Spirits of chaos and destruction, leave this village and never return." Once the couple disappears from sight, the men in our village bound into action. Within minutes, Ci-do and Deh-ja's newlywed hut has been destroyed. Then the men go in groups into the forest to collect *meh,* a magic vine related to the ginger plant with long stems and red flowers that spirits are very much afraid of, to wrap around the perimeter of Spring Well Village.

"You see, Girl?" A-ma says. "This is why the rule that babies must be born in the newlywed hut is a good one. Otherwise, the main family home would have to be burned instead."

"Where will Ci-do and Deh-ja go? Where will they sleep?"

"So many questions!"

I tug on her sleeve. "A-ma, will they ever come home?"

She clicks her tongue to show her impatience and bats me away with the back of her hand. I am so confused . . . I long to bury my face in her skirt.

THE LENGTH OF A SWALLOW'S BLINK

For the next twelve days, our village follows ceremonial abstinence. On Tiger Day, fetching water is not allowed. On Donkey Day, I'm sent to bring water, because donkeys carry things. On Rabbit Day—and the rain has not let up for one instant—I gather firewood. A-ma chooses not to notice or praise me, and her silence enshrouds me like a heavy cloud. I live in a house with many people, and yet no one speaks to me. I've never felt so alone or lonely.

On the fourth day, we hear the voice of the spirit priest. "It's time for the sacrifices," he calls. "I'll need nine sacks of grain, nine pigs, nine chickens, and nine dogs." But Ci-teh's family doesn't have nine pigs. Our entire village doesn't have nine pigs. Ci-teh's family turns over their grain, four pigs, and all their chickens, while young men go through the village to catch stray dogs. By the end of the ceremony, Ci-teh's family has lost a lot of its wealth.

Once our full cycle of ceremonial abstinence ends, life seems to return to normal. The women go back to embroidering, weaving, and doing chores. The men go back to smoking pipes, hunting, and trading stories. But the birth of the twins and what happened to them, although traditional, has transformed me as irreversibly as soaking cloth in a vat of dye. I cannot accept what I witnessed.

But while my soul has changed, my flesh and bones must still follow the course laid out for me, which means also returning to school.

A-ma and A-ba didn't learn to read or write. My brothers started working full-time with A-ba when they reached eight years, so they don't know much about reading or writing either. I'm the first person in my family to reach such a high level in primary school. I've always liked coming here; today it feels like a refuge. The one-room schoolhouse—which sits at the edge of a muddy lot—looks very much like houses on Nannuo: built on stilts, made of bamboo and thatch, and illuminated inside by a smoky fire pit. We're nineteen students altogether, ages six to twelve, all from villages scattered on our side of the mountain. The older girls share a mat, while three big boys huddle together on the opposite side of the room. The littlest children wiggle and squirm on their own mat. I sit with Ci-teh. We still haven't spoken about what happened to her brother, Deh-ja, and their babies. She must be reeling from shame and loss, and I don't think I could ever tell her what I saw in the newlywed hut.

Teacher Zhang shuffles into the room. He wears blue wool pants, a blue wool jacket, and a matching blue cap with a red star on the front. Everyone on Nannuo Mountain feels sorry for him. Ten years before I was born, during the Great Proletarian Cultural Revolution, he was pulled from his university post in the capital and "sent down to learn from the peasants." When the Cultural Revolution ended and others were called home, he remained unable to get a permit to return to his family. He can't have yet reached fifty years, but his bitterness makes him look like a village elder. So sad. But everything seems sad to me just now.

Those of us from Spring Well Village have missed two of what he calls weeks of attendance, but he neither welcomes us nor chastises us. Instead, he pins a map of China and its neighbors to the school's bamboo wall.

"Who can tell me the name of your ethnic minority?" he asks.

We've memorized the answer just the way Teacher Zhang likes to hear it. Today, I'm happy for the normalcy.

"Chairman Mao categorized us as Hani," we chant together, "one of fifty-five ethnic minorities in China."

"Correct."

Except it isn't. Mandarin speakers call us Hani. We are called Aini in the local dialect. But we are neither. We are Akha. When Chairman Mao proclaimed that China was home to fifty-five ethnic minorities, no one had found us yet. When we were discovered, powerful people elsewhere said we would become part of the Hani, because Chairman Mao could not be wrong. Over time another thirty peoples were added to the Hani, including the Juewei, Biyue, Amu, Enu, and so many more.

Teacher Zhang sniffs, wipes the back of his hand across his nose, and adds, "Since you are Hani, you must learn in Hani." Although the Akha and Hani share most of the same words, the pronunciations and the ways we end our sentences are so different that we wouldn't be able to understand each other if not for what we've been forced to memorize in school. Teacher Zhang looks furtively around the room, as though one of us might report him. "Be grateful. The Hani have their own written language—thirty-one years old. Do you not think it hilarious that it's written in the letters of the imperial West?" He laughs, shakes his head, and something comes into his voice that I can't pick apart. "But soon I'll switch all my teaching to Mandarin, the national language of the Han majority." He pronounces this carefully, making sure we hear the difference between the Hani (tiny) and the Han (huge, because they make up more than 90 percent of the population of China). "*To learn a different language is to learn a different way of living,*" he recites. "This, I'm told, will be your way to learn how to cultivate your fields scientifically and appreciate proper sanitation. It will also help with your political indoctrination, which will promote loyalty to the state."

Sometimes I don't know if Teacher Zhang is teasing or torturing us with his comments.

He turns to the map with its swaths of green, blue, and brown. He's marked where we live with a red *X*, although once, when I was called up to identify the capital of the country, I saw no written characters under the *X* to mark our villages or the names of our mountains. Even Jinghong, the largest town in Xishuangbanna prefecture, was not on the map. When I asked why, he explained, "Because where you live is unimportant. No one knows you're here."

Someone must have known, which is why Teacher Zhang was sent here, but I understood what he was trying to say. It's only through his maps and posters that I know anything about the outside world. He has described their contents, but why would I need a *hospital* when I have A-ma? Why would I want to work in a *factory* so far from the forest? I've seen drawings of *secretaries,* and I wonder why a woman would want to wear the same head-to-toe plain blue jacket and trousers that Teacher Zhang wears.

He now asks for a volunteer to come up to the map and point out the places where the Akha live. A weak man always seeks to hurt those lower than he is, so I suspect he's going to be tough on Ci-teh and me today. Hoping to protect my friend—she lost her brother and so much more—I quickly raise my hand. He calls on her anyway.

She goes up to the map and studies it. I know the answers and itch to help her, but I'm hoping she'll remember the stories she's learned from her a-ma about where our people roam, even if she can't point out the countries on the map. She surprises me, though, by putting the tip of her finger on the wrinkled paper.

"Here is Tibet," she says at last. "A thousand years ago, maybe less, the Akha grew tired of the cold." (This is the story we've learned from our elders. Our ancestors were *cold.*) "The Akha . . . I'm sorry . . . We Hani"—a few of the boys titter at her correction—"walked down from the Tibetan Plateau. Some of us settled in Burma. Some in Thailand. Some in Laos." Her finger moves from country to country, until finally settling on the red *X*. "And some came here, to Xishuangbanna prefecture."

"Is Nannuo included on the list of the Six Great Tea Mountains of Yunnan?"

"No, Teacher Zhang. Those would be Mansa, Yibang, Youle, Gedeng, Mangzhi, and Manzhuang, which lie on the east bank of the Lancang River. But here, on the west side of the river, we have the six second-greatest tea mountains: Hekai, Banzhang, Bada, Mengsong, Jingmai, and our Nannuo. There are even lesser known mountains where tea grows in our prefecture too."

When Ci-teh returns to our mat, I squeeze her hand, proud of her.

"I did it," she whispers. "I did it even better than you could have." Her comment stings, and I pull away. Doesn't she realize I'm sad too and need her love as well?

Of course, Teacher Zhang saw and heard everything. "Yes, Ci-teh, you're very smart for an Akha," he says, using our real designation. This is never a good omen, because he considers everyone in our province to be brainless and crude, and Ci-teh has just proved him wrong. "The world knows that the Akha are the butts of national jokes. Even the Hani are ridiculed as being *tu*." It's a Mandarin word, but one that everyone—including the youngest children here—recognizes. In Mandarin, *tu* means *earth,* so we're considered filthy, backward, and *of the dirt*. Teacher Zhang continues: "This is where poets and scholars were exiled in centuries past." (And where artists, teachers, and students like him were sent during the Cultural Revolution.) "If all that were not enough, your proximity to Burma is an added black mark, because the Akha there have built a bad reputation for opium growing and drug smuggling."

I glance across the room and see the older boys roll their eyes. People like Teacher Zhang can't know us, just as the Dai, the Bulang, or any other minority can't know us, let alone the Han majority. Yes, we grow opium and, yes, A-ma uses it in her medicines, but that's not the same as drug smuggling.

"None of the hill tribes like the Akha," Teacher Zhang continues. "You're stupid and violent. Ci-teh here wants to prove them wrong."

It's hard to listen to Teacher Zhang when he's like this, and I wonder if something more personal has happened—and not just mountain gossip about Ci-teh's family and my behavior in the newlywed hut—that's pushing him to be so cruel today. Was another petition to return to his home rejected? Did he hear that his wife, who divorced him long ago, remarried? Or is it the rain that's been coming down steadily for weeks now, leaving everyone and everything smelling of mildew, and all ears tired from the unrelenting deluge that spatters nonstop on thatch roofs and the trees of the forest?

All through the morning Teacher Zhang asks questions related to the map, and for a while I'm distracted from my feelings. "Yes!" we chant in unison. "We live on the Tropic of Cancer." And, "Yes! The Lancang River flows from Tibet." The river passes through our mountains, changing its name to Mekong where China, Laos, and Burma meet, before flowing through Thailand, Cambodia, and Vietnam, and eventually to the South China Sea. "Yes! It is called the Danube of the East."

The lunch break comes. The other kids run through the rain to an open-air canopy, but Ci-teh takes my hand and holds me under the overhang that protects the entrance to our schoolroom.

"What's going to happen to my family now?" she asks, staring out at the muddy landscape. "How will we ever come back from this? And my brother . . ."

I feel sorry for her, and I want to offer comfort, but it's harder than I thought it would be. Her cap is still better than mine. Her family still has its vegetable and opium fields. Her clan is still better off than any other in Spring Well. Despite my uncharitable feelings, she's still my friend. I try to offer her some sympathy. "We'll all miss Ci-do and Deh-ja."

She presses her lips together, visibly fighting her emotions. Finally, she mumbles, "Don't say anything more. It hurts too much." Then she releases my hand for the second time today, steps into the rain, and joins the other kids under the canopy. I wonder what it would be like to be so proud and then have your belongings, reputation, and status taken from you.

I go back into the classroom to speak to Teacher Zhang.

"I hear you had a hard time," he says somewhat kindly when I approach. "Your traditions can be harsh."

His sympathy for me, given how he treated Ci-teh, is startling. So is my response.

"Thank you for understanding."

"Work hard and you could go on to second-level school and beyond. You don't have to stay on this mountain forever."

I've heard there is a second-level school and even a third-level school. No one from our group of villages has passed the test to attend, so the idea is impossible to imagine, just as it's hard to imagine him ever being allowed to leave.

"So what do you want?" he asks when I don't say anything.

I reach into my pocket and pull out a small piece of cloth tied with a strip of dried corn husk. Inside is a pinch of tea my family processed from last-grade leaves. A-ma likes me to give Teacher Zhang some of this tea for two reasons. First, he is a sad and lonely man. Second, I must respect my teacher. And maybe it's just a dream, but today I would add a third reason: to distract him from Ci-teh, so she might have more time to deal with her family's losses.

In the afternoon, I see my leaves floating in the big glass jar he uses to drink his tea.

Every twelve days, the cycle begins anew with Sheep Day in honor of the god who gave birth to the universe. No work is done, and school is closed. A-ma waits until my nieces and nephews have settled and their mothers have begun their spinning before saying to me, "Come. You'll need your cape." I'm afraid of what she wants of me, but I bow my head, and follow her into the rain. We quickly pass through the spirit gate and leave our village behind. Her feet are sure and swift, even in the slippery mud, and I have to hurry to keep up with her. We climb the main trail that will eventually reach my brothers' tea gardens, but we don't turn onto the smaller paths that lead to them. The clatter of rain on the leaves of my cape seems to magnify A-ma's quiet determination. She crosses over the trail to the tea collection center without saying a word. We enter the clouds. Everything turns ghostly gray. The path narrows and then narrows some more. We've thoroughly entered the terrain of the spirits. I'm glad I'm with A-ma, because she'll always protect me and make sure I find my way home. I can't bear to think about what might happen if we were to get separated. With that, a frightening thought enters my mind. Maybe A-ma *plans* to leave me out here. Perhaps I've disappointed her that much. And still we climb.

After a while, she stops. An immense boulder blocks the last frayed remnants of the path. We have nowhere left to go. A chill runs through my body.

"Look around you, Girl," she orders. "What do you see?"

Rain . . . Rivulets of water streaming down the boulder's ragged skin . . . Ghosts of trees draped in shadowy mists . . .

I'm so, so scared. But as much as my body shivers and shakes, I can't make my mouth move.

"Look, Girl. *See.*" Her voice is so soft I barely hear it above the rain. "See deeply."

I lick the rain from my lips, close my eyes, and take a breath. When I open my eyes, I try to see the world as she does.

Ready, I try. "A hunter might call this an animal trail, but it isn't."

"Why do you say that?" she asks.

"I've seen broken twigs up here." I gesture to the height of A-ma's shoulder. "Someone comes up here often and passes too closely to the plants and trees. And look at those rocks." I point to some stones on the ground. "Someone placed them here to make this journey easier."

A-ma's smile is perhaps the most beautiful I've ever seen. "I'll need to be more careful in the future."

Feeling braver, I study the boulder. Huge trees—camphors—tower up behind it. The rock looks round, but a section juts out—a ledge over a steep drop—and curves to the right. I follow my intuition, put my hands on the face of the boulder, and follow the curve. What ledge there was disappears, leaving only hollows to tuck my toes. I slowly creep sideways around the boulder, my body flat against its ancient surface. Except it's not a boulder. It's more of an outcropping, a wall, a fortification made by nature, with a soul so powerful I feel it through my fingers and toes.

The ground comes back up to meet my feet, and I step into the grove of camphor trees I'd glimpsed earlier. Sheltered beneath the canopy of their great limbs are scattered about a dozen old tea trees. In the middle—surrounded by the smaller tea trees with camphor branches hanging above and the solid and well-cared-for ground beneath it—stands a single tea tree. Anyone would be able to tell how ancient it is by the twist of its branches.

"Is this *my* land?" I ask.

"When I went to your a-ba in marriage, the old traditions were supposed to be over. No more buying and selling of women into slavery or marriage. No more dowries either. But it doesn't matter what the government says. This land belongs to the women in our line. It is ours alone to control. It was given to me as my dowry as it will one day go with you into marriage."

I'm only half listening, because I'm so disappointed. It's just as A-ba and everyone else in my family has said. What I've been allotted is worthless. It will be hard to get a basket of leaves around the boulder and down the mountain to the tea collection center. The hope I've hidden that my land isn't as bad as everyone has always hinted has been smashed, but A-ma doesn't notice. Instead, she takes my hand and leads me farther into the grove. "Look how the stone on this side has opened to embrace this special place," she whispers. "See how part of the rock comes up and over, so you could sleep under it and stay dry, if you wished."

Yes, it's hollowed out on this side, forming a grotto, but what difference can that make to me?

She tells me the camphor trees are eight hundred years old or more and that the "sister trees" that surround the ancient tea tree are more than one thousand years old. My stomach sinks even further. Not only could no one find this place, but no one wants leaves from old trees. Tea bushes and pollarded tea trees bring money and food. Not *that* much money or food, but *something*. The leaves from these trees? The word that has been so much in my mind lately pounds against the inside of my skull. *Worthless. Worthless. Worthless.*

"And here is the mother tree," A-ma continues. Her voice is at once softer and filled with more emotion than it ever is during ceremonial sacrifices. She places her palms on the trunk as delicately as she did on Deh-ja's belly. "Isn't she beautiful?"

Not really. The tree is much taller than the ones A-ma called sister trees, but the years show in the way they do in village elders. The bark is cracked. The limbs are bent and gnarled by age. Some of the color has faded from the leaves. And it also has eerie growths—not moles or cracked toenails, but parasites and fungi—that mottle the bark and fester in the crooks of the limbs and at the base of the trunk. I've seen things like this before when we've tramped into the forest, but one characteristic is new to me. Bright yellow threads have crept into, over, and around the other parasites. The tree looks like it could die tomorrow. *Worthless.*

"Rice is to nourish," A-ma says. "Tea is to heal. Always remember that food is medicine, and medicine is food. If you take care of the trees, the trees will take care of you."

"But A-ba hates this place. I've heard the others call it unlucky. It's—"

"You don't know a thing about it." She takes my arm and pulls me—not so gently—out of the rain and under the crescent-shaped canopy formed by the boulder. "This tea garden has belonged to the women in my line since the Akha first came to this mountain thirty-three generations ago. The sister trees were still young back then, but the mother tree was already old. My grandmother told me it had to have lived more than one hundred generations already. And it has always been used for tea."

One hundred generations? For the first time, I use Teacher Zhang's math for something other than a class lesson. That would be over three thousand years old. The forest has been here since it was created by the gods, but did they drink tea?

"Do you see how the tree has grown?" A-ma asks. She strides back into the rain and climbs the tree! Each step is graceful and easy—from branch to branch, higher and higher.

"Footholds," she says when she returns to me. "Long ago, the tree's caretakers pruned and trained it for easy climbing . . . and picking. Look at any tea tree on our mountain, and you'll see the same thing. But this one is the most ancient."

"And most unlucky."

"Girl!" The look in A-ma's eyes tells me I've come close to making her break the taboo of hitting a child . . . again.

"I was told never to bring a man to this grove," she says after a long moment. "But after my marriage, your grandfather—

my father-in-law—insisted. He kept at me—every day, every night—claiming that now that I was his daughter-in-law the land belonged to him. I was only sixteen, and I didn't know how to say no strongly enough. I finally gave in. I brought him here, and he climbed up into the branches. When he fell . . ."

A-ma guides me back into the rain and through the trees to the opposite side of the grove to the very edge of a precipice. I've lived on Nannuo my entire life, but I've never seen the tops of so many peaks at the same time. Even I understand that this spot has ideal *feng shui* with its marriage of mountains, wind, and fog, mist and rain. Everything in this spot—trees, climate, insects, and animals—has existed in natural harmony for centuries, millennia. Except for what happened to my grandfather . . .

"He was dead by the time I reached his side," A-ma confides in such a low voice it's as if she doesn't want the trees to hear. "Broken neck. I had to drag him back to the village."

Around the boulder and down the mountain? How?

"This tragedy," A-ma goes on, "caused your a-ba and brothers to hate all wild tea. Since that day not even your a-ba has dared to follow me here. It's my duty to care for these trees, especially the mother tree. It will be your duty too one day. And you must promise that you'll never let a man enter this grove."

"I promise, but . . . A-ma, this tree is sick. Do you see those yellow threads? They're going to strangle the tree."

Laughter bubbles out of her. "If I let your a-ba and brothers come here, they'd spray the mother tree with poison to kill all the parasites who've found a home in her bark. They'd scrape away the fungi and molds and smash the bugs with their fingernails, but in the long-ago time, farmers let their tea trees grow naturally. Look above us, Girl. See how the camphors protect and hide the mother tree from spirits? The fragrance from the camphors is soothing to us, but it also wards off insects and pests. In other parts of the forest, poisonous plants can grow around the base of ancient and neglected wild tea trees, which means the leaves can produce stomach upset, even death. But do you see anything poisonous here? No. What I'm trying to tell you is that the men in our family wouldn't know what the yellow threads are, and they wouldn't like or trust them." The skin at the corners of her eyes crinkles. "I look at our trees differently."

Our trees. I'm still not sure how to feel about that.

"These trees are sacred," A-ma states simply. "And those yellow threads are the mother tree's most precious gift. I've helped many people with the leaves and threads from the mother tree when all else has failed. Do you remember when Lo-zeh had that growth in his armpit? My tea made it disappear. And what about Da-tu? His face would turn red and veins throbbed in his temple. Akha Law tells us no man should beat his wife, but we know it can happen. After the ceremonies for wife beating didn't work, the nima and the ruma sought my advice. I gave Da-tu my special tea. His face returned to a normal color, and his wild emotions calmed."

Those are two examples, but I can think of many people she hasn't healed, who've suffered terribly, who've died. I'm only ten years old, and I'm having trouble with the memories surfacing in my mind. The woman who wasted away to nothing . . . The man who accidentally sliced open his leg and eventually succumbed to the green pus that ate into the wound . . . Some of my own nieces and nephews who died in infancy from fever . . . No leaves or yellow threads or anything A-ma had in any of her satchels helped them, and they didn't help . . .

"What about Deh-ja?" I ask. "What about the—"

"You need to stop thinking about the human rejects."

"I can't."

"Girl, what happened to those babies was not about whether or not they could be healed. We have a tradition. This is our way."

"But Deh-ja and Ci-do were punished too—"

"Stop!" It takes a few seconds for her to still her frustration. Finally, she asks, "Do you remember the time Ci-teh ate honeycomb?"

Of course I do. We were around five years old. Ci-teh's a-ba had brought back to the village honeycomb from a hive he'd found in the forest. He gave some to Ci-teh and me as a treat. One minute she was talking. The next minute she struggled to grab breath and her arms flailed in panic. The ruma appeared right away and began chanting over her. Then A-ma came running . . .

"You put something in her mouth."

"If I'd waited for the nima to arrive and go into his trance—"

"You saved Ci-teh."

"Saved?" Again she makes that bubble laughter. "The spirit priest performed the proper incantations, and the shaman brings power with him wherever he goes." She kneels before me so we're eye to eye. "It's always better to let them take credit for a good outcome. Do you understand?"

I love my a-ma and I'm grateful she saved my friend, but I'm still struggling. I look around the grove and see not health and cures but superstition and traditions that hurt people.

"So," A-ma says as she rises, "you'll start coming here with me. I'll teach you how to care for the trees and make medicines."

I'm supposed to feel special—and I can see that the mother tree and this entire garden mean more to A-ma than her husband, sons, daughter, or grandchildren—but everything I've learned feels like a cut into my flesh with a dull knife.

"It's time to go," A-ma says. "Remember, Girl, no man can come here. No one should come here."

"Not even Ci-teh?" I ask.

"Not even Ci-teh. Not even your sisters-in-law or nieces. This place is for the women in our bloodline alone. You to me to my mother to . . ." Her voice trails off. She glides her hand down the mother tree's bumpy trunk. A gentle caress.

She's as quiet on the way down the mountain as she was on the way up. I can tell from the stiffness in her shoulders and the heaviness of her silence that she's supremely disappointed in me. I didn't react to my inheritance with enough joy, awe, or gratitude. But how could I, really? A-ma may be the most important woman in our village, but every single man and boy is above her. I would be violating Akha Law to believe her over anything one of them said, and A-ba says this grove is cursed, filled with old trees no one wants and one tree that caused the death of his father. For whatever reason—whether it's punishment against A-ma's female line for bringing the grove into his family or he just thinks so lowly of me because I'm a girl—this is what he has provided as my dowry.

My final acceptance of this allows me to see my future very

clearly. I'll have to hope for true love to find a mate, because I've been given nothing of value to take into marriage apart from my poor embroidery skills, a worthless grove of ancient tea trees, and my face, which may not be pretty enough to overcome my other disadvantages. The entire way home, I think about what I can do to change my fate. We Akha are meant to roam, and right now I feel anxious to escape. I have enough sense to know, however, that I can't go anywhere yet. I'm only a child, after all, and I wouldn't last many days alone in the jungle. Teacher Zhang said, "You don't have to stay on this mountain forever." Maybe education can help with my flight, if only in my mind.

The next day is Monkey Day. I leave the house when it's still dark. And, yes, it's still raining. I arrive at the schoolhouse wet but determined to enjoy the rhythms of learning. Teacher Zhang launches into a history lesson about the land. It's one we've all heard before, but today I hear it very differently. He begins by talking about how for centuries the people in these mountains worked for big landlords, who passed down tea tree gardens from generation to generation, keeping and hoarding everything.

"Peasants stayed poor," he drones. "They often starved to death. Life was not fair. But after Chairman Mao united the country in . . . What year?"

"Nineteen-forty-nine," we chant.

"All land was confiscated and redistributed to the masses."

I know this is so, because my a-ba's family was given a little land—not to own, all land belongs to the government, but to be responsible for. A-ma's family, who lived on the other side of Nannuo Mountain, also received land. They didn't tell anyone about the hidden grove. If someone had found out, they would have been classified as landlords. Luckily, the grove was, as I now know, so utterly hard to find that it had escaped detection by surveyors or other farmers. It wasn't on anyone's map, so it wasn't confiscated by a landlord, redistributed by Chairman Mao, taken back by him during the Great Leap Forward, or impacted by what Teacher Zhang is talking about now.

"Nine years ago, in a deal that was part of a nationwide program to return property to original owners, old landlord families in this area were once again allowed to work their ancestral lands. But they, and all Chinese, still had no rights to ownership. Neither do people like you."

Finally, he arrives at the most important part of his lesson: the Thirty Years No Change policy, which singled out the ethnic minorities in the tea mountains of Yunnan. I lean forward and listen hard. This policy affects each of us, and yet no matter how many times I hear it explained, I'm still confused. Once Teacher Zhang said it was supposed to be like that: "Confusing on purpose."

"Six years ago, the Thirty Years No Change policy divided the land yet again," he begins. "Each person—from infant to those in their nineties—received an allotment. The divisions were supposed to be fair, with each family receiving some land in the sun and some in the shade, some on steep slopes and some that could easily be cared for, some rocky and some with soil rich with nutrients, some with tea trees and some with terraced rice paddies." The stretch of his mouth sags as wilted and forlorn as a length of vine cut from its mother plant. "Are there problems with this policy?"

Yes, but no one would be foolish enough to say them out loud. No baby born since the policy was given to us has received an allotment of land. When an elder dies, the land is either kept in the family or returned to the village. When a woman marries out, she often loses her land to her father or a brother, but when she goes to her husband's village, she isn't given new land.

"Think, children, think. What repercussions has this policy had on your families?"

Still no one raises a hand. Teacher Zhang begins calling on different boys and girls. The stories are more or less the same. Once the land allotments were assigned to a family—maybe two people, maybe thirty people—the a-ba took charge and determined who would receive the land in the sun, the rocky hillside, and so on. My a-ba kept the best land for himself. He slashed and burned his tea trees to raise ducks, pigs, and chickens. The ducks died, he could never afford a pig, and we used our chickens for ceremonial purposes faster than they could lay eggs. He then tried to grow market crops. The monsoon season guarantees that the rice will turn out well, and we would starve if not for it, but otherwise A-ba does not have the gift for growing vegetables.

As the second most valuable person in the family, First Brother was given the second-best land. Like A-ba, he burned his tea trees. In their place, he planted tea bushes on terraces. Second Brother received the third-best land. He pollarded his tea trees—the tops were hacked off so that new and shorter branches would grow—making the leaves easier to pick and supposedly more profitable. So far that hasn't turned out to be so, because these plants are susceptible to diseases and parasites and require large amounts of fertilizer and pesticides. Third Brother received land immediately around our house and close to the village. He's the owner of many tea trees—two to four hundred years old. Since the tea collection center won't buy those leaves, Third Brother has done nothing to his groves. "Too much work," he says. This tea costs us nothing, so that's what we drink.

A-ba assigned A-ma's hidden land—with its worthless bride-price of ancient tea trees—to me. I was four at the time. Even if I'd been the age I am now, what could I have done to change the result? Nothing, because I'm only a daughter. I'll be thirty-four when the Thirty Years No Change policy ends. No one knows what will happen then. But one thing is certain . . .

"Everything always changes," Teacher Zhang says. "Now we've entered a new era. Paramount Leader Deng Xiaoping has given us a slogan to follow. *To get rich is glorious . . .*"

As he sometimes does when the last minutes before the lunch break near, Teacher Zhang points to the wrinkled posters of Beijing tacked to the bamboo walls. "If you study hard, maybe you could visit our capital one day." His arm drops limp as he stares at the images: thousands of people riding bicycles, everyone dressed alike. He looks homesick, but I would die if I had to live in a place like that. He sighs, blinks a few times, and then asks in the saddest voice, "Does anyone have any questions?"

In return, he gets only requests.

"Tell us about telephones."

"Tell us about television again."

"And movies! Tell us about movies."

A small smile lifts the corners of Teacher Zhang's mouth. "I'll have to use Mandarin characters," he says, turning to the blackboard. "The most important character to learn is *dian*. Who can tell me what it means?"

"*Lightning!*" The students sing out in perfect chorus.

"We can also call that *electricity*," he says.

"*Electricity*," we repeat as one, echoing his pronunciation as closely as possible.

"If I add the character—"

"*Speak*," we practically shout as he writes the character next to *dian*.

"I get—"

"*Telephone!*"

"If I add the characters for *vision* and *sowing seeds* to *dian*, I get—"

"*Television!*"

"And if I write *shadow* next to *dian*, I get—"

"Electric shadow! *Movie!*"

We don't have electricity, and we don't have telephones, television, or movies either. Until today I really and truly didn't believe they might actually exist. They had only been exciting things to hear about and much more fun than doing our math tables or identifying the countries around us that none of us have ever seen, will ever see, or can even imagine. Today, though, I understand just how sneaky Teacher Zhang is. He's made us beg him to teach us Mandarin. Or maybe he's tricky, which is why he was sent here in the first place and will never be allowed to return home. I hope so anyway, because I never want him to leave. I need him.

I run outside with the other kids, but I watch for Teacher Zhang to emerge from the classroom with his usual jar filled with hot water. Once he's settled on his own bamboo platform to eat his lunch, I walk over to him, reach into my pocket, and hand him a pinch of tea processed from last-grade leaves.

"Help me, Teacher Zhang. Help me."

Naturally, A-ba and my brothers are against extra schooling for me. "What husband wants a wife who thinks she's smarter than he is?" A-ba asks Teacher Zhang when he presents the idea, while A-ma looks at him as though he has plague pustules.

"A-ba, I will learn wife and mother responsibilities," I volunteer. "I'll continue to be a good daughter and help with tea picking. I won't miss a single chore or duty. If I do—even if it happens for the length of a swallow's blink—I promise I'll put away my books forever."

"No."

A half cycle later, Teacher Zhang goes around my father's back and invites the headman, ruma, and nima to our house to consult.

"The only education the girl needs is from her mother," the headman says. "A time will come when we will require a new midwife."

"I will learn those duties," I pledge. And I will too, because I don't see a way for my plan to work otherwise. That said, I won't meet A-ma's eyes for fear she'll see the truth in my heart. I can never be a midwife.

The headman, ruma, and nima glance at my a-ba to get his reaction.

"I have already said no," he says.

The village leaders seem willing to accept a father's decision about his daughter, but then Teacher Zhang starts rudely picking at the wound of inferiority we all carry.

"I've lived many years among you," he says, "and I can tell you this. Your people have no regard for education. You would rather let your children gather food, hunt, and nap than study. You boast of the Akha having one mind, but that mind is shy, closed, and suspicious. In this way, you ethnic minorities are all alike."

Embarrassed, the headman decides Teacher Zhang has hit upon a good idea: "She will bring honor to our village and inspire other children."

But the others remain silent in their opposition.

"To you, this meager girl is just another mouth to feed until she marries out," Teacher Zhang persists. "But if you let her continue her studies, she may help you one day." He mulls over the possibilities. "What if the government decides you need a village cadre as you did during the Great Leap Forward and the Cultural Revolution? Those were dark days, were they not? Wouldn't you prefer to have someone from Spring Well speak on your behalf?"

When the nima comes out of his trance, he says, "Let her go to second-level school, and later third-level school, if she qualifies. She'll become fluent in Mandarin. In later years, she'll be able to communicate with Han majority people."

"And, if they decide we need a village cadre to watch over us again, we'll present her as our candidate," the ruma adds, also agreeing with Teacher Zhang.

Sun and Moon! So I can take the blame and accept all the heat if the people of Spring Well Village don't obey the government's orders? Or did the ruma go along with the plan because I would be easily manipulated and controlled as a girl? Even A-ba saw that those men were looking out more for their own welfare than for mine. "No," he said, which was remarkable given that the headman, ruma, and nima were united. In the end, though, their interests were more important than rules for girls, and A-ba was only one man with too many powers against him. Teacher Zhang and I had won.

For the next two years, I work very hard: doing home chores, picking tea, following and learning from A-ma, attending school, and working privately with Teacher Zhang to improve my math skills. I take and pass the test that will allow me to go to second-level school. The headman, ruma, and nima call the village together to announce the news and present A-ba with a pouch of tobacco as praise for being such a farsighted father. Teacher Zhang gives me a copy of one of Lu Xun's books, "so you'll know our greatest writer."

Months later, when the new session opens, I walk alone to the second-level school. I'm very scared. I'm twelve years old and still quite small. Entering the school yard, I hear many different languages—Dai, Yi, Lahu, Hani, Naxi, and Mandarin. I don't catch a single word of Ahka. Only when I get into my classroom and we're assigned seats—something I've never experienced before—and I'm put in the back corner do I discover another Ahka. I recognize him right away: San-pa, the pancake stealer.

PART II

A BEAUTIFUL FLOWER CALLS

1994–1996

A BLIND KITTEN

Each year in the month of *Chor Law Bar Lar*—which is similar to what the Han majority calls the eighth lunar month and what I now know the rest of the world calls September—we have the Swing Festival. The four-day celebration always begins on Buffalo Day, exactly nine full cycles—one hundred and eight days—after the ruma has told the people of his particular village to plant their rice. The festival has yet another purpose beyond a sacred thanksgiving, and that is for boys and girls of marriageable age to meet. For this reason, some people call the Swing Festival the Women's New Year, because it can be the beginning of life for us. This year I turned sixteen, and now the women in my family have gathered to help me put on my headdress for the first time.

"When you reached twelve years, you discarded your child's cap so you might wear a simple scarf," A-ma begins. "Two years later, you tied a beaded sash around your waist, which hung down and kept your skirt from flying up."

She motions to Third Sister-in-law, who holds up my headdress. It's decorated with dyed chicken feathers, monkey fur edging, colorful woolen pom-poms, and silver coins, balls, and pendants that A-ma and others have given me over the years.

"The effort you've put into this will show your future husband and his family your meticulousness, willingness to do hard work, and knowledge of the Akha's path of migration through embroidered symbols," Third Sister-in-law says, proud of her teaching. "It will also announce your artistic sensibilities, which you can pass on in the unfortunate event that one day you give birth to a daughter."

She hands the headdress to A-ma, who gently ties it over my hair. Five kilos was a lot lighter in my lap than it is on my head, and my neck wobbles a bit.

"You have now received the gift of womanhood," A-ma says.

The sisters-in-law smile, and my nieces stare at me enviously. When I look in the mirror, I see a thin, but pretty, girl. My eyes are wide and shaped like leaves. My nose comes to a delicate point, unlike the mashed noses of Han majority women. My cheeks are tawny from the sun and mountain air. I'm most definitely ready for marriage. I wish I could run outside this instant to see if the boy I secretly love has come, but the ceremony isn't over.

"As promised," A-ma continues, "you've never missed a single chore or duty. You thresh rice and grind it under the house every morning. You haul water. You work as hard as your brothers during tea-picking season . . ."

Her voice trails off. This is to make me remember all the time we've spent on my useless land, tending to the mother and sister trees. Instead I think about all the classwork I completed aided by Teacher Zhang's ongoing tutoring and how I learned never to talk to my family about what I'd been taught. I made that mistake early on when I told A-ma and A-ba that a lunar eclipse was not caused by a spirit dog eating the moon and that Burma was now called Myanmar.

"You can now make potions," First Sister-in-law says. "You gave my daughter tea leaves to place over her pimples so they'd disappear quickly."

"And you gave them to me to reduce the circles under my eyes," Second Sister-in-law adds. "My husband benefited from the wild tobacco you told him to chew to help with his toothaches, and now he uses the gooey residue left in his pipe to kill leeches just as you recommended."

"You know the proper opium dosages to give to the dying," Third Sister-in-law says in awe. "And you've even learned how to extract and then boil the stomach contents of a porcupine to give to someone who is unable to stop vomiting."

A-ma holds up a hand to silence the others. "Most important, you have learned the skill of delivering babies."

It's true. When that mother in Bamboo Forest Village gave birth to a stillborn, I made sure that the tragedy was buried in the forest. The next year, she had a second stillborn. Tradition says that this child is the first baby returning. I instructed the father to throw the corpse in water to break the cycle of returning. The next year, the couple had a perfect baby boy. In other villages, I saw three human rejects come into and leave the world. One had a head double the normal size; one was too small; and the last had a particular look that A-ma said marked him as a future idiot.

"Never once have you faltered," A-ma says.

But what changes A-ma and I have seen since the birth of Ci-do and Deh-ja's human rejects! I now understand that I live in an area so remote that we didn't hear about the One Child policy for almost fifteen years. When the Family Planning Office finally opened at the tea collection center, it was only for Han majority workers, because this policy doesn't affect *any* ethnic minority *anywhere* in the country. However, if a Han woman gets pregnant with a second child, she'll be made to abort it and pay a fine. If she continues her reckless behavior, she'll be sterilized. But this talk of midwifery isn't just to praise me. It's the prelude to the warning every girl who puts on her headdress for the first time is given by her a-ma.

"Today, across the country, babies have a value they never had before, and we Akha get to have them," she says. "Even multiple litters of twins if we want! Our ruma and nima have accepted this—with sly male satisfaction—because this is the *one thing* we have better than the Han majority." When she says, "It is a shame this change didn't occur sooner," I know she's speaking of the one terrible time twins were born in our village. Then she adds, as if to comfort me, "Fortunately, our leaders were quick to embrace change. Other villages . . . Well, it can be hard abandoning something you've done and believed in for generations." She pauses to let me absorb her words. Then, "No matter what, though, we, like Han majority people, would not condone the birth of a baby if the mother was unmarried. Everyone knows that having a child without a husband is taboo."

This is one of our traditions that makes no sense. Boys and girls are encouraged to do the intercourse before marriage, but a girl is forbidden to come to a head. No matter. I'm too smart to let the second part happen to me. I've read novels, and studied history, math, and science. Together they have taught me the importance of independent thinking, watching out for my body, and looking to the future.

"You are a woman now," A-ma says, and the others nod their heads at the solemnity of the moment.

Just then, from outside, I hear Ci-teh call my name.

"May I leave?" I ask A-ma.

It's an abrupt end to the ceremony, but what else is left to say? I'm shooed out the door, with A-ma calling, "This is a big day for both of you."

Ci-teh waits for me at the bottom of the stairs. I'd like to tell her she looks beautiful in her headdress and festival clothing, but we Akha never use that word to describe another human.

"All the boys will want to take you to the Flower Room when they see you," I say in greeting.

"The Flower Room? I've already done that." She giggles. "I'd rather go into the forest to steal love. The question is when are *you* going to the Flower Room?"

I blush. Just the idea of meeting alone with a boy without our parents . . .

"Of course," she continues casually but knowing the effect her words will have on me, "if *he* comes, you might want to take him straight into the forest. There's nothing to it, you know. You need to stop behaving like a blind kitten and act your age. Otherwise you'll never get married."

Some boys and girls—like my friend—have been going into the forest to steal love since they were twelve. Not me. My free time was taken up with homework and studying. Over time, my seat in school was moved forward until I sat in the front row. San-pa also began to move forward, reaching the middle of the room. In another two years, we'll take the *gaokao,* the countrywide test to see if we'll be allowed to continue our education at a first-, second-, third-, or fourth-tier university or college. If we fail, we won't have a chance to take it again. If we make it, we'll be the first members of any mountain tribe on our mountain to be granted higher education. Then we'll get married, have as many children as we want, and be a part of all the changes that are still to come to our prefecture . . .

I'm not sure when I fell in love with San-pa. A week ago when he teased me about wanting to see me in my headdress? A year ago when I helped him for hours with his algebra homework? Or maybe six years ago when he gave me that bite of pancake? We have spent so much time together these past few years as the only Akha in our class. Together we studied the history of other countries beyond those that abut our borders but are still similar to China in outlook: Russia, North Korea, and Cuba. Together we struggled through the great Chinese novels—*Dream of the Red Chamber* and *Rickshaw Boy*—as well as those written by our Russian friends—Tolstoy and Dostoevsky. We've talked and talked. And we've spent hours together, just walking, partway to and from our first- and second-level schools. He's always been interested in what I have to say, and I've loved hearing about his hunting expeditions with his a-ba and other men in his village. I've been able to help him with his essays, and he's always shown his appreciation by bringing me a little treat plucked from the jungle—a blossom, a necklace of woven vine, or an egg from a nest.

"If San-pa asks me to go to the Flower Room or the forest, I'll go," I confide to Ci-teh in a whisper.

People in the next village can probably hear her laughter. Although we no longer spend the entire day together as we did when we were in Teacher Zhang's class, Ci-teh and I are still as close as two girls can be.

"If you don't like it with him, then steal love with one of the other boys who'll be here during the festival," she says once she's caught her breath. "You can do it as long as he isn't in your clan."

"Stealing love with San-pa won't be for me like it is for you and—"

"Boys try out girls. Girls try out boys," Ci-teh continues right over me. "If they both like the intercourse, then the boy will ask for marriage. If the girl comes to a head by mistake, then they will either get married or the girl will visit your a-ma for one of her special potions. If neither of them likes the intercourse, then why would they want to spend the rest of their lives together? Then it's only right to look elsewhere."

"I'm not of a mind to sample every pumpkin in the market. I only want San-pa. Until we become village elders. Until we die. Forever into the afterworld."

My admission sends Ci-teh into another spiral of giggles.

We climb a series of paths to a clearing that overlooks the village. Some men have already taken down the old swing, while others watch over a pit where pieces of a sacrificed ox turn on a spit. I look for San-pa in the crowd, but there are so many people . . . Women barter homemade brooms, embroideries, or dried wild mushrooms for silver beads and other trimmings for their headdresses. Men trade home-cured hides for iron to give to the village blacksmith to hone into blades for machetes and ax heads. Ci-teh and I are the only girls in our village who've put on our headdresses for the first time, and boys look us over like goats to be traded.

Ci-teh pulls on my sleeve. "When the time comes—and it will—you let him make a way down there first. It will still hurt, but it will hurt less. He's probably stolen love before. He'll know what to do."

Before I have a chance to ask what *make a way* means, whoops and hollers cut through the air as a throng of young men emerge from the forest with four thin tree trunks stripped of their bark. One member of the pack carries over his arm loops of magic vine. San-pa! I'm accustomed to seeing him in school in unadorned leggings and tunic, but today he's dressed as a man who wants to announce to everyone what a good family he's from. His mother has dipped the cloth of his shorts and jacket in indigo dye many times to get a deep and very rich color. Even from afar I can see that his jacket is built of many layers. And his mother or sisters or both have stitched his belt with five bands of intricate embroidery. Instead of a turban, he wears a cap sheathed with silver cutouts hammered into the shapes of acanthus leaves.

"Look at him," Ci-teh sighs dramatically. "He's definitely come to look for a wife. He's come for you! Why else would he walk so far? Why else would he join the boys from our village in going to the forest for the vine and to cut the trees? Hours on mountain paths and he still looks so . . ."

"Man beautiful," I finish for her.

"Beautiful?" Ci-teh covers her mouth to hide her giggles.

He spots me. He doesn't pretend indifference. His mouth spreads into a wide grin, and he begins threading his way through the crowd toward Ci-teh and me. She clamps shut her mouth, but I can feel her excitement. He stops a meter in front of us. His eyes shine like black pebbles washed by the rain.

"You have a nice village," he says, "but I look forward to the day when you come to mine. It's bigger, and we're on the crest of a hill and not in a saddle."

His meaning could not be clearer. He's telling me he'll make a good husband, because his village is better—wealthier and easier to defend—than mine. I blush so deeply that I'm sure I've turned the color of mulberry juice, which is so embarrassing that I feel my face burn even worse. Fortunately, the ruma arrives in the clearing.

The swing won't go up until tomorrow, so this part of the ceremony will be short. The ruma starts his ritual chanting, but we don't fully understand what comes out of his mouth. Our culture was built over many centuries by ancestors who lived on the earth before us. How they pronounced their words a hundred or a thousand years ago is only for the ruma to know. By the time he's done, I'm ready to have a proper conversation.

"May I show you my village?" I ask.

It feels natural to walk by San-pa's side, pointing out who lives where and telling little stories about our neighbors. He takes it all in, asking questions that in all the years we've known each other we've never discussed.

"How many brothers do you have?" he inquires. "How many sisters? How many cousins live in the main house?"

I ask him the same questions and follow up with "How many newlywed huts does your family have?"

"I'm the only son," he answers. "My three sisters have already married out."

So his a-ma and a-ba will welcome a daughter-in-law, be happy to build a newlywed hut, and eagerly await the sounds of grandchildren in the main house.

"I'll visit my sisters' villages on my way home," he goes on since I've been so busy figuring in my head.

"You're not leaving tonight, are you?" I stammer.

"If you'd like, I could stay for the entire festival."

"I'd like that very much." And another rush of blood floods my face.

We circle the village and return to the swing clearing, where everyone has gathered around a bonfire for the feast. San-pa joins the other unmarried boys, and I sit with my family. Our eyes keep meeting. Our silent communication is so deep that it feels as though we are the only two people here.

The music, singing, and dancing begin immediately after the meal. Someone hands San-pa a drum, and he joins the other men as they dance illuminated by the firelight. His body rises and falls with each beat of the drum. The warmth I feel comes not from the fire or my blushing cheeks but from below my waist. For the first time, my body fully understands why boys and girls want to go to the forest to steal love.

The next morning, everyone gathers again in the clearing, where the ruma supervises the men as the four poles for the new swing are put in place then tilted inward until they meet at the top. A man of small stature shimmies up one of the poles and secures them together. He then fastens a long length of vine to the top, letting the looped end hang down in the center of the pyramid. Last, the ruma makes offerings to appease earth spirits and protect us from any accidents.

"I am a-ma and a-ba to Spring Well Village," he chants. "Like a mother hen, I protect those under my wing. Like the father water buffalo, I protect them with my horns."

He grabs the vine, walks up the hill, and places his left foot in the loop. Then, accompanied by cheers, he careens down between the poles and out into the air over the ledge that overlooks the village. Next, every male—from eldest to youngest—takes a turn.

Finally, we girls get our chance. For reasons of modesty, a board is strung through the foothold for us to sit on. When my turn comes, Ci-teh and Third Sister-in-law give me a push and then I'm flying down between the poles and up and out into space. The wind rushes through my headdress. The bells and other silver ornaments jingle. The chicken feathers flutter. The silver on my breastplate catches the sun. I'm a soaring bird for San-pa, and I can't stop smiling and laughing as I pass back and forth over his head. He returns my smiles and laughs.

Later that night—after another feast—I take San-pa to the Flower Room. Some boys and girls have already paired off. I don't spot a private place for the two of us, but that doesn't matter. Our parents aren't watching, so we can do whatever we want. When San-pa pulls me into his arms, we both seem to know what to do. His lips are gentle on mine. With a moan that I've only heard coming from a newlywed hut, he buries his face in my neck and kisses me again and again. I feel like I can barely stand.

The next morning, as A-ma and I grind grain beneath the house, she asks, "Who were you with last night? Was it Law-ba?"

A-ma and A-ba have always liked Law-ba, who lives in Bamboo Forest Village. We went to the same primary school, and my parents have always hoped I'd marry him. He wears glasses with big black rims that make him look like an owl—but with none of an owl's intelligence—and I've never once thought about visiting the Flower Room with him.

I keep my head bent to the millstone, hoping she'll think of something else to talk about, but she's an a-ma and it's her duty to be nosy.

"Was it the stranger boy I saw gazing at you?" she persists.

"I guess so," I answer when I know perfectly well it was San-pa.

"But isn't he the one who stole the pancake all those years ago?" She doesn't chide me for taking him to the Flower Room. Instead, she cuts straight to the heart of the problem. "He was born on a Tiger Day. You were born on a Pig Day. That will never change. Your a-ba and I will never agree to a marriage."

"But I love San-pa."

"You love San-pa?" His name comes off her tongue like a bitter herb. "What you are doing is an irresponsible act of fate-tempting."

But I'm not going to give up. Not ever. "He will be a good husband. His family is better than ours. We are both educated—"

"None of that matters, and you know it! There is no purpose to his visit," she states with finality. "You will need to find another boy."

Hours later—after more swinging and feasting—I let San-pa lead me into the forest. The world shimmers with life around us: the fragrance of flowers, earth, and wild animals; the sounds of frogs in incessant song, animals howling in their mating, and the caws of birds who stare down at us with reflective eyes; the air itself bathes our skin with its warm breath. We walk until we find ground cushioned with leaves and pine needles softened by the passing of seasons. We sit side by side, staring out at a range of mountains that bank away from us, becoming more and more shrouded with mist, humidity, and distance until they melt into the blue-gray sky.

"Are you sure you want to do this?" he asks.

"I'm sure."

We turn to each other. He kisses me as he slowly lowers me to the ground. He fumbles with my clothes. His callused hands tell me that he works hard for his family. He squeezes one of my nipples, and a foreign-sounding yip escapes my lips. I haven't practiced with other boys, but I yearn to touch the flesh beneath his tunic. His chest is smooth. His muscles are firm under my palms. He pulls up my skirt, reaches above my leggings, and touches that part of me that has become slick and wet, but he's the one who moans. He stares into my eyes. I see all the way to his soul. Whatever he has between his legs has to find what I have between mine. I may not have done this before, but I've seen roosters mount the females of their species. Pigs, dogs, and cats too. San-pa helps me flip over until I'm on my hands and knees. Something hot and hard slaps against my rear end. I arch my back at the feel of his fingers. I'm so happy for Ci-teh's advice, because he's making a way exactly as he should.

"San-pa." His name is an ocean in my mouth, carrying me to a place I never knew existed. His hands come to rest on my hips. Then that hot thing back there finds my entrance and begins to push. I push back . . . *Waaa!* Such pain—like the blacksmith's poker stabbing me. I collapse to my elbows. We both hold completely still. He leans down over me, putting his mouth close to my ear.

"Should I continue?"

I take a breath and nod. Slowly, slowly, he moves back and forth. The startling pain is gone, but I don't feel anything close to the urgency I felt before. San-pa does though, and he picks up his rhythm—just as I've seen all those male animals do. When he's done, he falls onto on his back next to me, hiding the hot thing under his tunic before I get a chance to see it.

"Next time it will be better," he says. "I promise." He kisses me and smooths my skirt down my legs. "Will you stay the night with me?"

When I nod, he wraps his arms around me, pulling me to his chest. I close my eyes and listen to his heartbeat.

"I was an unmarried girl too . . . once," A-ma comments when I arrive home the next morning. "Just remember today is a day of ceremonial abstinence for the entire village. That means—"

"I know what it means," I retort. What I'm thinking, though, is that my sore parts will have a chance to heal.

"You were supposed to be different with your school and your plans—"

"None of that has changed."

She doesn't believe me. "You're no different than any other girl on this mountain. Stupid with love." She sighs and goes back to her grain grinding.

It may be a day of ceremonial abstinence—the requirement that we must be careful with our arms and legs has new meaning to me—but San-pa and I go to the forest anyway. "Just to talk," he says. We return to the spot where we did the intercourse. We sit, and he tells me how he's loved me since he first saw me at the tea collection center. He couldn't say anything to make me happier, and he couldn't do anything to make me happier than when he reaches into his pocket and gives me the eye of a peacock feather.

"For your headdress," he says.

"How did you get it?" I ask.

He juts his chin. "It's enough for you to know that I found something that might bring you joy."

Our future is clear. Now that he's given me a gift, all that's left is for his parents to send emissaries to ask my a-ma and a-ba if he can take me to his village in marriage. We'll graduate . . . Go to university . . . Join the market economy . . .

The following week, I'm surprised to discover Teacher Zhang in the school yard during lunch. Rumors travel fast, and I suspect he's come to congratulate me. I'm wrong.

"Are you sure marriage to this boy is what you want?" he asks. "You've worked so hard."

I try to be polite. "You've been my greatest teacher."

"What about the *gaokao*?"

"San-pa and I will take it together."

Teacher Zhang shakes his head sadly. "You know he'll never be invited to take the test, and even if by some miracle he is invited, he'll never pass, while you have a future. You could be the first on this mountain to go to Ethnic Normal College, or maybe even Yunnan University."

"You're wrong about San-pa—"

"If you marry him, tradition will weigh on you," he insists. "Your families will want you to stay home, have babies, and heal like your mother."

He hears what he's saying as a threat, but San-pa will never let those things happen.

"Tell me you won't stop studying," he persists.

"I won't stop studying," I promise. "I'll take the test even if San-pa doesn't."

Teacher Zhang nods his head three times very sharply, and then shifts his shoulders within his jacket. With that, he leaves, going back to the primary school for his afternoon class.

I look around the yard for San-pa. I spot him sitting on a wall with some other boys, their legs dangling. I realize he's watched my exchange with Teacher Zhang, but he doesn't cross the yard to ask me about it.

I still love my family and do my chores obediently. And I still cherish Ci-teh but reveal little to her of the dreams of the life I'll have with San-pa. Ci-teh, perhaps sensing this new and growing space between us, finds excuses for us to leave the village—"We're going to gather firewood. We'll be back soon"—so I can open my heart to her without fear of others eavesdropping. I understand her desire, because we've always shared everything. But even as Ci-teh wants to hear every detail, I find myself hoarding them, speaking insignificantly about my emotions and skirting her questions by asking if her father has received any proposals since the Swing Festival. (Her family is once again the richest on the mountain, having recovered from the setback caused by the sacrifices required to absolve and cleanse them of human rejects. As a result, Ci-teh will go into marriage with many gifts.) She tells me about this and that boy, but it doesn't make me any more forthcoming.

My evasions must hurt her feelings, because she strikes out at me by saying, "People say San-pa still visits other girls in their villages' Flower Rooms."

"I don't believe it," I tell her, and I don't.

When she hints at names and places, I can come to only one conclusion.

"Are you jealous?" I ask.

She gives me a haughty look. "Of what?"

"Of me, because you visit the Flower Room and steal love in the forest with different boys, and none of them have asked to marry *you*?"

"That's a mean thing to say when I'm just trying to be your friend."

"*Waaa!* Don't you think it's mean to repeat gossip? And even if he does those things, what makes him any worse than you—or any other boy or girl on Nannuo Mountain—who tries the intercourse? That's what we Akha are *supposed* to do before marriage."

She remains silent for a long while. Finally, she asks, plainly and simply, "Are you one of those girls who forgets her friends when she does the intercourse? I didn't forget you when I started doing it."

That I don't have an answer causes both of us anguish. But isn't this how it's always been between us—with one falling and the other rising?

San-pa comes often to Spring Well Village. We've met in the Flower Room. We've gone into the forest. I went ahead and asked him about other girls, and he asked me about other boys. My answer: "None." His response: "No other girls for me either." I've come to enjoy the intercourse, and we've even done it not like animals but face-to-face. I like that especially. Being able to look into his eyes. Kissing his mouth. Wrapping my legs around him. Afterward, when he walks home, I stay perched on our pine-needle bed, and we sing call-and-response love songs across the hillsides.

"The flowers bloom at their peaks, waiting for the butterflies to come—"

"The honeycombs wait for the bees to make honey—"

"A beautiful flower calls to her love—"

"The bee flies through the air to find her—"

"He drinks her nectar—"

"She holds him in her petals—"

We sing the refrain in unison, letting all who hear us know that our love is absolute. "Let us pick flowers together. Alloo sae, ah-ee-ah-ee-o, ah-ee-ah-ee-o."

We're happy, but one thing has not changed since the pancake incident. As A-ma reminded me, I was born on Pig Day, and San-pa was born on Tiger Day. This is not an auspicious match, so naturally our families are against a union. In the manner of all Akha fathers, A-ba sends messages to me indirectly. First Sister-in-law touches my shoulder and confides. "A weak boy grows up to be a weak man." Second Sister-in-law is brusque. "The whole mountain knows he's lazy." Third Sister-in-law, my favorite, mutters to me, "You won't have anything to eat if you marry that good-for-nothing." They can say whatever they want, but that doesn't make it so.

A-ba has allowed San-pa into the house, and the two of them have spoken. The situation for my family is better these days, which influences how the conversation proceeds. Three years ago, my a-ba was able to trade some of our extra rice for a young female pig. She grew up, was bred, and now we have three pigs sleeping under our floor. We'll never be as well off as Ci-teh's family, but A-ba's improved status gives him the confidence to hold out for the best marriage proposal that will arrive for me.

Sitting next to our home's dividing wall, I've been able to listen to the conversations between San-pa and my a-ba. San-pa announces that he's come to fetch a wife, which is how Akha men refer to marriage. "No," A-ba says. San-pa recites his male ancestors back fifty generations. "No," A-ba says. San-pa points out that we don't have any matching ancestors for seven generations, which means we've passed the incest taboo. But A-ba doesn't care. "No," he says. Adding: "It is not yet time for my daughter to go-work-eat," which is the way Akha women look at marriage. "My daughter plans to take the *gaokao* and be the first on Nannuo Mountain to go to college."

That's how much he doesn't like San-pa!

Five months later, the Month of Rest arrives. In the West, it would be considered comparable to February. Since the men don't have to work, they put their most formidable efforts into settling their marriage plans. Unmarried women spend their time weaving and waiting for proposals, which is why this month is sometimes called the Month of Marriage and Weaving. So far, I've done plenty of weaving but have seen no marriage arrangements made.

During the last half of the second cycle, San-pa comes to the house to ask yet again if we can be wed. He receives the usual answer: "No."

"I will be a good husband—"

"I don't think so." Today, instead of the usual mismatched-day argument, A-ba goes in a different direction. "You might think that you live far away and that we would not hear about you. But we have heard. You've been trading in things you shouldn't and trying things you shouldn't. If you were as respectable as you claim, then your parents would have sent two elders from your village to ask for Girl to become a daughter-in-law. They would have sent gifts. If we reached terms, then she would go to your home for a night, make sure she thought she could be happy, and three days later the two of you would marry. None of that has happened, because they disapprove too. I remember your a-ba, Boy, and he was an honorable man. Even all those years ago, he was prepared to protect my daughter's reputation from the actions of his own son."

San-pa has no way to defend himself.

My father speaks again. "The matter is finished."

Later, in the forest, I ask San-pa what my a-ba meant. "What does he think he's heard about you that puts you in such an inky light?"

But San-pa puts his mouth over mine, and we start conversing in other ways.

That afternoon we begin to make a plan.

"We'll move away together," I say. "We'll walk to Menghai. We'll be married there, and no one will stop us."

He tucks escaped wisps of my hair back under the protection of my day-to-day headdress. "I am a man," he says. "You are a woman. It is my duty to care for you. *I* will make the decision. You will stay here and take the *gaokao*. I will leave Nannuo Mountain to find work in one of the other countries where the Akha roam—"

"But can't we stay together? I'll go with you. Laos is so close. Myanmar too—"

"No!" His voice is surprisingly sharp. "It is not right. Your father would never forgive me. *I* will go . . . to Thailand." Does he decide on this country to remind me that he's in charge? "It's a long walk—maybe two hundred and fifty kilometers on a map, but much longer through the mountains. But what are mountains to me? I'll make it in ten days, maybe less. You keep studying and take the *gaokao*. When I return with my pockets heavy with good fortune, I'll find you at your college. I'll join the market economy and make even more money. After you graduate, we'll ask a village where people don't know us if we might be allotted a piece of land. I'll farm, and you'll be a leader of women." He stares into my eyes, surely seeking how deep my love is for him. "We'll tell people I was born on a more compatible day—"

"We could never lie about the lineage!"

"We won't have to. I'm suggesting the change of just one word from Tiger to Sheep. From now on, that's what I'll claim when I meet someone new. It will give us a fresh beginning."

I'm not sure this fabrication is a good idea or that the false label will change the essence of who he is, but I consent to his plan. He will one day be my husband, and I will be his wife. I must learn to obey, if we are to be happy.

He rips two thick threads from the hem of his tunic. "*When going far away, strings must be tied around wrists.* I'll be tied to you, and you'll be tied to me." He loops one of the threads around my wrist and makes a tight knot. As I do the same for him, he continues. "This proves we're human, because spirits don't have strings. I promise to come back with enough money to buy a rice farm and marry you, a girl I've known and loved since childhood. We're going to your a-ma and a-ba right now to tell them."

My entire family—all my brothers, sisters-in-law, nieces and nephews, and my parents—listens to us when we gather in the common room. There is a saying in the Han majority culture about a smiling face hiding bad intentions. That's what I see when I look at the faces that belong to my family. Their mouths say the correct words, but behind their tongues are deeper truths, and they permeate the room.

"Do you want to give up your opportunity to finish school and go to university?" A-ba asks San-pa, when what he really means is, *Go away and never come back*.

"Your parents will be proud of you," A-ma says, but her entire body radiates a message as strong as the sun: *You talk like a flying eagle, but your hands are like Chinese sour vegetables,* meaning, he can talk big all he wants, but he'll forever be a pancake stealer in her eyes.

"This will change the direction of your story," First Brother states, although he could just as easily be saying, *Once you leave here, you'll forget about my sister. So be it.*

My family walks San-pa to the village gate, which means that we don't have a chance for private goodbyes. Still, San-pa says loud enough for everyone to hear, "I promise to come for you, Li-yan."

He backs away, slowly, slowly, not for a second taking his eyes off me. I'm so blinded by tears that I don't see what's about to happen, and my family—curse them—doesn't call out to warn San-pa until it's too late. Instead of passing cleanly through the spirit gate, he backs right into it. It's the worst omen possible and strictly taboo. Even San-pa is startled and alarmed, so much so that he turns and bounds into the forest.

"I hope his parents perform cleansing rituals for him," A-ba comments.

"It doesn't matter. The damage has already been done," A-ma says, barely hiding her contempt. "Come. We must visit the ruma. We need to be cleansed."

THE GREEDY EYES OF A TIGER

The day after San-pa leaves, I visit Ci-teh. We sit on the floor and talk, as though my coolness toward her when San-pa was here never happened. "We are as jungle vines," she says, even though I've hurt her. "Our roots will forever be entwined in friendship."

"Our friendship will go on as far as the stars," I agree, and finally tell her everything about San-pa.

My friend doesn't warn me about him or criticize him. Instead, she closes her eyes and sighs. "One day I'll be as happy as you. Wouldn't it be wonderful if we could marry out to the same village, come to a head together, and help our children to be as close as we are?"

I squeeze her hand and silently make the same wish too.

A few days later, we're catching up on our home chores before tea-picking season begins when frightening noises come thundering from the forest. They grow louder and nearer. Small children cry into their mothers' tunics. Elders quake on their sleeping mats. Dogs crawl under houses, too afraid to bark. The sounds are mechanical but inconsistent—humming one moment, grinding the next. They abruptly end with a hideous cough. Everyone in our village must be inwardly thanking the ruma for building a spirit gate so powerful it barred whatever the horrible thing is from entering Spring Well.

No one ventures to the gate to investigate, but the birds begin to chirp again and the dogs come out from their hiding places. A few minutes later, we hear a male voice call . . . in Mandarin, "Hello, hello, hello!" No one answers. The voice rings out again. "Hello, hello, hello! Is anyone here? Come out. Let us meet." Again, the voice speaks Mandarin, but it sounds off, more melodious, as though he's singing. Still, the voice clearly belongs to a man, and not a spirit. Even I can tell that.

A-ba comes to the dividing wall. "Girl, what is he saying?" After I translate for him, he says, "You'd better come with me, since you've learned the man's tongue."

I meet A-ba outside, where the headman, ruma, and a few other men have already gathered. They all hold their crossbows. As we near the spirit gate, I see a man, a boy, and a car. A car! Green, with a tin red star attached to the front. It's an old People's Liberation Army mountain vehicle—something I've seen in school posters commemorating the War of Liberation. The car door opens, and another man, who's been sitting behind the wheel, steps out. We stay on our side of the spirit gate. The visitors remain on their side of the gate. In the silence, a lot of surveying happens. The driver is dressed nearly identically to Teacher Zhang: blue pants and jacket, like every other nonminority man I've ever seen. But the other two are as odd as can be. The little boy is bald, for one thing, but his father quickly covers his head with a tiny cap with a big brim in front. The child's pants—bright yellow!—are cut well above his knees. The tops of his shoes are made of cloth, but the bottoms look like bendable plastic. His shirt has short sleeves and hugs his body. No buttons or anything like that. Instead, a drawing of a yellow boy with hair that comes up in sharp spikes decorates the front. I try to pronounce the word that's been printed in Western letters coming out of the boy's mouth: *Cow-a-bunga!* It's not a word I know.

I step forward.

"I'm guessing, young lady, that I must speak to your elders through you," the man says. He strides straight through the gate—he must have been warned not to touch it—and extends his hand. "In Mandarin, my name is Huang Benyu. I'm from Hong Kong."

So he's a native Cantonese speaker—which explains his accent and extra tones—but his Mandarin is much better than mine.

"Hong Kong," I murmur. He could just as easily have said the moon.

"This is my son," he states, motioning for the boy to join him. "While we're on the mainland, we'll also use his Mandarin name, Xian-rong. He is five years old and my only son. My only child."

I translate this information for the men around me. I feel that we must all be staring at the strangers in the same way—our mouths agape, our eyes wide. Apart from Teacher Zhang, none of us has met someone from outside our province, let alone from another country. *Hong Kong*.

When no one says anything, he goes on: "I've come a long way to buy your tea. I'm a businessman. I make and supply cranes. China is in great need of those now."

Why are we in need of birds? No idea, but we listen anyway.

"That is my vocation. My avocation is tea. I am a tea connoisseur."

"Huang Xiansheng," I say, using the Mandarin honorific for *mister,* "I don't know how to translate all of this."

He throws his head back and laughs, exposing every single one of his teeth. The men around me edge back. I retreat even farther, wanting the protection of my a-ba and brothers. From my secure position, I take a closer look at the stranger. His head is shaped like a turnip—plump, with vaguely purple cheeks. His hair is as black as lizard eyes. He's chubby, like the posters I've seen of Chairman Mao. I never believed those images were real—that anyone could look like that, so fat, with a belly sticking out—but the way the stranger's belt circles his middle, emphasizing all the food that must have gone to build it, almost makes me want to laugh. His pants have sharp creases down the front and back. The material doesn't resemble anything I've seen before. His short-sleeved shirt is crisp, also with sharp creases.

The stranger regards us too, taking our measure in the way a farmer might look into the mouth of a water buffalo. I don't think he likes what he sees. But I have an idea of what he is: rich. Not well off like Ci-teh's family, but something altogether different.

"Is there a place where we can sit and talk?" he asks. "I'd like to sample your tea, possibly buy some."

After I translate, most of the men scurry back to the village. They want no part of this. Only the headman, ruma, and my a-ba and brothers (who must safeguard me) remain. The men whisper among themselves. We Akha are known for our hospitality, but they question bringing the stranger into one of our homes. The headman makes the decision.

"This girl speaks the stranger's language, and she has her clan to keep her from harm. We'll go to where she lives."

My brothers glare at me as though I've brought the worst disgrace possible upon the family. My father's eyes have the steely look they get when he guts a deer. They never approved of my education, and now it has placed the family in an uncomfortable position.

"All I want to do is buy tea," Mr. Huang assures us in his unnervingly friendly voice. "You have tea here, don't you? Yes, let us drink tea." (As though we wouldn't offer it.) "But made only with springwater. Do you have springwater?"

What other kind of water is there? Rainwater? Creek water? Pond water?

"Our village is called Spring Well," I say.

He laughs again. "Of course! That's why I chose your village to visit first."

We make a peculiar procession. The little boy skips ahead as though he knows where he's going. His a-ba doesn't seem particularly worried. One of our neighbors must have alerted A-ma and the sisters-in-law, because tea has already been brewed by the time we arrive. Once the men have seated themselves on the floor in the central room, the sisters-in-law are waved off. A-ma stands with her back against the bamboo wall, her hands clasped before her, watchful. I stay at her side and translate when necessary. A-ba gestures for the stranger to try First Brother's tea, but when he takes a sip his face crinkles as though he's rinsed his mouth with unripe persimmon juice.

"This must be terrace tea from bushes," Mr. Huang says. "It will have a monotonous flavor from the first brew to the last. It has no *qi*—no life force, no richness."

A new pot is brewed from Second Brother's pollarded tea trees. This time the stranger takes a sip, sets the cup back on the floor, and says, "Pollarding does not lead to strong roots, because they grow laterally to match what's aboveground. You'll get a sweet flavor, but it's an empty one. I'm looking for Pu'er. You know Pu'er?"

No, I don't know that word. It's as foreign to me as *vocation* and *connoisseur*.

He motions for me to approach. "Young lady, I can tell you've looked outward. You've studied the national language. You must make your family very proud, for you've followed the country's desire for transformation. You may not understand it here," he says with a wave of his hand, "but change is happening across China."

I translate this to make it sound more polite.

"You all must arise and greet the new day!" Mr. Huang exhorts the men. "This is the era of Reform and Opening Up. Even Americans are coming to China to see the Great Wall, the Forbidden City, and the Yangtze River."

The ruma clicks his tongue, then mutters in our dialect, "Too talky."

My brothers' snickers have a sobering effect on our guest.

"Where I come from," he continues, "we discuss business for many hours. I tell you some of what I want. You tell me some of what you want in return. This is how civilized men behave, but perhaps this is not your way. I'm not that familiar with the hill tribes. No one is."

The gathered men may not know the Mandarin expression for *hill tribes,* but Mr. Huang's insulting and condescending tone is one they recognize too well.

The ruma slaps the floor with his palm. "Ask the stranger what he wants."

After I relay this, Mr. Huang answers, "I already told you. I've come in search of your special tea. I've come to buy Pu'er."

I dutifully repeat the request. The ruma asks the question I've been too shy to ask. "Pu'er? What is Pu'er?"

Mr. Huang looks bewildered. "It's a special aged tea. It comes from here—"

"Maybe he means tea from old trees," Third Brother suggests.

The idea of serving the Hong Kong man tea from Third Brother's worthless trees amuses everyone. The tea is made and brought to the table. Mr. Huang and his son pick up their cups at the same time, drawing breath through their mouths as they noisily suck the liquid onto their tongues. The boy nods in appreciation, and his father smiles.

"This is better. When trees grow from seeds, the main roots extend endlessly, creating as much growth belowground as above. This gives tea flavor and depth," Mr. Huang says agreeably. "I've always heard that tea from Nannuo Mountain has special characteristics: it's more floral, and the mouth feel is medium. I can taste a hint of apricot, with some tobacco notes. And the astringency is moderate." He smells the empty cup, savoring the lingering aroma. The boy does exactly as his father does. Then Mr. Huang reaches into his pocket, pulls out a little box, and extracts two toothpicks. He gives one to his son, and the two of them pluck leaves from the pot, stretch them out on the floor, and examine them as A-ma might a boil or insect bite. "Look, Son. Brewing has returned the leaves to their original state, making them plump and pliable. That is exactly what we want to see." Then they each pick up a leaf and *chew* it. "This is not a bad raw tea," he proclaims, "but I'm still waiting to taste your aged tea."

"*Aged* tea?" A-ba asks, after I translate.

"I myself have tea cakes that are thirty years old, but there are others even older. They are antiques, but they are still alive."

"Who would drink such a thing?" A-ba asks, not bothering to mask his amusement.

My brothers laugh at the stranger's idiocy. Emboldened, First Brother speaks: "We pick our leaves. We process a few for our family, and they're drinkable after three days. If we left tea for six months, we would feed it to our pigs. No good."

"Pu'er, Pu'er, Pu'er," Mr. Huang repeats as though somehow we will have magically learned what it is. "Ponay? Could you have heard this word instead? It's Cantonese for Pu'er. No? No."

The bald boy casts a concerned look at his a-ba, who pulls his shoulders up to his ears and juts his chin. When Mr. Huang returns his gaze to me, he asks, "You mean to tell me you don't age your tea? How can this be? I've come a long way to find the birthplace of Pu'er. This is the place, I tell you."

Unimpressed by the stranger's bluster, the ruma scratches his chin and belches.

Mr. Huang spreads his hands, moving them outward as though he's erasing everything that's happened so far. He closes his eyes, takes a deep breath, and relaxes his shoulders. When he opens his eyes, a decision has been made. "Young lady."

"Yes?"

"I'm going to tell you a story." He's completely changed the tone of his voice. "I want you to pass it on to your father and the others with respect. Do you understand?" He draws his son onto his lap and begins. "For centuries, caravans with as many as a thousand men carrying one-hundred-and-fifty-kilo packs—twice their own body weight, maybe more!—filled with tea cakes journeyed fifteen hundred kilometers overland to the north and west along the Tea Horse Road to Tibet—"

"We know the Tea Horse Road," First Brother interrupts my translation. "My wife is from Yiwu, where the caravans left—"

"They encountered rain, heat, cold, and humidity," Mr. Huang carries on, undeterred, "which caused the tea to change its nature. It began to ferment. It *aged* naturally. Upon reaching Tibet, the fermented tea cakes were traded for warhorses."

"We—"

"The tea was also carried south along another route to Guangzhou and Hong Kong," Mr. Huang continues. "Those cities are known for their heat and humidity. The cakes were stored in dank basements, where they also began to ferment. In Hong Kong, we go to restaurants to eat dim sum, special savory dumplings that are very rich. We drink Pu'er—again, what we Cantonese call Ponay—to cut through the grease and oil." He chortles, and I'm thinking, *Restaurants?* "China was closed a long time. That means our tea has been aging in basements for decades. We go to certain restaurants for *that* particular tea, because each basement is different. The climate, the light, the packaging, what else was stored there, all had an effect on the taste of *that* restaurant's tea. You see?"

I answer for all of us. "Maybe."

"That tea has become more valuable over time. To us, it is a treasure."

"A *treasure*," I explain to the top men of my village, who silently contemplate the idea.

Mr. Huang glances from face to face. "It's not alcoholic, but you should think of it like French wine." (I don't attempt to translate that. What would be the purpose?) "As you know, Hong Kong will be returned to the mainland in three years. *One country, two systems*," he recites. "It sounds good, but can we Hong Kongers believe it? Many people are leaving the territory and taking their Pu'er with them—to Taiwan, to the United States, to Canada. Others are selling off their Pu'er stockpiles to finance their moves. Taiwan is the biggest buyer."

The outside world must be very strange.

"It seems to me there's only one thing to do," he continues. "You've never heard of Pu'er, but you have tea trees. You are poor and . . . unaware; I have capital and access to the market." He barely gives me enough time to finish translating. "Tea-picking season starts tomorrow, if I've been informed correctly. You will work for me instead of selling your leaves elsewhere. We must try to re-create aged Pu'er. No pesticides, all natural, using traditional methods. I've come to you first. Spring Well Village. The name appealed to me. I'm giving an opportunity to your family and your village."

After I translate this, A-ma, who hasn't spoken since the man entered our house, nudges me. "Tell him to go to Yiwu instead. There's someone there, a tea master, elderly now, who remembers the old ways of processing. For leaves, he should go to Laobanzhang. Their trees are ancient—"

"Shut up, woman!" A-ba cuts her off. "Let him buy his leaves from us. Third Son has old trees, and we can go into the mountains to pick leaves from wild trees. And—"

"Don't say it!" A-ma comes back sharply.

"We have Girl's trees. They have to be good for something."

A-ma's eyes flash. "Never!"

It's so rare to see an Akha angry that A-ba and the other men are taken aback, but the stranger knows he's hit on something even if he can't discern the meaning.

"How much do you currently earn per kilo of fresh leaves?" he asks.

I don't translate this for the men, but I start much higher than is true.

"Sixteen yuan per kilo." It's four times what we make at the tea collection center, an exorbitant amount when you remember that we can each pluck between ten and twenty kilos of leaves a day.

"I will pay . . ." He studies me with an intensity I don't understand. "Twenty yuan per kilo of perfect leaves from old trees."

Even more than I stated! Why would he do such a thing?

Mr. Huang knocks his knuckles on the floor. Is he doing this to ask for more tea, as is the custom, or is he impatient for an answer?

"For that price, I will buy all your leaves to make Pu'er," he adds, pressing me. "Together we'll save Pu'er from extinction."

I dutifully translate, once again.

"Our village will help you," the headman says.

I repeat his agreement in Mandarin. The little boy claps his hands. A-ma abruptly leaves the room. I stay behind to aid with the arrangements. Mr. Huang will go to Yiwu to find the tea master A-ma mentioned. He'll also scour the mountains—and even go to Laobanzhang—to find farmers who still have tea trees. He'll return to us every day to check our pickings. He also wants us to drink tea made from the leaves of wild trees to make sure they aren't poisonous or have bad flavors sucked in from surrounding plants. I'm not sure if he realizes what he's asking—or how dangerous it could be—but A-ba and the others are convinced the risk is worth it.

We walk Mr. Huang and his son to the spirit gate. Once the rattling of their mountain vehicle has been swallowed by the forest, we return to the village. A-ma waits for me at the top of the steps to the women's side of the house.

"You must stay away from that stranger," she orders. "I forbid you from meeting with him again!"

"How can I do that, A-ma? A-ba and all the men in the village will insist I help. I'm the only one who can."

A-ma squeezes her hands into fists and doesn't say another word.

Overnight, life in Spring Well changes as all regular routines are dropped. Yes, we still wake early and trek into the mountains, but we're no longer going to the tea terraces or pollarded gardens. Instead, we search the slopes, crawling like ants over rocks and through undergrowth, to find wild tea trees. I see even the very old scamper sure-footed branch to branch up into trees—just like A-ma showed me how to climb the mother tree to care for it—to pick the newest buds.

Someone must have told Mr. Huang about my grove or A-ma's special tea, because not a day goes by that he doesn't ask, "When are you going to take me to your tea trees, young lady?" or "I hear your trees are the oldest," or "People say your mother provides the best cures on the mountain. Tell me, where do they come from? Your trees?" Aware of his entreaties, A-ma doesn't allow me to give him even a single leaf.

I have no time to miss San-pa, but I carry thoughts of him always. I have no time to spend with Ci-teh, but I catch glimpses of her here and there. I might smile in her direction, and she'll wave back. Or Mr. Huang will ask her to do something, and I have to translate as though she's just another villager instead of my best friend. I have no opportunity to explain myself, because I'm always at Mr. Huang's side. In the mornings, his little boy stays close, and he so quickly picks up Akha words and phrases that I think soon Mr. Huang won't need my help any longer. In the afternoons, the boy rests in the women's side of our house. (Even though A-ma doesn't care for the father, she's become quite fond of Xian-rong, brewing him tea, and letting him stay with her when he needs to nap or requires a break from his father's obsession. "All Akha love their sons," A-ma observes, "but that man would take a life for his boy.") We also have a newcomer to our village—the tea master from Yiwu whom A-ma had recommended without considering that he might come *here*. Tea Master Wu is nearly blind, but he seems to know what he's doing.

Mr. Huang and Tea Master Wu inspect each family's baskets as they enter the village. Sometimes people bring leaves from trees they claim to be eight hundred years old. Some are; most aren't. Some promise that the leaves have grown in a completely natural environment. Again, some are; most aren't. Mr. Huang has an uncanny ability to see through the layers of declarations and lies.

The next step is a period of wilting. "So the brittle stems can soften," he explains, "while increasing resilience in the leaves and buds." Then comes "killing the green." Wood fires are set under woks stationed outside our homes. One family member stokes the fire, while another tosses and turns the leaves in the wok. It's hot and very hard work, and lasts long into the night. Then the leaves are dropped into flat baskets and kneaded. This is even harder work. By the next morning, the leaves are ready for their sunbath. "So they can absorb that great orb's fragrance," he tells us.

Most families decide that the area just outside their homes is perfect because it's flat, but the dogs, cats, chickens, and pigs all come nosing around, pawing, scratching, and doing who knows what else right on the exposed leaves. Others ignore the sun requirement and lay mats in their houses, where people are living, eating, and doing the intercourse, smoke fills the rooms, and kids are picking their noses, drooling, and crying. At the end of three days, each batch of twenty kilos of fresh tea leaves has been reduced to five kilos of what Mr. Huang calls *maocha*—raw tea made from the leaves of trees. Then comes the most tedious chore: sorting. Every woman and girl in Spring Well joins in this activity, sitting in groups around large woven trays to sort through every single leaf—one at a time!—to remove those that are yellow or otherwise defective.

At this point, Mr. Huang and the tea master divide the tea so it can undergo two separate processes to create two separate test batches. The first process is for natural fermentation. The highest-grade leaves are wrapped in muslin, which is tied into a distinctive knot, steamed, and pressed under a heavy stone into a flat cake round in shape. Once this is done, the cake is placed on a rack with other cakes to dry. In a day or so, the cakes are individually wrapped in paper on which we've printed a design from wood-blocks. These are bound together in sets of seven to seal in the flavors but still allow the tea to breathe. The tea is now ready to be stored to ferment naturally.

Mr. Huang is striving for something none of us have heard of—*huigan, mouth feel* or *returning flavor*. "The taste should be slightly bitter as the tea first enters your mouth, then will come the cool minty sensation that will linger on the sides of the tongue and open the chest, followed by a fragrance that will rise back up from the throat," he explains. "I'm hoping for specific flavors and scents to emerge: orchid, lotus, camphor, apricot, or plum." Time will tell if any of that happens.

The second method is for experimenting with artificial fermentation.

"We don't have time to wait decades for our tea to ripen," Mr. Huang says, "but I have a solution for that. Artificial fermentation was invented in Kunming almost twenty years ago. We'll use those techniques, and invent some of our own, to make the perfect Pu'er."

His enthusiasm never ebbs, but the results are disastrous. The sun-dried tea leaves are gathered into big piles, water is splashed on them, and then the whole mess is blanketed with cloth. The piles are uncovered every so often, the tea turned, more water sprinkled, and everything covered again. The stink! Like rotting forest undergrowth. Every so often, Mr. Huang and Tea Master Wu make a tea from one of the piles. They are less than satisfied. Mr. Huang calls some of the tea "too earthy," an insult we know all too well. Some piles smell like ox dung. Others are as moldy and foul as the armpits of a man's tunic at the height of monsoon season. One pile even catches fire!

The only thing we can do to his standards is provide springwater for brewing. "Springwater provides a flavorless flavor."

When A-ba says, "How fortuitous," I know he means, *Whatever the stranger says is fine, so long as he keeps opening his money pockets.*

Our water is acceptable, but we have to learn how to heat it! Mr. Huang lectures from *The Classic of Tea*, which, he tells us, was written in the eighth century by Lu Yü, "the greatest tea master the world has known." Mr. Huang instructs us on what to look out for. "First, the heating water should look like fish eyes and give off barely a hint of sound. In the second stage, the water should look like pearls strung together and chatter at the edges of the pot like a bubbling spring. Water has reached the perfect stage when it leaps and foments like the ocean and sounds like waves crashing on the shore . . ."

In the end he has taught us nothing, because what do we know of pearls, the ocean, or waves?

Mr. Huang talks about the connections between tea, Daoism, and Buddhism. Oh, how he goes on about *hua*—a Daoist concept he admires. It means something like *transformation,* and he applies this to the making of Pu'er in the sense that the astringent qualities of the raw tea are transformed—"metamorphosed," he enthuses—through fermentation and aging. "You see? Bad into good!" He believes tea can promote longevity, although people in our village don't live to be ancients. "Tea reminds us to slow down and escape the pressures of modern life," he says as though he's forgotten where he is and to whom he's speaking.

I have to admit I enjoy being needed, though. I like feeling important. Except . . . He never stops nipping at me about my hidden grove. "You don't realize how much I need this. I'll pay you good money, young lady. I'll pay you more than you ever dreamed of. Don't you have somewhere you'd like to go? Someone you'd like to marry?"

Mr. Huang is as persistent as a termite, and his questions eat at me. I have contradictory feelings. At night I lie awake and think of San-pa and what a few leaves from the mother tree might buy us. I still wouldn't know where to find him, because I don't know exactly where he went. But if I had my own money, I could help us get our start as newlyweds when he returns and later help pay my tuition. During the day I must be with Mr. Huang, so even if I want to, I can't sneak away. And if I did, and A-ma found out? I can't imagine the consequences.

In the end, I'm only a girl, and my heart's yearnings for the future triumph over my Akha morals. One day—and it only takes one moment to change your life forever—Mr. Huang goes to Menghai to buy supplies. While he's gone and A-ma's in another village setting a broken bone, I hike to my grove. I climb the mother tree and pick enough leaves to make a single cake. When Mr. Huang returns and we're alone, I sell them to him. He pays me far more than they're worth, saying, "I'm really thanking you for all your help. Now, let's see what we can do with these."

Every afternoon for the next three days, he takes me to a village on the other side of the mountain, where I can—as he puts it—process the tea in private. With the greedy eyes of a tiger, he watches everything I do. When the cake is finished, he hides it in the trunk of his mountain vehicle. I believe no one knows what I've done.

After three months, Mr. Huang comes to the decision that all the experimental fermented tea must be destroyed. Too many things have made homes in the odoriferous piles: worms, maggots, and strange-colored growths that if we saw them in the forest we would hurry away. Chickens, ducks, water buffalo, and oxen won't eat the garbage. That's how bad it is. Even the pigs turn away.

Mr. Huang refuses to give up, though. "You will spend this year tending to the trees. We'll try again next spring."

As his mountain vehicle is loaded, he grabs me by the shoulders. "When I return, you'll take me to your grove. You'll sell me more of your leaves."

His touch makes me feel as though a bad spirit has entered me. It's a sensation of disease and dis-ease. I cannot go to the ruma for ceremonial cleansing nor can I go to A-ma for one of her potions. To do so would be to admit I did something completely unforgivable. To do so would also mean that there's something dirty and fermenting inside me that wants what the foreigner has . . . Or my version of what he has, which is money to be with San-pa so we can follow our dreams together.

MOTHER LOVE

Waaa! But how quickly my hopes and plans fall apart. San-pa has been gone for a season's length of cycles. I've been away from school for almost as long and have lost needed studying time for the *gaokao*. "Your spoken Mandarin is much improved, but that won't be tested," Teacher Zhang says. "You've wasted your opportunity." The news is stunning, ruinous. After all my years of hard work . . . For days I languish in disappointment and regret for being so unthinking of the consequences of my new role in the village. Then Teacher Zhang comes again to visit. "You are not the kind of person who gives up," he tells me. "You are brave and tough and smart." His encouraging words give me strength. I can't allow this setback—as distressing as it is—to destroy my future. I force modern thoughts of opportunity to open my Akha eyes to see bigger and wider. *When San-pa returns, you'll be married. You'll work for Mr. Huang. You don't need college or university.* I resolve to stay positive—good *will* come.

And then, because I'm back to my regular routine—going to school even though I won't be eligible to take the *gaokao,* doing home chores, and not thinking outward for Mr. Huang every minute of the day—I notice something I should have noticed a long while ago. I have not had my monthly bleeding. I've been so busy and filled with self-importance, that I ignored my body entirely. I thought I'd gained weight because Mr. Huang made sure I was fed. That my breasts hurt because they were growing fast as a result of the extra food that filled my bowl. That I was tired because who wouldn't have been exhausted if they'd been following in my footsteps? With horror, I realize I've come to a head. That A-ma and the sisters-in-law haven't caught on is just another sign of how occupied we've all been.

I temporarily fell apart when I learned I wouldn't be able to take the *gaokao,* but I don't panic now. I have my money, and I'll go to San-pa once I find out where he is. The next day, I tell A-ma that I'll be in the forest digging for tubers. She lets me go without a single suspicious look. I walk through terrible heat and humidity to Shelter Shadow Village. It's just as San-pa described it—on the crest of the hill, easy to defend, with views in all directions. I am not someone San-pa's a-ma wants to see, but she invites me into the women's room anyway. Her hands show a lifetime of work, while her eyes reveal the concerns of motherhood. I must wait a suitable length of time before I ask about San-pa, but she surprises me by inquiring about him first.

"Have you heard from my son?" She may not want me as a daughter-in-law, but, I realize, her worry about San-pa is as deep as my own. "Has he sent word to you? At least we would know where he's living."

This information causes water to form in my eyes.

Tiny muscles in her cheek twitch at my response. "He's so far away. And Thailand . . ." Her voice trails off. Then, "You know better than most that he can be called to mischief . . ."

I cry the entire way home. The knowledge that San-pa is unreachable is devastating. The idea that something evil might have happened to him is crushing. Either way, I'm alone and pregnant with a human reject, making me doubly cursed.

I wish I could confide in Ci-teh, but she might let my secret slip by accident. I can't seek advice from my sisters-in-law, because it would be their duty to tell their husbands, who would tell A-ba. When girls find themselves in my condition they go to one person for help. This is the one person I absolutely cannot tell. A-ma would be so angry with me; I'm too afraid and humiliated to consider confiding in her. I do my best to hide the evidence of my pregnancy under my day wear: plain leggings and a tunic designed to hide a woman's procreating status. I don't know what will happen. I can't *think* what will happen.

For the next three cycles, everyone in Spring Well Village goes about their daily tasks—preparing the paddies for planting, pulling weeds from vegetable plots, and, for the women alone, spinning thread and weaving cloth to have material to sew and embellish when the rainy season starts. In addition, we have new responsibilities: to care for the tea trees so they'll be improved when Mr. Huang returns. A-ma shows Third Brother how to prune his previously insignificant trees, straightening branches and trimming diseased or withered twigs and leaves. My first and second brothers ignore their bushed terraces and pollarded gardens, instead turning over and feeding the soil at the base of the old tea trees that dot their allotted lands. I go to my hidden grove—sometimes with A-ma, sometimes alone—to do the chores I inherited from the generations of women before me. Sometimes I sit under the mother tree and stare across the mountaintops. San-pa is out there somewhere. He must return soon.

A day comes when the sisters-in-law are inside weaving and A-ma and I are outside dyeing cloth in vats. A-ma is poking at the cloth with a stick, not even looking at me, when she says, "I see you've come to a head."

"A-ma—"

"Don't try to deny it. I may be your a-ma, but I'm not a fool. The three child-maker spirits that live in all women have released your water from the lake of children. You have a baby budding within you."

All the worry I've held inside now pours out with my tears.

A-ma pats my shoulder. "Don't worry, Girl. I have a potion to help you."

I shake my head. "It's too late for that."

A-ma sighs. "How long?"

"Thirteen cycles."

She accepts my assessment. "You're not the first girl to have this happen. You'll marry the boy. All will be fine."

But when I reveal the father is San-pa, her eyes go as black and opaque as tar. "I told you . . . You were forbidden . . ." She purses her lips. "And he's not even here to fix it . . ."

I'm crying hard now.

"You can still marry Law-ba," A-ma suggests. "Take him to the Flower Room. Take him to the forest. Let him steal love. He's not so clever, and you wouldn't be the first girl I've advised to do such a thing— "

"But I love San-pa, and he loves me," I sob. "He'll come back. We'll get married."

"You'd better hope so," A-ma says darkly. "Otherwise . . ."

She doesn't need to say it: *a human reject.*

I stop going to school. No point.

Teacher Zhang himself comes to Spring Well to talk to my a-ma and a-ba. "She's been my brightest student. She's been the light that kept me going— "

But A-ba crows, triumphant. "At last she's ready to prepare for being a wife." Ha! What he means is he needs me to be here next spring and every spring after that when Mr. Huang returns to Nannuo Mountain.

Teacher Zhang doesn't give up so easily. "She could still go to trade school. It's a four-year program. I can secure a place for her at any time. She could become a secretary, typist, or clerk."

Those are all jobs I've seen in school materials, but A-ba crushes the idea when he asks, "What use are those skills here?"

"Besides," A-ma adds, "we cannot bear the idea that we would lose our daughter to the outside world. If she went away, she might never come home."

By the time Teacher Zhang leaves, I'm fully back to helping A-ma.

The months pass. Every day I hope I'll hear San-pa's voice call to me in song across the mountain, reaching me long before I see him walk through our spirit gate.

"The flowers bloom at their peaks, waiting for the butterflies to come—"

I'll sing back, "The honeycombs wait for the bees to make honey—"

But the melody never reaches me.

A-ma carries the burden of my secret. During our meals, she complains loudly to the rest of the family in an effort to explain my weight gain. "Girl thinks she's risen above the rest of us now and eats all she wants. Look how fat she's getting. When her tea benefactor returns they can act as two fat pigs together." Later, she sneaks me extra vegetables. She also watches to make sure I don't eat anything I shouldn't. When First Brother comes home with a porcupine—a forbidden pregnancy food—he caught in a trap, A-ma orders me to help my sisters-in-law serve the meal instead of eating with my natal family. "If Girl is to become a proper wife," she explains to A-ba, "then she should start learning what it means to be one." When Second Brother butchers a barking deer he shot with his crossbow and discovers two forming fawns, A-ma sends me to Ci-teh's house to visit for two days and nights for fear I too might have a litter. I gain very little weight. No more than five kilos. But should that minuscule weight gain spark the sisters-in-laws' curiosity, despite everything A-ma has done to point them in other directions, she provides me with bloodied rags at the appropriate intervals. Where she gets the blood she doesn't tell me.

Some taboos I cannot avoid. Under no circumstances may a woman return to her father's home when she's pregnant, since the other term we use for pregnancy—one who is living under another—clearly spells out I should be with my husband. It's also forbidden for a girl's a-ma to be present at the birth of a grandchild. If I were to give birth here attended by A-ma, then the men in my family would die for three generations and the rest of the family would suffer tragedies for nine generations. So A-ma and I have begun making plans for the birth in case San-pa doesn't return in time.

"The killing of a human reject is a father's responsibility," A-ma whispers to me one night. "It is his duty and his sorrow, which is why he must always show anger at the baby for making him do such a terrible thing. But in cases such as yours, it falls to the mother to remove the human reject from the world of the living."

This knowledge is crippling. I'm so numb with foreboding that I mix ash from the fire with ground rice husks as though I'm in one of the nima's trances. A-ma uses her finger to swipe the paste out of my bowl and into a little box, which she tucks away with her other potions and medicines. From that moment, not a second goes by that I'm unaware of its presence. The box and its contents are tiny—just enough to fill the nostrils and mouth of a newborn—yet it looms, a growing shadow over everything I do.

Sometimes at night, lying on my sleeping mat with my palms spread underneath my tunic against my bare belly, I feel my baby jut its elbows and knees, as though it's trying to touch my fingers. Deh-ja, Ci-teh's ill-fated sister-in-law, used to chant, "Let it be a son. Let it be a son. Let it be a son." My chanting is simpler. "San-pa, San-pa, San-pa." No matter how far away he is, surely he must hear the call of my heart.

Then, on a day that is dead still without a whisper of a breeze—suffocating, really—the first spasm of labor starts in my spine, grabs around my abdomen, and presses down. When the second pain arrives, followed by so many others—the relentless pushing of a baby ready to come out—I try everything I can to keep the baby inside. I cross my legs. I use my hands to lift my belly against the spasms. A-ma is too knowledgeable about these things not to notice. When she approaches me to say, "It's time," despair whooshes through me, draining whatever hope I had. I fight back tears. I mustn't cry. I absolutely cannot cry, if A-ma's and my plan is to work. We'll go to the forest, I'll expel my human reject, and kill it before it has a chance to cry. "Quick," A-ma has said, "so you'll suffer the least amount of anguish."

Seemingly out of nowhere, A-ma announces to the rest of the family that she and I will be gone for a day or more to care for the tea trees on my land. The men hardly pay attention, while the sisters-in-law stiffen their shoulders to show their irritation at the extra work they'll need to do in our absence. A-ma puts a few things in her satchel, including a hard-boiled egg wrapped in protective cloth. I see her palm the tin with the ash and husk mixture just as the worst spasm yet grips around the thing inside me. I try to keep my face relaxed so no one will notice. A-ma says our goodbyes and pulls me from the house. Once on the veranda, I scan the lane that divides the village, hoping to see San-pa. He's not there. How could he have failed me—failed us—so?

I choke back my emotions. I must leave the village looking as I usually do if I'm to come back and resume my life without being tainted by my mistakes.

Our progress is slow. I'm filled with dread and sadness, but I'm as scrabbly as a crab, climbing the mountain, grabbing for rocks, hunched close to the earth every time another pain disables me. If anything, our journey is speeding my labor.

"We must hurry," A-ma urges, clutching my arm and dragging me up the path.

The hardest part is edging around the boulder that hides the entrance to my grove, because my belly, facing that immutable wall of stone, upsets my balance and threatens to throw me off the cliff. When we enter the clearing, I'm too weak to make it to the shelter of the grotto. Instead, I collapse under the mother tree. A-ma spreads a mat, and I roll onto it. She helps me out of my leggings. She opens her satchel and lays out her knife, the tin with its deadly contents, and a few other small bags and boxes that hold the herbs that will help stop bleeding, fight pain, and tranquilize my mind after I've done what will be required. My circumstances are calamitous, but in the mother tree's spreading branches above me, I see a dome of protection.

A-ma follows the proper rituals, monitoring the messages my body sends her. She has me squat and brace myself against the trunk of the mother tree. The spasms are strong and frequent until my body is reduced to that of any animal. Strange sounds escape my mouth. My water breaks, rushing forth from my body, seeping through my birthing mat, and into the soil. A-ma's fingers feel around beneath me.

"You may push," she says.

I grasp a low branch. My back presses against the trunk as I push as hard as I can. A second push. A third push.

"I feel the head," A-ma announces. She massages my opening. "You can do this without my cutting." A fourth push. "The head is out. The shoulders are the hardest, Girl, but you can do it." Gods and spirits must be looking out for me, because none of this is as painful as I anticipated. A-ma seems to read my mind, because she says, "You're lucky. Now push!"

I suck in air and hold it for one last push. The feeling? The one I've sensed from births I've witnessed, only this time it's from the inside out—like a fish slipping through greased fingers. *Whoorp*.

"It is a girl," A-ma announces. What should follow is "You and your husband will always have water to drink," meaning that she'll fetch water for us, as is proper. Instead, A-ma mutters, "A little happiness." Does she realize she's quoting the Han majority saying for the birth of a girl? I don't think so. Rather, she's reminding me how fortunate I am that my human reject is a daughter instead of a son. *A little happiness* that I will only have to kill a worthless female.

The plan was for me to act quickly. Instead, I find myself staring at my daughter on the mat. The cord still spirals from her belly to my interior. She's covered with the white wax that's protected her inside my body, smeared with blood, and speckled with yellow threads that have shaken loose from the mother tree. Even if my baby were not a human reject, no one would be allowed to pick her up until she cried three times. But she doesn't cry. Her arms don't flail. She looks calmly up at me. Perhaps it's because the day is warm and the labor was fast. Perhaps it's because she knows she's a human reject and her time on earth is numbered in minutes. I've been told that newborns can't see, but if that's so, then how can my daughter be staring into the depths of my soul?

I have a duty, a responsibility, but I don't move.

Then, completely unexpectedly, A-ma flicks the nail of her middle finger against the baby's foot. The little thing startles, and her first cry cuts through the stillness of the grove, surprising the birds out of the trees, the flapping of their wings stirring the air around us. There is no recitation of the customary words.

A second cry, irritated to have been disturbed.

A third cry, desperate to be held.

Inside my body, a part of me so deep I didn't know it existed stirs, jolts, wakes. Before A-ma can stop me, I scoop up my baby and hold her to my chest. The cord pulls on my insides. A-ma—she cannot be thinking either, but also moving from some buried part of herself—gently dabs the baby's face with a cloth. A-ma has a look I've never seen at a birth—not even at those for my nephews and nieces. The baby eerily returns the gaze. Tears glisten on A-ma's eyelashes, then overflow down her cheeks.

"A long, long time ago," A-ma begins, following a custom as old as the Akha people, but her voice is unsteady, "a vicious tiger prowled the mountains, searching for the blood-perfumed scent of newborns. The tiger snatched these unfortunates to eat before they could receive their permanent names. One gulp. Nothing left. The ruma tried to cast protective spells. The nima went into trances, searching for the cause of the tiger's ceaseless hunger. Mysteriously, whatever remedy the ruma and the nima implemented only emboldened the animal. He became hungrier and hungrier. It could have been the end of the Akha people."

A-ma should not be telling this story to a human reject. I should not be opening my tunic and exposing my breasts. Neither of us should have touched her. I can't imagine a cleansing ceremony exists strong enough to erase our offenses.

A-ma presses on, never hesitating in telling the traditional story. "Then, in a village so remote the people did not yet have clothes to wear and protected themselves from the elements with only palm fronds and kneaded bark, a woman like me—a midwife—gave the child the temporary name of No-food-no-tiger. From that day forward, that tiger—and all tigers born from the creature—have been repelled by the strength of temporary names carefully chosen: No-bite, Mildewed-rice, Soured-tofu." She puts a fingertip on my daughter's forehead. "Your temporary name is Spiny-thistle."

The baby nuzzles my breast and finds my nipple, seeking the healthy drops of yellow fluid that will nourish her until my milk arrives. How serene she is. How small and perfect. The pulls of her mouth are surprisingly strong, and they trigger a spasm that pushes the friend-living-with-child out of my body. I loosen my arms so A-ma can reach my baby's stomach, cut the cord, and tie it. We cannot take the friend-living-with-child home to bury under the ancestor shrine, so A-ma buries it under the mother tree.

A-ma hands me a jug of water and walks to the edge of the grove, leaving me alone with my daughter. I suck some of the liquid into my mouth, spray it on Spiny-thistle's body, and use the corner of a piece of cloth to clean the birthing muck from her skin. How can this tiny bundle of flesh be so precious to me already? I understand in all my sore and aching parts, including my pathetic little heart, that this is why the mothers of human rejects may never touch or hold them.

A-ma returns and squats next to me. She peels the heart-forget egg and hands it to me. Numb, I take a bite. It may help me forget the physical pain of childbirth, but I'll never lose the agony of *this*. A-ma searches my eyes. I search hers. *What are we going to do?* My emotions are jumbled. Love for my daughter. Terror that A-ma will insist I use the ash and rice husk mixture on my baby. Concern that A-ma is going to remove Spiny-thistle from my arms and do what I cannot. I don't have the strength to fight A-ma for my daughter when I just gave birth. And even if I fought her and won . . .

I say to A-ma the obvious thing. "I can't keep the baby—not without a father."

"If you take her back to Spring Well, your a-ba or one of your brothers will need to complete . . . the ceremony. The headman, ruma, nima, and village elders will see to it."

Tears course down my cheeks, fall from my chin and onto my daughter's face. She blinks at the interruption of her sucking.

"Maybe for once the Han majority laws can help," A-ma goes on. "The One Child policy doesn't apply to us, but suppose you give her away—as so many Han women must do when they birth an unwanted daughter. I have heard it happens."

Yes, we've heard it happens, but is it so? Could a mother abandon her baby? Look at me. I couldn't do what Akha Law told me to do. Maybe Han majority women can't do what Chinese law tells them to do either.

But when I say this to A-ma, she responds, "It is the only hope for you or the baby. We must try."

"But where can I leave her?" My voice trembles. If someone on Nannuo Mountain found an infant abandoned in the forest, he would immediately recognize it as a human reject with a father too weak to do what needed to be done. It would be up to that stranger to make sure the rite was carried out. Akha Law is immutable when it comes to human rejects.

"There's a place I've heard the family-planning women talk about at the tea collection center." A-ma takes her time to pronounce the Mandarin word. "Orphanage. You will find one in Menghai—"

"Menghai?" It's the nearest big town, where the tea factory is, and where I begged San-pa to take me. The only people I know who've been there are the mountain traders who bring goods to us; Teacher Zhang, who passed through when he was sent here to learn from the peasants; and Mr. Huang, his son, and their driver.

"They say it's about twenty kilometers or a day away by horse cart," she says. "You ought to be able to walk there and back in three nights."

We make a new plan. It must forever stay a secret—to protect my reputation, if I hope to marry one day, and to keep A-ma from being disgraced as a midwife and woman, who, until now, has been an ideal of our Akha ways.

When she goes home for supplies, I stare into my daughter's face and tell her how much I love her, hoping my words will seep into her flesh, blood, and bones to be held within her forever. "You have been born on Chicken Day," I whisper tenderly. "This is wonderful, because you'll always know the opening and closing of the sun." I tell her how sorry I am that I won't be able to chew food for her when she reaches four months or feed her fish when she's older so she becomes adept at fishing. "Always remember that if you're afraid a spirit is coming toward you, spit at it, because spirits are afraid that if saliva touches them they will get leprosy."

I teach her the sounds of the forest around us: how to distinguish the rustling of the wind in the trees from the crackle of an animal brushing against shrubs and vines as it makes its way on a wildlife trail; how to look at the sky and estimate from the number of stars if there will be rain, fog, or a blanket of humidity at dawn;

and, most important, how to understand her place in the world. "From my a-ma to me to you, know that every plant, animal, and mote of dust has a soul. You must make correct choices for the world to remain in balance." As I murmur these words, I'm on guard for a spirit to swoop down and suck the breath straight out of my lungs as punishment for keeping my daughter alive instead of sending her to the great lake of boiling blood.

Hours later, A-ma returns with a tea-picking basket strapped to her back. She makes a camp for us in the rocky grotto, where we'll be protected through the night. She unpacks clean clothes for me, as well as rags to place between my legs to catch blood. For the baby, she's brought some swaddling, including a cap with charms. A-ma inspects the place where the baby came out. I have bleeding, but nothing excessive or uncontrollable. I haven't had need for opium or any of her poultices, but I'm exhausted from the months of hiding, from the disappointment that San-pa didn't return in time, from the trek to my land, and from expelling my daughter. I lie on my side with Spiny-thistle cradled to my breast. The moon illuminates the trees, filtering leafy shadows across the grove. If only there were a way to make her remember this moment.

A-ma has already made a fire and heated water by the time I wake. I feel far worse physically this morning: sore, tired, empty. Mentally, it's as though I've been inhabited by a spirit: lost, confused, but determined to carry out my misdeeds.

A-ma holds Spiny-thistle while I eat. "Look around you," she coos to the baby. "This is the mother tree. These are the sister trees. You may never see this place again, but it is yours by right. Our blood is in this earth. It has nourished these trees. You are a part of them, and they are a part of you." She pauses before continuing. "There can be no proper naming ceremony for you, since neither your father nor one of your grandfathers can perform the rite. You'll live outside our Akha traditions, but you'll take two gifts with you when you leave our mountain today."

A-ma glances at me, commanding my attention. I put down my cup to listen.

"First, I name you Yan-yeh. You are the first daughter of my only daughter. Li-yan to Yan-yeh—"

With no father to properly name her, my daughter will never learn to Recite the Lineage. The sharpness of regret stabs into my chest, cleanly, cruelly, irrevocably.

"Second," A-ma goes on, "I'm giving you the most precious gift we women have in our line." With one hand, she reaches into the picking basket she brought with her and pulls out a round cake of tea. Wrapped in rice paper, the cake is not so big—maybe eighteen centimeters across and two centimeters thick. Age has faded the ink drawings. All my life I've lived in the same house with my a-ma, but I've never before seen the tea cake. And, not that it's all that important, I thought we Akha didn't make tea cakes, let alone wrap them in decorated papers. That's why Tea Master Wu had to show everyone in the village what to do.

In answer to my unspoken thoughts, A-ma says, "Since I came to your a-ba in marriage, I've kept this hidden in the most powerful and safe place in our home—the space between the family altar in the women's room and the friends-living-with-child that came from me and your sisters-in-law buried in the soil directly below. Girl, you think you learned so much about tea when the stranger was here with his son. He says he came here to save Pu'er from extinction." Even in this most profound moment, she snorts her distaste for Mr. Huang. "He *knows* nothing. He *learned* nothing. He was looking for aged tea? *This* is aged tea. It has survived many changes and threats. Your great-grandmother secreted it away from the Japanese in the thirties. Your grandmother hid it from revolutionaries in the forties. It was my responsibility to protect it during the dark years of the Great Leap Forward in the fifties, when tea tree plantations were razed and replanted with tea terraces. We were forced to change our old ways and make vast quantities of inferior tea to sell to the masses. We worked so hard, and we were so hungry. Many people starved to death."

A-ma is usually so careful with her words, releasing only those that are necessary. Not this time, and her urgency is marked by my need to absorb this new information about her and this strange tea cake.

"Then came the sixties and seventies," she continues, "when the Red Guards sought the Destruction of the Four Olds of ideas, culture, customs, and habits. We were no longer allowed to drink tea, because it was seen as recalling hours of leisure, as though we'd ever had those. We were forced to tear down the spirit gate and the village swing. To keep the old ways would have been to commit a political crime, but for anyone to think someone like me would forget? Or let something as precious as tea become extinct, as that stranger-fool said?"

All this time, she could have said something to Mr. Huang. She could have helped him more.

"This cake," she says, turning her attention to Yan-yeh, "goes back many generations of women in our family. It is the best gift I can give you, my granddaughter, yet it holds many secrets and much suffering. Carry it with you wherever you go as a reminder of who you are and where you came from."

A-ma places my baby on the tea cake so that it serves as a shield on which to rest her neck and fans above her head like a halo, and then binds them together with a handwoven blanket. She picks up Yan-yeh and gives her to me. "You must go."

I shake my head. I'm terrified.

"Keep walking down the mountain." A-ma gazes out across the peaks, blue and hazy in the distance. Her jaw tightens as she pulls her knife from her belt and tucks it in mine. "Protect yourself," she says, and I clutch Yan-yeh closer to my body. "When you see people, ask the way to Menghai. Mark your route for your return."

Getting around the boulder is hard with the baby, but A-ma is at my side, steadying me, keeping me from falling. As soon as we reach the old and faint path, she places on my back the basket packed with the necessities for my journey.

"Support her neck," she instructs. "Keep walking. I told the others we would be gone for four nights. That gives you three more nights to get her to a safe place and then come home. I will wait here for you." Then she turns her back on me, grabs on to the boulder, and shimmies out of sight.

I feel like a girl in an Akha fable.

The tiny trail that leads away from my grove joins the larger path. I bypass my village entirely, always heading down. Where the path branches, I build a pile of rocks or cut into the bark of a tree. I stop every once in a while to clear my throat three times and rub the hair on my arms and legs. The world knows that spirits are not that clever or brave. They are frightened of saliva and the sounds of human hairs are excruciating to their ears. When Yan-yeh whimpers, I hunker down and bring her to my breast. I lay her on pine needles when I need to relieve myself and change my bloody rags. I eat rice balls as I walk.

Night falls. I wend my way deep into the forest to find what I hope will be a place safe from the worst outside spirits. I strike three trees with my fist. "You be my home! Watch over us." I roll out my sleeping mat and curl around my daughter. As soon as dawn brightens the sky, I'm up again. I hurt all over and my body screams for more rest, but I have to keep moving if I'm going to give Yan-yeh a chance at life. The mountains are still steep and should be unusable, but tea terraces undulate, following the curves of the hillsides and climbing until they disappear into the morning mists. The farmers have triumphed over nature as I must now conquer my physical pain and weakness.

When the sun is high, the mountain path widens and I start to hear rumbling sounds. I reach a dirt road with a truck going one way, a tractor going the opposite way, and a few people bearing wares trudging in both directions. I need to find this spot when I come home. I can't leave a pile of rocks by the side of the road, because what if someone or something tips it over? I struggle to find a landmark, but I see nothing different from what I've been passing through all morning. I take one of the rags A-ma gave me and tie it to a branch. *Please let it be enough for me to find on my return.*

I step into the road, not knowing which way to go—left or right. I ask a woman wearing Dai nationality clothes and carrying a basket heaped with corncobs the way to Menghai. "We're going there too," she answers. "You can follow us if you'd like." I feel better to be walking with someone from a hill tribe—a stranger but still familiar—because every step reveals something completely new. The land turns to gentle slopes and what's planted on them changes. The impossibly towering tea terraces are far behind me now. Instead, trees I don't recognize rise up in neatly planted rows. Now, when I stop to mark my route with a slash from A-ma's knife, thick white goo oozes from the trunks like white blood. The Dai woman tells me they're rubber trees. "Are they for eating?" I ask. She laughs and shakes her head. I begin to see houses, which are unlike any in the mountains—made of stones, clay bricks, and some type of smooth gray material. Then I see my first two-story building. And then the most astounding sight. Way above my head. My first airplane.

Yan-yeh stirs and squawks in her birdlike way. I say goodbye to the Dai woman and step off the road to find a spot of shade. I unwrap my baby and set the tea cake on the ground. I bring her to my breast. My milk hasn't come in yet, but she sucks and sucks and sucks—my baby is strong, and she'll need courage to survive what's coming—while my insides wring and constrict. I have to bite my lips from the double pain, and yet the way she looks up at me . . . Her eyes are so clear . . . When she falls asleep, I wrap her back up, making sure to support her neck as A-ma showed me. Then it's back to the road.

Two hours later, as darkness falls, we arrive at the city. Dust churns and swirls as cars, trucks, motorcycles, tractors, donkey- and horse-pulled carts, bicycles, and so many people bump along the dirt road. Even in my despair, the sight is amazing, but the first time I hear a horn, I almost faint I'm so scared. Nearly everyone is dressed like Teacher Zhang—in a Mao suit and cap—but some men wear gray pants, white shirts, matching gray jackets, and knit vests. That too looks like a uniform. Here and there, I spot someone like me—a member of a hill tribe, immediately identifiable by our embroidered indigo clothes and the special headdresses that mark us as Bulang, Dai, or Akha.

I recognize things I've learned about in school: apartment buildings, petrol stations, dress shops, restaurants. (Restaurants! Imagine going to a store like that, sitting down, telling the man what you want, and then he brings it to you.) But it's the electric lights that are most alarming and fascinating. White lights. Yellow lights. Orange and red lights. Green lights. Glowing from buildings. Illuminating roadways. Shining like evil eyes from cars.

I stay on the main thoroughfare, afraid that if I turn off it I'll never find my way home. I don't know how to locate the orphanage. I'm surrounded by strangers in a place that could never even come to me in a nightmare. I'm hungry. My private parts hurt. I'm weak from giving birth and all the walking. And I absolutely must not be caught, because even for Han majority people what I'm about to do is against the law. I've heard of jail, prison, and labor camps—who hasn't?—but no Akha has ever survived being sent to one. Not that I've heard of anyway.

An image of A-ma gazing out over the mountains before she handed me the knife comes to me. The way she set her jaw . . . Anguish. Courage. Sacrifice. This is mother love. This is what I must find in myself now.

I come to a tiny roadway that divides a block. It's also unpaved but empty of people and bicycles. I creep into the shadows and sit shielded by a discarded cardboard box with my back against the wall. From here, I can watch the street without being seen. Surely those people will need to sleep. I eat some rice balls, ration my water, and nurse Yan-yeh again. I tell her everything I can about Akha Law, about her a-ma and a-ba, about the lineage, and what it will mean to become a woman one day. How I will always love her. How I will think of her every breathing minute of my life. I whisper endearments into her face, and she looks up at me in that penetrating way of hers. Her tiny hand grips my forefinger, searing my heart and scarring it forever.

I'm awakened later—who knows how much time has passed?—by her mewling. I feel dawn coming in the quiet around me, but for now the night is still murky and dim. I must act now. Already tears pour from my eyes. I make sure her blanket is tight around her and the tea cake secure. I put her in the box. She doesn't cry.

At the corner, I peer in both directions. To the left, in the distance, two women approach, sweeping the powdery dust from the surface of the dirt road with brooms made of long thatch—slowly from side to side, *swish, swish, swish*. I step out, turn right, and scuttle forward. I pass over two more streets, both deserted. All the while, I'm whispering, "Your a-ma loves you. I'll never forget you." I place the cardboard box on the steps of a building. No more words now. I must run, and I do—to the next corner, right, then right again, and to the next corner, so that I've returned to the edge of the main street. The two sweepers come closer—*swish, swish, swish*. I dart across the road and hide on that side so I can see the abandoned cardboard box. Its sides tremble. My daughter must be moving, realizing I'm gone. And then it comes—a terrible wail that cuts through the darkness.

The two sweepers look up from their work, cocking their ears like animals in the forest. And then another croaking shriek. The women drop their brooms and come running. They don't notice me, but I see them clearly—two elders with faces like rotten loquats. They drop to their knees on either side of the box. I hear them clucking, concerned yet comforting. One picks up the baby; the other scans the street. I can't hear their conversation, but they're decisive and knowing, as though they've encountered this situation before. Without hesitation, they begin marching back the way they came, back toward me. I slither farther into the shadows. When they pass me, I watch them until they reach their discarded brooms and continue on. I leave the safety of my hiding place and follow, creeping from doorway to doorway. They arrive at a building I passed earlier right on this same main road. The woman holding Yan-yeh sways and pats her back. The other woman bangs on the door. Lights come on. The door cracks open. A few words are exchanged. My baby is handed over, the door closed, and the two old women walk back to their brooms. The sign on the door reads: MENGHAI SOCIAL WELFARE INSTITUTE.

I stay until the sun comes up. Grocers set baskets brimming with vegetables on the sidewalk. Barbers open their doors. Children walk hand in hand to school. The door to the Menghai Social Welfare Institute remains closed. I can't stop crying, but there's nothing more I can do. I begin my long walk back up Nannuo Mountain. I get lost only a few times. When I feel I can't take another step, I venture into the forest. I fall asleep holding A-ma's knife. The next day, by the time I reach my grove with the mother tree, where A-ma is waiting for me, I'm empty of tears. From now on, I cannot—I must not—let anyone see my sorrow. The loneliness of that . . . like I'm drowning . . .

Social Welfare Institute
No. 6, Middle Nanhai Road
Xishuangbanna Dai Autonomous Prefecture
Yunnan province, China

Report on Baby Girl #78

Today a baby girl foundling was delivered into our care by Street Cleaners Lin and Hu. They report they did not see a mother, father, or any other person of interest. They are fully aware of the penalties for lying and have been honest in similar past situations.

Baby Girl #78 arrived with part of her umbilical cord still attached. It looks four to six days dried. From this, I am giving her a birth date of November 24, 1995. Baby Girl #78 weighs 2.77 kilograms and is 47 centimeters in length. She has black hair. She does not have a birthmark or other identifying marks.

As required, we have cataloged and stored her possessions, except for a cardboard box, which I sent to the kitchen to be used for vegetable storage:

1 cake of tea, 1 blanket, 1 shirt, 1 pair leggings, and 1 cap with charms. These items will remain with the child.

The charms on the hat and the indigo coloring of the handwoven blanket and clothing suggest that the child was born of an ethnic minority woman.

Two photographs and a footprint of Baby Girl #78 were taken during intake and will be added to her file.

Signed,
Director Zhou Shue-ling

SHREDDED OUT OF EXISTENCE

The next three months are terrible. In the beginning, my breasts turn as hard as rocks with the arrival of my milk, and my insides continue to leak red tears. Even after the physical discomforts pass, I ache for my lost baby. Waves of grief wash through me—sometimes with such cruel force that my eyes pool beyond my control. When A-ma sees me thus, she pinches the exposed back of my neck or snaps at me to do my chores more carefully, all to help me gather myself in front of the rest of my family. A-ba, noticing I'm more subdued, decides I'm ready for marriage: "It's time for you to start contributing to the increase of people," he declares.

In the fourth month, Mr. Huang and his son return. Mr. Huang looks the same; the boy looks completely different, with a full head of hair instead of a shaved dome. A-ba shows off his new hand-operated rolling machine, for which he traded his best crossbow. "Now we can process an entire kilo in a half hour!" he boasts.

Mr. Huang shakes his head. "Nothing mechanical can touch our leaves."

A-ba, his shoulders slumped, puts his machine under the house with the pigs and chickens; the stranger hires me again; and his son follows A-ma nearly everywhere she goes. Xian-rong has retained the Akha words he learned last spring and now picks up even more. Tea Master Wu arrives from Yiwu to supervise the killing of the green, kneading, drying, and sorting. He watches every step of the artificial fermentation process too. We happily take Mr. Huang's money, and he gets to act like a big man. Beneficent.

After three months, we know that the fermentation results are far better than those from last year. Once the cakes are made, Mr. Huang arranges for them to be transported off Nannuo Mountain and out of the country for storage and aging in Hong Kong.

"But I'm still missing my favorite leaves." Mr. Huang needles me at the end of his trip. "How much will you make me pay for them this year? Double? Triple? This time, will you take me to your grove? I'd like to see how you care for your trees."

I'm about to go to pick leaves when A-ma stops me. She seems to have a magical sense when it comes to our trees. "The grove is special to our family. It is special to you. Never let an outsider have it. Never let a man see it."

"I would never take him there, but if I sell him some of my leaves, San-pa and I will be able to—"

"San-pa," she nearly shouts. "He's never coming back! And even if he does, do you think we would allow you to leave with him? Where would you go? What would you do?"

I have answers to her stinging questions: He is coming back, they can't stop me from leaving with him when I've walked to Menghai and back alone, we would go wherever he wants. We could start a life in his family's newlywed hut or go to a whole new village, as he once suggested. But why bother trying to turn a monkey into a goat? A-ma will not change her mind about Mr. Huang or San-pa: "Stay away from that tea man. And forget about San-pa."

But the temptation and my dreams are too great. I climb the mountain and fill a basket with unfurling leaves from the very tips of each branch of the mother tree. I tell myself these are not the best leaves. Those would have come in the first ten days of tea-picking season, but Mr. Huang buys them, paying me even more than he did last year. Once again, we visit the faraway village so I can process the tea in secret.

One day later, A-ma goes to the grove and discovers what I've done. I wish she would shout at me, but that's not the Akha Way. Instead, she punishes me with quiet words. "Was it worth it? Did it make that boy return for you? It's been more than a year. You sold your greatest gift. You sold your honor."

In my shame and despair, I finally accept he's never coming back. Anguish nearly destroys me. I'm like a leaf that's fallen from its home branch and now spirals down, down, down, floating out over a cliff, buffeted by winds, shredded out of existence.

A-ma stops asking me to accompany her on healing visits. The sisters-in-law, following A-ma's example, pretend I no longer exist. My brothers ignore my face swollen from so much crying. A-ba doesn't even notice what's happening to me. I feel too guilty to go to my grove for solace and solitude. I can't talk to Ci-teh, because where would I start? And even if I could confide in her, she's never around. These days she's spending every free moment stealing love in the forest with Law-ba, the boy A-ma and A-ba once wanted me to marry. She's turned into the type of girl she once accused me of being: one who discards the comforts of friendship to give her full attention to a boy.

I end up spending my days and nights under the house with the dogs, pigs, chickens, and ducks. The smell is rancid and foul, and the animals stare at me with baleful eyes. If Akha Law is correct and everything on earth is connected, then our animals are aware of my humiliation. I feel as low as a human reject. And yet life continues around me. Ci-teh's family announces she'll soon marry Law-ba, and the whole village enjoys a celebratory feast. I must attend the festivities, but they are heartbreaking for me. Not so long ago, A-ma and A-ba intended this joyousness for me. Soon after the banquet, all three sisters-in-law come to a head in the same cycle. The news is greeted by great rejoicing in hopes of the arrival of new grandsons; sacrifices are made to ensure good deliveries; and *everyone* in my family eats proper foods, because these simultaneous pregnancies are so auspicious. Joy and optimism spread through Spring Well. Even in my hiding place, I can't avoid the sounds of pigs being bred, cats yowling that they've found mates, and boys and girls singing their attraction to each other from hilltop to hilltop.

"The flowers bloom at their peaks, waiting for the butterflies to come—" The first line of the love song reaches me. How unfair.

The next line belongs to the girl. It should be "The honeycombs wait for the bees to make honey," but I can't hear it. She must be singing away from my direction. A relief.

"A beautiful flower calls to her love—"

The male voice comes closer. I cover my ears.

"Alloo sae, ah-ee-ah-ee-o, ah-ee-ah-ee-o."

The song tortures me. I hum a planting tune to drown out the pitiless sounds of ardor. Later, I feel the thumps of footsteps climbing the men's veranda and remove my hands from my ears. The singing is over, at least. The bamboo floor above me squeaks and heaves as my father and brothers pace back and forth. Footsteps rattle down the stairs. Third Brother's feet come into view.

"Girl, you'd better come."

I go around to the women's veranda. A-ma and the sisters-in-law are all standing when I enter the house. A-ma wears one of her impenetrable expressions.

"He's returned," First Sister-in-law states.

I rush to the men's side of the house. San-pa! He looks thinner. Wiry. Older. A man now. I run into his arms. He holds me tight. His heart beats into me. He speaks over my head to the men in my family.

"I've Recited the Lineage for you. Your daughter and I have no matching ancestors for seven generations. Your daughter does not have seizures nor is she troubled by insanity. Neither do I have these afflictions. I went away to earn money so I can take care of her when she's at university."

"My daughter didn't take the *gaokao*." How is it that A-ba can so easily use against me something that he once opposed? I notice, though, the long silence from San-pa.

Finally, San-pa sputters, "I've come with the proper gifts for your family to seal the arrangement."

A-ba clears his throat, but when San-pa won't allow him a single objection, I know my future husband has forgiven me my failings as a student. But can we have a life together if I don't tell him about our baby?

"Most important, your daughter is older than thirteen," he goes on, gaining momentum again. "You and I both know that we could have married in the past without your permission, but I sought it anyway. I respected your wishes. Now you must respect mine. I have come to fetch a wife, and I expect your daughter to go-work-eat with me."

Look how San-pa has changed! If only he'd spoken this forcefully sooner. We would have been sleeping and doing the intercourse in his family's newlywed hut until our daughter's birth.

When A-ba addresses the traditional phrase to me, "Go get married to him then," I understand that San-pa and I have finally won. Without another word, San-pa takes my hand and together we run out of the house and into the forest. We don't stop until we reach our special clearing. Panting—from excitement, from our running—we stare into each other's faces. He's dirty from his travels. And I'm . . . My hands shoot to my cheeks. I must look—and smell—dreadful. But he doesn't seem to mind. He grabs me, and we fall together on the bed of pine needles. We don't even take off all our clothes. He's even thinner than I thought when I first saw him. I can feel his sinews and bones under his skin. Once the intercourse—lovely and urgent—is over, we lie together.

I've experienced numerous adversities in my eighteen years, but telling him about Yan-yeh is one of the hardest. He tightens his arms around me when I weep out the truth.

"I'm sorry this happened," he says when I'm done. "I failed you, but that doesn't mean I'll fail our daughter. We'll go to Menghai and get her."

Why hadn't I thought of this? Because my despair had forbidden me even to hope for a chance to get Yan-yeh. But is it still possible to change her from a human reject into a daughter?

"People will know she came before our wedding—"

"If we could have lived in the city near your school," he says, his tone surprisingly sharp, "we would have avoided that problem . . ."

This reproach stings more than it should when all I should be is happy to get Yan-yeh.

"And we can't stay on Nannuo or any nearby mountain where people might hear about us." His brow furrows as he ponders the problem. After an uncomfortably long pause, he comes to a decision. "We should go back to Thailand. I can get work there, and she will not yet be so big. In Thailand, they will think we were already married when you gave birth, just as they already think I was born on Sheep Day. So propitious for a sheep and a pig to share a home, don't you think?" He smiles reassuringly. "And here? By the next time we come back, you will have borne me a son. My a-ma and a-ba won't bother counting her teeth to judge her age after they see him."

He has taken charge of our lives as all husbands should. How I love him in that moment.

"Can we go get her right now?" I ask.

San-pa laughs and pulls me back into his arms.

Akha weddings are complicated and drawn out for days, sometimes weeks. Not ours. Everything happens over three nights, because we're anxious to pick up our baby.

I'm dressed in a white wedding skirt, a gaily decorated kerchief, and my usual tunic and leggings, when two elders from San-pa's village arrive in Spring Well to set the rituals in motion. They present A-ba with coins. These are not a bride-price in the traditional sense. Rather, they are, as the older man says, "To pay for the mother's milk your daughter drank." Then come the yips and yelps of a group of young men, who shepherd San-pa into the village. A-ba announces that our family is going to host a Fill the Carry Basket ceremony so I might gather a proper dowry, which tells me he has accepted the circumstances. Ci-teh sits with me when the ruma recites a special poem about me, listing my attributes from the time of my birth to today. "She only got in trouble one time. She is a good worker." And so on.

The ruma then asks San-pa, "Do you need to test the machete before you buy it?"

This sends Ci-teh into a spiral of laughter, because he's asking if San-pa and I have yet stolen love. If not, we'd be required to go to the forest right then. Still, I'm a bride, so I turn crimson when San-pa answers, "The machete has been tested, and the rice already cooked."

A-ba presents me with a carrying basket to take to my new home. A-ma gives me a rain cape and a new set of clothes, plus her silver bracelet with the two dragons facing each other nose to nose. It's beyond what I could have hoped for, considering her feelings about San-pa. My brothers contribute packets of rice seed that San-pa and I will be able to plant when we reach our new home. First Sister-in-law and Second Sister-in-law each cut a bangle from their headdresses as tokens for me to remember them by; Third Sister-in-law presents a blanket decorated with her fine embroidery and appliqué. I pack these things in my carrying basket, tucking the money Mr. Huang paid me at the bottom. (I haven't yet told San-pa about my savings. I want to surprise him if a time comes when we need it.) And while most brides must relinquish their rights to the property they were allotted in the Thirty Years No Change policy to their a-bas or brothers, A-ma promises to care for my grove.

She also gives me some last-minute advice, and it's as traditional as can be. Next come the messages that A-ma actually wants to give me, passed through intermediaries. She pushes First Sister-in-law forward: *"Remember that if you want to terminate your marriage, you can always run away, but you can't come home."* From Second Sister-in-law: *"Remember that if you have children, you will need to leave them behind when you run away."* Third Sister-in-law's message must not be a good one, because she looks embarrassed. She whispers in my ear: *"If a gopher does not have his escape route dug and ready ahead of time, then it will be difficult to run away when he needs it."*

These are the last things A-ma wants to tell me as I leave home? Does she really think that after all San-pa and I have been through I would ever follow the Akha rituals that would give me a divorce? Never. Neither will I give him cause to divorce me by being lazy, arguing with his parents, stealing love with another man, or not giving him more children in addition to our Yan-yeh, who is days away from my arms.

Then it's time for goodbyes. A-ba and my brothers blink back emotions, the sisters-in-law openly weep, and A-ma dabs at her cheeks with the hem of her tunic. I see the headman, the nima, the ruma, Ci-teh and her family, and so many others. Even Teacher Zhang has come to wish me farewell.

The voices of the women in my natal family rise up in song:

"When living under your father-in-law's roof, you must obey his rules.
When living next to your mother-in-law, you must follow her instructions.
When living near a brother-in-law, avoid him as a pestilence.
When living with your son, know his life comes first."

San-pa and I reach the spirit gate. I should be crying loudly to show the pain of leaving my family and my village. But I don't cry. I don't even look back.

When we arrive in Shelter Shadow Village, San-pa's mother greets me with a boiled egg, signaling her acceptance of me. Mothers-in-law are difficult the world over, and I've seen how severe A-ma can be with my sisters-in-law, but so far my future mother-in-law seems determined to put aside her past disapproval.

A few hours later, Ci-teh comes to perform the next part of the ritual. She's brought with her the heavily decorated headdress that first announced my maidenhood and will now mark me as a married woman. *"Remember that a wife must never overstep her husband's knowledge,"* she recites. I'm glad she's here, and I try to absorb her words—which she herself will receive upon her marriage to Law-ba—so that I'll become a perfect wife. As soon as I have that thought, a realization comes to me. "I'm sorry, Ci-teh, that I won't be able to deliver your headdress when the time comes."

"That is a pain beyond imagining," she admits.

"Please know that into every life my soul is born, I'll always be indebted to your soul—whatever form it takes—for all the ups and downs we've shared."

She nods tearfully before resuming her marriage duties. *"Remember never to overtake your husband on the path,"* she says. *"Remember never to crow like a rooster. Remember always that you are only a hen."*

San-pa's a-ma takes the headdress from Ci-teh and places it in the newlywed hut. Ci-teh gives an almost imperceptible nod: *Good luck. I hope you'll be happy. We'll be friends forever.* I smile at her and try to memorize every detail of her face, not knowing how long it will be before I see her again. As she turns to begin her journey home, San-pa and I enter the newlywed hut. The village ruma waits for us. He gives us our Meal of Joining—a single cooked egg, a single glass of rice wine, and a single cup of tea—to share. Once I put on my headdress, our wedding ceremony is complete. I am now Wife-of-San-pa and Daughter-in-law to his parents. I'm happy, but a part of me—that hard stone I carry within me at all times—reminds me of our daughter. *Why couldn't things have happened differently? Why couldn't San-pa have come sooner?* But then another thought: *Only two more days and I'll have her next to my heart again.*

San-pa and I go back outside. A group of men herd a pig to our door. San-pa stabs his knife into its throat. The men restrain the animal so its blood can spurt into a bowl. Once the pig dies, San-pa slits it open and removes the liver. This is taken away for the ruma, nima, and village elders to examine for good and bad omens.

Each minute that passes is another minute of joy. Our marriage feast begins with a soup, followed by fried potato wedges, bitter melon with scrambled egg, sautéed eggplant and garlic, pickled mustard greens, and special meatballs made from minced meat from the slaughtered pig mixed with its blood. The people of Shelter Shadow complete their welcome of me by singing a wedding song filled with good wishes:

"*You are the new bark on the tree of our village.*
May your life together become strong as wood,
Rings growing one link at a time,
A part of the Akha line."

That night, San-pa sleeps in his parents' house, and I retire to the home of one of his uncles. To say this is difficult . . . *Waaa!* Tradition!

The next day, a woman elder escorts me into San-pa's family house to bathe me. I feel embarrassed for her to see me naked. Will she be able to tell I once had a child? Meanwhile, villagers hit the eaves with long sticks. "Move in, soul. Move in! Move in!" I wish I could tell them that they don't have to work so hard at this, because my soul moved in with San-pa's a long time ago. Once I'm dressed, I return to the main room. Three elders take turns circling an egg around us. It sounds easy, but it's hard for one elder to pass the egg to the next elder without dropping it. I hold my breath, so nervous. I look over at San-pa for encouragement, but he's even more anxious than I am. If one of the elders drops the egg and it cracks, then we would not be able to have any (more) children, have a happy life, or live to become elders ourselves.

At the end of the evening, I'm invited to sleep on the women's side of San-pa's family home, while he sleeps on the men's side. How tantalizing it would be to slip out, run into the forest, and do the intercourse, but if we did that our newlywed blessings would decrease. We've already had such ill luck that I don't want to attract bad spirits intent on troublemaking.

On the third morning, San-pa and I go door to door to Beg for Blessings. We carry bowls of chopped pig meat and liver, as well as a bottle of liquor to share. In exchange, people give me gifts of money and silver trinkets. Again and again, we hear, "May you have a long life. May your animals multiply. May your tea pickings and rice crops be plentiful. May you have many children."

Finally, *finally*, at the end of a night of feasting and dancing, San-pa takes me to our newlywed hut. I feel nervous yet eager, shy yet bold, as I start to undress.

The next morning, Shelter Shadow's ruma kills a chicken and inspects it for bad signs. The tongue is in the normal position, which is fortuitous. If it had been twisted, it would mean that San-pa and I would argue on our journey. I can't imagine ever arguing with my husband.

"Has a tiger ever killed an animal in or around our village on this day of the cycle?" San-pa asks.

The ruma and nima consult and agree that no such thing has occurred. With no more rituals left to complete, San-pa and I lift our baskets to our backs and depart.

San-pa has told me that it's 250 kilometers from Nannuo Mountain to the village outside Chiang Rai in Thailand where we're going. First, though, we head in the opposite direction, to Menghai. After a half day's journey, we join the path I took when I carried Yan-yeh off the mountain. When night falls, we sleep among the rubber trees. In the morning, San-pa uses his machete to scratch the dirt where we rested. "Wake up! Wake up! Let's go!" He smiles at me and explains, "All hunters do this to make sure we don't leave our souls behind." I'm not a hunter, so I didn't know this ritual when I came this way with our baby. What if Yan-yeh's soul got lost? What if mine ran away? What about all the ways both small and large that San-pa and I have skirted fate? By the time we reach the Menghai Social Welfare Institute, I'm both hopeful and frightened.

As we enter, the smell of urine hits my nose with a powerful slap. On the floor in front of us, a scramble of babies and toddlers. There are so many of them! Even as San-pa talks to the woman in charge, I dart from child to child. They're all girls. This one too old. That one too young. Eyes too squinty. Ears too pronounced. Too much hair. Not enough hair. All this, as though I would recognize Yan-yeh after leaving her months ago in a cardboard box down the street. But, I tell myself, a mother would *know*.

"Wife!"

When I turn, I expect to see San-pa with our baby in his arms. Instead, he anxiously shifts his weight from foot to foot. Next to him, the woman has puffed her cheeks in anger.

"Did you leave a baby here?" she demands shrilly. "Do you know that is against the law? I'm going to call Public Security!"

"Wife!" San-pa calls again. "We must go! Hurry! Now!"

But I can't move, because a couple of the toddlers have latched onto my legs. But even if I could move, would I? I came here for Yan-yeh.

San-pa crosses the floor and grabs my hand. The babies and small children startle at his abrupt action. Two begin to wail. Then another two. And more after that. Caretakers in pink smocks come running from other rooms. In a different situation, San-pa and I would look comical the way we tiptoe in and around and over the babies. The woman in charge crosses her arms indignantly as we approach.

"We have a child here," I confess, my voice coming out as breathless as if I'd raced Ci-teh up a mountain. "We've come to get her." Only the truth will help me, and maybe this woman will have a kind heart. "We're just married. We're beginning our lives together at last, but we need our daughter with us. If we take her, you'll have one less mouth to feed. And"—I pull one of my new silver wedding bracelets off my arm and offer it to her—"we can pay."

Babies howl. The caretakers scoop up the loudest screamers. San-pa glances apprehensively from the woman's face to the door, ready to bolt. I hold the woman's gaze. "I want my baby, please."

"My name is Director Zhou, and I prefer that bracelet," she says, pointing to the one A-ma gave me just days ago. It's my most valuable possession, but I readily give it to her. "So tell me," she asks, slipping the bracelet onto her wrist, "what day did your baby come to us? Does she have any scars or a birthmark?"

"She was wrapped with a tea cake—"

Director Zhou instantly brightens. "I remember that one!" But as memories of Yan-yeh return, her face falls. "We sent her in a caravan with other infants to Kunming two months ago."

I reach for San-pa. "We can go there—"

Before San-pa can respond, the director continues. "She's been adopted. She's no longer in China. She has new parents in America."

The world around me goes black, and I feel myself falling to the floor.

I follow San-pa on mountain path after mountain path. Up. Down. Up. Down. My mind is deadened from heartbreak. San-pa keeps his thoughts to himself. He's barely spoken to me since I fainted in the Social Welfare Institute. A few times a day, he wordlessly flicks his fingers at me—*Stay!*—before disappearing off the path and leaving me alone with my anguish. I'm a wife now, and I must grow accustomed to his male ways, but I worry he won't come back and I'll be lost out here, alone, forever. While I wait, I mark a tree or build a stack of rocks, just in case. But he always returns, jittery and anxious or sleepy and lethargic. I've been married only a few days, so what do I know? Maybe A-ba was like this to A-ma when they first wed.

We reach Daluo, on the border between Yunnan and Myanmar. San-pa asks some men if there's been any recent movement along the border because we don't have papers, but nothing has changed since he last passed this way. After we make our camp back in the jungle, he sits down across from me.

"Wife, we must forget the human reject. We'll have more children."

He's trying to be kind and soothe my pain, but how can I forget Yan-yeh? I lost her once, and suffered. I had hope, and then I lost her again. She's so far away now, it's as if she's dead. That knowledge—sharp as a knife—twists in my heart, doubling, tripling, the pain I had when I abandoned her.

When San-pa says, "We should start right now, trying to make another baby," I turn away from him and weep into the crook of my arm. When I recite, *"No wife should deny her husband in the first cycle of married life,"* he wordlessly accepts the depth of my guilt.

The next morning, "Wake up! Wake up! Let's go!" We traverse thick jungle—reeking with rot, heavy with humidity, and empty of people. At some point we pass an unmarked border and travel on to our first Myanmar village, where San-pa leaves me to buy supplies. I'm standing in the path that divides the village, staring at nothing, my mind with my baby and her "new parents in America," when a woman's voice speaks my name. "Li-yan." My eyes try to focus. I see a woman in filthy rags. Her face is thin and worn. It's Deh-ja, and it's been eight years since she and Ci-do were forced out of Spring Well for having human rejects.

"Are you real?" I ask. "Is it you?"

"I shouldn't have spoken." She lowers her eyes, humiliated for me to see her in such abysmal circumstances. "Forget you saw me."

"Forget?" My body surges with sudden urgency. "Destiny—my a-ma would call it coincidence—has brought us together, for only you can understand what I'm feeling now." I glance down the path that separates this hideously poor village. "Where is Ci-do?"

Instead of answering, she takes hold of my arm—more forcefully than is necessary—and pulls me with her to the right, past a few molting chickens and a single house, and into the jungle, where ruthless greenery instantly swallows us. Above us, a thick canopy of branches blocks the sky. Mosquitoes whine, and tropical birds screech. We reach a lean-to made of bamboo and thatch. A fire pit is dug in the ground before it. Trash has been tossed here and there. A few pieces of clothing hang from low branches. The person who lives here has no respect for nature or herself, and that person is Deh-ja. Together we squat on our haunches. How long will it be before San-pa wonders where I've gone?

"Did Ci-do go back to Spring Well?" Her eyes gleam with an unsettling combination of desperation and loyalty. When I tell her we have not seen him, she remains silent for a long while. "I hoped he'd gone home," she says at last.

"What happened?"

"Where do I start?" she asks. "When my monkeys were born"—I wince at the euphemism for her human rejects—"no one would look at us. You know that Ci-do wasn't allowed to wear his turban nor I my headdress. He didn't carry a crossbow, and I had milk leaking from my breasts. It wasn't hard for people to guess we'd been banished for having human rejects. We kept walking until we reached Thailand."

"San-pa says life is good there."

"You're here with *him*?" she asks, surprised. Of course she'd remember the incident of the stolen pancake. "But how—"

"Finish your story, and I'll tell you mine."

She sighs. "Life for the Akha is bad in Thailand—"

"But San-pa says—"

"We circled back to Myanmar. We never entered a village, but we kept looking for one where we might be accepted. We built this place between this village and the next. The people here are all Akha, and I began to barter with them. My embroidery skills have always been praised, so I made pouches and kerchiefs, which I traded for eggs. Eventually, I was able buy Ci-do a crossbow—not as good as his old one, but he was always a good hunter and we no longer went to sleep hungry."

In the distance, San-pa shouts, "Wife! Wife!" I don't respond. A part of me hopes he'll come looking for me, and yet I need Deh-ja's advice.

"Tradition demanded we could not speak to anyone for twelve months," she continues in a monotone, "so we gestured and grunted to make ourselves understood. One morning I woke up, and he was gone. That was seven years ago."

I should offer comforting words. Instead, I weep at the inescapable brutality of fate. "I also had a human reject. I didn't perform the rite. I took her to Menghai. Now San-pa and I are married, but she's gone. To America."

Deh-ja draws the back of her hand across her mouth. How can I know which part of the story shocks her most? That the little girl she once knew had a baby without marriage? That I didn't rid the world of my human reject? That I gave her away?

"Wife! Wife!"

I ignore San-pa. I'm less than one full cycle married and already I'm disobedient.

Now it's my turn to grab Deh-ja's arm. She doesn't pull away, but her muscles tense under my fingers. *I've been through too much already. Leave me be.*

"What do I do?" I ask. "How do I go on?"

Her laugh carries weariness and despair. "All you can do is live," she says. "You don't have a choice. Life continues whether we want it to or not. The sun will rise despite our suffering." She pauses. Her eyes take in the meagerness of her surroundings. "Maybe this is better than nothing. Maybe this is all we deserve. No nima can find a cure for us. No ruma can mix a potion. But isn't *this* better than no life at all? Isn't it better than hearing the tree that represents me in the spirit world crash to the ground?"

I don't want to accept her words, but a part of me knows she's right. I remember that woman who had multiple stillborn babies but kept trying until one lived. And Deh-ja has been through the very worst that can happen to a woman and yet she's still scraping by.

It's getting dark now. I must get back to my husband. Before leaving, I dig through my carrying basket, pull out the hidden pouch, and offer some money to Deh-ja. At first she doesn't want to take it, but I insist.

"When—*if*—San-pa and I come this way again, may I visit?"

"Of course. And if you ever encounter Ci-do . . ." She juts her chin, and the light in her eyes fades.

"But *we* found each other," I respond, wishing good omens for her. "Anything can happen."

She walks me to the edge of the village. "Be careful," she says before disappearing back into the jungle.

I find San-pa, sitting on the ground, sound asleep, his head resting on his folded arms. I have a hard time waking him. He slowly nods at me, trying to bring me into focus, as if he's still dreaming. No. I understand now. He's found someone to sell him opium as anyone suffering from grief might seek out my a-ma for the same dulling remedy. I don't need to question him about it. To my eyes, he's far more upset about Yan-yeh and the whole turn of events than I could have imagined. I love him for that, and I understand his need to numb his sorrow. I've had months to try to accept the loss of our daughter. He's had days. Later, after we've made camp, I reach out to him. I don't enjoy the intercourse, but it's something I must do to quiet my emptiness and help my husband too. *Bring me a baby. Let it be a son.*

The next morning, we continue south. We ford what San-pa says is the Nam Loi River. He tells me we've gone too far east when we reach the Mekong River. We work our way back into the dense greenery, staying out of sight, but keeping the river to our right. The border into Thailand? I don't know when we reach it. I don't know when we cross it. We're on just another trail snaking through the creeping vines and densely growing trees as wild animals call their indignation at our presence.

On the last day of our journey, we begin to encounter other travelers. I can't identify the dress or language of the tribal people; and I really don't understand the language or ways of the native

Thai. At one point, San-pa, who's walked ahead of me the entire way, abruptly stops. He's always been a good hunter and he cocks his head, listening intently to the jungle sounds. When he sniffs the air, I'm instantly petrified. Has he caught the scent of a tiger? He turns to me, his eyes sharp, his jaw tight.

"Run!"

I bound off the path and up a steep slope. San-pa catches me, pulls me up the hill with him, and yanks me down to hide in the undergrowth. I try to swallow my panting breaths, knowing that tigers are the greatest hunters of all with their sensitive ears. But no tiger would make this much noise stalking through the jungle. Soon a group of men, talking in subdued voices, tramp down the path. Next to me, San-pa crouches, one hand pressing down on my shoulder, keeping me hidden, the other holding his knife, blade out, ready to defend me. The men cannot be hill people or they would have noticed our fresh footprints. Only when the sounds from the caravan subside does San-pa loosen his grip on me. As he does, my body rises just a little—released—and I peer down the trail to see the last of a chain of men dressed in military fatigues, some carrying baskets on their shoulders, others swinging machine guns from left to right.

"I know them," my husband whispers, his voice rough. "You are not allowed to go anywhere near those people. You understand?"

Roger Siegel, M.D.
Mattel Children's Hospital UCLA

August 5, 1996

Sheldon Katz, M.D.
800 Fairmount Ave.
Pasadena, CA 91105

RE: HALEY DAVIS

Dear Sheldon,

Thank you again for referring the above named patient, estimated DOB 11/24/95. Records indicate that she has now been my patient since 4/20/96. To review: Family medical history is limited, as we have no prenatal or delivery information from the birth mother. The adoptive parents, Constance and Dan Davis, went through IVF and IUI, with no success. Father is an arborist, whose clients include Caltech, the Huntington Library and Botanical Gardens, as well as estates around Southern California. Mother is a professor of biology at Caltech. They reside at 2424 Hummingbird Lane in Pasadena. Parents chose adoption from China to minimize the risk of birth parents showing up and asking for their daughter back. Parents were told there were two hundred couples ahead of them on the China waiting list.

Parents took classes on adoption procedures and potential pitfalls. They gathered letters of reference, composed a personal essay, provided financial details and proof of employment. Parents were examined by their personal physicians, fingerprinted, and met with a county social worker on three occasions, where they detailed physical and mental health problems, thoughts about children, and their relationships to their respective parents (living and deceased), as well as past lovers. They chose Bright Beginnings as their adoption agency. They were told the patient would cost approximately $20,000, including travel expenses.

Parents received paperwork listing the baby as four months

old. The adoption agency told Mother, "You get what China feels like giving you. There is no negotiating. No second chances. This one or none." My initial examination on 4/20/96 suggested that patient was considerably younger than her reported age, as she weighed just ten pounds. As you know, patient presented as extremely malnourished and sick. She could not hold up her head or roll over by herself.

Parents were part of a group of six couples to pick up babies in Kunming, China. Parents came prepared with diapers, baby food and formula, energy bars, toys, clothing, and graham crackers. They were told to bring $5,000 in crisp $100 bills, of which $3,000 was given to the orphanage director as a cash donation. The babies were brought to a hotel and handed out "seemingly randomly." Mother states she is unsure if she got "the right one." Father describes all the babies as being filthy. Many had lice. (Patient did not.) Parents were instructed not to wash patient or clothes she came in, because familiar smells would be helpful for transition. This no doubt exacerbated patient's impetigo and scabies.

From Kunming, family flew to Canton (Guangzhou) to pick up an exit visa for patient at the U.S. consulate. On the flight to Los Angeles, patient turned blue and stopped breathing. An EMT on board performed CPR and monitored her progress until landing. Baby was first seen at Centinela Hospital Medical Center near the airport. Patient's parents had her transferred to Huntington Hospital near their home and your office in Pasadena. Patient was diagnosed with antibiotic-resistant *Clostridium difficile* and nearly died a second time. You referred her to me. I admitted her to our pediatric intensive care unit.

Clearly, patient had been in the presence of infected fecal matter, unclean water, and unsanitary food supply. Diagnoses of *Ascaris lumbricoides, Entamoeba histolytica, Giardia intestinalis, Helicobacter pylori, Sarcoptes scabiei* followed. I'm treating the roundworms with mebendazole. The other intestinal parasites have been harder to address given the limitations caused by the ongoing protocol for her *C. diff.*

Although she has been moved down to specialized care, morbidity rates are high for each condition, especially in a patient so young and immunocompromised. While I explained to parents that I cannot be confident of recovery, I hope you will more fully prepare them for the worst.

I will keep you posted as to patient's progress.

Sincerely,
Roger Siegel

P.S. Would you and Millie like to drive out our way one evening for dinner? It's been ages.

PEACE, QUIET, AND SANCTUARY

This morning, as every morning, I meet neighbor women, and together—safe in a group—we forage for wild yams, mushrooms, and birds' eggs in the mountains. I like Wife-of-Ah-joe, Wife-of-Shaw-kah, and Wife-of-Za-po. They've held me when I cry from homesickness and for the sorrow of my life, which has not turned out as I imagined. Recently, however, Wife-of-Ah-joe, the strongest and eldest of us, has become impatient with me. "Wife-of-San-pa, do you think your story is worse than mine? Have you suffered more than any other woman in this buffalo sputum village?" She is right, of course.

San-pa and I have been here three months. When he came to get me, he told A-ba that he'd gone away to earn money, not that he'd made much money. Only when we arrived in Thailand did he confess that he'd counted on my taking the *gaokao* for our future. "Now your wedding cash will have to do," he said. I gave it and the money I earned from Mr. Huang to San-pa. He used it to rent a plot for us to build a small bamboo and thatch house barely larger than a newlywed hut, without even space beneath our floor to protect chickens and pigs, if we had them. But he hunted, keeping us well fed, and he promised to look for a job soon. He continued to lament the loss of our daughter, but we sought the remedy for that sadness by doing the intercourse almost nightly, fully naked, staring into each other's eyes, trying to make another baby. But by the end of one Akha cycle—twelve days—I understood exactly where San-pa had brought me.

The Akha who live in Thailand have strayed so far outside our culture and so against nature that we're under constant threat. Here, we are the poorest of the hill tribes. We aren't allowed Thai citizenship. We can't own property. We're at the mercy of developers who can confiscate land we've slashed, burned, and planted. We can also be displaced by soldiers, businessmen, and drug runners on a whim. The first time I heard the words *Golden Triangle,* I understood the darkness of this place. I remembered when San-pa and I saw the men with their machine guns and mysterious baskets the day before we arrived here. He *knew* who those men were and what they were carrying. He tried to protect me, but I wish he had warned me of the world we were entering *before* we left Nannuo Mountain. How could he have ever thought this was a place to bring me or our daughter? When I asked him this question, he answered, "We had to conceal your disgrace, and I knew I could get work here." When I asked why he didn't have a job, he looked at the ground and turned away from me.

Over the next few weeks, San-pa stopped hunting and chopping firewood. I reminded him of old sayings: *If you work hard, you will eat easy. If you work easy, you will eat hard.* He responded with the words from a love song that dates back to the time of our great-grandparents: *True lovers will love each other unto death. Even if both are buried alive, they will not be afraid.* This did not give me confidence. Without money or food, we were, I realized, poorer than my family was when I was a little girl. Hunger, familiar as an old friend, began to gnaw at my insides. I've lost weight, but I'm still not as thin as my husband. "Does your stomach speak to you too?" I asked him one night as we lay together on our sleeping mat. When he didn't answer, I believed he was in his dreams. By dawn, I thought better of asking such a question again.

No wife wants to poke at her husband's manliness with a sharp snout, but I couldn't help myself. Every time I ask him to pick up his crossbow, he comes back at me with inquiries weighted by two different thoughts spread apart: "Why didn't you perform the rite?" or "Why did you abandon our baby?" With either question, he had the answer: "You cursed and ruined us." This was his grief speaking, and I caused it. When he began to steal away into the jungle and not return for a day or two, I blamed myself for that too. Such sadness I have brought to my husband.

This morning, I asked why he'd married me. He answered, "You were supposed to change my fortune. You were supposed to grow from the number one girl to the number one woman. The first from Nannuo Mountain to go to university. The first to be a leader of women. With me standing proudly at your side." With a chill, I remembered San-pa's moment of hesitation when he heard that I hadn't taken the test. As if reading my thoughts, he added, "I was trying to be honorable. I was to marry the number one girl, but I ended up the number one fool. Now all we can do is hide from your mistakes." My mouth could not form a response. The worst part? Everything he said was true.

Now, as I dig up a mountain tuber with the tip of my knife, I try to think of ways to bring him back to the person he was. *Have a son. Have a son. Have a son. Make your husband happy. He will love you again.*

After our hunt for food, my friends and I return to the village, change into our wedding attire with our glorious headdresses, and meet at the spirit gate, where we join other women similarly outfitted. We're supposed to be watching the mountain path for the arrival of our daily visitors, but we're also casting wary looks at the skinny men who lounge before their huts. They need to disappear before our guests get here.

I grew up believing that opium was for rituals and medicine only, but on my first day in this village I saw that some men smoked it for pleasure. Many cycles later, when my friends and I were looking in the jungle for thatch to reinforce our roofs, I found a syringe. When I showed it to Wife-of-Ah-joe, she batted it out of my hand. "Don't ever touch one of those! They're used by men who cook opium into a liquid to inject in their veins." I thought, *Why would an Akha do such a thing?* Sadly, I already knew the answer: no future. Opium and heroin had not caused our poverty and hopelessness. Rather, poverty and hopelessness had brought about an unquenchable desire to forget.

After that, Wife-of-Ah-joe took me to the village ruma. He warned me about our men working for the drug traffickers. He told me about husbands selling their wives and fathers selling their daughters into prostitution to earn money to buy drugs. He explained that after Chairman Mao took over China, the imperialist West—America—sponsored the Nationalists in the mountains of Thailand. Those men stayed and began to cultivate opium. By the time of the Vietnam War, the Golden Triangle supplied half the world's heroin. "You are now living in the midst of that," he told me wearily. It was nearly impossible to believe. *Be grateful,* I told myself. *San-pa may not have a job, but at least he doesn't work for the drug men.*

The announcement of our guests' arrival comes first through our feet—*thud, thud, thud.* A toothless woman helps her grown son, sick with a disease that comes from the needles, into the privacy of their hut. As the sounds of thrashing and honking reach us, followed by laughter and chatter in languages none of us comprehend, other men sidle wordlessly into the jungle. The lead elephant comes into view, his immense body swaying delicately from side to side, his trunk constantly searching. A handler, bare feet dangling, perches between the elephant's ears. Behind him, white foreigners sit on a painful-looking platform shaded by a canopy: tourists. (The first time I saw a foreigner, I thought it must be a spirit, for no one living could be that tall, white, or fat. Fatter than pictures of Chairman Mao. Fatter than Mr. Huang. So fat that sometimes I even worry for the elephants, which is silly, I know.) Once all the elephants have been tethered and the tourists helped down—with much laughter and cameras snapping—my friends and I approach.

"You want to buy?"

"You want to buy?"

"You want to buy?"

We've learned the English words, which all foreigners—no matter where they're from—understand. To tourists like these, we sell woven pouches for their sunglasses, laptops, and cellphones. Sometimes sophisticated buyers—who call themselves dealers—come, and they wheedle us to sell our wedding headdresses, embroidered tunics, silver-adorned breastplates, and our baby carriers woven and decorated with special charms and good wishes, representing all the love a mother can give.

A huge man shouts at me and waves his camera in my face. *Garble, garble, garble.*

"Photo five baht," I recite in English.

I pose with him, then with a family from America with two sour-faced sons, then with an elderly couple with gray hair, sunhats, and legs so white I can see the veins under the surface of their flesh. I secretly hope that one day a tourist family will arrive with an Akha child in the wife's arms. Yan-yeh would be almost a year old now.

I go home with fifty baht, my minuscule earnings from posing and selling, which is not enough to live on if your husband isn't hunting or working. At least I'm not a beggar. No Akha anywhere has ever become a beggar. *Always keep your pride,* I remind myself as I hide half the money where San-pa will never find it—not with my clothes or even with my cookware, not anywhere he would suspect me of concealing something of value. I hide it at the bottom of *his* carrying basket with *his* belongings.

When San-pa arrives, he demands that I give him what I earned. "I need it. Give it, Wife." When I don't hand over what he considers should be the full amount, he makes other impossible requests. "Give me your bracelets. Give me your headdress. I'll sell the silver."

I try reason. "If I don't have those, then the foreigners won't want to take my picture. If they don't take my picture, then how will we have money to eat?"

The look on his face tells me I've gone too far.

"You know what happens to wives if they don't obey," he says in a low voice. "It can happen this quick!" He brings his hands together for a single loud clap. I can't believe he'd beat me, but three months ago I wouldn't have believed I'd be as hungry as I am now. I give him the money from my pocket. I'll use coins from his carrying basket to buy rice and oil.

Later, on our sleeping mat, he nuzzles against me. "Forgive me, dear one," he whispers tenderly. We do the intercourse, and he's as gentle as ever. But afterward, when he slinks out the door to smoke his pipe, I'm left with suspicions. He never tells me how he spends what I give him. Maybe he loses it gambling. Maybe he purchases rice liquor or a woman's time. Maybe he buys opium. But he couldn't be taking opium, because I would have noticed. Or maybe that's why he stays away for days at a time. To recover before coming home. I reject the idea. *He wouldn't do that to me.* Soon, though, my mistrust returns. *He did it that time in Deh-ja's village . . .*

I go outside and ask directly: "Have you tried opium again?"

His eyes become hooded. "On rare occasions," he admits, "when I want to get away from the misery of my life."

As his wife, I long to help him, but what can I do?

The next day follows the usual course: foraging, followed by selling trinkets. In the late afternoon, after the tourists have returned to their hotels and we've gone home to change, my friends and I gather outside once again. We sit on logs to embroider, trade stories, and sing. We're united by sorrow, and I'm comforted by the fact that we all speak the same language and follow the same traditions. We all wish for the bounty of the earth to reward us. We all hope for peace, quiet, and sanctuary. We just want to be left alone to sojourn through our lives—apart from lowland dwellers, apart even from other hill tribes. We want to be embraced by the warmth of the earth's soil, the energy of its trees, and the fragrance of its blooms. But since our lives are out of alignment with the world, today we must endure a visit from the strangest creatures of all: missionaries. Akhas are taught never to hate, but this particular group of foreigners, who tell us our practices are evil and there is only one god, challenge my patience.

"No god would permit the killing of twins," the white man yammers at the four of us, as though the practice still continued. His wife tries to talk to us about babies who are born with other problems. "These children are God's special gifts." They spend another half hour belittling us for our "foolish superstitions." To them, we are not just *tu*—backward—we are sinful.

When I first encountered the couple, I saw people who didn't know how to exist in harmony with the earth, the animals, or the rain, wind, and sun. I ignored the gossips who told me that missionaries kidnap Akha children and send them to orphanages and forced labor camps, but today, after the couple leaves, Wife-of-Shaw-kah tells us what happened to her.

"When I was full with child, they encouraged me to go to their clinic to have my baby," she confides, trying unsuccessfully to keep her emotions hidden. "They said that if it was born with a cleft palate or an extra finger, their doctors would fix it. So I went to the clinic. They put me to sleep. When I woke up, they handed me my baby. She was perfect, and I had not suffered. But they did something to me when I was asleep, and I have not been able to come to a head again."

I've now heard variations of this story too many times to doubt their truth.

I change the subject by seeking my friends' advice. "I think I made a mistake in marrying my husband, but what can I do about it now?"

"You need to be careful in what you say," one of the women warns. "He could sell you."

I hadn't considered that this could happen to me, and the idea—suddenly too real—makes me even more desperate. "But what if I could find my way back to Nannuo Mountain? I could return my wedding gifts to my in-laws to signal my divorce. I might be accepted back into Spring Well Village—"

"Those things are not possible." Wife-of-Ah-joe cuts me off. "Even if you follow the rituals for divorce, you can never go home. Too shameful."

I remember First Sister-in-law warning me of that but in more traditional words. Other things A-ma and A-ba relayed to me through the sisters-in-law also come back to me: *A weak boy grows up to be a weak man* and *The whole mountain knows he's lazy.* And that was before the heartbreak of Yan-yeh.

"At least he hasn't taken your bracelets or the silver from your headdress," Wife-of-Za-po offers helpfully. "When that happens, you'll have nothing left."

That evening, after a dinner of soup made with no more than hot water and jungle tubers, San-pa takes the money I give him and pulls on his cape.

"Will you be gone long?" I ask.

"Do not ask me one more question," he yells. "Do you understand? Not one more!"

He storms out of our hut. I doubt he will be back tonight. He might not even return tomorrow night. Fighting despair, I repeat in my mind what Deh-ja told me. *All you can do is live.*

Deep in the night I have a terrible dream. Deh-ja's human rejects come out of her body. They are not babies, though, but yapping, miniature, yet somehow full-grown, dogs. A-ma puts them in a bag and sits on it until their yelping quiets. Deh-ja, as in real life, weeps. Ci-teh reclines in the corner, giggling. A-ma pushes medicine down Deh-ja's throat. Her head begins to nod. She looks at us sleepily. Then San-pa appears. He takes the sack of dogs outside, strings the carcasses end to end on a spit, and roasts them over a fire for his evening meal. He tears the animals apart with his teeth. His mouth is as greasy as the first time I saw him. He stares at me, begins to nod, finally dozing off. Then he jerks his head up and grins, showing me all of his shiny teeth . . .

I jolt awake. I feel more alone than I thought possible. I'm unable to return to sleep, because the dream felt so real. In the morning, I can't bring myself to go foraging, but at noon I put on my tourist costume—my wedding clothes and headdress, which once meant so much to me—and go outside. As my neighbors and I pose for pictures and pocket tips, I continue to ponder the significance of my dream. I look at it from every angle. I think about how A-ba, my brothers, and my sisters-in-law would decipher the messages. And then, of course, my mind goes to A-ma, the best interpreter of dreams on Nannuo Mountain. She would see the violation of Akha Law in every image, just as I do. For all the visions, though, only two matter in the end. The way both Deh-ja's and San-pa's heads nodded so dreamily. I'm shoving a handful of woven sunglass cases in the face of a woman with hair the color of wild mustard—"You want to buy?"—when the meaning becomes clear.

My husband is a heroin addict. This is not going to get better. Things can only get worse.

I manage to complete my sale and then walk back to my house, in a daze, without saying goodbye to my friends. Maybe I should be more upset. Maybe I should be pulling my hair, screaming down the path, or sobbing in a heap at the feet of an elephant. But I'm not the girl I once was. I'm still only eighteen years old, but I'm many decades older in my heart.

I enter the single room that is my home. San-pa has returned and is stretched out on our sleeping mat, an arm draped over his eyes.

"Wife," he says, acknowledging my presence.

"Husband," I say, kneeling on the edge of the mat.

There must be something in the way I speak the word, because his arm drops to his side and he stares into my eyes. Despite everything, he can still read me very well. A second or two, and he understands that I *know*.

"I thought coming back for you would change everything." His breath still smells sweet, yet his excuses for his drug use merely incorporate variations of the same familiar torments. "But you doomed us by having the human reject. Then you made it so we couldn't fix our mistake and save our daughter."

I have a lot of remorse for the things I've done, but I won't allow San-pa to make me feel guilty any longer.

"I'm the one who suffered. I carried Yan-yeh within me. I gave birth to her. I was her mother, and I did everything I could to save her. I needed you, and I still need you."

Tears pool in his eyes. "You did this to me."

"I didn't make you into the man you are," I say sadly. "You've always been exactly who you are. A weak man. A pancake stealer."

They're such gentle admonitions when I could say so much worse, but they cut to the very heart of who San-pa is. His eyes go cold, and he rolls away from me.

I lie down next to him. A canyon of sorrow and regret fills the space between us. By the time he sneaks out hours later, I know what I must do.

Still dressed in my wedding clothes, I pack the rest of my belongings in my carrying basket. I need to be gone from the village before others rise, but I'm not hurried or frightened. I calmly rummage through San-pa's basket to retrieve my hidden money. We don't have any food, but I'll be able to survive in the jungle as long as I have my knife. Beyond that, I don't have a plan. I can't go home. Maybe I'll end up living in a lean-to next to Deh-ja. Even that would be better than this.

I don't bother to glance around the room to collect memories. Resolution guides me now. I brush off my skirt three times and recite the words that will begin to set my divorce in motion and instruct my soul to accompany me and not be tempted to remain behind. "I'm leaving, leaving, leaving." I'm so very thankful I don't have children, because custom would force me either to maroon them with San-pa or to give them to his parents.

I slowly walk down the lane that divides the village, careful not to rouse the dogs. But as soon as I reach the last house, I gallop for the dense protection of the jungle. My husband may have his drugs, but I feel something pulsing through me, giving me the strength to flee. At the top of a rise, I pause, crouch, listen. Nothing. I run again. I'm familiar enough with where I live from the long hours spent foraging that for now I know which direction to go. That doesn't mean I'm confident. San-pa might come looking for me. I try to move carefully through the jungle, but I'm in a hurry and he is a good tracker when he wants to be.

The descent of fog over the mountain comes as either a gift or another danger. It will give me the ability to hide, but it's also disorienting. Spirits lie in wait for the weak, the sick, the frightened. I try to build courage by reminding myself I'm Akha. We live in the jungle. We get food and medicine from the jungle. If we're careful, we can protect ourselves from bad spirits, wild animals, and fateful accidents. But in running away from my husband, I'm not being careful. Then it hits me. *What if he finds me?* He has to know I won't go back with him. My blood chills. If he finds me, I've left him with two options: sell me or kill me. Both would be his right.

Yunnan lies to the north. I follow mountain paths from dawn to dusk, watching the way the sun moves across the sky: to my right in the mornings, to my left in the afternoons. I drink water from streams and eat plants. I loop magic vine over my shoulders, hoping it will protect me from bad spirits and my husband. I walk—and sometimes run—until I can't go another step. Then I veer off the trail and find a place to rest. I'm exhausted, but I barely sleep. *If a gopher does not have his escape route dug and ready ahead of time, then it will be difficult to run away when he needs it.* If I'd had an escape plan, I could have protected myself with rituals and talismans. Now I'm scared, never an emotion to have in the jungle. I spend the black night hours listening to every snap and creak coming from the shadows. On the fourth day, I feel San-pa's presence. If he sang to me, I fear I would hear him. But there's something else too. The wind shifts, and I catch the smell of wildness. A spirit or spirits?

Terrified, I sprint into a small clearing with high grass and hunker down. Hidden. Safe. But then, like a rabbit, I can't keep still. I bolt up out of the grass and run as fast as I can back into the jungle until I reach the trail. I jump from rock to rock, scramble over outcroppings, slip in mud, pick myself up, and keep going. My legs and lungs ache with fiery pain.

My mind races with sick knowledge. If it's true that A-poe-mi-yeh—the supreme god of the Akha people—has placed a stamp inside every person's head that says how long he or she will live and that we each have a tree in the spirit world that represents us, then the due date on my stamp must surely be coming and my tree must have shed its leaves. So many aphorisms A-ma used to recite come back to me as recriminations. Why didn't I listen? Because I was like every other girl. Stupidly prideful. Too sure of myself. Foolish in love. Yes, I've sinned—against my a-ma and a-ba, against my husband, against my baby. Now that the end of my life feels so close I inwardly beg for it to last a little longer. *Let me go back home. Let me find my baby. Let me survive what is hunting me. Give me a chance. I will fight. I will be better. Sun and Moon, help me.*

Behind me I hear someone—something—crashing through the dank undergrowth. I duck behind a tree, as if that could hide me from a hunter. I hear the hum then *thwack* as an arrow embeds itself in a tree near me. The thought that I won't see death coming—that I'll end my life with an arrow in my back—hurts more than I could have imagined. I want to see San-pa. I want to look in his eyes when he pulls back the arrow and lets it fly to my heart. When I die, I want to face all the mistakes I've made.

I step from my hiding place. There is San-pa. His crossbow is raised. He loved me once, and I loved him. And now here we are. His arm begins to draw back the arrow.

"Cat!" he says sharply in warning.

My eyes move to my right, to where I heard the first arrow hit. There, by the tree, a tiger crouches, ready to pounce. His golden eyes hold me still. His whiskers twitch.

San-pa calls again, this time for the tiger's attention. "Cat!"

The beast shifts his gaze from me to the nuisance who's interrupted his hunt. San-pa shoots the arrow just as the tiger lunges. Another *thwack* as the arrow misses its intended target. The tiger passes so close to me that I feel the hard slap of his tail. Two bounds, and he reaches San-pa. The first scream is one of anger. But as the tiger bites into San-pa's thigh, his screams turn to pain and terror. The tiger backs off, then playfully swats San-pa with his paw. A sound grates out of the tiger's throat—*rrrrrrr*. He turns his head to make sure I'm still here.

San-pa manages to grab another arrow, holding it before him like a spear. So pathetic. The tiger pounces again. He doesn't go for San-pa's throat. Instead he bites into San-pa's stomach and yanks with such ferocity that my husband is lifted off the ground and tossed hard against a tree. His agonized groan tells me he's still alive, but even if the tiger doesn't attack San-pa again, he will die. A terrible death. And I'm next.

With the stronger of the two of us incapacitated, the tiger returns his attention to me. His mouth and whiskers are stained with blood, but he has such a regal and powerful face. I close my eyes so my mind can go one last time to my daughter. *Wherever you are, always remember I loved you.*

"Cat!" San-pa screams.

I open my eyes to see the tiger glance back at San-pa. This time the hum is short. *Thwack*, as the arrow enters the tiger's eye. The animal stands perfectly still for a moment, then his knees crumple. I collapse too. My fingers grip the ground. My heart pounds. Carefully I crawl past the tiger to San-pa. His guts lie about him like jungle vines. Blood is everywhere. His eyes are wide and unblinking. His last breathing act was to save my life.

Roger Siegel, M.D.
Mattel Children's Hospital UCLA

November 5, 1996

Sheldon Katz, M.D.
800 Fairmount Ave.
Pasadena, CA 91105

RE: HALEY DAVIS

Dear Sheldon,

On November 3, I saw your patient, Haley Davis, for a follow-up with respect to the management of her parasites and accompanying infectious diseases. After a lengthy stay in our pediatric intensive care unit, I am most pleased to report that Haley no longer exhibits any symptoms. Her stools are normal. Her lung fields are clear. She has not developed secondary complications: her heart is normal in size and configuration, her renal and liver functions are normal as well.

I have gotten to know Constance and Dan, who are delightful people and, I believe, very good parents. They will vigorously carry out all instructions to ensure Haley's continued health and well-being. As for Haley, rarely in my professional life have I seen such a fighter. She's not only responded to treatment, she's begun to thrive. She's gained weight and has caught up to her age-appropriate developmental milestones: she can roll over and sit up unassisted, and she's become a master creeper. I expect she will have begun walking on her own in time for her first birthday in a couple of weeks, to which the family has invited me. Haley is very eager to please. The nurses in the unit love to make her laugh, but I'm her favorite. When she touches my nose, I stick out my tongue. She giggles so hard she tips over. Her verbal skills are coming along, but I was one of her first ten words. She calls me Da Ta, for doctor. All who have treated Haley consider her to be a bright and very cheerful child.

Since Haley is doing so well, I make no further recommendations at this time. Many thanks for allowing me to follow this nice youngster with you.

With warm personal regards,
Roger Siegel, M.D.

GOODBYE TO THE TEARS

What am I to do now? We Akha have many customs, but none are more sacred than those for the dead, because these are souls who've moved from the living world to the spirit world. For a normal death, the ceremonies are ten times greater than those for a wedding. For someone who's died a terrible death, though, traditions are severely simplified. Still, all dead must be treated with reverence and accord to clear their passage and see them settled in their new home, but there are too many things I can't do for my husband. No songs of mourning will shudder along the hillsides telling everyone on Nannuo Mountain of our tragedy. I can't weep—as a proper widow—as his family sacrifices a water buffalo, chickens, and other animals to make amends to the universe for their son's terrible death and to prevent him from causing trouble in the village. Most of all, I can't stay in this spot for three days and three nights with San-pa's body. I just can't. Nevertheless, I need to make sure his spirit is in his corpse and that both are completely in the ground, because his nature in the life he lived—and not his last moments—are what will drive him now.

I wash what's left of his body as best I can with water from a nearby stream. Never before have I seen anything so horrible. His flesh has been torn and ripped. I don't know what to do with his innards, which don't want to fit back in his stomach cavity. I place a coin on his tongue and bind his jaw closed with a length of vine. "May you use that money to buy clothes and food in your new home," I recite. I pull two threads from my skirt. One I use to tie San-pa's thumbs together; the other to tie his big toes together. We do this to remind the dead that they are indeed dead. Surely San-pa knows he's dead, but I perform this small act for him out of gratitude for his saving me.

Tradition says those who've died a terrible death must be buried right where they fell, but I have no digging tools. After searching the area, I find a small depression that might serve as a burial place. I manage to drag San-pa to the hollow. But once he's there I can't just pile stones over him, because one special rule applies to the interment of those who've died a terrible death. A sacrificed dog must be placed over the corpse to serve as a barrier so that the disturbed spirit won't feel a need to roam and cause trouble for humans. There are no dogs in the jungle. I'm a woman, so I'm not a hunter either. I sit on my haunches, think, and wait. Finally, it comes to me. The tiger. I could never move it, but its power, even in death, might be strong enough to work. I try to cut off one of the tiger's paws, but the sinew between the bones is too gristly. The thinnest part of the tiger is his tail. I wedge my knife between two of the bones, pry and pry. The length comes loose at last. As quickly as I can, I toss the tail on San-pa, then hurriedly cover his body with rocks, branches, and thatch. Anyone who passes the mound will know that someone is buried in this spot. They will recite incantations, seek ritual cleansing when they return home, and, I hope, remain safe.

I say a few last words to my husband. The first are phrases I've heard the ruma speak at proper funerals. "When you were alive, your a-ma and a-ba loved you, and you loved them. Now you are dead. When you were alive, you liked to hunt. Now you are dead. When you were alive, you liked to sing and dance. Now you are dead. It is time for the living and the dead to separate. May you travel to your ancestors. May you never disturb living people."

Next I add a few words of my own. "You must forget all about me. You are dead completely. Do not try to follow me. I say goodbye to the tears you caused. I thank you for saving my life, but do not come back to earth again—as a spirit or in your next incarnation—until I am dead."

I want to leave this place, but I'm covered with dirt and dried blood. At the stream, I bathe fully clothed so I can retain some decency in case someone should come upon me. My husband's blood tints the water. My wedding clothes will never be completely cleansed, but my headdress is fine. Dripping wet, I gather wood for a fire, collect some tubers, find a patch of sun, and make a simple meal. Afterward, I lie down—hoping the sun's rays will dry my clothes—and fall into a sleep as deep as death.

In the morning, I pick up San-pa's crossbow and arrows, pass by the tiger's corpse one last time, and find my way back to the path. I search the shards of sky peeking through the branches above me so I can track the arc of the sun as I continue my journey.

I never find the village where I saw Deh-ja. I get lost. When fog descends or a storm washes through, I end up walking in circles. I ask people for directions, but rarely do I find someone who speaks Akha or Mandarin. Surrounded by the thickness of the forest, I spend hours trying to make sense of all that happened as things I should have paid more attention to crowd my eyes. Two years ago, I overheard A-ba saying to San-pa, "You've been trading in things you shouldn't and trying things you shouldn't." I didn't ask either of them about it, but could it mean San-pa was already involved with the drug? When San-pa hid me from the drug traffickers, did he recognize them because he'd worked for them? Was that how he'd earned money to come for me? Even if we'd gotten Yan-yeh, what did it say about San-pa as a father that he'd been willing to take her to that awful village? Would he have eventually become the kind of man who would sell his wife or daughter? These are questions for which I'll never know the answers, and that knowledge is a torment. But the memory that cuts the worst is in many ways the simplest. I married a man who lied to change the day of his birth as a way to fool the universe. That act was a pure violation of a most basic tenet of Akha Law. And for what? To marry what he called a number one girl? I find myself speaking aloud to A-ma Mata, the great mother of the Akha people. "What does it say about *me* that I went along with his lie?"

After days of walking, I reach the trails I know so well. It's all I can do to keep from running home, but I do what I know I must and go straight to San-pa's village. The story I tell my in-laws is short and simple, revealing only that their son died a terrible death. And while I avoid details that will haunt their sleeping hours, they can see from my stained clothes that their son must have suffered greatly.

"We knew he'd get in trouble in Thailand," my father-in-law comments, resigned but accepting, "but we didn't think it would be this."

I hold my mother-in-law's hand while she weeps. Since San-pa died a terrible death, he will not be worshipped and no offerings will ever be made to him. Rather, incantations will be recited to keep him away, and his name will never be mentioned again. If he'd had a younger brother, then I would have been asked to marry him, but he had no brother.

Once my mother-in-law and I have retreated to the women's side of the house, she gives me a change of clothes. Later, we stand together as I feed my marriage leggings, tunic, and skirt to the fire. All I have left is my headdress. San-pa's mother hands me a pair of embroidery scissors, which I use to clip off the silver balls and coins. This is my final act of dismantling my husband from my life. I tuck the silver pieces in my pocket and drop the now worthless headdress into the flames. My dreams—and that's all they were—of happiness are soon ashes.

Unsure of what to do next, I seek the solitude of my grove and fall asleep under the grotto's canopy, feeling the age and protection of the trees around me. Many hours later, the smell of food cooking over a fire reaches into my slumber. I can tell by the warmth of the air that it must be midday already. I open my eyes, see a pair of legs, and follow them up.

"A-ma . . ."

"Girl." She squats next to me and rests her elbows on her knees. Her eyes pass over my wrists, notice her dragon bracelet gone, and then drift away. I sense her hardening herself against the miseries I will tell her. "People saw you on the mountain. Word reached me last night. I knew I would find you here."

I tell her more than I told my in-laws, but I keep it just as basic: my baby was given to a family in America, my husband was an addict, I ran away from him, he was killed by a tiger. She could say many things, all of which could begin with "I told you . . ." Instead, she says, "We Akha believe that every human lives and dies nine times before becoming a special kind of spirit, which is like the wind blowing, unseen yet comforting and necessary. Even San-pa will reach that level one day. But your daughter's path . . . I don't understand it."

We sit silently for a long while.

"May I come home?" I ask at last, knowing the humiliation I'll face from my family and neighbors for the rest of my life.

"I wish you could—"

"It's against tradition," I acknowledge, "but I've seen enough of the outside world to know that it is not something I wish ever to see again."

"No place is as beautiful or as comforting as our home, but—"

"I don't have to marry," I hear myself begging. "I can work hard. I'll become the midwife you always wanted me to be."

"Girl—"

"If you don't want me in Spring Well Village, I could live here in the grove."

"You could, but people on Nannuo will hear what happened to San-pa. They'll blame you for his terrible death, and your life will not be what it should."

She pours tea made from big leaves from old trees. The taste of my childhood. The taste of home. The taste of sorrow.

"You are my daughter," she picks up. "You and I are connected by blood. We are also joined by this grove and your daughter. When you were gone, not a day passed that I didn't worry about you. And not a day went by that I didn't know you would come back. It took longer than I thought." Her smile is sad. "So . . . I've had much time to think about what should happen when I next saw you. I wish with all my heart that you could stay here—despite the embarrassment for our family and the regrets for you—but you must leave."

I haven't cried once since deciding to run away from San-pa, but now that all hope has vanished, I weep.

"Don't." A-ma nudges me with the back of her hand. "You must listen. Teacher Zhang and I have prepared for this moment."

"Teacher Zhang? But how could he know anything about— "

Again, she gives me that sad smile. "We know you, and we knew San-pa." She puts her hands on her knees and pushes herself up. "You're going to that trade school— "

"What?" I can't believe what I'm hearing. "How?"

"Teacher Zhang always said he had friends there. He was right. He secured a place for you for whenever you returned."

"But you never wanted me to go— "

"That's correct. As your a-ma, I didn't want you to be away for four years. Who knew how you would change or if you would ever come home? But now I need to make this sacrifice if you are to have any chance at life. And you need to do this so maybe you can return one day. People will forget eventually . . ."

Will they? They never forgot about Ci-do and Deh-ja.

She glances up at the sun, judging the time. "I was awake all night. Third Sister-in-law helped me gather clothes for you. We've also packed a basket of tea. The best. I made it myself from the sister trees. This morning, I went to Teacher Zhang's house. He's waiting for us now at the tea collection center. But before we leave, I must tell you some things."

All this is happening too fast. I don't know what to think or how to feel. Disappointment. Confusion. Guilt. Worry. Fear. Sadness. Grief. And more. But one emotion overrides them all: deep love for my a-ma. Tears of gratitude streak my face.

A-ma stares down at me and shakes her head tolerantly. "Just sit. Just listen." Then she begins. "You've heard the stories of how the Tea Horse Road spread civilization through the trade of salt, matches, and so many other necessities. None was more important than the exchange of our tea for Tibet's warhorses. I can still remember the caravans from when I was a girl. Some had mules to help them, and they were decorated with beautiful stirrups, embroidered breastplates, and tasseled reins. Other caravans were composed solely of men, who carried heavy packs of tea cakes on their backs for fifteen hundred kilometers through jungle and rocky passes, across rivers and around lakes, over icy peaks, until reaching the treacherous plateau that is Tibet."

I've heard all this before. Why is she telling it to me again?

"Each caravan might take six months to reach its destination," she continues. "One part was so steep that it took twenty days to go two hundred and twenty-five kilometers, with rests every hundred meters or so. Many died from the hardship, falling from cliffs or freezing in blizzards, but those who survived to come home would turn around after a few days and start the trip all over again. Back and forth. Never ending. The road was also a way for monks, pilgrims, armies, and peoples to move. For the Akha, the road gave us a path to follow when we fled down—"

"From Tibet a thousand years ago."

"Exactly. Now, Girl, think of your female ancestors thirty generations back, walking all that way. As they traveled, they picked up wanted and unwanted guests on their bodies and in their belongings—pollens, seeds, and spores. Now look at the mother tree."

It's as gnarled and twisted as ever. The trunk and branches are still infested with various types of fungi, molds, orchids, and, of course, the yellow threads.

"All the life on the mother tree came from somewhere else. It was transported by our nomadic ancestors. You could say the tree shows the history of our female line. You must remember, Girl, that not only men Recite the Lineage. We women do it too. For generations, the nima and ruma of Spring Well and so many other villages have sought the help of the women in our family. We give them leaves, bark, and even the yellow parasite from the mother tree to use as medicine."

She puts up a hand to stop me from stating the obvious: *I know all this.*

"If you were to open the tea cake I gave your baby," she continues, "you would see yellow threads twisted and growing throughout. That cake is a link to time and to the women who came before us." She taps my chest right above my heart. "You've had difficult times. No question. But you, Li-yan, are unique."

It's the first I've heard A-ma speak my real name, and it's overpowering.

"You have special abilities," she goes on. "I don't mean you are a witch or a fox spirit. And you've never seemed drawn to the special gift of healing or magic. Rather, you are like A-ma Mata, who gave birth to the Akha people, who pushed against her restraints, who said, 'No, I will not accept my bad fate,' and who endured against all odds with her intelligence, compassion, and perseverance. All that comes from this grove. And the mother tree."

A-ma had told me some of this the first time she brought me here. All I remember is my disappointment. Maybe I had to suffer to hear the words in a new way.

"Your a-ba didn't give you this land because you're worthless. He had no rights to it at all. *I* insisted that it go to you. It can only belong to you, as it will belong to your daughter one day." She has to correct herself. "The daughter you will have one day."

She hastily kicks dirt over the fire, not giving me a chance to comment. "Now, come. We can't keep Teacher Zhang waiting." Only as I'm about to begin shimmying around the boulder does she hold me back. "Take one last look. Remember."

I try to absorb everything that I see with new eyes: the mother tree standing with such dignity, the sister trees offering their protective embrace, the camphor trees hiding them all, the ancient strength of the boulder, the cliff at the edge of the grove, the mountains in the distance.

My riot of emotions is no less jumbled when we reach the tea collection center, but seeing Teacher Zhang looking exactly the same in his blue Mao suit and cap is comforting. I'm in my borrowed outfit, with a basket of tea over one shoulder, a basket of new clothes over the other, and clutching a small woven bag filled with rice balls, fruit, and an earthenware jug of water. The courtyard bustles with activity as families bring in their autumn pickings to be weighed. Even the old Dai woman is here, and the aroma of her scallion pancakes is as tempting as ever.

"You'll be taken by truck to Menghai," Teacher Zhang explains.

"When you get there, ask the way to the bus station. Buy a ticket to Kunming. From Menghai, the trip will take another eighteen hours."

"I'm scared," I whisper.

He pats my arm awkwardly. "You've already been far away," he says gently. "You will manage."

A-ma gives last-minute advice: "Always follow Akha Law. If you adhere to our ways, you'll be protected from problems whether from the spirit world or the human world. Never forget us."

"I'll come home one day—"

A-ma places her fingers lightly on my lips as if to stop me from making a promise I might not be able to keep.

"I'll be waiting to see your face," she says. I hear hope below her deep melancholy. She folds money into my hand. "I'm told you'll need two hundred yuan a month for room and board. I promise to send more each month through Teacher Zhang."

I clamber onto the back of the truck. Teacher Zhang and A-ma pass up my baskets, which I secure in the bags of tea bound for the factory in Menghai. The driver starts the engine.

"Always remember how to behave, how to speak to people, how to respect the world around you," A-ma calls up to me, fighting the sound of the truck's engine. "No matter where you go or what you do, don't abandon our customs."

"I promise to do my best, A-ma," I say. Then I recite, "*A good Akha no more has the ability to throw away the customs than a buffalo has the ability to place his footprints in one spot while having his body somewhere else.*"

Sun and Moon! Am I sick! I'm so sick going around the curves and over the bumpy roads that I think I might die. I hang my head over the edge of the truck, and everything pours out of me. This is so much worse than Mr. Huang's mountain vehicle, which was small and I could sit in the front seat. Even when I'm empty, the nausea doesn't leave.

For every kilometer, I feel the past stalking me. As we veer ominously close to the edge of the steep mountain road, I recall yet another mistake I've made. At every jolt over rocks or dip through rain-eroded holes, I have to accept in my bones the price I've paid. A-ma said, "Always follow Akha Law," but all my errors have stemmed from ignoring the very principles that make me who I am. I've learned and been scarred by the inevitability of pain and defeat. Now that I'm totally alone, I feel the blessings of my culture feeding me strength. I gave birth to a daughter and lost her. I married the man I loved and lost him—in so many ways. I may be separated from my family, my village, and my mountain, but in my heart I'm connected to them more than ever.

We finally arrive on flat land. The truck grinds past the Social Welfare Institute. My daughter is not there. She's journeyed afar. This knowledge gives me the last bit of courage I need to find the bus station after I'm dropped off, buy my ticket, and suffer more sickness all the way to Kunming.

The bus pulls into Kunming late at night. I thought Menghai was big, but it is a fleabite compared to Kunming. Most of the roads are paved with cobblestones or asphalt. The crooked lanes are crowded. Concrete buildings six stories high loom over houses made from mud. I find my way to the trade school, show the letter from Teacher Zhang at the guard gate, and am escorted to a dormitory, where beds are stacked two high, side by side, down both sides of the room. I lie on top of the blanket. I hear other girls breathing. Teacher Zhang comes into my mind. Over the years, as he tutored me, I realized how much he lost by being sent to Nannuo Mountain. I also remember how Ci-teh and I used to speculate about why he never returned home to Beijing and what he possibly could have done to have been forever exiled. But what if remaining with us was his choice? Maybe he understood that he could never go home. What if that happens to me?

I roll over and cry into my pillow, hoping no one will hear my misery. That thought moves in a new and even sadder direction: perhaps they hear me but don't care enough to inquire if they can do anything to help. I squeeze my eyes shut, willing the tears to stop. *I won't allow them to see me ache. I won't allow them to see me suffer.*

PART III

THE OUTSIDE WORLD

1996–2006

Selected e-mail correspondence over eight years from Constance Davis to her mother

November 24, 1996

Mom,

Haley's first birthday party was a huge success. A true celebration of life, good health, and thankfulness. I wish you and Dad had been here.

Haley's doing extremely well. What a difference it makes to read *Goodnight Moon* in her room instead of in the hospital! And you should see Dan. He's got her in the backyard all the time, talking to her about trees, as though she understands every word he says. We're so happy. She's a miracle that's come to make our lives joyous. I wish she'd sleep a little, though. What an insomniac! (I can practically hear you laughing. What goes around comes around.)

I don't know how I would have gotten through the past months without your help and support. I bet Dad's glad to have you home, but I sure miss you.

Constance

———

September 20, 1997

Mom,

We've joined a group called Families with Children from China—just in time for us to celebrate the Moon Festival. Everyone in FCC has adopted baby girls from China, now ranging in age from a few months to around ten years old. There are another four families with daughters Haley's age. Seeing the way the kids' eyes light up when they see each other makes me realize that Haley—and we—will never be alone. I'm so grateful for this community, because I now know we've got a rougher road ahead of us than we imagined.

A policeman came up to me the other day and asked what

I was doing with Haley. He thought I was a kidnapper! I was totally shocked. Then he tried to make up for his mistake by asking if I had any children of my own. Haley *is* my own! I've already told you how total strangers ask, "Where did you get her?" like she's a purse or something. And you should hear what people have said to some of the other moms.

"Are you the babysitter?"

"Does this one belong to you? I thought she might be lost."

"How much did she cost?"

"Is it hard for you to love her when she doesn't look like you?"

People can be so cruel and unthinking. But here's what bothers me the most. Haley doesn't yet realize what they're saying, but she will. What will I tell her then? How will I comfort her? She'll *always* know she was adopted, because she *doesn't* look like us. I don't want her to be hurt. We went through so much to get her. And all the medical stuff. We almost lost her *five* times. If I punch out some dope in Trader Joe's, will you come and bail me out? (Just kidding. Or not. We'll see.)

I'm really missing you right now.

Constance

June 3, 1998

Hi, Mom,

Sorry I haven't answered your e-mails, but I've been bogged down with end-of-the-year stuff—grading finals, writing recommendation letters, etc. Dan's also been busy. It feels like half the women in Pasadena have been calling him to deal with a new invasive mite from Mexico that's attacking everyone's citrus trees. Haley tags along with Dan everywhere he goes. She's inherited his love of trees. There's magic in that, don't you think? (I know. I know. I'm a scientist. But still . . .)

Now that Dad's fully retired, why don't you move out here? Maine is so far away. Don't you want to see your granddaughter grow up?

Constance

October 31, 1999

Dear Mom,

Today Haley's preschool celebrated Halloween. The other girls did all the usual things—princesses and the like—but Haley wanted to be an astronaut. She said, "Girls can be astronauts too, Mom!" I'm so proud of her! (See attached photo.)

Hugs and kisses to you and Dad,

Constance

March 15, 2000

Mom,

Haley's having a recurrence of her C. diff. Dr. Katz has been great. Dr. Siegel too. We're all working really hard to keep her from having to be admitted to the hospital again. God damn superbug. Oh, Mom, it's just so scary.

Constance

August 21, 2001

Dear Mom,

You're always so astute. In your last e-mail you asked if I was worried about something. You know me. I can always worry. And I worry best and deepest about Haley. She's just a couple of weeks away from starting kindergarten. She already recognizes her letters, can read a few words, and knows how to write her name. I feel really good about all that. Her November birthday meant she couldn't start kindergarten until she was two months away from turning six, so she'll be on the older side. Dan says it's for the best. He's concerned about her size, since she's so tiny. Dr. Katz doubts she's small from all the medical setbacks she had starting out. He thinks maybe her parents were small. But we'll never know for sure, will we?

But here's what I'm anxious about. Haley doesn't look like other Chinese kids. We've been in FCC for four years now, so we have the other adoptees to compare her to. And the way things are changing in the San Gabriel Valley? We see lots of Chinese children, and Haley doesn't look like any of them either. She's darker for one thing, her nose isn't as flat as theirs, and her eyes are shaped more like leaves than almonds. We went out for dim sum last weekend, and a Chinese woman walked up to Haley and asked, "Where did you come from? Mongolia?" The comment went over Haley's head, thank God. I know what it's like to be teased in school, and I'm scared Haley will get picked on for her size and how she looks—not only by whites (although everyone says she's adorable), but by the Chinese kids in her class who'll notice she's different than they are.

Advice please!

Constance

November 29, 2002

Hi, Mom,

Did you and Dad have a nice Thanksgiving? I wish you could have come out and celebrated with us. Dan took us to the Raymond Restaurant. Haley chitter-chattered the whole time. She's so talkative!

It's hard to believe she's already in first grade. I had thought she was advanced, but she wasn't nearly as prepared as the other Chinese kids. Haley and I have spent the weekends and vacations working to catch up. I can't say this to anyone else, but I can brag about your granddaughter to you. Now she's the best at math in her class! Want to know what her teacher said to me the other day? "She might even outdo you one day, Mrs. Davis, and win a Nobel Prize." Wouldn't that be a kick?

I almost forgot to mention how well Haley's doing with her violin lessons. Thank you so much for suggesting the idea. Sometimes it's hard for me to remember that just because Dan and I aren't musical doesn't mean Haley wouldn't be either. Who knows? Instead of a Nobel Prize, maybe she'll become the next Sarah Chang.

Constance

October 12, 2003

Oh, Mom,

The saddest thing has happened. I'll call later, but if I write this out maybe it will help me get a better handle on the situation. Remember when I told you that all the kids in Mrs. Johnson's second-grade class had to do a cross-disciplinary "roots" project, combining history, art, and geography? Dan and I spoke a lot with Haley about it. We showed her how far back she could go on *both* sides of her family. I didn't think a single kid in her class had family here in colonial, Revolutionary, or Civil War times. (I was right.) Dan and I didn't know which side she was going to choose—his family or ours. It was going to be a big surprise.

Today the class gave their presentation at the school assembly. Parents were snapping photos and shooting video when their kids got up to give their presentations. And really, the children are smart, and their families are interesting too. Anyway, the assembly sped along, because the teacher's aide held up the object each kid made to represent something the first immigrant in his family brought with him to this country, while the kid read two or three sentences from one side of a large piece of paper. The side facing the audience showed a map with an arrow pointing to the country of origin.

Finally it was Haley's turn. The aide lifted above her head a drawing of the tea cake that came with Haley. Here's what she wrote: *I am the first person in my family to come here. I came from China. I brought a tea cake with me.*

It was such a heartbreaking thing to hear. I love her so

much, but will she never see herself as part of our family? We've tried to keep her connected to her Chinese background and we've always felt really good about that, but what if, instead of building her Chinese identity, it's only served to make her feel separate from us and not 100 percent our daughter? I had to fight to keep myself from crying in front of everyone. Dan and I knew we had to talk to Haley. All the experts say to keep it simple, but honestly, Mom, I think we really messed up.

We divided the conversation into two parts. First, what we thought would be easy—the tea cake. We've never hidden it from her. In fact, we encouraged her to keep it in the bottom drawer of her dresser. Some mornings I find it in her bed, which means she's gotten up in the middle of the night to pull it out and sleep with it. Well, *not* sleep. I always joke with Dan that Haley must still be on China time. The point is, she's *up* at night looking at it. I've even seen her trace the characters and decorations on the wrapper with her finger. You remember what it looks like, don't you? There are *V*'s like cartoon birds, those repeating lines like *S*'s, another stroke that meanders uninterrupted all over the place, and that thing that looks like a fork drawn in the center. More than once, Haley's said to me, "The squiggly lines have to mean something, but what?" Dan and I tried to find out when we first got her, but no one could tell us. Tonight, it was hard because Haley kept repeating, "My mother is sending me a message." My mother? *I'm* her mother. Oh, Mom, it hurt so much, but I ache even more for Haley. I mean, what if I didn't have *you* in my life? You made me the woman, wife, and mother I am. Haley has Dan and me, but knowing your mother—your parents—gave you away must be . . . what? A heavy burden? A hole in the heart that can't be filled? A universe of unknowns? I can't stop weeping at the sorrow of it, but in the moment I just kept repeating how much I love her.

The second part of our discussion went even worse. No matter how many times we said that we were a family and that she was our daughter, Haley came back with "But I *am* the first person in my family to come here." Her logic is correct, and I'm proud of her for that. But her insistence really stung and she must have seen something in my face even though I was trying as hard as I could to be supportive and loving, because she asked, "Are you going to send me back?" It was a crushingly sad thing to hear. We spent the rest of the evening trying to convince her that we'd never send her back. How many times can we say "You're our daughter. We're a family" before she believes it? Not enough apparently, because last night she just kept sinking deeper and deeper into her chair. She must feel like she let us down, but how could she *ever* think we'd send her back? What more can we do to make her understand how much we love her? That she is and always will be a part of our family? That she is what *makes* us a family?

I've gone on too long. Maybe I should have called, after all. Let's talk when you get home. Hearing your voice . . . I need to be strong for my daughter as you've always been strong for me.

Constance

November 1, 2004

Dear Mom,

We're still going to FCC events. Right now Haley's taking a Chinese brush-painting class. The girls have been practicing painting bamboo leaves and flowers. (Don't be surprised if you see some of her artwork at Christmas.) Master Lee also does calligraphy, so I thought, *Let's show him the tea cake.* Haley so loved the idea that I couldn't help beating myself up a bit for not thinking of it sooner.

We showed the tea cake to Master Lee. He studied all the designs, while Haley stared at him hopefully. Finally, he pronounced in his heavy accent, "They're meaningless." Another disappointment. The only useful thing he said is that tea aficionados—did you know there was such a thing?—like to take tea cakes on pilgrimages to their places of origin. Now not five minutes pass without Haley asking when we're going to China to find the cake's place of origin. Dan and I have always wanted to take Haley on a roots trip. There's even a tour company that specializes in vacations for families like ours, but even if we go, how is she going to get any closer to finding where the tea cake came from? The only silver lining out of all this: Haley has taken it out of the drawer and put it on her dresser. It's a huge step for all of us, although Dan and I have to play it cool.

As long as I'm here . . . You asked if you should bring Haley's birthday presents to Colorado over Thanksgiving. (Nine years old! Can you believe it?) Wouldn't it be easier if you mail the big things here to the house and she opens the small things at the ranch? She's going to love the little chemistry set, microscope, and telescope you bought. She'll say you're the best grandparents ever, and you are.

Really looking forward to all of us being together.

Constance

P.S. You and Dad are really going to like this year's Christmas card. It's the best of Haley yet.

A DRINKABLE ANTIQUE

The light changes, and I zip through the intersection on my moped. I've just finished my shift at King World Hotel, where I work at the front desk, and I don't want to embarrass the people who've arranged this interview by being late. At a stoplight, I glance at my reflection in the window of the car next to me. A flowered silk scarf protects my hair from the dust and exhaust. My pink blouse is clean and perfectly ironed. My skirt will have wrinkles from sitting, but I can't do much about them. I don't care for makeup, but hotel management likes us to wear it for our guests' enjoyment, and I learned in my course on how to achieve a successful job interview that potential employers like it too. Luckily, my roommates have taught me about mascara, eyeliner, and eye shadow—just enough, not too gaudy. For lipstick, they prefer me in a shade of light coral. They say the color makes me look Han-majority pretty. That's as high a compliment as I'm ever going to get as a member of an ethnic minority my roommates have never heard of.

I made so many resolutions on my journey here eight years ago, but I didn't know a thing about anything. I promised A-ma I'd always follow Akha traditions, but these things I could only do in my heart, for I had no ruma, nima, or family to perform rituals or encourage me. (And Kunming didn't have a spirit gate, village swing, or any building or place I could go to feel connected to or even sense my culture.) I needed to forget the tragedies of my past, but the only way to do that successfully was to build a brick wall around my heart. I arrived at the trade school thin from my deprivations in Thailand, but I lost even more weight because I didn't have enough money to buy food in the cafeteria. When A-ma promised a monthly allowance of two hundred yuan, it seemed like a fortune. It was a fortune—as much as my family had lived on each month when I was little—but the girls in my dormitory each received eight hundred yuan every four weeks. When I ran out of money, I drew slowly from the bank account that was made up of the silver pieces I'd saved from my wedding headdress. After I sold the last of those, I practically lived on tea alone.

Most of my classmates saw me as a country bumpkin and the most *tu* person they'd ever met. They teased me when I performed a cleansing ritual to prevent myself from being paralyzed after the shadow of a crane in flight touched me. They made fun of me when I asked what was done to protect the dormitory from spirits. A few girls felt sorry for me and gave me advice. "Don't worry so much," one of them said. "We don't have bad spirits here. And even if one enters Kunming, don't let on to others you believe in them." Slowly, I began to forget about spirits. It was my only choice.

If I was thankful to A-ma for my monthly stipend, I was even more indebted to her for the loose tea she gave to Teacher Zhang to mail to me in pretty homemade packets each spring. I gave these gifts to my teachers in the same way I once gave our humble homegrown tea to Teacher Zhang: as a sign of respect and gratitude. Those instructors are my friends to this day, and we still get together to drink tea—sometimes in one of their apartments, but mostly in tea shops. It is to them that I must give my thanks for this new opportunity. Yunnan Agricultural University here in Kunming is opening a Pu'er Tea College, and they've suggested me as a candidate.

"It is to be the first such program in the world," Teacher Guo told me last week. "They're going to offer two tracks: one to learn the art of tea—brewing and etiquette—to become a tea master; the other to become a tea evaluator—so you'll be able to oversee tea production, as well as advise collectors and connoisseurs on what to buy. We've heard that over two thousand people have applied, but they're accepting only sixty students for each program. When we were asked to recommend a pupil—present or past—we knew exactly who that would be: you, because you're the only one we've taught who comes from the tea mountains."

I pull through a gate, park in the open courtyard, and enter a nondescript building. I follow signs that read: INTERVIEWS THIS WAY. I'm one of fifty people in the waiting room. A woman with a clipboard calls applicants in one by one. Some of the interviews are as brief as ten minutes. I try not to be nervous. When my name is called, I follow the woman down a hallway painted pea green and into a large room, where a single chair faces a table with five examiners: two women and three men. The man seated in the middle position motions for me to take my place. Once I'm settled—my ankles linked and tucked modestly to the side, my hands resting delicately in my lap—he goes over the basics, confirming my name, ethnic status, and where I was born.

"And your age?" he asks.

"I'm twenty-six."

"Married then? With a child?"

"Unmarried," I answer.

"So old!" a woman wearing a red sweater observes.

How am I supposed to respond to that?

The questions shift to my educational background.

"I didn't finish third-level school," I confess, altering my voice to sound as though I'm speaking to a hotel guest. I've found that this—and the way I've taught myself to move as though I'm a maiden painted on a ceramic vase from Ming times—helps people forget that I'm from a hill tribe. "But at my trade school I learned how to organize files, create a spreadsheet, and send e-mail."

I make it sound easy, but I struggled with so many things. Learning how to use an indoor toilet? Do you squat facing the wall or the door? Taking a shower? *Waaa!* And the idea that I could turn an electric light on and off? In my dormitory, we had electricity for an hour in the morning and an hour in the evening, but I flipped the switch on and off so many times in the first week that the matron threatened to shut down the power to the entire building for a day if I didn't stop. My roommates made sure I didn't touch the switch again, but they let me watch them turn it on and off at the beginning and end of the morning and evening allotted hours. Yes, I was very *tu* back then.

The man in charge stubs out his cigarette and gives me a hard stare. "Teacher Guo claims you're proficient in English, but are you really?"

I respond by switching to English. "I can't be sure why English came easier to me than to the other students. Maybe it's because I grew up hearing the different languages of the hill tribes. Or maybe—and this phrase I learned from a hotel guest just yesterday—I was in the right place at the right time."

The other two men snicker, which causes the man in charge to lose face. He writes something on a pad of paper.

No position or educational spot is possible without answering political questions, and they can be tricky. My interrogator thrums his fingers on the table.

"How do you feel about the changes in Kunming?"

I smile, showing enough teeth to appear friendly but not so many that I'm tempted to cover my mouth. "Ten years ago, a man from Hong Kong came to my village." I lower my eyes to illustrate my modest personality. "We didn't know what was happening in the rest of China. He told us about the new era of Reform and Opening Up. Everything he said would happen has happened, and more. Tourists have come from all over to see the Great Wall, the Summer Palace, and the terra-cotta warriors in Xian. We can be grateful that later the central government enacted the Opening the West Campaign. As you know, it was intended to boost foreign tourism to the western provinces."

I pause to weigh how they're reacting. I feel like I'm not impressing them, which is strange because I've already lasted longer than any of the other candidates.

"Then," I hurry on, "just three years ago, our beautiful province was given permission by the central government to change the name of the city of Zhongdian to Shangri-La—"

"Beating out Sichuan and Tibet for the honor!" the man who sits at the far right finishes for me. "We can now claim the world's paradise as Yunnan's!"

The boast is greeted by indifference as the others stare out the window, suck their teeth, examine their pencils.

"May I ask a question?" I can't help being curious. "Why have a college for Pu'er?"

"Ah! Trying to be a clever girl," the man in charge says, scribbling again on his pad. Another demerit? He makes me wait as he finishes writing, lights another cigarette, takes a drag, and blows smoke toward the ceiling. "I suppose where you're from Kunming must seem very modern, but it—and all Yunnan—has been slow in developing, while the world has rushed into Beijing, Shanghai, and Guangzhou."

As he speaks, I remember the posters I used to study on the bamboo walls of Teacher Zhang's classroom, believing what I saw in them had to be made up. Now I go to movies and watch television. And I do so with very different eyes; all those images—as unbelievable as they appear—must be real.

"The roadways have traffic jams, polluted air chokes babies and the elderly alike, and everyone is rushing, rushing, rushing to get rich," he continues. "The people who live in those places? They long to visit Yunnan, because the streets are quiet, the air is fresh, and the day-to-day life is peaceful. All of that has become embodied in, of all things, Pu'er."

I wonder what would happen if I told him how all the changes he mentioned have affected me. Since the Shangri-La renaming, the government has been talking about rechristening the city of Simao to Pu'er. I bet that will happen in a year or so. These new labels, though subtle, telegraph messages to China's Han majority people, which they embrace as they are meant to do. Today, many of the words that were once used to degrade the province are used as praise. Yunnan is no longer considered a backward province, where the people are *tu*. That's not because Yunnan or its people have changed. Rather, the meaning of *tu* has changed. Now *tu* means *untouched by the evils of civilization*. Tourists—Chinese *and* foreign—started visiting Kunming, Lijiang, Dali, and the Tiger Leaping Gorge. They even wanted to encounter the hill tribes! They begged to participate in the Dai people's Water Splashing Festival, see Jinuo women's teeth painted black with the sap of the lacquer tree, and buy Miao weavings. Men—young, with backpacks and few brains—sought directions to Mosuo villages, because in that matriarchal culture, the women choose their bed partners . . . and those women choose *a lot* of different lovers—whether Mosuo, Han, or foreign—just for their own pleasure. *Tu* is now so valued that this year on National Day, the government announced a countrywide search to find a set of twins from each of China's fifty-five recognized ethnic minorities to be paraded four years from now at the Olympics. Since we Akha are grouped together with the Hani, I suspect the government will look to them to find a set of twins old enough to represent us.

"To answer your question in a different way," the woman in the red sweater comments, "visitors to Yunnan—whether Han majority, German, French, or American—need souvenirs to take home. What better souvenir could there be than Pu'er? A tea cake is small and fits easily into a suitcase. For Chinese people, tea is always an appropriate gift. For foreigners . . ." She sniffs. "They like things that reek of the hill tribes."

For some, intolerance and discrimination are just a part of their natures.

"Had you heard before of Pu'er?" she asks in her superior way.

"I grew up drinking it, even though we didn't call it that."

The man in charge clears his throat. "The program will begin after Spring Festival. The Year of the Monkey will start early, on January twenty-second in the Western calendar. Applicants will be notified on January fifteenth. If you are accepted . . . Well, we have applicants who have good *guanxi*—connections—and you don't have those. We have applicants who come from prominent families. You don't have that either. You're a climber. This we can tell from the way you sit and from the soft quality of your voice. You may have learned to illustrate self-possession, but you don't have a chance—"

The door swings open, and a whirlwind of people and objects sweeps into the room. Five young women, carrying papers, a kettle with a cord dangling from it, a tray, and bundles in different sizes, orbit around a small man: older, with baggy pants bloused at the ankles with elastic, kung-fu slippers with no socks, and a flowing shirt.

"Are you the girl from Nannuo Mountain?" His eyes glitter with mischievousness. A single long hair sprouts from his right ear—a sign of wisdom . . . or poor grooming. "You look very young. Maybe *too* young."

Since I've come to Kunming many people have accused me of this. Even I've wondered why all the things that have happened to me don't appear on my face. Mostly it has worked in my favor—the manager at the hotel wants only pretty girls at the front desk—but other times, as now, it makes me feel less worthy. And that is an emotion I do not like. I manage to find my voice.

"I'm not young. I already told the others I'm twenty-six."

"You look like you're fifteen."

"I'm not."

"Then tell me. Why do you look so young?"

He's beaming like a fool, while the people behind the table exchange irritated glances and I feel humiliated.

"I'm Tea Master Sun." He scuttles behind the table and motions for the man seated in the middle to move. The tea master sits down, and the man I thought to be in charge stands with his arms folded, a new cigarette drooping from his lips, trying, unsuccessfully, to cover his annoyance. "Let us drink tea. What have you brought?"

"I wasn't told to bring tea."

"But you carry some with you always, I hear. What we have in our cafés and teahouses isn't good enough for the Akha lass."

"I prefer to drink what my mother sends me," I admit.

"Good. Then let us taste it."

"Do you have springwater?" I ask.

"Only." Tea Master Sun grins first to his left, then to his right, sending a message to the people on the panel that he's pleased with my question. "But circumstances force us to accept some modern elements." He snaps his fingers and one of the helpers plugs in the kettle, while the other young women unwrap the various packages: teacups, a bowl, and rounds of tea cakes.

I pull a packet of A-ma's tea from my purse. When Tea Master Sun buries his nose in the bag to smell the leaves, his impishness departs. He piles about eight grams of leaves into the bowl of a *gaiwan*—a three-piece slightly oversize teacup with a lid and saucer—until they rise up and out of the vessel like a hill of threads. The room falls silent as we wait for the first sounds of simmering to come from the pot.

When the water lets us know it's ripened, the tea master asks, "Do you see how I keep my left hand on the table at a forty-five-degree angle, while my right hand lifts the pot?" He pours the hot water into seven tiny cups to warm them. Then he pours water over the leaves in the *gaiwan*. "As I set down the pot, I resume with my left hand. If you're accepted into the program, you'll need to develop strength and agility on both sides of your body." He rotates the edge of the *gaiwan*'s lid along the surface of the water-soaked leaves to clear the bubbles. Then he covers the cup with the lid and tips it so that the water flows out and into the discard bowl while keeping the leaves in the cup.

"Why am I disposing of this liquid?" he asks.

"To wash the leaves," I answer.

"Why?"

"Do you know where Pu'er comes from? And how it's processed?"

He cackles at my questions. "Exactly! Hygiene matters. But we're also opening the aromatic properties of the leaves. Now watch what I do. You must look at serving tea as though it's a dance. Every movement must be fluid. See how my actions flow from my right hand to my left hand, with everything smooth?" As he talks, he pours more water over the leaves and covers the *gaiwan* with its lid. "Brewing will last fifteen seconds. How will I know when those seconds have passed?" I have no idea, because he isn't wearing a watch. "By my heartbeats! I can teach you to tell time this way too."

He pours the tea into a glass pitcher, symbolizing that every person is equal and together we can all view and drink the same brew. While we appreciate the honey-yellow color of the liquid, he uses tongs to pick up each tiny teacup and toss the warming water into the discard bowl. He finally pours the tea into the cups. "Notice how I'm moving counterclockwise. This is called the welcome style. Now I'll put every object back in its original position." All this he does with ease, ending by graciously drawing his arm from left to right, taking us all in. "Please enjoy."

Then I sit there as the others discuss the *maocha* made from the sister trees.

"I can taste the ions," the man I'd thought was in charge comments. "The longer the liquor rests on the tongue, the more I taste the fresh air of the mountains."

The woman, who'd previously been so disdainful of me, agrees. "The warm and fragrant flavor strokes every cell in my mouth. The *huigan*—the returning flavor—comes quickly."

"Your tea is better than satisfying," Tea Master Sun observes. "There's some astringency and a good amount of initial bitterness, but overall I like the clear purity of the flavor. Collectors prize tea from Laobanzhang, calling it the king of teas, because the taste is musky, masculine, and daring in the mouth. They call tea from Yiwu the queen of teas, because the taste is as alluring as a radiant woman awaiting her lover, but you can be proud of the tea that comes from Nannuo Mountain for its smoothness and subtlety. One day people will prize it as much as, if not more than, the king and queen of teas. Do you still spend a lot of time on Nannuo?"

"I haven't been home in eight years."

The tea master sucks in his cheeks as he considers my answer. What daughter wouldn't return home for Spring Festival, a wedding, or a funeral? Instead of commenting on what is a clear breach of daughterly manners, he chooses to go in a different direction.

"I want to see what you think of these." He tosses the leaves A-ma sent me from the *gaiwan* even though another ten infusions could be made. "Your *maocha* is good, as I said, but I personally prefer a naturally long-aged Pu'er. *Man becomes wiser and more mature through life experience.* The same can be said of tea."

We sample five teas. Each time, Tea Master Sun guides me through the flavors. "I can brew these particular leaves up to fifteen times. With each new infusion, the taste will change, coming from different parts of the leaf and invigorating different parts of the tongue. Terrace tea is cloned, so the flavor is very consistent, but tea from wild trees is complex and enticing."

The more I taste, the more captivated I become. The tea itself is physically seducing me. The third tea, he tells me, would cost the equivalent of two hundred yuan for a cup if I drank it in Hong Kong. It's delicious, but to me it's not the monetary value that's important. I know from living in Kunming that this is arbitrary. Do you want a yellow or blue T-shirt, when a decade ago I didn't even know what a T-shirt was? Guests at the King World Hotel have a peculiar view of value. They refuse to stay in a room if it doesn't have a sit-down toilet. This took me the longest time to accept, because who would want to sit in the same place where someone else's rump has been to do your private business?

The tea master once again empties our cups, rinses them, and then brews a new tea. The *huigan* from my first sip opens my chest so quickly that I feel I might faint. Warmth washes up from my chest and flushes my face. What's happening to my body feels as potent as those early days when I first fell in love with San-pa.

The tea master chortles at my reaction. "Is it smooth?" he asks. "Does it have good *qi*—life energy? Examine your emotions. You're hearing nature sing through the leaf."

"The taste is light—like dew on flower petals," I say. "Elegant—"

"Elegant! You're right! This is Truly Simple Elegant tea. Have you tasted it before?" When I shake my head, he continues. "I thought you might have. Eleven years ago, a certain Mr. Lü from Taiwan went to Luoshuidong, then an isolated village in the tea mountains."

That was a year before Mr. Huang came to Spring Well.

"Mr. Lü wanted to make a batch of tea from old trees in the traditional style," the tea master goes on. "He found a retired tea master. He—"

"Mr. Lü?" I interrupt. "Are you sure you have the correct name, country of origin, village, and year?"

Tea Master Sun gives me a dismissive look. "Yes, and I've met Mr. Lü many times, which is how I came to buy several of his cakes."

Could there have been two men around the same time doing the same thing?

"Have you ever heard of another tea that was made—"

The tea master cuts me off. "The world of tea is very small, so I know the tea of which you speak. I have some of that too. If it had been the only tea made after so many years, it would have become iconic. But Mr. Lü used leaves solely from Luoshuidong. As I said earlier, leaves from Nannuo Mountain are good and one day they'll be prized, but for now they cannot compete—taste to taste—with Truly Simple Elegant. However"—he leans forward to confide—"the creator of the tea you mentioned has a separate vintage which he has not shared with anyone. He made just two tea cakes . . ."

The ones I processed using the leaves from the mother tree.

"Rumor has it that the man who made them has not even tasted tea brewed from those cakes," he says. "If they're so special, then he should share them with people who'll appreciate them, no?"

This topic is making ghost spiders crawl along my arms and legs.

"Now for one last tea," he announces. "Before Liberation, our province had many private labels for making tea. After Liberation, we had just four state-owned tea companies. One of them was in Menghai."

"The tea collection center where I grew up sent all of its leaves there—"

"This is called Hong Yin—Red Label—and it was the first batch to be made after Liberation," he continues over me. "A single cake like this one, forty-five years old, sold this year for eighty-five thousand yuan. That's over ten thousand U.S. dollars! Now we will try it."

The color of the brew is rich and dark with mystery. The first flavor is peppery, but that fades to divine sweetness. The history of my people shimmers in my bones. With every sip, it's as if I'm wordlessly reciting the lineage. I'm at once merged with my ancestors and with those who'll come after me. I grew up believing that rice was to nourish and that tea was to heal. Now I understand that tea is also to connect and to dream. That seduction is deeper and more profound than could happen with any man.

Tea Master Sun seems to comprehend that I'm being transformed, yet his words are as colorless as can be. "So, Pu'er. Tell us what you know about it."

The minute he asks this question, I understand two things. First, I want this opportunity so much more now. Second, I may be the lone applicant from a hill tribe and unacceptable to the others on the panel, but the tea master is the only person in the room who matters.

"Not everyone is looking for aged Pu'er these days," I answer. "They want raw Pu'er—*maocha*—because it's considered healthier and richer in cultural meaning. Still, no matter how a person looks at Pu'er—raw, artificially fermented, naturally aged, young tree, old tree, ancient tree, wild tree, cultivated tree—no one is throwing away tea after six months any longer. Everyone agrees: the older the better."

"You're telling me two contradictory ideas."

"Two contradictory ideas can exist at the same time. Maybe more than two."

He laughs; the others don't.

"You asked why I look so young," I say. "Would it be too bold of me to ask your theory?"

He sweeps his arm around the room, echoing the welcome style. "Everyone here knows why. You drink Pu'er. If all women in our country followed your regimen, we would have the most beautiful women in the world."

The two women on the panel give me sour looks, and the tea girls blush, but the master isn't done.

"As China gains prosperity, our people want to appreciate the finer things in life. Pu'er is seen as a way for the newly wealthy to triumph over the poverty of the past. It's also a channel for investment in a country where our citizens are wary of what the government might do. It's considered a 'drinkable antique.' Tea, a beverage that had been ignored for decades, has become collectible once again. But even though it's classified as an antique, it's still *alive*. And every sip—through the powerful senses of taste and smell—opens our hearts to remember family, love, and hardships that have been overcome. Our ancestors believed that the best teas could eliminate arrogance, dissipate impatience, and lighten our temperaments. You seem to understand all that, but I believe my colleagues still have much to learn about our beautiful drink. What do you think?"

First he comments on the lack of beauty of the other women not only in the room but in all China. Then he sharply criticizes the members of his panel. I was raised never to say anything that would be humiliating to others, but when I recite, "*If you strike with the right hand, you must soothe with the left,*" the room goes stunningly quiet. In publicly chastising the tea master, I've put myself in his same category, either ruining or securing my prospects.

Haley Davis – Miss Henderson's third-grade class, December 10, 2004

Things I need—huge	**Things I need—big**	**Things I need—small**
Liquid	Good education	Ski boots
Food	Parents	Friends
Sun	Peace	Violin strings
Earth	Body	Dress for Easter
Air	House	My stuffed bunny
Moon	Whiskers (my cat)	New Harry Potter book

THE WORLD HAS COME

I begin to wait. *I want this.* I lie awake at night, weighing my chances of getting into the Pu'er program, doubting the answers I gave Tea Master Sun, and questioning why I had to be so rude to him when all he had done was show interest in me. After five days, I'm distracted, impatient with guests, and sharp with the maids. I've never taken a vacation from my job, but I need one now.

When I first heard about vacations I was surprised, because the closest we Akha had to anything like that was rainy season—the months of darkness when spirits were considered to be mischievously active and we worked on our weaving, sewing, and embroidery. Hence, I've always turned down the opportunity to go on holiday. Even if I'd been forced to take one, where would I have gone? Home, to where people might still blame me for San-pa's terrible death? To tourist sites, alone, to remind myself that I have no one to love me? So I've earned the gratitude of my co-workers, because I cover their shifts when they take time off. But now I need my family. I want them to see how far I've come, but I also need their good wishes. It's a momentous decision and the outcome may not be what I hope for, but I ask my manager if I might return home for three weeks. "It's spur of the moment," he tells me, "but how can I say no? You've been an exemplary employee for many years, and you've never asked for a single favor." I leave on the eve of what Westerners call Christmas, promising to be back in time to cover the absences of others who wish to visit their families during Spring Festival.

I buy a ticket for the evening bus to Menghai. The road has been improved, so the trip lasts just twelve hours. In the morning, after an uncomfortable and mostly sleepless night, I board a minibus, which takes me and about a dozen others into the mountains on a new, roughly carved, extraordinarily bumpy, and very narrow dirt road. After a few hours, I get off at the stop for Bamboo Forest Village. When I was a girl, the village was nothing—no better or worse than Spring Well. With the new road and the bus stop, Bamboo Forest has opened a small café and started a morning farmers' market. About half the women wear their traditional Dai, Bulang, or Akha attire. The rest are dressed like me, in blue jeans, T-shirt, and tennis shoes. I'm taking in the surprising changes when a motorcycle skids past. The rider shouts at me to get out of the way. I'm stunned.

I swing my knapsack onto my back and head out of Bamboo Forest. Not long after I dip onto the trail that will lead to Spring Well, I pass a construction site with bulldozers moving earth and workers building massive retaining walls. The main structure is still a puzzle, shrouded in bamboo scaffolding on which dozens of men crawl like ants. I can't imagine what it is or why it's here. But soon enough the noise and ugliness are behind me, and I'm on a quiet forest path. People are out, tending to their trees. Songs come to me on wafts of air. It's winter, but tea-picking season is around the corner and each tree seems ready to burst forth with emerald-green buds. Every leaf—so alive—reaches for the morning sun and sends forth a fragrance that's light and brilliant. I pick a leaf and chew it. With each breath, another layer of *huigan* is released. I am home.

I know things are now better for my family. When I was first hired at King World, I worked to repay A-ma. Then I sent money to help the family. But two years ago, Teacher Zhang wrote to tell me that life was going so well at home—income from tea work had increased fiftyfold, an amount difficult for me to absorb—that I no longer needed to worry about my family. Still, I expect everything to be more or less the same, believing that our culture and traditions are so old and deep that they would withstand all attempts to transform them. I'm reassured when I arrive at the spirit gate that protects the entrance to Spring Well. But as I walk farther? Dogs nap in the middle of the lane that divides the village and chickens peck at the ground, but everything else is different. Many of the bamboo and thatch houses have been replaced with gray brick boxes. Plastic troughs in pink, orange, and green lie about—filled with soaking laundry, vegetables to be washed for the evening meal, or animal feed. Empty plastic water bottles stand at attention in a neat row on one veranda. And just like in Bamboo Forest Village, many of the people wear Western-style clothing, although every woman still covers her hair with a scarf of some sort. I don't recognize a soul; no one seems to recognize me either. But what's most shocking is the number of people sitting on the ground with piles of tea leaves spread before them, negotiating with outsiders. I pass one group of visitors bargaining hard. They're Korean!

When I reach my home . . . It's gone, as are all the newlywed huts. Where our house once stood is a building that resembles a greenhouse—glass panes held together with aluminum struts. Nearby are four stucco structures—all of the cheapest and ugliest materials, soulless, antiseptic, not one with glass in the window frames. None of them are built on stilts, so there's no place for livestock to live. One is slightly larger than the others. I don't see separate verandas for the women's and men's sides of the house. The single door stands open.

"Hello," I call at the top of the stairs. I peer into the interior of the house, where people bustle back and forth. "Hello?" I say again, uncertain.

Young and old, men and women, all stop what they're doing to glance in my direction. After a long moment, someone says, "It's Girl." I recognize A-ba's voice. The others part, clearing a way for him. He wears plastic sandals and jungle fatigues, as though he's in a war movie, which is about as disconcerting as anything I've seen so far. Otherwise, he's still my a-ba—small and wiry. Then A-ma comes to his side. She wears her indigo tunic, skirt, and leggings, and her headdress is as magnificent, welcoming, and comforting as I could hope.

That night, A-ma and the sisters-in-law prepare a meal unimaginable when I was a child: pork four ways (crispy skin, barbecued ribs, braised belly, and meatballs in clear broth), a soy-sauce roasted goose, bitter melon with scrambled egg, rice, and a fruit plate. Instead of eating on the floor around the warmth and glow of an open fire in the main room, we sit on tiny chairs at a small table. This furniture—built little to save cost and for easy storage—nevertheless shows my family's improved circumstances. During dinner, my relatives pepper me with questions about the world beyond Nannuo Mountain. My brothers ask about banks and loans, because they now have so many expenses. The sisters-in-law want to know about cosmetics, and I give them my lipstick to share. Their three daughters, who were all born within one month of each other, are now eight years old, attending Teacher Zhang's class, and irrepressibly inquisitive:

"Do you think I can go to secondary school, Auntie?"

"How old should I be when I first steal love, Auntie?"

"When can I visit you in Kunming, Auntie?"

After dinner, we gather around a space heater with a single bare—and very dim—lightbulb hanging from the ceiling. Electricity! When tea is poured, I gather the courage to question the changes in Spring Well, pointing out that after centuries of steady life, so much has been upended during the eight years I've been away. "And it all started with Mr. Huang—"

"Our lives changed rapidly after the Hong Konger came to us," A-ba agrees, "but we haven't seen him in years. You know how he is—always looking for something no one else has. He's probably experimenting with leaves in a village on one of the other tea-growing mountains. So be it. With all the traders and collectors visiting us, we don't need him anymore."

"But what about our traditions?" I ask.

Faces stare back at me silently, but their message is clear: *Who are you to ask this question with your city ways?*

"Everyone changes," A-ba says at last. "We still live in the forest, but the world has come to us. We continue to have the Swing

Festival, build a new spirit gate each year, and consult with the ruma about when to plant our crops, pick leaves, and select propitious marriage dates, but we don't have time for all the cleansing ceremonies, sacrifices, or worrying about Dog Days and Buffalo Days when we have so much work to do. Tea growing is very lucrative, you know."

Truly, what is stranger—the matter-of-fact way he's just dismissed our customs or the way he speaks about business? *Business!*

"We have to guard our product," he continues. "Some especially greedy tea traders have sent hooligans onto our mountain to look for the most ancient trees and chop them down, because it's easier to harvest their leaves that way—"

"They would chop down a tree?" I ask, shocked. "What about its soul?"

But no one seems interested in that.

"When the government instituted the Quality Safety Standard," First Brother carries on, "we could no longer dry our leaves or artificially ferment them on the ground or on the floor of the house. All tea processing had to be done fifty meters away from animals, so we were forced to sell our livestock. The new rules turned out to be good for us, because now nothing can taint the flavor of our tea. We borrowed fifty thousand yuan to build the drying and processing building, where our old home once stood."

"And we all have our own houses with indoor plumbing!" Third Brother chimes in.

Their optimism and free-spending ways have been buoyed by an early thirty-year extension to the Thirty Years No Change policy. Knowing he would "own" land until 2034, First Brother ripped out the tea bushes on his terraces, while Second Brother took out his pollarded trees so new tea trees could be planted from seeds. A-ba gave up on his vegetable plots—"We can buy what we need in Bamboo Forest Village"—so that he too could plant tea trees. For all three of them, the few wild tea trees on their respective properties have helped pay for these improvements, while Third Brother's once worthless old tea trees are now the most valuable asset in the family . . .

"His trees, and your grove," A-ba adds pointedly. "Of course, we can't get your a-ma to let us take a look—"

Mercifully, First Brother cuts him off. "None of us could have predicted today's situation. Buyers now visit from all over Asia to buy Pu'er to drink, sell, and collect. We have to host big banquets, hoping to make them happy. There's a lot of competition. That's why we need to borrow at better rates."

"And the price of tea keeps going up and up and up!"

Everyone pesters me about my chances of getting into the tea college.

"If you do well," First Brother exclaims exuberantly, "you can sell our family's tea and make it famous!"

I have only one response to that: "I have to be accepted first."

No one embodies the changes in Spring Well more than Ci-teh, whom I see the next night at a banquet my family hosts for a buyer from Japan. Her giggling ways seem to be gone, and any embroideries that would mark her as an Akha have been packed away as well. She's gained weight—as has almost everyone in Spring Well—and her stomach and breasts push against the buttons of her flowered cotton blouse.

"Visit me tomorrow!" she urges. And I do. Her house is the nicest in the village, naturally. "The first with electricity," Ci-teh boasts. She's also the first person in Spring Well to own a cellphone. She insists we exchange numbers. "So we never again lose our connection."

We were once very close, but our lives have taken different paths, which she reminds me of again and again. "You abandoned me. You left without a word. So hurtful you are." While the things that happened to me remain a secret, the steps in her life are well known by all on Nannuo Mountain. After her parents died, Ci-teh consolidated the land awarded to her family in the Thirty Years No Change policy. In addition to her own groves, she also leases stands of tea trees from other families, which has earned her the title of the single largest grower on Nannuo. She further strengthened her status when she paid the ruma and nima to allow her brother, Ci-do, to return to Spring Well after a spiritual cleansing—of what degree or intensity no one tells me—plus nine days of feasting provided to every man, woman, and child in the village, all paid for by her. The things money can buy . . .

"He has a new wife and two children. Times change, but the stain on him from fathering human rejects will never be completely erased," Ci-teh confides in an offhand manner. "It's best for everyone that he and his family spend most of the year visiting the great sights our country has to offer."

But for all her money, success, and power, she's been unable to control or influence the child-maker spirits. She and Law-ba have three daughters and have broken with Akha naming practices to show their disappointment: Mah-caw (Go Find a Brother), Mah-law (Go Fetch a Brother), and Mah-zeu (Go Buy a Brother).

"Why haven't you remarried?" she asks me another day when we sip tea in the bamboo pavilion she's built to entertain her international buyers. "If a wife dies, a man can remarry in three months. When a husband dies, a woman must wait three years, but that has come and gone for you."

Does she spout these old-fashioned aphorisms just to goad me? She's obviously let go of many traditions herself, but our loving but contrary relationship is the same as ever. I give a bland answer. "I want to get ahead in life." The reality is something murkier. I've been alone and lonely for eight years. I've blinded myself to the advertisements for online dating. I've also learned how to walk through parks and ignore the middle-aged mothers who approach me with photos of their sons and lists of their accomplishments and possessions: a bicycle, a motorcycle, or a car; living with parents, renting an apartment, or owning a condo. "You're too old not to be married," more than one mother has told me. Unasked, by the way. Then, "Please consider my son." But I can't allow myself to repeat the mistakes of the past. If I were ever to fall in love again, it would have to be with someone who'd be accepted by my family. Otherwise, too much heartbreak.

"Do you date?" Ci-teh persists, using the Western word. "Do you go to the movies and have noodles with men?"

"Most men don't want to go out with an Akha," I say, hoping to end the subject.

She nods knowingly. "You look so young, and you're too quiet. You are *tu,* and not in an admirable way. What about stealing love in the forest while you're here? Surely our men will overlook your faults, and you can have fun too."

"I don't want to steal love."

She ignores that and asks, "What about a foreigner? You work in a hotel. Maybe you could marry one of them and move to America."

I couldn't do that either. It's hard to explain to Ci-teh how it feels to be separated from the mountain, my family, and our customs—even though so much has changed.

She cocks her head, appraising me. "Have you become one of those women who hates men?"

As I look back at my years in Kunming, I can be grateful that, despite everything, I'm not bitter. I'm not like Deh-ja—wherever she is—either: crippled by Ci-do's abandonment. But I must protect my heart, even if that means being alone.

"I'll never hate men," I answer. I'd never confide all that happened to me, but I add, "I just don't want to make another mistake."

She waves off my words as though they mean nothing. "Look at me. I'm fat, but you're still beautiful. I could find someone to marry you by nightfall."

She could too, but I'm not interested.

Ci-teh's inquisitiveness spreads to others. The sisters-in-law, A-ba, my brothers, even some of the nieces and nephews buzz their noses at me like persistent gnats, asking why I haven't remarried, giving me advice, and trying to prove how much they care for my well-being.

"We don't want you to be lonely," Third Brother says.

Second Brother takes a more practical approach. "If you don't get married, who will look after you when you get old?"

First Brother is even more frank. "If you don't get married, who will care for you when you go to the afterlife? You'll need a son to make offerings to you." He shakes a warning finger at me. "You can only be a leftover woman for a limited time. After that, it will be too late for you. No one will want to marry you."

A-ba, who shouldn't speak directly to me on such matters, sends messages through the sisters-in-law, as is proper.

Third Sister-in-law speaks to me one morning as we gather firewood: "You can't act too picky."

Second Sister-in-law passes on the following: "No man wants to marry a woman who is overly ambitious or wants to outshine him."

A-ba has First Sister-in-law deliver the bluntest caution: "People will say you don't like to do the intercourse, but it is your duty to the nation and to the family to have a child."

Their talk leaves me feeling both irritated and insecure.

During the third week, I walk to Shelter Shadow Village to pay respects to San-pa's parents, only to find they died five years ago in a typhoid epidemic. I also visit Teacher Zhang at the primary school, where the same old maps and posters hang on the bamboo walls as when I was a girl. I confide in him my concerns that I failed my interview and will let my family down again. Here's what he says:

"There's nothing you can do about it now! But if you ask me—and I guess you are—I believe you will get in. Who is more qualified than you, after all?"

Which lifts my spirit.

I don't get to see or talk to A-ma much at all. She's the only person, apart from Teacher Zhang, who seems unchanged—from the way she dresses to the way she moves to the way she ignores the spiraling world around her. She's as busy as ever, though, cooking for the family, settling arguments between the sisters-in-law, washing clothes by hand, spinning thread, weaving cloth, embroidering and decorating caps for her grandchildren, delivering babies, and mixing potions for those who come to her ill or injured. She's so busy that I'm alone with her only once—when we visit the mother and sister trees on my last day. As we wander through the grove, she stops here and there to stroke a branch, clip a few leaves, or pick some of the parasites that cling to the mother tree for medicinal concoctions. The last time we were here together . . .

"Nothing will take away the pain of a lost child," A-ma says. "My feelings for your daughter are always strongest here. In nature. In the atmosphere. Because that's where Yan-yeh has gone. Into the ether."

"For me, my grief is like a huge hole. Everything flows *around* that hole. I have forced myself to move forward, but I can never move on."

A-ma regards me, weighing so much. When she finally speaks it's to drive forward the theme that has come at me from every direction since I've returned home.

"You shouldn't be alone. You cannot let memories of what happened in the past turn you into someone *you* wouldn't recognize. Be who you are, Girl, and the right person will find you and love you."

While I still don't think love will happen for me again, her words give me strength—to say goodbye, walk alone back to Bamboo Forest Village, board the minibus to Menghai, and travel on to Kunming.

When I enter my apartment, I find a note from Teacher Guo, asking me to visit him immediately. He breaks away from dinner with his family to give me the news. Of the two thousand people who applied, I'm the only student accepted into *both* programs. I'm ecstatic. I sell my moped and most of my belongings so I'll have money to live on without taking an extra job to support myself.

For the next twelve months, I'm rarely apart from Tea Master Sun. In the first track, he teaches me how to buy raw tea, store it, and let nature do its job of aging. I learn to judge the minutes required for wilting, killing the green, kneading, the sunbath, and fermentation. (I've had a head start on some of these things, which gives me an advantage over the other students.) In the second track, I study the best qualities of tea so that one day I might become a tea master myself, like—and here's my first French word—a wine sommelier.

"Taste requires a lifetime of dedication," Tea Master Sun instills in me. "You have a simple palate shaped by your childhood, cultivated by mountain springs, and enriched by the soil. I like this about you, but you must learn subtlety and refinement. You'll stumble and make mistakes, but as long as you're humble and honest, you'll learn. You love tea. I see it in your face. Always remember *If you don't love tea, you can't make good tea.*"

Nothing romantic grows between my tea master and me, but after months of being around him the last of the sadness and loneliness I've felt about the past dissipates like clouds after a storm. When I look back at my life—all twenty-six years of it—I see the many men who've helped me, but none of them will ever be as important as Tea Master Sun, who opens my eyes, heart, and soul. The things he teaches me range from the practical to the spiritual.

"Confucius taught his followers that tea could help people understand their inner dispositions," he tells me, "while Buddhists grant tea the highest spiritual qualities, ranking it among the four ways to concentrate the mind, along with walking, feeding fish, and sitting quietly. They believe tea can link the realms of meditation. Just the physical process we experience when we drink tea—our search for *huigan*—causes us to turn inward and reflect as the liquor coats our tongues, shimmers down our throats, and then rises again as fragrance. The Daoists see tea as a way to regulate internal alchemy, be in harmony with the natural world, and serve as an ingredient in the elixir of immortality. Together, these three disciplines have taught us to look upward to see the state of the heavens and downward to observe the natural arrangement of the earth. But whatever you believe or however you view life, the quality and goodness of a tea are for the mouth to decide."

My mouth does learn to find the best flavors, distinguish the body (light or heavy), discern texture (like water or velvet), as well as detect the most disagreeable notes—chalky, dusty, and rancid, or petroleum, disinfectant, and plastic. I become adept at identifying the differences between Pu'er, Iron Goddess of Mercy, Dragon Well, Silver Needle, and White Peony teas by taste alone. I study auction prices and have seen how values change and surge. In 2001, a special Iron Goddess of Mercy sold for 120,000 yuan, but just one year later a three-year-old Pu'er sold for 168,000 yuan. Two years ago, in 2004, when the yuan was at a historic high against the

U.S. dollar, a mere three grams of a Pu'er once stored in the Palace Museum sold for 12,000 yuan—thirty-two times the price of gold! And now, just as I'm graduating, another 100 grams of Pu'er has sold for 220,000 yuan or about $28,000.

How can I not rejoice in my good fortune in living with this particular leaf, celebrate my knowledge of it, and show courage in revealing it to others? It's time for me to start "plucking the hills and boiling the oceans" by entering the tea trade, and I have many options to choose from in Kunming alone. More than four thousand wholesale and retail tea dealers, as well as countless teahouses, have sprung up in the city like frogs after the monsoon. But before I can apply to any of those establishments, Tea Master Sun presents me with an offer from a business that wants to invest in the future of Pu'er by bankrolling a shop in the Fangcun Tea Market in Guangzhou, the largest wholesale tea market in China. "They'll put up the capital—not much, but enough to rent a space and buy product—and you'll produce the sweat and have all the worry," Tea Master Sun explains. "You'll make money on commission until you've paid back the initial investment. Then you'll own the business fifty-fifty. I don't think you'll find an opportunity better than that."

Who can question fate? Bad things happened to me; then my fortunes turned when I went to the trade school and Pu'er Tea College. Now another propitious moment blossoms before me. Perhaps what the Han majority say is true: *Good luck comes in threes.* I sign the contract with Green Jade, Ltd., on my tea master's advice.

Before taking the train to Guangzhou, I write a note to Teacher Zhang:

> Please ask Ci-teh, my family, and our neighbors to find me the best teas, and I will sell them.

Birthday letter to Constance from Haley, March 1, 2006

Dear Mom,

I am ten years old. Dad is sixty years old. And today you turned fifty years old. We all have zeroes in our ages. I think that's cool. Zero is my favorite number.

I like skiing with you. I like riding horses with you. You drive me lots of places. You let me and my friends eat lots of ice cream! Jade and Jasmine like you a lot. You also take us to the movies. You let us talk in the backseat of the car and don't tell us to be quiet like Jade's mom. You help me with the computer. I like science just like you.

You are the best mom in the world. No other mom could have taken her daughter to the Observatory to look through the telescope, like you took me, when no one else was there. I love you as much as the whole universe.

Happy Birthday, Mom!

Haley

THE SWEETEST DEW OF HEAVEN

I've been in Guangzhou two weeks, and every morning I wake up with a knot in my stomach. Even seven floors up I can hear the inelegant thrum of the city and knowing I have to venture into it—be a part of it—is a challenge. I get dressed, eat breakfast standing up, and leave my apartment. The hallway reeks of garlic and cigarette smoke. I squeeze into the too-small elevator with other people who live in the building. When we reach the ground floor, I'm pushed from behind as my neighbors hurry to be first through the lobby and out the door. Once they're gone, I linger for a moment. I take a breath to fortify myself. *You can do this!* I step outside and am immediately swept into a current of thousands of people heading to work and school.

Not even in my dreams could I have imagined such a big city. It's loud and crowded, with more than double the population of Kunming. Instead of eddies of bicycles like I used to see in Teacher Zhang's posters, the road is solidly packed with cars, at a standstill, their horns blaring. I pass restaurant windows filled with big aquariums in which sea creatures I don't recognize wait to be scooped out by the chef for a family's lunch or dinner. (Why would anyone *eat* those things?) Stores sell all manner of goods—more than anyone could ever want or need. *To get rich is glorious!* But the success of the campaign has also brought a dark side: beggars. China isn't supposed to have them and the government is supposed to keep peasants in the countryside, but with so many people and not enough watchers . . .

It's a short walk to my subway stop near the Martyrs' Memorial Gardens. Once I reach the platform for Line 1, I let the tide of humanity draw me with it into the car that will take me seven stops to the exit for the Fangcun Tea Market in the Liwan District. We are so jammed together that the other passengers and I sway as one entity through every acceleration, bump, and turn. Things are quieter once I'm back on the street, but not by much, because hundreds—maybe thousands—of people work in the market. It's still hard for me to grasp its vastness. It covers several blocks and does big business. This year it's on target to sell 67 billion yuan worth of tea, with Pu'er making up a third. Each block contains a cluster of four-story buildings. On each floor, in each of those buildings, on each of those blocks, are dozens upon dozens of shops. Some are just four by four meters. Others take up half a floor. Still others are little more than a couple of stools surrounded by bags of tea overseen by a single family in the open hallway, and banded together with similar smaller dealers. The long hallways are dimly lit by fluorescent tubes. Shipping containers—crates, cardboard boxes, and stuffed burlap bags—create obstacles outside nearly every purveyor's door. But not every shop sells tea. Some offer cups, pots, glass pitchers, picks to break apart tea cakes, tables and trays for tea pouring, in every price range imaginable.

When I unlock the door to my Midnight Blossom Teashop, I'm greeted by the intoxicating aroma of Pu'er, the only type of tea I sell. Knowing the rest of my workday will follow *my* rhythms allows me to relax. My first customer is from Beijing. We exchange business cards, each of us making internal calculations as happens in every transaction across China these days. His belt buckle has been let out a couple of notches, which tells me that whatever his business is he must be doing well but not so well that he feels comfortable buying a new belt. Is he a collector or an amateur trying to get in on the action? I learn he's serious when he says he's looking to buy a *jian,* which holds twelve stacks of seven *bing* to a total of eighty-four cakes of Pu'er to give as gifts to people in the government to help him build *guanxi*—connections. It quickly becomes evident, however, that he doesn't know a thing about tea. I could take advantage of him—sell him an inferior tea or overcharge him—but in just two weeks I've already started to gain a reputation for being fair and honest, something that can't be said for some of my competitors. Besides, if he's an entrepreneur on his way up, this could be the first of many purchases.

I brew tea; we taste it. I make a different infusion; we taste that, and so on, for a couple of hours. I teach him a popular saying that has recently sprung up: *You'll regret tomorrow what you don't store today*. The idea encourages him to exceed my expectations. He buys a kilo of loose tea for his personal use. An hour later, we get down to real business: he orders twenty kilos of Spring Well Village Pu'er to put on the menus at his eight cafés. As I copy down his shipping information, he asks where I'm from.

"I was born in Yunnan," I reply.

His nose prickles enviously. Then he asks the question I hear nearly every day. "Why would you move to Guangzhou? Every person who lives here longs for the tranquillity of your province. Remote and untouched. With clean air and wild forests."

"I miss it," I admit, "but I'm helping my family by selling the natural gifts of our mountain." Actually, I'm selling treasures from the Six Great Tea Mountains plus another twenty tea mountains, including Nannuo. Ci-teh has found some wonderful teas from Laobanzhang. What she sends isn't the highest quality, but the liquor is good and the name value unsurpassed. I think of my Laobanzhang Pu'er as a small but surprising vintage from an area that produces some breathtaking products.

After my customer departs, the afternoon stretches out before me. I fetch bottles of springwater, wash and dry serving utensils, and package tea in single servings to sell or give as samples. I lock up at 5:00. I jump back on Line 1, and it's as awful as it was this morning. My attitude about it is better, though, because at the end of the ride I will reward myself. I get off at the stop for Martyrs' Memorial Gardens. I buy a bottle of water from a woman who sells commemorative key chains, pinwheels, and other items from a cart. I wave and say hello in my pathetic Cantonese to three retired men—wearing their old People's Liberation Army uniforms—who bring their caged finches to the park, smoke cigarettes, and share stories. I stroll along the walkways to one of the benches that ring the memorial. I sit, breathe, listen. There's no escaping the rabid roar of the city, but the rustling of the breeze through the trees sweeps away the stresses of the day.

I found this spot a week ago, and already I've learned the patterns of others like myself, who seek comfort in the park's embrace. On the bench to my left sits a woman around sixty. She wears the costume of her age: a short-sleeved white blouse and gray trousers. Past hardship has set lines in her face. I'm most struck by her eyes, which are surprisingly wide for a Chinese. Her purse serves as a paperweight to keep what I assume are copies of her son's biography and photos of him from blowing away. She has none of the desperation or pushiness of the mothers in Kunming's parks who used to hound me, looking for daughters-in-law for their sons. Rather, during the past week, she's placidly watched young women meander by, never once approaching or speaking to one of them.

A month later, I arrive at the park, ready to let the hustle of the long day fall from my shoulders, when the woman on the bench next to mine motions for me to join her.

"I'm Mrs. Chang," she announces in English. "I've noticed you don't know much Cantonese and my Mandarin is abysmal. English will work for me, if it will work for you." She pats the seat next to her. "Please sit down."

I obey because I don't know how to avoid her invitation politely, but I take care not to glance at the pile of papers between us. If she's been watching me as I've been watching her, she has to know I'm not interested in matchmaking.

"I'm a widow," she tells me straight off.

Her revelation causes me to be equally blunt. "So am I."

"Such a shame when you're so young." She blinks a few times. "I was young when I lost my husband too."

All these weeks from my spot on my bench, she's seemed nice enough, but if she thinks I'm going to talk about San-pa . . .

"Years ago," she continues, "I was a high school English teacher and my husband taught philosophy at South China Normal University. Have you heard of it?"

"No, but I grew up far from here."

"I can tell."

Tu. My cheeks burn.

"I've spent time in the countryside myself," she goes on, ignoring my discomfort. "During the Cultural Revolution, my husband and I were labeled black intellectuals and sent to the countryside to learn from the peasants. I was six months pregnant. Have you ever been pregnant? Do you have a child to care for?"

"Yes. And no."

She searches my eyes to make sure I'm telling the truth. "No secrets between us. I like that." After a pause, she says, "My husband and I—two bourgeois revisionists—learned to grow sweet potatoes and millet."

She's talking, and I'm thinking, *So much confiding, and we don't even know each other!*

"Five years after our son was born, my husband caught a cold, which turned into pneumonia." Her throat hitches. Then, "After his death, I forced myself to survive." Much like I had to do . . . "I needed to raise and protect my son. I petitioned the authorities to let us come home to Guangzhou, claiming unreasonable hardship. But I wasn't invited back until after President Nixon's visit to China. I was told the country would once again be joining the international community. China would need English teachers. My son and I have been here ever since."

"I'm glad you were able to return. My teacher where I grew up never went home. He couldn't get permission."

"That happened to a lot of people. My son and I were lucky."

The next night and the night after that, I sit with Mrs. Chang. We share stories of the countryside. She doesn't miss a single thing about it. She's never been to Yunnan, and although she's heard of its beauty, she has no interest in visiting.

"When I think of the countryside," she says, "I remember only suffering."

Two months later, my day-to-day routine has barely changed. The noise and crowds are still difficult for me, but I'm adapting. I ride the subway to the tea market, work, ride the subway to the park, and walk straight to Mrs. Chang's bench. We meet every evening, except Sundays, talk for a half hour or so, and watch the passing girls to evaluate who might make a good daughter-in-law for her. Oh, the laughter! This one's too skinny; that one's too fat. This one wears too much rouge; that one's too pale. This one looks spoiled; that one looks like a factory girl sniffing for a man to buy her gold and jade. Not everything is about matchmaking, though. The more she's confided in me, the freer I've felt to unburden myself of my past, which, until now, I've never been able to do. Mrs. Chang knows everything about me. *Everything*. Never has she criticized me or made me feel ashamed, but once she said, "You did the best possible given your circumstances. Sometimes all we can do is count ourselves lucky to be alive."

Tonight, as usual, we're making our assessments of the girls who pass by—too studious, too vapid, too clumsy, too sure of herself—when Mrs. Chang suddenly blurts, "Are you ready to meet my son?"

I stiffen, insulted that she thinks so little of our friendship. "I haven't been talking to you so I might find a husband."

"Of course you haven't," she responds calmly. "But the two of you might make a felicitous pair."

"I don't want to get married again—"

"Because of what happened to you—"

"It's not that. The way I live now . . . I have the freedom to do as I please."

"To me, that's just another way of saying you've seen hardship. I too have survived hardship, as has my son. Don't you think we've all earned a little contentment?"

I like Mrs. Chang, but she's wrong if she thinks I want to meet her son. Let alone marry him! Still, in her own clever way she's been working on me since the first moment she saw me enter the park. She picks up the pile of papers that's sat untouched between us all these weeks and scoots closer to me.

"Let me show you some photographs," she says. "Here's Jin when he graduated from primary school. We hadn't been in Guangzhou very long. See how thin he was?"

I've enjoyed Mrs. Chang's companionship and I don't want it to end, so I look at every photo with absolute courtesy but zero interest.

In June of the Western calendar—two weeks after being presented with Mrs. Chang's scheme and three and a half months after arriving in Guangzhou—the heat and humidity of this subtropical city has permeated the Midnight Blossom Teashop, as it has every shop in the Fangcun Tea Market. The unbearable climate doesn't keep people away, though. By 10:00, every chair and stool around my table is occupied by an international assortment of buyers—from Korea, Taiwan, and Japan. The late afternoon sees the departure of these buyers and the arrival of my regulars.

Mr. Lin—in his sixties, lean, and successful in our new economy—was the first to bring his laptop to my shop so he could monitor his stocks while speculating on tea futures. The next day, Mr. Chow brought his laptop. He looks like he's in his sixties too, but not a single strand of gray threads his unruly black mop. He's an entrepreneur—what else?—and he owns a string of five shoe stores around the city. He's remained a humble man and is easily awed. Mr. Kwan is the youngest by a few years and the only one who's had to take mandatory retirement. As a former schoolteacher, he can't afford a laptop, but the other men share what they find, and all activity is focused on Pu'er.

The three men all have their own special cups. Mr. Lin, the wealthiest of the three, opens a bamboo box and lifts from the silken cushions a cup made of blanc de chine—perfect for appreciating the clarity of liquor in the bowl. Mr. Chow and his newer money also bought a cup in white porcelain, only his has calligraphy in blue on the exterior. It's a sad couplet, fit for the widower he is: *It was hard to meet you and harder to bid farewell. The east wind blew weak and all the flowers fell.* Mr. Kwan's teacup is a cheap copy of a Ming dynasty "chicken cup," showing a hen tending her chicks.

My tea men gossip as though they've known each other from childhood. They discuss the final bids at tea auctions, international tea prices, the effect of the weather on terrace and wild tea in Yunnan, Fujian, and other tea-growing regions around the world. Today they debate the health benefits of Pu'er. Mr. Lin, the most highly respected and educated of my tea men, delves deep into the past to press his beliefs.

"Lu Yü, the great tea master, wrote that tea can alleviate the stoppage of the bowels, relieve melancholy, and remove aching of the brain, stinging of the eyes, and swelling of the joints. He said that tea is like the sweetest dew of heaven, so naturally it can only do us good."

"Tea helps us to think quicker, sleep less, move lighter, and see clearer," Mr. Chow agrees.

Mr. Kwan, who always tries to best his betters, adds, "Our traditional Chinese medicine doctors tell us that tea—Pu'er in particular—has more than one hundred proven purposes: to boost the immune system, balance the body's hot and cold temperatures, lower blood pressure and blood sugar, and help melt away hangovers as well as tumors."

"It didn't help my wife," Mr. Chow reminds them.

"How do you know?" Mr. Kwan asks, not unkindly. "Perhaps the tea prolonged her life."

"Myself?" Mr. Lin cuts him off. "I no longer go to the herbalist or acupuncturist. I believe in Western medicine—"

"You can afford it," Mr. Kwan remarks defensively. "But let me point out that American scientists are now studying catechins and polyphenols. You must have read about them. They're the compounds in tea that provide the antioxidative, antiinflammatory, antimicrobial, anticancer—"

Mr. Chow sinks into his stool. It's clear that memories of his wife are still distressing.

"Anti-this, anti-that, anti-everything," I jump in, trying to lighten the mood. "Yesterday I saw a 'medicinal' Pu'er in the drugstore guaranteeing weight loss—"

"Of course!" Mr. Kwan enthuses. "Because it cuts through

grease. The world knows *that*. My cholesterol is much lower. My lipids too—"

"But what do these claims matter in the end?" I ask. "Shouldn't we just enjoy it? Where I come from, we always drank raw tea. You tell me you prefer the stomach-warming and mouth-smoothness attributes of a Pu'er that's been naturally aged for five years or more. Let us discuss the merits of each."

I pour one of the Pu'ers Ci-teh sent from Laobanzhang. In the time I've been here, the wholesale price for this tea has jumped five, then ten times. As a result, I've been able to pay back Green Jade's initial investment, so I now own 50 percent of a thriving business. My success has rippled out. My father and brothers are enjoying what to them are instant fortunes. I can proudly say I helped make that happen. As for Pu'er's supposed health benefits, it's hard to know what to make of them. A-ma made potions from the mother and sister trees, but maybe the people she gave them to would have healed anyway. Maybe her elixirs gave comfort like the nima's trance or the ruma's chanting. We *believed* we'd get better. No one was overweight in my village, but that's because we were poor and didn't have enough to eat. For me, I'm content to see my tea men sipping their tea appreciatively—and quietly.

The next Sunday, my only day off, I walk to Martyrs' Memorial Gardens to Mrs. Chang's bench. The old woman has gnawed at me nonstop—"Meet my son . . . Just once . . . We'll have dim sum together . . . If you don't like him, you and I will still be friends"—until I'm little more than a chewed down corncob. Now here we are, waiting for her precious Jin to arrive. From photographs, I know what to look for: a man of medium height, average build (I wouldn't be able to stand one of those heavy Cantonese businessmen), and a full head of hair. From Mrs. Chang's stories, I know he's thirty-eight and an entrepreneur, like just about everyone else in China these days. He exports America's trash—old cardboard and other types of used paper—to China to be recycled into new boxes to ship consumer goods back to the United States, which seems like a utilitarian, if not terribly interesting, thing to do. As a result, he travels often. Mrs. Chang has promised that she's told him nothing of my "adversities": "I would never speak of your past nor would I reveal his," she said. "These things are for the two of you to come to yourselves. But why worry about that now? Let's first see if you like each other." So for all I know, he may be just as guarded and mistrustful as I am. Maybe he's coming here with the sole purpose of getting his mother to leave him alone about *me*! I can practically hear Mrs. Chang: "Meet Li-yan . . . Just once . . . We'll have dim sum together . . . If you don't like her, nothing is lost . . ."

Jin waves as he comes into view, and I have the benefit of watching him stride purposefully toward us. He wears his clothes comfortably—suede loafers, navy blue slacks, and a Polo shirt—the real thing, not a knockoff. A few strands of gray at his temples catch the light. His wide and intelligent eyes prove him to be his mother's son. Beyond that, something deep within them instantly puts me at ease. He's arrived with gifts, which he juggles in his arms so we can shake hands. He's a businessman, but his palms reveal the calluses of hard work. He isn't shy, but he isn't too forward either. He's brought his mother what I've already learned is a traditional Cantonese gift: a tin of imported Danish cookies.

"And for you, Li-yan, some tea. You're a young tea master, my mother tells me, so I hope you'll accept my modest gift."

The label says it's a naturally aged Pu'er from Laobanzhang made from the leaves of a single four-hundred-year-old tree. The tea itself is set in an exquisite red lacquer box whose price may equal my monthly income, which tells me that either he's trying to show off or he's honestly interested in me because of his mother.

"Shall we try it at lunch?" I ask.

Before he can answer, Mrs. Chang says, "You absolutely should. I've arranged a table for you at the Southern Garden Restaurant. You two go along now."

Jin and I protest. She was supposed to join us, but she's like a snake that's swallowed a mouse. As she sets off toward the subway stop, he says with humor edging his voice, "Together we've just lost our first battle with my mother."

He owns a car, which might impress some women. Sun and Moon! Who am I fooling? A Mercedes? I'm *very* impressed. Mrs. Chang told me her son was doing well with his recycling business, but this is very well. But the last thing I'm interested in is money. I like the way he drives, though. Casual, with his wrist draped over the top of the steering wheel. He doesn't honk like a maniac or swerve in and out between cars to gain an extra few meters either.

The restaurant is large—and jam-packed. We're led through a labyrinth of courtyards, banquet halls, waterfall grottoes, and gardens. We cross over a zigzag bridge and enter a small room built to resemble an ancient pavilion. We're seated at a table that overlooks a weeping willow whose tendrils drift languidly above the surface of a pond filled with lotus in bloom. The waiter brings hot water for me to brew the tea. When I open the lacquer box, however, I'm assaulted by an odor of dirt and mildew.

"What's wrong?" Jin asks.

"I don't know how to say this . . ."

"You won't hurt my feelings," he coaxes.

"I'm afraid someone sold you a fake."

His expression falls. I wouldn't be surprised if this news ended our lunch before it began, but then he smiles. "Taken again! I thought those days were behind me."

"There are a lot of fakes," I console him. "Even connoisseurs buy fakes sometimes."

"From now on, you'll always choose our tea, and I'll take care of other things—like ordering our meals."

I spot a good-quality Pu'er on the menu, and he orders an intriguing assortment of dumplings. I expect him to talk only about himself, but he keeps the conversation going by asking me questions. Do I like Guangzhou? Do I know how to drive? Would I like him to teach me how to drive? Have I gone to Hong Kong? I end up enjoying myself much more than I thought I would. After our meal, we meander back through the courtyards, stopping to watch the water tumble over the rocks at the main waterfall. When the valet brings around the car, Jin holds my elbow as he directs me into the front seat.

"Would you like to go for a walk?" he asks once he's behind the wheel. "Maybe visit the Orchid Garden? Or we could go to Shamian Island, sit outside, and have American coffee. Oh . . . Do you drink coffee?"

"I like coffee, but maybe another time."

He must think I'm trying to get out of prolonging this day or seeing him again, because his expression collapses as quickly as it did when I told him he'd bought fake Pu'er.

"I mean that," I say. "Another time. I'm free every Sunday—"

"Then next Sunday—"

"And I'm free every evening," I add, which makes him smile.

He offers to drive me home, but I ask to be dropped off at the Martyrs' Memorial Gardens. We shake hands. He drives off. Before going to my apartment, I sit on a bench and punch in Ci-teh's cellphone number.

"I went on a date," I tell her. "My first ever."

She laughs in her distinctive way and asks to hear every detail.

Over the next months, Jin and I see each other twice a week after work and every Sunday. I don't go to his apartment, and he doesn't come to mine. He may have an expensive car, but I sense he's modest in his aspirations, for he often wears the same clothes—clean, but the same nevertheless. (That, or he's trying to show me that he doesn't mind that *my* wardrobe is limited.) I teach him to drink tea properly, and he's got a fine palate, easily distinguishing between raw and ripe Pu'ers by whether they taste grassy, floral, fruity, and sharp, or dark, of the forest floor, cavelike, and smooth. He takes me to restaurants all over the city, where I try clams, sea cucumber, and jellyfish. Every bite is strange, and a lot of things I don't like . . . at all. "It's true a crab looks like a spider," he says. "If you don't like it, then you never have to eat it again." On those evenings when we don't meet for dinner, a concert, or a movie, I go to the park and chat with Mrs.

Chang. She's a clever matchmaker, because the more I ask about him, the less she says, which means the only way to know more is to spend time with him.

Jin and I return again and again to Shamian Island to take in the crumbling beauty of the deserted English colonial mansions, Western banks, and consulate buildings. We always stop for tea or coffee at an outdoor café open for tourists who also like to visit these modern ruins. "Years ago, only foreigners could live here," Jin explains one evening. From our table, we can see down the tree-lined cobblestone pathway, where a young mother chases after her one child. "Chinese could not step on the island without permission. At night, the iron gates on the bridges were locked and guarded. I wonder what it would take to restore one of these houses and bring back its garden." The idea sounds wonderful but outlandish, so I just nod agreeably.

While Shamian Island is charming and peaceful—my favorite place in Guangzhou—we explore other parts of the city too. We take a boat excursion along the Pearl River to look at the high-rise apartment buildings that sprout from the banks, and he showers me with questions: "Do you like the water? Have you seen the ocean? Can you swim?" When I answer, I don't know, no, and no, he comes back with "Ah, so many adventures lie ahead of us." It seems like he's made a decision about me, but so much remains unspoken.

On Sundays, he drives me into the countryside. We pass what are called villa parks, where rows of identical houses sit in neat lines. Between those enclaves are rice paddies and other fields, where farmers carry buckets of water hanging heavily from poles strung over their shoulders. We visit White Cloud Mountain. It's more like a hill to me, but the views over the Pearl River delta are pretty. We go to the Seven Star Crags, which, Jin tells me, are like a miniature version of Guilin, with their mist-shrouded peaks and rivers. "One day I'll take you to the real Guilin," he says. "You'll love it."

Today, in what seems like the worst torpor and stickiness of the summer, we drive to Dinghushan, another popular mountain resort, to see the Tang and Ming dynasty temples. Although it feels like half of Guangzhou is also here, trying to escape the swelter of the city, we stroll along the trails, and Jin takes several photos of me.

"Would you rather live in a villa park surrounded by fields and drive to your shop every day or would you prefer to have an apartment in the city and visit nature on weekends?" he asks.

"As though I would ever get to live in a villa!" I manage to get out through my laughter. "Or own a car! Or have an entire weekend without work!"

"But what if you could live in the countryside, would you want that? A villa park is not far from the city . . ."

He's so earnest, and this excursion reminds me how much I love the purity of clean air, birdsong, and the calming sounds of bubbling brooks and waterfalls. Driving back to the city, I feel refreshed and ready to start the new week, but I also feel homesick. How can I explain to him that while Dinghushan is lovely, the mountains are not as beautiful or as tall, isolated, or pristine as my childhood home?

He reads my mind, and remarks, "Maybe one day you'll take me to where you grew up and I'll get to meet your family."

I don't even know what to say. What *if* he came to Spring Well and experienced what I love—the mossy cushion of the forest floor, leaves fluttering in the breeze, and birds and monkeys chattering in the trees? Or would he see my village—and my family—as backward and crude? So much of my time with Jin, I realize, is spent with contradictory thoughts like these. His comments and questions make my heart feel both sweet and bitter and leave me confused, but not so confused that I ever say no to his invitations.

I've never told him about my marriage to San-pa or our trip across Myanmar and into Thailand, but the following Sunday when he announces, "You should have a passport in case you want to travel to another country someday," I go along with the idea. Of course, it's not easy to get a passport. He seems to know people who know people, though. He introduces me to one cadre and bureaucrat after another. "She's a businesswoman," he explains to them, following up with "Do you like Pu'er? Naturally! The health benefits alone! Please accept her gift . . ." And so on.

Once I get my passport (amazing!), he advises me to get a single-visit visa to the United States, because "You never know what can happen in this country." He isn't aware that I have a daughter in America, but I fill out the forms, go to the interview, and quietly begin to save money for a plane ticket. After I get the United States of America visa stamp on my passport, I take it out every night just to stare at it. If I went there, could I find her? Jin remains ignorant of the gift he's given me—hope—but I'm indebted to him for it nevertheless.

I often remind myself of what Mrs. Chang said: those who suffer have earned contentment. Maybe I have earned it. Although Jin and I are getting to know each other, as Mrs. Chang asked, I worry what will happen if I share my life story. Maybe a time will come when we'll want to tell each other everything, but maybe not. He seems to feel the same way, because our conversations look inward and forward but never backward. Every word exchanged reveals something—from the insignificant and even silly to the more profound admissions that get to the core of who we are. Who knows? Maybe we are less interested in infatuation or romantic love than in understanding, compatibility, and companionship unmarred by the past.

"I like yellow," he answers when I ask his favorite color. "I don't have many good memories of being in the countryside as a boy, but I did enjoy the spring when the rapeseed was in bloom."

"I'll always love indigo," I tell him. "One might think I'd be tired of it. I wore that color every day until I went to Kunming, and every person I knew as a girl wore that same color. Instead, it reminds me of tradition and the comforts of home."

He asks if I like dogs.

"I prefer cats, because they're useful and mind their own business," I explain. "Dogs are only good for omens and sacrificial eating."

"Promise me you won't eat my dog."

"You have a dog? I love dogs!"

It's not a concession. I'm not changing who I am to please him. I'd walk a dog and clean up its poop, like I see people do here in the city, because I like Jin and I want to spend time with him. (Turns out he was joking. A relief!) But every revelation is weighed. Could I bear that? Could I live with it?

By fall, my feelings for him have grown and changed. He hasn't tried to kiss me. I understand we're from different cultures and that it's unusual for Han majority people to kiss or hug in public or for the most traditional couples even to show physical affection in private. Still, every time he uses the tip of his finger to slide a loose strand of hair behind my ear or takes my elbow to help me into his car, I feel the warmth that got me into so much trouble with San-pa. But I'm not a young girl anymore. I go to a Family Planning Office for birth control pills. If we ever decide to steal love, I'll be ready. But *when*? I consider how much time we've spent together, and that's when it hits me he's holding something back far worse than his family's tribulations in the countryside. Of course. So am I. Many things . . .

Haley's Fifth-grade Spelling Words

Scrape	Cruel	Millionaire	Criminal	Annoy
Spain	Plastic	Boycott	Cauliflower	Tragedy
Homeless	Communicate	Imagination	Career	Youth
Professional	Ghost	Desalination	Groundwater	Sponge

1. Office buildings scrape the sky.
2. Friends can be cruel.
3. Most parents are millionaires.
4. If you ask a criminal what kind of job he has, he will say a government job.
5. I wish I had a sister to annoy me.
6. Will you send me a sister from Spain?
7. Grandma's face looks like plastic.
8. Dad says people can boycott things they don't like.
9. I want to boycott cauliflower.
10. A tragedy is when my violin teacher passes gas.
11. Homeless people must feel terrible.
12. I want my own phone to communicate.
13. Grandpa says I have an imagination "this big."
14. All girls should have a career.
15. Youth in Asia is different from euthanasia.
16. Every year my mom hires a professional photographer to take pictures of me.
17. I wish I had a ghost to play with.
18. I will never use desalination in a sentence again.
19. I'm learning about groundwater in Miss Gordon's class.
20. If I had a little sister, I would wipe her mouth with a sponge.

PART IV

THE BIRD THAT STANDS OUT

2007–2008

A CHICKEN, A GOAT, AND A COIN

To celebrate Western New Year's Eve, Jin takes his mother and me to a restaurant at the top of a fancy hotel, which allows us to see the fireworks—giant blooms of light and stars—bursting over the city. He orders champagne, which I've spoken about to my customers but never tasted. Once it's poured, he toasts us, wishing all prosperity, happiness, and golden health in the new year.

My toast is to Mrs. Chang. "Thank you for befriending a stranger."

"May this be the first of many New Year's celebrations—Western or lunar—we share together," she says when her turn comes.

Her words are so bold. She's a wishful mother of an unwed man in his late thirties, but I worry her pushing could drive him away. I try to compose myself—hiding my embarrassment behind a pleasant expression—before glancing in Jin's direction. When I do, he's right there, staring at me with such intensity that I immediately lower my eyes to the salted prawn on my plate.

A week later, on the first Sunday of the new year, Jin flies to Los Angeles for a series of meetings. When Mrs. Chang and I visit in the park during the week, we don't discuss the awkward moments after her toast, but my mind is full of unspoken truths. I've fallen in love with Jin, but I'm not sure the feeling is reciprocated. I could try to shield my heart and say I don't want to see him—or her—again, but what would that bring me? Immediate loneliness.

I want to prolong this emotion as long as I can, even if it will cause me pain in the future.

That's when my a-ma comes into my mind. Two years ago and now nearly ten years after San-pa's terrible death, A-ma cautioned me, "You shouldn't be alone." She also said I shouldn't let memories of the past turn me into someone I wouldn't recognize, and I guess this proves I haven't, because I'm as foolish and reckless as ever. But she also said, "The right person will find you and love you," and I have to believe that's happened, because, truly, won't Jin have a moment when he realizes what he feels for me? What if he proposes, we go to Spring Well Village, A-ma and A-ba like him, and we're married in a full Akha wedding—the kind I should have had all those years ago? What if, when we come back to Guangzhou, we find an apartment together? He certainly won't have a crossbow, but what other possessions might he bring to our home? How will our lives unfold? What if we have a child? Just the thought of that . . .

See? Foolish and reckless.

On Saturday, I work in the tea market but my mind is elsewhere. Jin returns today, and we're set to meet this evening at our favorite café on Shamian Island. My shop is busier than ever. I work—pouring, measuring, and selling tea, listening to the conversation between my three favorite tea men. Mr. Lin brags about how many kilos of a twelve-year-old Pu'er from Laobanzhang he's stored. He points to his laptop screen. "Come see how much money I made—overnight!" Mr. Chow says, "Only on paper." Mr. Kwan jokes, "Only on screen, you mean!" Then they shift—as they often do—to the size of their temperature-controlled vaults. It's a normal day, except for the thoughts about Jin that keep me from joining the banter.

It's a normal day, that is, until two new customers enter the shop. The sight of the older man jolts me out of my daydreams. Mr. Huang! Next to him, a teenage boy, who has to be his son, Xian-rong. A little more than a decade has passed since I last saw them. I'd recognize Mr. Huang anywhere, but these days he doesn't look so startlingly different compared to the other men in my shop. He's still well fed, but here in the city he wears white pants, a striped shirt, and white patent leather shoes. The boy—thin, gangly, with a mild case of acne spotting his face—slouches, keeping his eyes on the floor. They don't recognize me, of course. But seeing them brings back all the ways I failed as an Akha, as a mother, and as a wife: selling the leaves from the mother tree, abandoning my daughter, and San-pa's addiction and death.

"I'm looking for something truly unique—the more artisanal and rarer the leaf the better," Mr. Huang announces, proving that his desires are the same as ever.

My trio of tea men take up the challenge.

"I have tea picked from thousand-year-old trees," Mr. Lin brags.

Mr. Chow goes a step further. "I have tea picked from a *single* thousand-year-old tree."

Mr. Kwan can top either of those. "A farmer in Fujian province sold me tea picked by trained monkeys."

A bemused expression spreads across Mr. Huang's face. He raps on my table with his knuckles, commanding attention. "But does anyone here have tea picked by the lips of doctor-certified virgins?"

My tea men murmur among themselves. Who hasn't seen articles on the Internet about this tea? Not only do they have to be virgins, but they're required to have a C-cup bra size as well. Some reports claim that the girls even sleep with the tea on their breasts to infuse the leaves with vitality and virility.

"No one believes those stories," Mr. Lin scoffs. "If you do, my friend, then you've been duped. Do not feel bad. Even I have bought a counterfeit on occasion from a dealer who claims the material came from forest tea trees, but was not, or was naturally fermented but was sentenced to extreme wet storage, with high heat and high humidity to achieve the proper color but not the depth of taste. We must always remember what Lu Yü, the great tea master, told us thirteen hundred years ago: *The quality and goodness of a tea are for the mouth to decide.*"

"How to authenticate . . . That's the question!" Mr. Chow chimes in. "Is the seller telling the truth about the vintage? Is the rice paper wrapping original? But like Mr. Lin says, you must know by taste. Your body will tell you. If it doesn't taste right, it isn't right."

"Buyer beware!" Mr. Kwan concludes.

Hearing Mr. Huang's laughter transports me back many years. The skin on my arms reacts, contracting beyond my control, as though I've stepped on a bamboo pit viper. He's a physical manifestation of all my mistakes, even if he wasn't at fault for everything I associate with him.

"I like wise men," Mr. Huang says, "and everything you say is true. We're like art collectors, no? We taste every day. We know our own teas. No one believes in tea picked by the lips of virgins, because are there any of those left in China these days?" He tucks his chin as he asks, "But will you doubt me when I tell you *I* was the first to return to artisanal methods to create Pu'er?"

Xian-rong rolls his eyes, as though he's heard the story a thousand times, but Mr. Lin responds with a bland "How interesting." Then, because he can't help himself, he adds, "Tell us more."

"If you're a true connoisseur, then you've heard of me," Mr. Huang says. "I started a new era—to make private-label tea again."

"Are you Mr. Lü, the creator of Truly Simple Elegant tea?" Mr. Chow asks in unveiled awe.

Mr. Huang's crowing goes mute, and his shoulders sag. Then his eyes get the steely look I remember so well. "Mr. Lü and I were in the tea mountains around the same time. My leaves also hadn't been picked for forty years—"

"Were they picked by virgins or monkeys?" Mr. Lin teases.

Mr. Huang visibly bristles. I wish he'd leave my shop so tranquillity could be restored.

"The tea I created is special, very potent—"

"Dad," Xian-rong interrupts, speaking perfect English. Then to the others, he says, "Please forgive my father."

"We have our stories too," Mr. Lin says good-naturedly. He clasps a hand on each of his friends' shoulders. "Come, let us leave the strangers to conduct business with our maiden."

Despite my begging them to stay, my three tea men pack up their laptops, cellphones, and cups.

"We'll return after lunch," Mr. Chow announces, whether to warn Mr. Huang and his son or to reassure me, I'm not sure.

As soon as they're out the door, Xian-rong turns to me. "I apologize for my father. He's like the fisherman who let a big one slip off his line. For him, it's always the one that got away. Every year since he made his first blends, he's traveled to other mountains, trying to re-create one particular tea, which he made into only two cakes—"

"But I've been missing one special ingredient," Mr. Huang cuts in. "The leaves from your grove."

A chill runs down my spine. They knew who I was all along.

"How did you know I was here?" I ask.

Mr. Huang laughs. "I returned to your village last spring. Didn't your family tell you? And then there's my old friend, Tea Master Sun."

My stomach lurches. He was back in Spring Well? And he *knows* my tea master? I thought Tea Master Sun had only tasted Mr. Huang's tea.

"Don't let my father bother you, Auntie," Xian-rong says, again in English, this time using an honorific to address me. "He made the mistake of selling most of the tea cakes made on Nannuo Mountain to a Korean collector. Can you imagine what they're worth now? I'll tell you: one thousand three hundred U.S. per cake."

Waaa!

"Forget the fisherman," Xian-rong goes on. "My father is more like Ahab in search of his whale."

All right, so that stumps me.

I want them out of my shop. Sweat dampens my armpits, and I tremble despite my best efforts. It's not a big room, and the three of us are standing together: the man staring at me, the boy embarrassed by his father, and me, feeling reduced to an inconsequential, uneducated, *tu*, hill-tribe girl. But rather than push them out, I elect to appear friendly and helpful.

"Please sit, and we'll have some tea," I say, keeping my voice steady as I motion to the stools in front of my tea table.

We spend the next two hours drinking tea and "catching up,"

as Mr. Huang puts it. He still lives in Hong Kong, but he has so many construction projects in Guangzhou that he now maintains an apartment here. He sent his son to Andover, a prep school in America, where he was one of many overseas students. "But the boy fell in love with a white girl," Mr. Huang complains. "I had to bring him home. Now he's at the American International School in Hong Kong." (Doesn't Mr. Huang realize that his son will have an equal chance of falling in love with a foreigner at the American school?) "He's a senior. Seventeen years old! We come here on the hydrofoil every Friday afternoon and stay the weekend, so I can teach him the business he'll inherit one day."

The son in question looks about as interested in that prospect as in digging ditches.

"*The unridden stallion gets lazy,*" Xian-rong recites in Akha. His voice still sounds weary, but for the first time since he entered my shop, his eyes have lit up, sparkling with our secret communication. "*A boy who does not have skills will have difficulties.* This is true the world over, is it not, Auntie?"

I love hearing the Akha coming from his mouth, and it pleases me that he's retained what he learned as a youngster. In the future, if they visit again—and knowing Mr. Huang's persistent ways, I expect him to come back next Saturday and the one after that—Xian-rong and I will have a way to converse without his father understanding.

Mr. Huang ignores his son, shifting the conversation to memories of the tea mountains and what it was like for them when they first came to Spring Well Village. On the surface, it all sounds polite and harmless, but the whole situation is disconcerting. Mr. Huang pokes at me with our connections: Why didn't I know he did business with my a-ba and brothers last spring, what did I think of Mr. Lü's iconic Pu'er, and why do I suppose Tea Master Sun never told me that the two of them have known each other *for years* from time spent in the highest circles of tea connoisseurship?

"I opened one of the cakes we made from your special leaves," he confides, so sure of my interest. "Do you care to hear what I found?"

I jut my chin, pretending indifference.

"The entire cake was flecked with yellow—"

The threads from the mother tree must have spread and grown. But what's even more striking is that this is what A-ma told me was in my daughter's tea cake.

"The aroma was . . ." His voice drifts off. "Sublime."

I can't help myself. "How did it taste?"

He laughs all the way from his belly. "I didn't drink it!" This is what Tea Master Sun told me had been rumored during my interview, but I still find it incomprehensible until Mr. Huang continues. "I wrapped it up again. That's what you'd do with gold, isn't it?" He turns to his son, pinches his cheek affectionately, and then lets his hand come to a rest on the boy's shoulder. I remember how A-ma always said Mr. Huang loved his boy, and it's still so clear.

But Xian-rong is now of the wrong age for such fatherly tenderness. He waits a minute or so before edging away from his a-ba's protective touch. In many ways, though, the boy, still unformed and underdeveloped, is more sophisticated than his father when it comes to tea. His ability to taste the brews I pour is unusually refined. At the end of the visit, when his father goes down the hall to the WC and Xian-rong asks if he might return—without his father—I listen warily. Once Mr. Huang reappears, strutting down the dim hall, reflexively checking his fly as he stares through the windows of my competitors' shops, Xian-rong's pleas turn desperate.

"I beg you, Auntie. Please let me visit. We'll speak the language of the mountains and share our friendship through tea."

He seems so lonely and frail that against my better judgment I agree.

The subway is packed, but it feels even more suffocating than usual as I make my way to the stop closest to Shamian Island. Walking alone to the café to meet Jin, I struggle to rein in my emotions. Mr. Huang. Why did he have to come to my shop? When the café comes into view and I see Jin sitting at our favorite table under the colored lights with a single cup of tea before him, it's all

I can do to keep from running to him for solace. Instead, I take a deep breath to fortify myself, mortar into place another brick to hide my secrets, and settle my face into what I hope is a pleasant expression. When he sees me, he rises, drops a few coins on the table, and leaves the café before I reach it.

"Li-yan," he says, his voice serious, "will you come with me?"

My mind is in such turmoil that I automatically think he's going to tell me he no longer wants to see me. We walk together side by side. I try to memorize the moment: the height of his shoulder next to mine, the occasional brush of his sweater against my jacket, the sound of our footsteps on the cobblestones, the way the trees rustle above our heads.

When he passes through an iron gate and into a courtyard, I have enough sense to call out, "Wait! You can't go in there!"

He doesn't respond or even glance back at me. Instead, he strides along the rose-lined pathway and up some steps to the porch of a colonial mansion I've admired, despite its run-down condition. Now the layers of peeling paint have been stripped away and replaced by a coat of yellow, with the shutters and other woodwork shining glossy white. Jin opens the front door and extends his hand for me to join him. He must know what he's doing, I tell myself, but a part of me is terrified we'll be arrested for trespassing.

Once I reach him, he takes my hand, pulls me through a small entry, and brings me into a large room to the right that overlooks the garden and the tree-lined pedestrian walkway. I soak in the details in seconds: Fragrant freshly cut flowers in crystal vases. Handwoven Chinese silk carpets in intricate designs. Antique lamps on the end tables, but recessed lights to create atmosphere. A pair of ancestor scrolls hang on one wall. The opposite wall is dotted with small paintings of life in the city that must have been done when this house was first built.

"What is this place?" My voice shakes. "What are we doing here?"

"For months we've visited spots in the countryside and neighborhoods in the city," he answers. "I've shown you villa parks and apartments abutting the river, but always you've seemed happiest on this little island, which is why I bought this house a while ago. I've been restoring it since. I hope we'll be happy here."

I'm too stunned—beyond stunned, really—to speak. My confused silence sends a flicker of doubt across his face. Then he sets his jaw.

"I'm asking you to marry me, Li-yan," he forges ahead. "What I mean is, will you marry me?"

I answer without hesitation. "Yes, I'll go-work-eat with you."

We kiss. I'm dizzy with emotion as the walls I've built to guard my heart crumble. In my chaotic mixture of confusion and joy, I manage to put together a clear thought.

"I once promised myself I'd never marry unless my mother and father thought it was a good match." I leave out the word *again*, as in *I would never marry again*. Jin can't possibly know that, but a knife of guilt slices into my happiness. Before it can overpower me, Jin delivers into my hands a large and surprisingly heavy package wrapped in homemade indigo fabric.

"Open it," he says. "Your parents' blessing is inside."

I fold back the layers of fabric to find a new headdress decorated with trinkets I immediately recognize: a silver fish from First Sister-in-law, a string of silver balls the size of peas from Second Sister-in-law, a burst of appliquéd butterflies done in Third Sister-in-law's fine stitches, a coin from A-ma, as well as feathers and colorful pom-poms. Beneath that are folded a traditional wedding skirt, tunic, and leggings, plus a belt buckle, earrings, breastplate, and necklaces. All in all, there's perhaps fifteen kilos in silver—so much heavier than when I married San-pa—between the headdress and accessories. While I'm trying to take it all in, Jin is still talking.

"I've lied to you about some things," he begins. "I'm rich, as you can see. I didn't tell you, because I wanted you to love me for *me* and not just for my money. But that's not my only lie. This week, I wasn't in Los Angeles. I was in Spring Well."

My cheeks flush in embarrassment to think of him in my backward village.

"It wasn't my first visit," he continues, purposefully ignoring my obvious shame. "In the last six months, I've traveled four times to Spring Well to meet your family and ask permission to marry you." He pauses to let that sink in. Then, "Your father kept telling me to come back another time."

I cover my eyes and shake my head. "This is too much."

"They wanted me to prove to them you were happy. I brought photographs I'd taken of you. I wouldn't accept no. I even met with your . . . What is he called? The person who selects propitious dates? Like a *feng shui* diviner?"

"The ruma."

"He gave me a date."

That Jin's been planning this moment for such a long time . . .

"And that's not all," he goes on. "It seems a spirit incantation needed to be held for me. No one told me why, but it included the killing of a chicken and a goat and the passing from hand to hand of an old coin. What was all that about?" he inquires genially.

"Are they asking us to come home for the wedding?" I manage to choke out, because I'm not about to tell him that a special ceremony must always be performed when a widow remarries so her new husband won't have his life cut short. The goat is added to protect the new husband of a widow whose first husband died a terrible death.

"Your mother had a different idea. It seems she's heard about honeymoons," he says, bemused. "She thought you might like a honeymoon in America." He grins as he confides, "She pulled me aside to tell me that the *first* time I visited."

Which means she liked him from the beginning . . . Which is why I now have a wedding outfit, as well as a passport and visa . . . But which also means she deliberately wanted to remind me of Yan-yeh . . .

"Even before I met you," he says, "my mother made me love you. Then, when I saw you the first time, sitting on the bench with her . . . You were even more beautiful than she'd described."

"Beautiful?" Since we Akha don't use this word to describe people, this is the first time it's been applied to me. *Beautiful.*

"My mother liked you because she saw you as hardworking and honest. Please forgive me for my lies. I promise they won't happen again."

I have to bite my lips to hold back my emotions. He's been keeping secrets, but they've come from a place of goodness and kindness, while mine . . . How could I have said yes to him when I don't deserve him? I bow my head, and let the tears come. He pulls me into his arms, probably believing I am overcome by happiness. I lay my head against the softness of his sweater. I feel the warmth of his body and the beat of his heart. For a few seconds, I allow myself to relish what might have been. Then I make myself pull away. I cannot go into marriage with lies and secrets as my only dowry.

"I love you," I say, "and I would love to marry you, but you may not want to marry me when you know the truth about me."

"Nothing you could say would make me think less of you."

"You haven't heard my story yet."

We sit on the couch, facing each other. Jin holds my hands, and I hesitantly begin to speak. I start with the easiest and least damning sin I've committed: that I broke a promise to my a-ma by selling leaves from my grove which should only be used for medicinal purposes and shouldn't have gone to *any* man, especially someone like Mr. Huang. Jin easily accepts this, saying, "You were young and poor. You made a mistake. And it sounds like the mother tree was not permanently damaged." Next, I tell Jin about being married and widowed. His eyes widen with each new detail. When I get to the end, he takes time to compose his response. "I've never been married," he says at last, "but would it be fair for me to look into your eyes and deny that I've been with other women before you? If I'd grown up on your mountain, I would have been married too."

"Whatever happens next," I say, "I want you to know that I'll always think of you as an honorable man." He squeezes my hands, giving me strength. "Before San-pa and I were married, I got pregnant. I didn't realize it until after he'd gone to Thailand, so he didn't know. I gave birth in secret and abandoned my daughter. By the time San-pa returned to Nannuo Mountain, she'd been adopted by a family in America."

Jin slowly releases my hands, stands, and crosses to the window.

He keeps his back to me, as though I no longer exist. I don't blame him. I sigh and get up to leave.

"Wait," he says, swiveling to me. Twin trails of tears trickle down his cheeks, which he roughly wipes away. "You're very brave, Li-yan. Far braver than I am. We both have secrets, but you had the courage to be honest with me." He visibly struggles. "One mistake can change the course of your life. You can never return to your original path or go back to the person you were."

"That's how I've always felt. If I hadn't taken a bite of San-pa's pancake. If I'd only listened to A-ma when she said she didn't want me to see him. If I hadn't let false ideas of the future compel me to sell leaves to Mr. Huang— "

"But nothing you did resulted in death." He pauses to make sure he has my full attention. "I'm responsible for my father's."

"How can you say that?" I ask, bewildered. "Your father died of pneumonia. You were a child when he got sick— "

"Perhaps you can understand a little of what it was like for my parents. They went from Guangzhou to a village in Anhui province called Moon Pond. Such a pretty name, but it held only darkness. I was born there, and we lived in a one-room shack made from mud bricks. It was more miserable and wretched than anything I've seen in your village."

That stings, especially since he didn't see Spring Well before all the changes. But this is not the time to take offense.

"My parents lost their positions, clothing, papers, photographs, friends, everything," he goes on. "The only tokens from the past they carried with them were five of my father's philosophy books, which they kept hidden under the wood platform that served as our bed. My mother learned how to haul water, wash clothes by hand, and make soles for our shoes from whatever scraps of paper she could find. My father gathered night soil from different families and hoed it into the fields. My parents weakened from the physical demands of working under a merciless sun or being soaked to the bone during the monsoons. My earliest memories are of having dysentery from the bad water and poor sanitation. We were all sick." He takes a moment to ask, "What do you remember of the Cultural Revolution?"

"I was born not long after it ended," I answer softly. "Besides, we were peasants already. My family and all our neighbors had always lived that life. But I have a friend, Teacher Zhang. He was sent to Nannuo Mountain. He suffered—"

"Suffered," he echoes. "Suffering takes many forms. Hunger. Cold. Fear. Physical and psychological pain. The villagers were bad enough. They had opportunities each day to torment us. But sometimes a Red Guard unit would visit. Everyone was forced to gather together so that my parents could be publicly punished and humiliated. They endured numerous self-criticism sessions. I don't remember much about my father anymore, except that sometimes, late at night, I'd wake up and see him reading one of his books by the light of our oil lamp. He'd quickly close it, put it back in its hiding place, and say to me, 'You're only dreaming, Son. Go back to sleep now. Forget everything.'"

Jin falls into melancholy silence. I suspect where his story is going, which doesn't make it any easier to hear.

"The Red Guard came again just after my fifth birthday," he resumes at last. "They were so young, you know? They played with me. They gave me a piece of candy—the first I'd ever tasted. I thought they liked me. When they asked if my mother or father kept anything hidden, I eagerly volunteered what I knew. After that, they dragged my father from our home and made him kneel in broken glass. They tied his arms up and back into the airplane position. Then they beat him with switches. They tore every page out of his books and set them on fire. They made me stand right in front of him, so he would forever know who'd betrayed him."

"You were only five. Just a boy—"

"But what son does that?" he asks, tortured. "I broke his heart and his will to live or fight for us. The rest is as my mother told you. My father got pneumonia and died very quickly."

My heart aches for him. "Those were deviled times filled with very bad people," I say, trying to offer comfort. "You were a little boy, and you were tricked. Tragedies of this kind happened to people who were far older and with far more knowledge than you had. You can't blame yourself."

But of course he can, because I blame myself for so much too.

I take hold of his arms, and our eyes meet. What I'd always seen in them, I now recognize from looking in the mirror at my own reflection: pain and guilt.

"You said earlier that one mistake can change the path of your life forever," I say. "It sounds like it did for you. I *know* it did for me. But what if *this* is an opportunity to do something purposefully right? Won't that put us on an entirely new path? A good path? Maybe even a happy path? Will you still have me?"

My new life requires adapting to one surprise after another. The next day, Jin and I drive to the airport to pick up Ci-teh, who's agreed to leave her husband and daughters for a month to take care of my shop while I'm on my honeymoon. She's arranged to have the most recent batches of tea my family made, as well as several kilos of Pu'er from Laobanzhang, sent directly to Midnight Blossom. My impression, seeing her for the first time out of Spring Well Village? Chubby and *tu,* with her ill-fitting Western-style clothes and numerous overstuffed bags made of red, white, and blue plastic mesh hanging from her arms. Ci-teh catches the judgment in my eyes, so the first thing she says to me is "I'm the first person from Nannuo Mountain to fly on an airplane." Ours is a long and complicated friendship, and I'm beaming at the joy of it.

Next, we pick up Jin's mother and continue straight on to the marriage bureau. Ci-teh and I peel off to the ladies' room so I can change into my Akha wedding clothes and she can ask what feels like dozens of questions.

"Has your future husband tested the machete yet?"

The last time I heard that phrase was when the ruma asked it of San-pa as part of our wedding ritual. When I tell her no, her eyes go as wide as soup bowls.

"Don't they have a Flower Room in Guangzhou?" she asks.

No, but there are many equivalents where boys and girls, men and women, can be alone together for talking and kissing: bars, nightclubs, a friend's apartment. I apply lipstick so I don't have to answer the question.

"Then you must have stolen love in the forest by now," she presses, so nosy.

"Do you see forest around you?" I ask, starting to get irritated. "Besides, I already told you. He hasn't tested the machete."

Undaunted, Ci-teh changes the subject. "So how rich is he?"

"Rich enough to buy you an airplane ticket," I answer.

"I didn't need him to fly me here. I could have bought my own ticket," she brags. "My family now makes one hundred times what we did just five years ago. All because of Pu'er." She laughs, giddy, I suppose, at the craziness of the changes we've seen. But crowing about her own wealth serves to bring her back to her original subject. "Really, how rich is he? A millionaire? A billionaire?"

"I don't know, and it doesn't matter to me anyway." I've been reciting these phrases to myself the past twenty-four hours. In truth, I wouldn't mind having the answers, although a part of me is afraid of them.

"Would he invest in a business with me?"

As I put on my headdress, I meet my friend's eyes in the mirror. "Ci-teh, you already sell your teas through my shop. Are you hoping to compete with me?" I've kept the question light and teasing.

Ci-teh frowns at my reflection. I hope I haven't gone too far and insulted her. "Why aren't you having a Western wedding with a big white dress?" she asks, ignoring my question. "That's what I see in the magazines. That's what everyone wants."

I stare at myself in the mirror. I look young and unmarred by my experiences, which is both unsettling and a relief. The clothes remind me of all I've lost, but also gained, and all I'll need to forget . . . and remember. It feels strange to leave the ladies' room and walk down a public hallway wearing something that so marks me as an ethnic minority. I worry about Jin's reaction, but he lights up when he sees me. That he's happy makes me happier still. He holds my hand through the five-minute ceremony. Mrs. Chang dabs at her eyes with a tissue. Ci-teh's laughter feels as light as air. Jin can't stop smiling, and neither can I. Our banquet is small—just four people sharing a moment of supreme joy.

We drop my mother-in-law at her apartment. Alone in the backseat, Ci-teh chatters like she's had too many coffees, pointing excitedly at the skyscrapers, neon lights, and limousines. When we pull into the motor court of a hotel next to the Fangcun Tea Market where she'll stay—too hard to teach someone so *tu* how to use the subway or hail a taxi—she leans over the front seat to whisper in my ear. "Tell him to make a way down there first," she advises in Akha, as though I've never done the intercourse before.

An hour later, Jin and I are sitting on our veranda, overlooking the tree-lined pedestrian walkway outside our beautiful home, and drinking champagne. I excuse myself to change into a cotton nightgown I bought at a night market. Ready, I open the door into our bedroom. Jin has closed the shutters and lit candles.

"I'm not a girl anymore," I remind him.

He takes me in his arms. We don't steal love or do the intercourse. We make love.

Three days later, I'm in Beverly Hills, having dinner in a restaurant called Spago. I'm still struggling with how to use a knife and fork—which my husband finds supremely amusing—and worrying that the meal will make me sick. Everything is too rich and too heavy with cow: cow meat, cow cream, cow butter. And why can't the dishes be served all at once in the middle of the table to be shared by the two of us like a normal meal? Later, after the main course plates are removed, Wolfgang Puck himself comes to the table to shake Jin's hand and kiss me on both cheeks. He promises to send over a special dessert that isn't on the menu—a Grand Marnier soufflé. If I don't spend the night throwing up, I'll be happy. Every wife must adapt, but the food part has been hard for me. But the rest? *Wow!* I so like this American word. *Wow! Wow! Wow!*

We're staying at the Beverly Wilshire Hotel, which makes the King World look like a guesthouse. My husband took me shopping on Rodeo Drive, where he bought me new clothes, because, he said, "We don't want you to look fresh off the boat." I tried on clothes made with a quality of textiles—silk, cotton, and cashmere—I didn't know existed and fit me in a way I didn't think possible. Dior. Prada. Armani. He even took me to a store to buy new underwear and a nightgown so pretty I can't imagine sleeping in it, to which he whispered in my ear, "I don't expect you to *sleep* in it." I got a new haircut too. By the end of the first day—and I was completely jet-lagged, something tourists at the King World used to complain about—I looked like a different person. Jin couldn't stop grinning, or saying, "You're beautiful." I'm a married woman, and my life has been totally transformed.

But those are only outside things. Now, as we sit in this elegant restaurant, I *look* like I belong, but inside I feel out of place. Maybe it's the jet lag or the shock of encountering so many new things at once, but I feel myself beginning to spin with unwanted questions. Do I need to be changed this much by Jin for him to love me? Am I being as easily corrupted by his money as I was by Mr. Huang's offer to buy leaves from my grove? How rich is my husband anyway? Village rich? China rich? America rich? Self-doubt and distrust are a bad combination.

As we wait for the mysterious dessert to arrive, I gently ask Jin about his business. Without hesitation, he answers my questions, saying, "You need to know everything about me, just as I need to know everything about you." Some of what he tells me I already know. Jin was ten years old when he and his mother were allowed back to Guangzhou. His mother had a job, true, but they were allotted only a single unfurnished room in the worst of the faculty dormitories, which also served the most meager food.

"In the countryside, I'd learned to save everything I found, because we never knew when it would come in handy," he explains. "Nothing could go to waste. Not even a scrap of paper."

"I grew up the same way—"

"Which is why I love you." He pauses for me to take in the statement I'll never tire of hearing. Then, "So, as a boy newly arrived in the city, I began to collect paper trash, bundle it, and sell it to a recycling mill to earn extra money. It had to be completely under the table, because all enterprises were still state-owned."

"Was it dangerous?"

"Definitely! But you have to remember that our country's need for cardboard, lumber, and pulp was growing quickly. Where were factory owners going to get the materials when so many of our forests had been cut down during the Great Leap Forward?"

With the money he earned, he was able to buy necessities and extra food. He kept up with his classwork too. Armed with good test results, he got into a local college, where he studied engineering.

"Engineering?" How could I not know even *that*?

"All through those years," he continues, "I kept my little business, hiring kids like me, who were poor and hungry, to collect discarded paper and cardboard. I would have been sent to labor camp if I'd been caught, but I had to do what I could to help improve my mother's life after what I'd done." His eyes flit off to the side for a moment, then return to me. "Besides, when you're desperate, you'll do anything to make life easier, even if it's dangerous."

When he graduated, his education and his own connections got him a job at the recycling mill, but still he kept his side business. The kids who collected paper grew up, moved on, and were replaced by new kids who were in such sad circumstances that they too risked being arrested for collecting and selling paper to him.

"When Deng Xiaoping began his economic reforms in the mid-nineties," he continues, "I was eager to participate, and I already had my own business. I easily got an EB-5 visa to come here under the U.S.'s Immigrant Investor Program. What better place to look for trash than in America—the land of consumption and waste?"

His laughter booms through the restaurant. The people at the next table glance in our direction. I blush and stare down at the tablecloth. Will I ever feel comfortable here?

"Of course, Zhang Yin had a head start. Have you heard of her?" When I shake my head, he explains. "She's the queen of cardboard and the richest person in China. She's the second richest self-made woman in the world, after Oprah." (I have no idea who that is, but no matter.) "When I met Zhang Yin, she said, 'Other people see scrap paper as garbage. You and I see it as a forest of trees to be utilized.' I was only too happy to sell to her. I now send container ships filled with trash across the sea to China, where her Nine Dragons Paper Holdings turns it into cardboard. Goods are placed in those boxes, loaded onto other shipping containers, and sent right back to America to become trash again. The cycle continues day after day, and as Deng Xiaoping predicted, we've gotten rich. You'd be too modest to ask me directly, so I'll tell you. If Zhang Yin is the queen of cardboard, then maybe I'm her two-hundredth princeling."

I can't begin to untangle in my head just what a two-hundredth princeling might mean.

When dessert arrives, Jin abruptly switches subjects. "I want to take you all across this country to see places for yourself, but do you already have an idea about where you might want to live?"

"*Live?*"

"We should buy a house here too," he says matter-of-factly. "I already have a small house in Monterey Park—"

"A house *here*?" He needs to stop surprising me . . . "Why aren't we staying there now?"

"Because this is our honeymoon! Later, I want us to have a new house, where we can start fresh together." He hesitates before continuing. "But that's not the only reason. You never know what can happen in China. *Dog today; cat tomorrow*. As entrepreneurs, we need to think about how to protect our money." *We.* I like how he includes me as an equal. "So what can we do? Buy jewels and gold? Buy a hotel? Buy art? Buy wine? I've done a little of all that."

"You *own* a hotel?" I need to break this habit of repeating what he says.

"Half the Chinese I know own hotels here."

But that can't possibly be right.

"I want to make you happy," he goes on. "I want you to *feel* beautiful. I want us to have a glorious life together."

When he puts it that way . . . *Wow!* I'm swept up. It's very easy to be loved this way. I could even eat that dessert again too.

Mr. Kelly's fifth-grade American history unit: Choose a person or event from the Revolutionary War to write about. Divide your report into three sections: background, the person or event, and how this person or event continues to have an impact on you, America, and/or global life today. Due January 10, 2007.

The Boston Tea Party
by
Haley Davis

Background

China is the birthplace of tea. The botanical name for tea is *Camellia sinensis*. It is an evergreen plant. In 782, during the Tang dynasty, China put the first tax on tea. In history, many other countries have placed taxes on tea. In the ninth century, bricks of tea began to be used as money. Some people thought this was better than gold or silver, because if you were starving, you could eat it. In the sixteenth century, tea was introduced to Portuguese priests and merchants traveling in China.

In 1650, the Dutch brought tea to New Amsterdam (what is now New York City) on sailing ships. When England acquired the colony, they discovered that the small settlement drank more tea than all of England put together! The colonists didn't have very much to eat and drink, and they really liked tea, but in England tea was only for rich people. In 1698, the British Parliament gave the East India Company a monopoly on tea importation. Even though there was a monopoly, smugglers brought tea to the colonies at a much cheaper price. On May 10, 1773, Parliament passed the Tea Act, which was supposed to help the English government pay for its wars with France and help the East India Company survive. People said that the East India Company would last forever because it was so big and strong, but actually it was failing. (My dad says that today we would call what happened a bailout.) Now the Thirteen Colonies and the colonists had to pay a big tax on top of buying their tea.

The Boston Tea Party
The colonists didn't want taxation without representation. Their motto was "Anything but British tea." They boycotted the taxed tea. It became the symbol of rebellion. New York and Philadelphia sent tea ships back to London. In Charleston, tea was left on the dock to rot. In Boston, the colonists wouldn't let three ships unload their tea. On December 16, 1773, some colonists dressed up like Native Americans, climbed on the ships, chopped open 340 chests of Chinese tea with tomahawks, and threw the contents into Boston Harbor. The tea weighed 90,000 pounds. In today's money, the value would be one million dollars. Founding Father John Adams called the event "the Destruction of the Tea in Boston." Today we call it the Boston Tea Party.

England got really mad and enacted the Coercive Acts. The colonists called them the Intolerable Acts. The laws punished the people in Boston by ending all commerce and closing the harbor until the bill for the lost tea was paid. They punished the state of Massachusetts by abolishing self-government. Now all Thirteen Colonies got mad. There were tea parties in other harbors. In September 1774, the colonists met at the First Continental Congress. They wanted to fight back. Seven months later, the Revolutionary War began.

How the Boston Tea Party Affects Me Today
For a very long time, the United States, England, and other countries could only buy tea from China. Emperors in China said that anyone who tried to take a tea seed or plant out of the country would have his head cut off. Finally, the British people stole some plants and took them to India. One of the tea gardens there was started by Sir Thomas Lipton, a grocery store owner. My grandma and grandpa still drink Lipton tea.

Tea is the second most popular drink in the world after

water. The biggest tea-growing countries are China, India, and Kenya. Overall, China is the biggest tea-drinking country, but the largest per capita countries for tea drinking are Turkey, Ireland, and the United Kingdom. In Turkey, they consume seven pounds of tea leaves a year per person. Per capita means that every person in Turkey, even if they are babies, drinks ten cups of tea a day. The United States is the sixty-ninth per capita tea-drinking country. Americans only drink twelve ounces of tea leaves a year per person. (Americans aren't in the top ten countries for coffee drinkers either.) My mom and dad like coffee, but they drink tea when we go to a Chinese or Japanese restaurant. Sometimes they let me have tea with sugar for a special treat, but not very often because I get too excited and can't go to sleep. We may not drink tea that much in the United States, but it is still very important around the world.

TALL TREES CATCH MUCH WIND

The day after our dinner at Spago, I insist—yes, *insist*—that we visit Jin's house in Monterey Park. He'd called it a "small house." It's larger than anything I've lived in, and it has to be larger than anything he lived in growing up too. The day after that, we cancel the rest of our trip, check out of the hotel, and move into the house. He drives me to the market, and everyone there is Chinese. That night, I make Jin dinner for the first time: pork belly braised in chilies, *ong choy* with preserved tofu, scrambled egg with tomato, and rice. For the next week, we leave the house only to go shopping. And then we go home, lock the door, make love, eat, watch the Mandarin-language channels to see what's happening in China, sleep, and repeat it all over again the next day.

In the second week, he insists—yes, *insists,* and I, as Wife-of-Jin, go along—that we look for a new house. As we crisscross the San Gabriel Valley, I begin to understand the differences between the neighborhoods of Arcadia, Rosemead, Monterey Park, South Pasadena, and, of course, San Gabriel. Everything we look at seems grander than I could have imagined. My favorite, though, is a 1920s one-bedroom bungalow—cozy, and perfect for the two of us.

"But we're going to need more than one bedroom!" Jin exclaims. Then he frowns as he realizes we've never spoken about children. "I hope you want children."

Sun and Moon! How can he know how much this has been in my mind? On our first day here, when we were walking down

Rodeo Drive, I saw an older man and woman—white—with a girl with long black hair walking between them, holding their hands. *Yan-yeh? Could it be?* As Jin and I passed them, I turned back to look. That girl had to have been adopted, but she was clearly Han majority and not Akha. After that, I stayed alert, searching always for a white mother or father or both with a girl with black hair, who'll be turning twelve later this year. Would she be Akha small? Or would her lifetime of American food have given her extra height? I've spotted girls here and there: too old, too young, nose too flat, breasts too big. Besides, my daughter could be anywhere in this big country. She could be in New York City. She could be living with a cowboy family on a ranch. She could be in Alaska or Hawaii. Knowing I'll never find her—and loving Jin as much as I do—has stirred a desire in me to have a baby. But it's only now as Jin asks the question that I wonder how the One Child policy will apply to us. As an ethnic minority, I could have multiple children. Jin, as a member of the Han majority, will be allotted one child.

"Why worry about the rules?" he asks. "We can have as many children as we want, if they're born in America. And they'll be American citizens too. And even if we have them in China, what will the authorities do to us? Make us pay a ten-thousand-dollar fine? We aren't peasants. We can afford *many* children."

We get to work making a baby that afternoon. I sense old emotions and traditions bubbling to the surface. I don't say this to Jin—he might think me too backward—but inside I call to the three child-maker spirits that live in every woman to release my water from the lake of children so I'll become pregnant quickly.

Perhaps Jin is motivated by a similar urge, because by the end of the third week, he's found our new house: a pretty four-bedroom Spanish-style home on a street planted with jacaranda trees in Arcadia. For the first time, I observe my husband as a businessman. He's a tough negotiator, and honestly, I don't know what all the things he talks about are: deeds of trust, CC & Rs, escrows, title searches, insurance—none of which we have in China. No matter. It turns out that if you do an all-cash deal, you can buy a house very quickly.

Jin calls his mother to tell her we won't be home before Chinese

New Year after all. When I phone Ci-teh and explain the change in plans, she says, "I was hoping to see you soon so we could catch up. I miss you." Before I can respond, she hurries on. "That's okay. I'll make us rich instead." I try to suggest that she keep her aspirations modest. "It's only tea," I caution. When she comes back with "It's so much more than that to me," I know I've left my shop with the exact right person.

We cancel our flight back to China and move into our house. The myrtlewood-paneled library on the ground floor doubles as Jin's office, and I also have a room—what the agent called a solarium—where I have a desk, phone, computer, fax line, and Internet connection. I talk to Ci-teh nearly every day.

"These weeks leading up to the holiday have been very busy with shoppers buying hostess gifts," she gushes. "I've sold all the tea from Laobanzhang and have ordered more."

It's impressive, but I have to ask: "Don't you miss Law-ba and the girls?"

"Not one bit!"

I hope she's telling me the truth, because having her at Midnight Blossom allows me to focus on my husband and my home.

One week later, on February 18, Chinese New Year arrives. We Akha have our own cycles and our own new year, so I always ignored the Han majority's celebrations when I was in Kunming and Guangzhou. "Now that I'm married to a Han majority man," I confide to Ci-teh one night on the phone, "I want to give him a proper holiday. To figure out how to do that, I've been watching the pre–Year of the Pig holiday shows on TV and looking at the other houses on our street to see how they're decorated."

"You should also spy on what women buy in the shops," Ci-teh advises.

I do exactly that and purchase couplets to hang on either side of our front door and a ceramic pig painted gold and tied with a red ribbon to set on our dining table. Jin and I put together a small altar to commemorate his ancestors. We're only two people and don't have family and friends to celebrate with, but a neighbor, Rosie Ng, invites us to join her family for dinner at one of the big Hong Kong–style restaurants on Valley Boulevard in Monterey Park.

Jin and I settle into a routine. A-ma has sent tea from Nannuo and I've had Ci-teh mail a few special teas from my shop, so we now start the day sitting at a small table by the window that overlooks the back garden, sipping golden liquid from small cups, and drawing inspiration from the old aphorism *An hour spent drinking tea is the hour when the prince and the peasant share thoughts and ready themselves for the commonalities and woes of their separate lives.* This allows the rest of the day to unfold in a relaxed manner, with no worries or anxieties. Around noon, Rosie picks me up, and we go grocery shopping. Jin and I take walks together in the afternoons. After dinner, we make our calls to China. It's gratifying to know that my shop has done so well in my absence. Well? I mean great! Ci-teh has done an impressive job and taken advantage of every opportunity.

"Prices for Pu'er have skyrocketed," she tells me. "In March, during the ten days of tea picking, thousands upon thousands of traders, connoisseurs, and journalists from all around the world climbed the tea mountains of Yunnan. Some people even brought old cakes of tea with them. They said they were on a 'pilgrimage to the place of origin.' "

She sounds like a completely different person, but everything she's said is true. I saw it on TV. Big crowds stepping from buses, elbowing each other to have a chance to try out killing the green and shouting ever-soaring prices in the faces of bewildered growers. Teacher Zhang sent word that tea from wild forest trees was the most popular. Third Brother sold a single kilo of raw tea from one of his old trees to a dealer for 570 yuan, the equivalent of seventy-five dollars!

I'll always have tea from Nannuo in my shop, because I still believe what Tea Master Sun told me—that one day people will prize it as much as, if not more than, the king and queen of teas—but I agree to let Ci-teh send her husband to Laobanzhang to buy more product. Later in the week, Ci-teh calls to give her report.

"Don't be mad, but he spent a lot."

"How much?"

"Eight hundred yuan a kilo—"

"No!"

"Listen. I told him to do it, and it turned out to be a good deal, because the next day the price jumped to twelve hundred a kilo."

"*Waaa!*"

"Don't worry. I can sell those teas for even more money."

There's only one thing left to say. "You're clearly a much better businesswoman than I am, because if I'd been there I'd probably be thinking too much about flavor, aroma, and provenance instead of higher profits. Thank you."

"No. Thank you."

I may have misjudged Ci-teh when she landed in Guangzhou, but now I'm grateful for her cleverness and fortitude.

When Rosie's golden retriever somehow manages to get up on the roof of her home, Jin and I meet several other neighbors—all Han majority Chinese. We stand on the sidewalk to laugh and point as Rosie's husband runs a ladder to the roof to rescue the animal. Tea is poured. Snacks are shared. We gather on the street another time when the limb of a jacaranda snaps and closes the road until Street Maintenance comes and clears it away. At American Easter, Rosie hosts an egg hunt for children in the neighborhood. We're invited even though we don't have a baby. When Rosie drops her son's basket and several of the hard-boiled eggs break open, her relaxed attitude about the mess relieves my shyness about being an outsider. I help her clean up the eggs and sweets called jelly beans and Peeps. She's grateful—and friendly. By the end of the day, she's given me a Western-style name: Tina. Jin likes it, and the neighbors pick it up in days. I practice saying my name over and over again in the same way I once memorized English phrases at my trade school: Tina Chang, Tina Chang, Tina Chang.

Every moment of every day seems perfect, except I don't come to a head. Getting pregnant isn't so easy when you're trying. The more weeks that pass, the more I seek answers in Akha beliefs. Although I never once dreamed of water when I was pregnant with Yan-yeh, I go to sleep every night, hoping I'll dream of rushing water, which will announce that a baby has been released from the baby-making lake. Jin knows me very well already, so whenever he sees me leave the bathroom looking worried, he reminds me that we've only been married four months. His words are meant to be reassuring, but they make me even more anxious because they let me know he's been counting too.

At the beginning of May, Rosie tells me about a Mandarin-speaking doctor—an ob-gyn—but before I can make an appointment two unfathomable things happen. First, an all-time record is set when four hundred grams of *maocha—raw* Pu'er—sell at auction for 400,000 yuan. Nearly $53,000! I'm thinking I may end up as rich as my husband in my own right—kidding, but still fun to fantasize about—when a Chinese-language channel airs a special called *The Bubble of Pu'er Is Broken,* which I watch in our living room as Jin naps on the couch next to me.

The show begins in the Fangcun Tea Market with the reporter claiming that Pu'er prices are inflated. At first, I tell myself that this isn't the worst criticism. In fact, something like this might have even been expected. After all, *Tall trees catch much wind* and *The bird that stands out is easily shot*. Then the show takes an even darker turn.

"Not only are the prices inflated but many teas claiming to be Pu'er are fakes," the reporter says. "These would include ninety percent of tea bought in Yiwu—the so-called home of the queen of Pu'er. It's been labeled as 'authentic forest tea' but is actually just terrace tea from elsewhere."

Another accusation has to do with Pu'er from the Laobanzhang area. The camera follows the reporter as he walks a few meters and then plants himself directly in front of Midnight Blossom. My stomach tightens. I shake Jin awake. He groggily sits up as the reporter says, "The Fangcun Tea Market alone claims to have five thousand tons of Laobanzhang tea, yet the entire village harvests only fifty tons a year. That means that the vast majority of Laobanzhang Pu'er in the Fangcun Market is fake."

I clasp a hand around my throat, hoping to steady my voice. "Ci-teh has been selling Pu'er from Laobanzhang. She even had her husband buy more recently. She wouldn't have sold counterfeit tea, would she?"

"No, she wouldn't. She's your friend . . ."

"Other teas from other villages also declared Pu'er are not," the reporter continues. "Many of the teas being sold as naturally aged have been artificially fermented. Many of the health claims are false as well. Contrary to popular opinion, some scientists have suggested that drinking artificially fermented Pu'er can *cause* cancer . . ."

With each new revelation, another wave of panic washes over me. Throughout the special, proprietors try to hide their faces from the camera. Some are successful, but others spit out denials in high-pitched angry tones, while shaking their fists at the camera. Nothing, however, can hide the names of shops or stands. Midnight Blossom. The conclusion—and it's one I've come to myself—is that my business must be one of the worst offenders.

I repeatedly call the shop and Ci-teh's cellphone but never get an answer.

"What am I going to do?" I ask my husband.

Jin tries to sound unfazed. "Maybe the show won't mean anything. People are watching now, but they'll forget about it tomorrow." After a pause, he asks, "Wouldn't Ci-teh call if there's a problem?"

I ponder the idea, playing it out in my head. "A better question might be why she hasn't called already." I point to the screen. "You can see my whole shop, but where is *she*?"

Jin's mouth tightens into a grim line. Without another word, he goes to his computer and begins looking for flights.

Walking into the tea market two days later is like entering a tomb. The lights are dim, as usual, but the aisles are completely empty of people and goods, and many of the shops have already been vacated. We turn onto the corridor that leads to Midnight Blossom. Someone sits on the floor outside the shop, legs stretched before him. He jumps to his feet as I approach. It's Xian-rong.

"I didn't know how to reach you," he sputters. "I've been asking Ci-teh for your contact information for weeks, but she wouldn't give it to me."

I peer through the window. Large bags of loose tea rest open on the floor and the shelves have their displays of tea cakes, but my shop still manages to look ghostly.

"My father and I tried the hotel where you first went on your honeymoon—"

"So long ago?"

He's only a teenager, but his eyes are hollow with worry. I glance at Jin. He's set his face into an impenetrable mask. Inside, I feel as though everything I've worked for is being swept down a river. I fumble with my keys and unlock the door. Wordlessly, the boy slips behind the table. Jin and I sit opposite him. I feel strangely detached. It's my shop, but Xian-rong is in charge. He shows me a tea cake. The rice paper is printed with the distinctive Laobanzhang label, with a date and a stamp of authenticity.

"You can't fake that," I say.

"Someone must have sold her unused wrappers," Xian-rong replies.

He opens the cake, uses a pick to break apart the leaves, puts a few of them into a little dish, and hands them to me to smell. The odor is of dirt and mildew, but that doesn't necessarily mean that what Ci-teh bought—and what my shop has been selling—is counterfeit. Irrepressible hope flickers from deep inside. Maybe this Laobanzhang Pu'er is of minor quality, picked at the end of the year or during the monsoon. He brews the tea and pours it. The smell of jungle rot—the telltale giveaway of a badly artificially fermented Pu'er—assaults my senses. My worst suspicions are confirmed.

"Where is she?" I ask.

"They started doing interviews about ten days ago," Xian-rong answers. "She left the next day."

"Did she fly back to Yunnan?" The idea that Ci-teh could manage to buy a ticket and get to the airport on her own, even after what I now know, seems impossible, beyond her.

Xian-rong lifts his shoulders in response. After a moment, he says, "Nannuo Mountain is her home—"

"And her husband and children are there."

"I never thought an Ahka could be so devious," he adds.

I can't believe it either.

What happens over the next couple of days is worse than my worst imaginings. The world market for Pu'er collapses, falling in value by half. It's estimated that dealers like me have between one hundred and three hundred tons of Pu'er in storage that they'll now be unable to sell. In Guangzhou, reports reveal that it would take every single resident of the city drinking Pu'er every day for eight years to deplete the excess stock. Most damning, *New Generations Magazine* reports that the number of people in China speculating on Pu'er has reached 30 million, and that dealers, bankers, and government officials have all worked together to cheat them. This cascade of news causes several more emporiums in the tea market to go belly-up. I close mine too, never once having met my partners. Nearly all my stock goes into trash bins. My three tea men, sensing a unique opportunity, buy my best teas at rock-bottom prices with plans to store them until the value rises again to that of gold. "You'll make even me rich one day," Mr. Lin tells me. I need to bite the insides of my cheeks to keep from weeping.

Jin and I retreat to Shamian Island. When he's asleep or out, I go into the bathroom, lock the door, and sob. I'm nearly torn apart by sadness, regret, and guilt. I'm Akha, but in my new and pretty life—one seemingly removed from the danger of spirits—I ignored signs that I should have instantly recognized as bad omens: the dog who mysteriously mounted Rosie's roof, the tree limb that blocked our street, the cracked hard-boiled eggs. I didn't pay attention. I was so happy . . .

My life is not over, however. I have a wealthy husband so I won't be poor again, but back home my a-ba and brothers—and probably everyone in Spring Well Village—who were already in debt after the building expenses required by the Quality Safety Standard, have lost their income. Will everyone be thrown back to living hand to mouth? My mind spirals with worry but also suspicion. Is the money Ci-teh had been depositing my cut for selling the fake Pu'er? Could my family and others in Spring Well be a part of this? Again and again, I circle back to Ci-teh. How could she have done this to me?

When I tell Jin that I need to go home for a few days, he agrees, saying, "I'll come with you. Maybe I can help." We take a flight to Kunming, and then on to Jinghong. It's evening, pouring rain, and very hot and humid when we step off the plane. Jin hires a driver to take us to a small hotel for tea dealers and collectors in Menghai. "It's an easy drive to your village—only about an hour and a half," Jin explains. "We can stay in the hotel in town, have creature comforts, and go back and forth to your village as needed." That's not how I remember getting in and out of Spring Well, but he seems very sure. The driver loads our bags in the trunk, Jin and I get in the backseat, and then we're on our way.

In the three years since I was last here, the changes are dramatic. The road from Jinghong to Menghai is jammed with trucks, tractors, buses, and private cars. The street itself has been paved and the berms planted with palm trees, hibiscus, and bougainvillea. Hawkers sidle through the traffic selling grilled meats and soda pop. We pass billboards advertising motor scooters, a transmission repair garage, and baby formula.

We turn onto Menghai's main street, illuminated by the yellow glow of overhead lamps. My breath catches as I'm thrown back to the night I walked along this road, searching for a place to hide before I abandoned my baby. As we near the Social Welfare Institute, I grip the piece of plastic that edges the passenger window. On the steps, someone sleeps in the rain under a broken-down cardboard box. Jin puts an arm around my shoulders and pulls me to him. I bury my face in his shirt. Why is this hitting me harder than the times I passed through when I was waiting to hear if I'd gotten into the tea college? Ever since I left this place, my life has been one of *up, up, up.* I'm married to a kind man, whom I love deeply. We have two homes—an idea inconceivable even a year ago. I'm so very lucky, but I'll never escape the regrets I have for leaving my daughter on this very street. Ci-teh's betrayal has complicated and multiplied my emotions. My insides are raw with pain.

We check in to the hotel. Our room has a squat toilet. The promised hot water is lukewarm, and our bath towels aren't a millimeter larger than kitchen towels. Jin paces, looking worried. He wants to talk. I don't. When he gets in bed, I roll away from him. He puts a hand on my hip to comfort me, but I don't acknowledge him. I'm so down—my business failed, my family and village back on the path to poverty, all the memories this town brings up about Yan-yeh—and now I'm an ungrateful wife. My jet lag is terrible and my emotions are jumbled, but I can't fall asleep. The mattress is too hard, the rain batters the window like knocking spirits, and my mind is awash in reminiscences. How could I have thought that the happiness I've felt with Jin these past months could ever erase who I am or what I've done?

Morning comes, and the rain still pours down. In the dining room, Jin orders tea and spicy noodle soup. I rinse our eating utensils with the hot tea to kill germs. Our napkins are lengths of toilet paper.

"If you don't want to talk to me," Jin says into the bleak silence, "you don't have to, but I hope you'll listen to what I have to say to you. We both know that wealth, privilege, hard work, and luck do not heal a heart, nor can they save us from sadness, loneliness, or guilt. Before we go to your village, let's visit the orphanage."

I shake my head. "No, we should go to Spring Well right away. We've come so far, and I have to make sure—"

"All that can wait another hour or so—"

"I have to go home," I plead. "Please, Jin."

The muscles in his jaw tighten as he considers his response. Finally, he says, "We'll go to Spring Well first, but sometime while we're here, we're going to the orphanage. You're in a different position now than you were when you went there with your baby's father. And you have me."

Despite promises that this is now an easy drive, the torrential rain has turned the unpaved road into slippery muck. We get stuck in the mud, tires spinning, the driver cursing. Jin and I get out and fill the sludge with stones and thatch. The tires catch, we get back in the car, and we're on our way. But it's not far before we get bogged down again. Then more skidding and shimmying. On a particularly steep curve, the car slides to the edge of the precipice. I scream as one tire slips out into space. For a moment, we sit absolutely still, desperately hoping the other three tires hold. Carefully, we all get out of the car. The driver moans and groans about his most prized possession, Jin promises to buy him another car if this one goes over the cliff, and I feel as sick to my stomach as when I left Nannuo Mountain in the back of the tea delivery truck.

We're grateful to be alive, but we're three drenched cats, soaked clean through, muddy, indignant—and very funny to look at. How do I know? Because the road is busy, although no one but us would be fool enough to drive an automobile or motorcycle in this weather. But even in the misery of the monsoon season, farmers have plots to work, mothers and their babies go visiting, and children have school to attend. We're a hilarious diversion. At last, a tractor rumbles up the road. Jin flags down the driver, and I speak to him in our local dialect. A few minutes later, Jin and I climb on the back of the tractor and hang on to the rain-slick steel. Our driver remains with his car with promises that we'll send the tractor back to help him.

A half hour later, we come to another obstacle. A portion of the road has washed out. Jin and I decide to walk the last few kilometers. At least the rain is warm. We pass through Bamboo Forest Village and turn onto the trail that will lead home. To our right, on the construction site I remember from my last visit, rises something I never thought I'd see on any tea mountain: a villa as huge as the ones Jin and I used to see outside Guangzhou. It has a tile roof, large patios extended on massive retaining walls, and bright lights blazing from every window on this dark and rainy day.

I peel off onto a smaller path. Jin follows behind me. We each have to catch ourselves several times from falling down the slippery embankment. Soon we pass through Spring Well's spirit gate. The track that divides the two sides of the village is deserted and dismal. Dogs and chickens have found shelter under the remaining bamboo and thatch houses. The gray brick and stucco structures look bleak, already old somehow. Rain streams down the glass panes of the tea-drying sheds. An odiferous smell seeps from them. Yes, they're fermenting tea here.

Jin veers toward my family's new home. Not me. I go straight to Ci-teh's house. The door is open, and I enter without announcing myself. Ci-teh sits alone at a table with a cup of tea and a pile of papers before her. She's dressed in the same outfit she wore to fly to Guangzhou for my wedding. Rain batters the roof but otherwise I hear only echoes of emptiness. It's just the two of us.

"I wondered how long it would take you to get here," she says, not even bothering to look up.

Passed class note from Haley to Jade, May 18, 2007

Jade,

Why are you and Jasmine being mean to me? You won't even look at me in class, but I see you passing notes with Jasmine. You said you, Jasmine, and I would go to Old Town together and hang out next weekend. You said we'd all buy matching outfits so we could be samesies. You said we should ask our moms and dads for Tamagotchis for sixth-grade graduation presents next year, so we could take care of them together.

You said I was fresh off the boat, because I wasn't born here like you. I said Jasmine wasn't born here, and you said it didn't matter because her parents are real Chinese, not like mine. All three of us look Chinese, and you know it. You and I have been best friends since kindergarten. When we got into Westridge School in fourth grade, you said we would always be best friends. At our sleepover, you said you and I were like twins. You're a big fat liar.

And I'm not a midget. I'm not a dwarf either. You are the meanest person ever.

Haley

ONE LONG CHAIN OF LIFE

Ci-teh stares at me coolly. She looks as *tu* as ever, but for the first time I see her differently. "You've always underestimated me," she says. "Ever since we were girls, you acted like you were smarter than I am."

"And you were richer, but I thought we were friends."

"You know nothing, Li-yan—"

She's interrupted by the spirit priest's shouts.

"Ci-teh! Li-yan! Everyone! Come out!"

Akha Law wouldn't allow me to confront Ci-teh alone, but I'd hoped for a little private time with her. Ci-teh nods. She slips on a rain jacket, steps outside, and opens an umbrella. I follow behind her. As wet as I am, I'm grateful for the constant washing of the rain. Beside us, in the mud, stand the ruma and the nima, my a-ma and a-ba, my three brothers, their wives, and all their children, and everyone else who lives in Spring Well. Some are dressed in Western-style clothes and, like Ci-teh, have umbrellas. Others—A-ma and A-ba included—wear their capes made of leaves. The ruma and the nima haven't donned their ceremonial garments, although the ruma has brought his staff. I glance at my husband, who doesn't understand Akha. He's going to have to follow along solely by body language and mood. That realization saps some of my strength.

"Whatever you have to say to each other needs to be said in

front of everyone," the ruma begins, "because your actions have tipped the forest and all who live in it out of balance."

"I've done nothing wrong," I object.

Ci-teh points a finger at me. "She's done everything wrong."

"That's not—"

Ci-teh interrupts. "She will accuse us of making counterfeit tea. But we made artificially fermented tea like Mr. Huang showed us so many years ago."

I put up a hand to stop her from speaking. "Please don't put words in my mouth. There's nothing wrong with fermenting leaves as long as you do it correctly and make a good product. That's what Laobanzhang did and what you used to send to me. But to put a label on inferior tea made in Spring Well, say it's from Laobanzhang, and sell it *as a fake* to customers at an inflated price . . . while I'm away. And now you blame me?"

Ci-teh waves off the suggestion. "Everyone's been doing it, not just our village."

"Yes, plenty of villages have made false products," I reply, "but that doesn't make it right. We're Akha. We don't deceive people."

"Li-yan," a man calls out, "not everyone did what she wanted."

"We turned down her request too," the woman next to him adds.

"Our family refused to sell our *maocha* or lease our land to her," First Brother says, and several other heads bob to let me know they too held out.

I knew that Ci-teh had been subleasing land, but I didn't know how widespread it was.

"If Li-yan hadn't asked us to send an unreasonable amount of tea to her shop," Ci-teh says, "then we wouldn't have done what we needed to do to fill her demand. She just wanted to get rich!"

I wish it hadn't come to this, but I'm seeing something new about Ci-teh. She's savvy and selfish. I hope I can find the girl inside her who I used to know.

"Ci-teh," I say, touching her arm. "You know that's not what happened. I trusted you, my oldest friend, to help me. We have something valuable to sell, but you corrupted that."

She pulls away just as someone in the crowd shouts, "Who are you to tell us how to do business?"

People murmur. I worry they don't trust me.

"We've *all* benefited from the popularity of Pu'er," I say. "I tried to share my good fortune with you—"

"She's an outsider," Ci-teh tells them, defiant.

"Yes, I've lived outside, but answer me this: How much did she pay for your artificially fermented tea that you then wrapped in counterfeit paper, knowing your finished product was also not from Laobanzhang?"

A faceless voice reveals "Two thousand yuan a kilo."

"A lot of money. But do you know what she told me she paid the farmers in Laobanzhang? Three thousand yuan. At the very least, she was stealing one thousand yuan from me per kilo of the fake Pu'er. As we stand together now, only one person knows how much she asked customers to pay for that same tea. Ten, twenty, fifty times what she paid you?"

The grumbling begins again, but this time I sense the tide turning.

"Ci-teh's made a lot of money by acting against Akha Law," I press on. "*I* made a lot of money too. Your lives have been boosted as well. New houses. Electricity. Motorbikes. We can each take some responsibility. But these fakes have caught up to *all* of us. Outside, the price of Pu'er has fallen by half and is continuing to tumble."

"It can't be true."

"How can we trust *you*?"

"You can't," Ci-teh jumps in. "We have a ton or more of fermenting tea in our sheds. Think about that. Tomorrow she'll be gone, but I guarantee I'll pay you one thousand yuan per kilo."

That's half what she previously paid but still the equivalent of a little over $130,000 for Spring Well's ton of tea at today's exchange rate. That translates to around $3,250 for each of the village's forty households, and that doesn't include teas made from the lesser pickings throughout the year. I remember when my family was lucky to earn 200 yuan a month—$300 a year—and we were thankful for it.

"If everyone wants to make fermented tea," I say, "then let's do it the right way. I'll pay you well—maybe not one thousand yuan to start, but we could build back to that and higher. Let's never again try to pass off our tea as something it isn't—"

"I've promised to sublease land from every family here," Ci-teh interrupts. "Let's say what she's told you about the price of Pu'er is true, then your tea trees and the land under them have no value. I want to help you. Don't let an outsider who's been influenced by bad spirits trick you."

"Do you realize what she's doing?" I ask Spring Well's families. "She's trying to steal your land!"

"I'm not stealing," she answers. "I'm subleasing. I'm volunteering to take responsibility for every lease until the next renewal of the Thirty Years No Change policy."

"You're trying to become a landowner!" It's the worst accusation I could make.

I search out Jin. He gives me a subtle nod. *Say it. Go for it. You're strong.*

"Your family was always better off than others in Spring Well," I say, "but now you would take the leases of every family here? At the bottom of the market? Betting that the price of tea will come back?"

She laughs derisively. "You don't know a thing about it. I've decided to tear out the tea trees once and for all. I'm going to help the people convert their land to rubber and coffee."

"But we're at too high an elevation to grow rubber! And it destroys everything around it. As for coffee—"

"Starbucks and Nestlé have already approached me," she says smugly. "Everyone here will make money, because the worldwide demand for coffee—"

"You'd deprive the people of the one thing they have—land with our special trees?"

"But you'll have money," Ci-teh says, speaking again to the villagers. "I can pay you more than you'll ever earn from tea."

"You'll have money for a couple of years, but then what?" I appeal to the crowd. "Will your sons and daughters have to go out as I did? You can look at me now and say, Oh, she's an outsider. Or, Oh, her fate has been easy. But I know what's out there for Akha who have no education or opportunity."

How can I make them understand?

"There's more to us than cash," I say, "and there's more to our tea trees than profit. We Recite the Lineage, but our lineage is in our trees too. We can start again, but we should do it the right way, by treasuring what is most valuable to us. Every tree has a soul. Every grain of rice. Every—"

Ci-teh opens her mouth to object, but before she has a chance, A-ba calls out, "Listen to my daughter. She is still the only person from our village to go to second- and third-level school. She went out, just like Teacher Zhang said she would. We need someone who can represent us and look after us."

I'm overwhelmed that he would speak this way on my behalf, but I have the sense to add, "But only if we can behave as proper Akha—"

"Look around," A-ba continues. "My daughter's entire clan is here, but where is Ci-teh's clan? Where are her husband and her daughters? Who—*what*—is an Akha without family?"

A man who defended Ci-teh earlier steps forward. "She leased my land three years ago. It's the closest to Bamboo Forest Village, where her husband is from. She built herself a house on it."

That would have to be the monstrosity Jin and I saw on our walk here. Whatever improvements have been made in Spring Well—as dramatic as they are—are dwarfed by the riches suggested by Ci-teh's new home. All of this makes me feel like a fool. If Ci-teh had been anyone else, I would have asked questions, but I never looked beyond the surface of our friendship. Ci-teh was right when she said I underestimated her.

Leave it to the women to know what's happening with Ci-teh's family members.

"Her brother and his family are at Disneyland in Hong Kong."

"Her husband and their daughters are in Myanmar, buying rubies."

"Child of a dog!" someone shouts. Others call out even harsher epithets, but that doesn't mean the tide has fully turned. Many people here earn their livelihoods from Ci-teh. If they abandon her, then what will become of them? The tension is palpable. I worry a physical fight could break out.

The ruma stamps his staff. The crowd falls silent as he consults with the nima. After considerable whispering and gesturing, the ruma announces, "We'll hold a ceremony in my house."

We make a somber procession to the ruma's home, where he and the nima slip on their ceremonial cloaks. The elders sit in a circle around us. Once everyone is settled, the nima beckons Ci-teh and me to kneel before him. He rubs soot from my forehead down to the tip of my nose. He repeats the process with Ci-teh.

"These two with the marks are who you are to look at and examine," he notifies A-poe-mi-yeh—our supreme god. Next, he ties string around Ci-teh's and my wrists. "Let them be joined together for the journey to the netherworld." Last, he pours a little alcohol on the floor, where it seeps through the bamboo to the ground below. "I call on you, ancestors, to help us look for the truth. What, if any, spirit has been chewing on these women's souls and strangling our village?"

His eyes roll back until we see only the whites. His arms and legs tremble, causing the coins and bones on his cloak to rattle. Unrecognizable words escape his mouth: *"Ooh, aww, tsa."* The ceremony continues for three hours, during which the rain finally lets up. The absence of the constant clatter only amplifies the nima's groans.

When he comes out of his trance, Ci-teh and I are ordered outside so he can confer with the ruma and village elders. Every man, woman, and child of Spring Well Village still waits in the misty drizzle. The divisions are obvious: the group that's most benefited from Ci-teh and the group that's held on to their land and the old ways. I've been away for more than a decade, while she's been a constant and influential presence. I'm promising something intangible for the future, while she's already changed many lives. I'm asking for honor; she's guaranteeing livelihoods.

The ruma, nima, and village elders join us. As is tradition, it's the ruma's responsibility to declare the outcome and announce the nima's recommendations.

"Accusations have shot back and forth like poisoned arrows," he begins, "but we've weighed everything, including what the nima saw in the netherworld." When he asks, "Could a spirit have entered Ci-teh?" I feel a touch of optimism. "If the nima told me that her spirit was gasping for breath, then I would take banana leaves stuffed with ash, husked rice, and coins and rub her body with them, but she is not suffering thus. If she'd become wild, tearing off her clothes or howling like an animal, I would ask three honorable women of our village to urinate on a broom, which I would use to brush away Ci-teh's problems, but she is not suffering thus. If she had seizures, I would wrap her in magic vine, then sacrifice a goat, a pig, and two chickens, but again, she is not suffering thus. Ci-teh does not suffer from a spirit affliction. Everything she has done has come from her own hands, heart, and mind—"

Relief floods through me, but Ci-teh is outraged. "How much did Li-yan pay you to say those things?"

"Shamans and spirit priests don't lie," the ruma replies indignantly. "We can't lie. If we were to lie, the spirits would vex us. Now please, let me continue. A spark lights a fire. Water sprouts a seed. The Akha Way tells us that a single moment changes destinies. Therefore, the nima and I have searched through time to find the instant that changed every person in Spring Well, but these two most of all. I am speaking of the occasion when evil spirits forced the birth of twins upon us."

Everyone instinctively recoils, but I'm thrown back in time not to the birth of Deh-ja's babies but to my cleansing ceremony after the pancake-stealing incident. I'd felt the ruma had magically understood everything that had happened, but now I realize his gifts may have less to do with magic than with interpreting the world around him in a magical way.

"For Li-yan, the arrival of the human rejects caused her to begin looking beyond our spirit gate to the outside world," he says, and I see how clever he is to allot a portion of responsibility to me. "For Ci-teh—"

"We lost our wealth, our reputation, and my brother," Ci-teh finishes somberly.

"Which caused you to work hard to regain your family's prosperity and position. You've even been able to bring your brother—if not all the way back into village life—closer to you." He stamps his staff. "Let us now, as a village, chase away the evil spirits who have haunted these two women. Release them! Be gone! Be gone forever!" He pauses before adding, "We will now practice ceremonial abstinence."

Once the routine requirements might have settled things, but this hasn't been a simple matter of someone touching the spirit gate or a dog climbing onto a roof.

Someone yells, "What about my land? Will Ci-teh sell it back to me?"

The suggestion jags through the crowd.

"That might work for you," another farmer shouts, "but I can't return money I've already spent."

"Shouldn't Ci-teh be banished?" another man calls out.

Then a person from Ci-teh's faction lets his views be known. "Why should she go? I leased my land to her. Why can't I work for her and grow coffee?"

"Make the outsider leave! Look at her. She's not a true Akha."

Several click-clicks of tongues reveal support for this last suggestion.

"If a woman marries out, does that mean she's no longer Akha?" the ruma asks. "In the past, when our men traveled the Tea Horse Road for months or years, were they no longer Akha? If Li-yan wishes to stay among us, she's welcome. As for Ci-teh . . . She's not a human reject. She's not a murderer. I cannot banish her. She has her own home outside the protection of our spirit gate. Let her continue to live there. Those who want to do business with her know that good and bad spirits are watching."

None of this absolves Ci-teh, and it's clear she could easily rile the crowd again. Instead, she straightens her back and begins threading her way through the crowd, stopping here and there to speak to her supporters. Knowing the effect the birth of the twins had on me, I feel empathy for her and the losses her family endured as a result. I even grudgingly admire the desire that ignited in her when we were girls to help her family. But as she walks away, I know the two of us will never again be friends.

Having exposed Ci-teh, I feel I need to be more present in the village. I want to help the people of Spring Well regain pride in our tea trees, help revitalize the Pu'er business, and stabilize and bring back the money everyone has come to rely on. Fortunately, Jin agrees. During the following weeks, as the monsoon season continues and little can be done for the trees themselves, I go from household to household trying to build trust, while Jin makes business calls on his cellphone and occasionally meets associates in Menghai or Jinghong. At night, we sleep in an abandoned newlywed hut. It's not the time of year to build a house, but the ruma and Jin begin to seek a proper date for construction. On the appointed day, men go into the forest to cut bamboo. We women gather thatch and fashion bamboo lashing. Our new house—minus the modern conveniences Jin promises he'll provide eventually—is completed by lunchtime. We move in that afternoon. That night I dream of water. Two weeks later, I wake up sick to my stomach. I've come to a head.

Jin is delighted. He calls his mother, and I can hear her joy through the line. A-ma's smile is open and wide. She says, "It took you this long to figure it out? The sisters-in-law and I could tell a half cycle ago." Her words sound matter-of-fact, but her happiness radiates like the sun on a spring morning.

And this is what I've wanted. This is what will make our lives complete, but the worries my condition stirs up are troublesome. What if I have a girl?

"I don't need a son," Jin reassures me. "You don't need to do that for me."

But he doesn't understand that every Akha wishes for a son first, followed by a girl, followed by a boy, followed by a girl. It's how we keep balance in the world. I had a daughter; now I *must* have a son.

Teacher Zhang inadvertently adds to my anxieties when he and two old women from the Family Planning Office at the tea collection center visit Spring Well to paste posters on the sides of buildings, marking the launch of a new campaign seeking to address "the dark side of the miracle" of the One Child policy. "China already has a huge surplus of men over women, and that number is expanding by about one million each year," Teacher Zhang announces. Each poster has a different slogan, all bearing the same core message: *Daughters constitute the next generation. Men and women build a harmonious society together. Nature will decide the sex of the newborn. Giving birth to a girl is the will of nature.* The villagers don't remove the posters, because all the slogans are in accordance with Akha Law. Then my three eleven-year-old nieces come home with memorized sayings, which they recite with alarming frequency.

"*Care for girls. Support the girl class.*"

"*Protect girl children. Benefit the state, the people, and families.*"

"*To care for today's girls is to show concern for the future of China.*"

All this should make me want to have a girl, but the more I'm encouraged to give birth to one, the more apprehensive I become.

Let it be a son.

In October, five months after the confrontation with Ci-teh, Jin and I feel comfortable enough to go back to Guangzhou so he can take care of business and I can visit the tea market to research what it would take to open a new shop. We have to pass through Menghai to get to the airport in Jinghong, so, as promised, Jin and I stop at the Social Welfare Institute. The rains should be over, but today they've reappeared. A beggar woman sits under a makeshift shelter on the steps of the orphanage . . . in this weather, with no one about. I wonder if she's the same person I saw sleeping under the cardboard sheets when we drove through Menghai on our way to Spring Well. Jin splits off, drops a few coins in her cup, and bounds up the steps to catch up to me as I enter the institute.

As soon as the door closes behind us, I'm overcome by the smell of urine, which seems exponentially multiplied by the day's warmth and humidity. Toddlers scurry across the floor in walkers, foundlings squirm in metal cribs, and older children—most with physical or mental disorders—linger at the edges. One child—a boy—sits crumpled in a heap against a wall, his atrophied legs like broken twigs beneath him. Although leftover New Year's couplets and other decorations festoon the walls, the room, while clean, lacks toys or books. Three women, wearing matching pink smocks and kerchiefs, hang diapers on a clothesline strung from ceiling hooks. One of the women leaves her chore when she sees us. As she wipes her hands on her smock, my a-ma's bracelet slides into view. It's Director Zhou. The room begins to swim.

"Welcome to Menghai's Social Welfare Institute. Do you drink tea? Have you eaten yet?" she asks politely.

We're shown to a sitting room with two overstuffed couches upholstered in faded fabric. Antimacassars cover the armrests and drape over each head position. The other two caretakers bring tea and a platter of sliced watermelon and lychees. The tea is poured, adding more heat and dampness to the chamber. Once everything is served, the two women join us, ready to be part of the conversation.

"Are you looking to adopt a boy or a girl?" Director Zhou inquires. "Many Chinese couples are adopting now, because they don't want our children to leave the home country. Most want a boy, but all of ours have special needs. We are told they are the 'rubbish of society.'" She sighs. "If you can only have one child, you want it to be perfect. For birth parents and adoptive parents alike, no? I can offer many choices for girls. Do you want a newborn or one who can already do chores and care for herself?"

"We're here on a different matter," I say. As I recite the facts, Director Zhou nods slowly in recognition. The cardboard box was not unique—many babies probably arrive similarly—but the tea cake was. More important, San-pa and I were the only parents brave enough—or foolish enough—to come here to track down an illegally abandoned daughter.

"None of us have forgotten that day," the director concedes. "I should have called Public Security to come and arrest you. Then you fainted. I am not without heart."

The two other caretakers exchange furtive glances as the director pushes A-ma's bracelet into her sleeve with her unadorned hand. This isn't like last time, though. I have Jin with me, and he takes over. Sure, the women cover their mouths and tip their heads as if in deep contemplation over the ethical dilemma, but the cash he holds in his hand is too great a temptation.

"We were told she was sent to Hao Lai Wu—Hollywood," the youngest one blurts.

Hollywood? I grip the armrests.

"Have you been there?" she asks.

I nod, unwilling to give away anything more.

All the women, including Director Zhou, brighten. Does everyone own a car? Do all the women paint their nails? Then the questions become more sinister.

"Is it true that Americans adopt our girls so they can raise them until they're old enough to have their organs harvested?"

"Or do they adopt our girls purely for sex?"

"That's government propaganda," Jin chides. "You shouldn't repeat such things."

"Are you sure she's in Hollywood?" I ask.

"Everyone wants to go to Hollywood!" the youngest caretaker exclaims.

"She knows not one thing about it," Director Zhou says gruffly, drawing attention—and the offered bribe—back to her. She waits as Jin counts out bills and lays them in a stack on the table. When she's satisfied, she says, "I told you last time that the baby was sent to Kunming. From there she went to Los Angeles. Somewhere in the Los Angeles prefecture," she clarifies. "We like to think it was Hollywood."

Los Angeles isn't a prefecture, but the city is huge, and really, that could mean Yan-yeh's anywhere from Venice Beach to San Gabriel, from Woodland Hills to . . . I don't know. Disneyland?

"Will you show us the file?" Jin asks.

The director locates it easily and hands it to me. The folder contains a photograph—showing an infant a few days old with her head wrapped in an indigo cap decorated with silver charms—a footprint in red ink, and a single sheet of paper, which outlines the basics of Yan-yeh's arrival at the institute. These three items constitute the only tangible proof of my daughter's existence.

"Shouldn't there be more?" I ask, running a finger over the photograph.

The director smiles at me sympathetically. "One of the photos and the rest of the paperwork went with your daughter to the Social Welfare Institute in Kunming for identification purposes, but a fire seven years ago destroyed their records. You could visit the new facility to see if anyone remembers something, but babies are sent to them from all over the province for foreign adoption. I don't see how they'll remember one out of so many."

So no easy answers or traceable clues. Still, I now know where my daughter is—if this information is accurate, and if she and her parents have never moved. How could my daughter be in Los Angeles, of all places, and I haven't been looking for her every moment? I begin to cry. The ladies are kind, patting me on the back, cooing, pouring more tea. The director even offers to return Jin's money, saying, "We don't often see the suffering of mothers here. We only see the babies."

She gives me the photo and the footprint, then the three women escort us to the front door. Babies wail in their cribs. The toddlers in their walkers push their way toward us. The older children seek our eyes, hopeless, knowing we haven't come for them. The director puts a comforting hand on my shoulder. The ridge of A-ma's bracelet presses into my flesh.

"I would help you if I could," she says.

Through my tears, I ask, "If I can't have my daughter, is there something I can do for the other children?"

"Oh, no. We're fine. We're given everything we need."

"Maybe . . ." I try to think big. "What about a washing machine and a dryer?"

"We could never accept such generosity," she says, but she's just being Chinese-polite.

So our flights back to Guangzhou will be put off another day. We open our umbrellas and step out into the rain. The beggar woman, who's been here all this time, waves to Jin to approach. He gave her money earlier, but he reaches into his pocket again and begins to move laterally over the steps to her. It hurts enough to see beggars in Guangzhou and the homeless in Los Angeles, but to encounter one in my prefecture? We grew up living on the land. If we caught or found food, we ate it. If we had nothing, we ate nothing. But the idea that one of us would beg?

"Sir, please come a little closer," the woman entreats in broken Mandarin. "Let me show you something. I've been waiting for the right buyers. You and your wife look like people of fine standing. I know there are collectors from afar who will pay good money . . ."

I only had to hear the first few words to recognize the voice, and they catch me like a spring trap. It's Deh-ja. The irrevocable loss I feel about my daughter followed by this chance encounter with Deh-ja, again, feel as humbling and cleansing as a tidal wave. For a moment I can't move, because it's all so hard to take in. When I saw her on San-pa's and my way to Thailand, she was barely surviving, but this is different. Deh-ja—an Akha—has become a beggar. Unheard of. I sweep in a deep breath to steady myself and then walk to my husband's side, where Deh-ja—filthy, nearly toothless, and as brown and wrinkled as a salted plum—holds out her most special possession for sale: her wedding headdress.

She doesn't recognize me until I speak. That's how much *I've* changed.

"Fate sent you in one direction," she says, showing no embarrassment about her circumstances. "Destiny sent me in another. Now, would you like to buy this headdress? I think you remember it."

"Of course I remember it, but I'm not going to buy it. You're coming with us."

Jin raises his eyebrows, clearly surprised.

"*No coincidence, no story,*" I recite before going on to explain. "Deh-ja once lived in Spring Well. She and I have been together at our worst moments." I pause to look in her eyes. "We've also bumped into each other in the most unlikely places. That has to mean something, doesn't it?"

The next two hours should be filled with the sad tale of Deh-ja living as a hermit in the jungle for many years before traversing mountain trails—always alone—back to Xishuangbanna prefecture. Instead, a cacophony of laughter and hoots of surprise stream out of Deh-ja as she experiences her first shower, her first flush toilet, her first restaurant meal, her first television program, her first mattress, her first air-conditioning, her first nightgown, and her first use of electricity, flipping on and off the bedside lamp.

"Why are you doing this for me?" she asks as I sit next to her on the bed, holding her hand, trying to assure her about sleeping inside a room with four solid walls for the first time in her life.

"Maybe it's not for you. Maybe it's for me. Tomorrow, we're going home—"

"To Spring Well Village? I can't go there!"

"We're going to Guangzhou—"

"Sun and Moon! Not possible!"

"As Akha, we're linked in one long chain of life. Do you still believe in the malevolence of spirits and the power of our ancestors to overcome them?" I ask.

Of course she does.

"We were both on those steps today," I continue. "We don't have to know why. All we have to do is accept that our spirit ancestors must want us to be together. Akha Law tells us never to ignore portents or coincidences."

The following morning, Deh-ja gets her first experience in a car as the driver takes us to Jinghong to buy the appliances. Terror turns her face as white as a phantom. I keep reminding her that we can stop if she needs to be sick. The appliances cost barely three hundred dollars—a modest amount for us, but a washer and dryer will change the quality of everyone's lives at the Social Welfare Institute. Not wanting to take any chances, we follow the truck back to Menghai and watch as the items are hooked up and proven to work. The three caretakers smile through their tears. The older kids shoulder in, wanting to get a closer look. The toddlers surround Deh-ja with their walkers, and her laughter is as light and clear as water tumbling over rocks in a stream.

It's close to 4:00 when Jin gives the installer a tip and sends him on his way. Director Zhou offers more tea and a meal. Now that she sees we've adopted a beggar, she expects us to take a child with us too. When I tell her I'm carrying a baby, she exclaims, "Wonderful news! Later, when you want him to have a little sister, you'll know where to come." She walks us to the door, takes my hand,

and transfers something into it. A-ma's dragon bracelet. "You have a big and generous heart," the director says. "I'm sorry for your sorrows and for whatever part I may have had in them, but we're required by the government to do our jobs."

The weight of the silver on my wrist soothes my spirit, as though I'm setting things right.

Although Guangzhou is shockingly large by any measure, Deh-ja barely notices because she's so busy taking care of me. The phrase we Akha use for pregnancy is "one living under another," meaning a wife lives under her husband and won't be able to run away. But really, Jin and I are both living under Deh-ja. She's so bossy! We don't have a cat, but she reminds Jin at least once a day not to strike or kick one or else our baby will act like a cat when it comes into the world. She forbids Jin to climb trees, which would cause our baby to quake with fear and cry endlessly. (But Jin isn't likely to climb a tree any time soon.) When I reach five months, she bans him from cutting his hair. But she saves her strictest admonitions for me for even the most minor things. "You were raised to walk at an angle when you carry a baby," Deh-ja scolds, "so your belly will be less prominent." I'm careful about that, but it's hard when so many mothers-to-be walk around Guangzhou in tight T-shirts and leggings, proudly announcing to the world the imminent arrival of their one child.

Dr. Arnold Rosen's Group Therapy for Chinese Adoptees
Transcript: March 1, 2008

*Emphasis has been added in an attempt to accurately show the moods and affect of participants.

DR. ROSEN: I'm glad you young ladies agreed to see me in a group setting. Of course we've been meeting individually—some of us for years and some, like Haley, for just a few sessions. Let me go around the room and introduce everyone. Jessica, you're the oldest at seventeen. Tiffany and Ariel are next at sixteen. And Haley and Heidi will be turning thirteen this year. Who would like to start?
JESSICA: I don't know why I have to share stuff with a couple of crappy-ass tweens.
TIFFANY: Me either.
DR. ROSEN: Putting the age differences aside, the five of you have many things in common. You all live nearby—in Pasadena, Arcadia, and San Marino—
JESSICA: Great, so we'll get to run into each other on the street—
DR. ROSEN: You all have similar educations. You've gone to Crestview Prep or Chandler, Westridge or Poly.
JESSICA: I'm intimidated already.
DR. ROSEN: You're all Chinese—
JESSICA: Duh.
DR. ROSEN: And you were all adopted from China.
JESSICA: I still don't see why *they* have to be here.
DR. ROSEN: They?
JESSICA: The little girls.
DR. ROSEN: They're a bit younger than you, but they won't be afraid to speak up.
JESSICA: You mean, they won't be afraid to speak up around *me*. You must have invited them to learn from my bad example. Hey, what are your names again?
HALEY: Haley.

HEIDI: Heidi.

JESSICA: Let me give you my advice and then you can go home to your mommies. Don't give a random blow job at a house party just because some guy asks for one. Don't drink your dad's best scotch if he's the kind of person who'll notice a drop missing in the bottle. Actually, don't drink scotch, period. Don't bother to self-medicate. You're seeing Dr. Rosen. He gives way better meds.

DR. ROSEN: Thank you for your input, Jessica. I can see you're angry—

JESSICA: You always say that.

DR. ROSEN: Can you think of another reason why Haley and Heidi are here?

JESSICA: Nope.

HALEY: Maybe you older girls can learn from us too.

DR. ROSEN: What do you mean, Haley?

HALEY: My mom and dad sent me to you because I was having problems with my friends. I've had other problems too. Things I don't like to talk about. Maybe Jessica, Tiffany, and Ariel will hear what Heidi and I have to say and . . . I don't know. Maybe our lives are like gigantic jigsaw puzzles. You find the right piece and suddenly the whole picture has meaning.

JESSICA: Whoa! Isn't she the smart one?

HALEY: I bet every person in this room has had to deal with that label.

TIFFANY: I have.

HEIDI: Me too.

JESSICA: I *hate* labels. I hate the word *labels*.

ARIEL: Just because we're Chinese doesn't mean we're smart.

JESSICA: Yeah, but the expectation is there. The high school girls know what I'm talking about. God, all the hours I've spent going to Kumon, and now I have an SAT tutor. This year I doubled down on extra AP classes. The school called my mom to say they were worried about me. "If she takes all APs then how will she have time for extracurriculars? How will she make friends and become a *whole* person?" Of course my mom and dad got all worried, but it's a little late for that, don't you think? After their pushing . . .

TIFFANY: What'd you say to them?

JESSICA: What could I say? "Working hard makes me happy, Mom. Do I get into trouble, Dad?" And they bought it, because we've been in this pattern since Day One. Now it's going to be all work until I get into college. Debate, tennis, making blankets for the homeless, and all that crap. I'm sticking with my cello lessons too. I'm busy promoting the Asian stereotype!

HALEY: But are your parents Chinese?

DR. ROSEN: Interestingly, you were all adopted by white families.

HEIDI: I'm a super student—

JESSICA: Brag about it, why don't you?

HEIDI: There's a big difference between bragging and the truth. I'm great at math and all the sciences. I have to play an instrument—

TIFFANY: So do I. What do you play?

HEIDI: Piano. My parents want me to be like Lang Lang.

JESSICA: For me, it's cello and Yo-Yo Ma.

ARIEL: Violin. Sarah Chang, you know, and she's not even Chinese! She's Korean! But I have to keep up with my violin because it'll look good on my college application. Like every other Asian kid in the country doesn't also get straight A's and play an instrument too? I don't know. Maybe I should stop with all the academic stuff, focus entirely on the violin, and go to Juilliard instead of Stanford, Harvard, or Yale. Man, what a burn that would be!

DR. ROSEN: What about you, Haley?

HALEY: I started violin lessons when I was six. My mom and dad also said I could be like Sarah Chang. My dad inherited a ranch near Aspen—

JESSICA: Great! A brainiac and rich too—

DR. ROSEN: Jessica, please let Haley finish. Go ahead, Haley.

HALEY: Last summer we were in Aspen, like usual. They have a big music festival up there. We're in the tent listening to Sarah Chang. My mom has this thing where she'll lean down and whisper, "That could be you one day." She does it all the time, and it's always really bugged me. But that day, as I listened to Sarah play Sibelius's Violin Concerto in D Minor, I realized that was *never* going to be me. Not ever. I haven't picked up my violin since.

ARIEL: And they let you?

HALEY: They didn't "let me." I just stopped.

ARIEL: Weren't you scared? I mean, what if—

HALEY: They send me back?

JESSICA: *I'd* send you back.

Tiffany: C'mon, Jess. Who *hasn't* felt that? When I was little, Mother and Father thought they were helping me by telling me how lucky I was to have been adopted. "Your parents wanted you to have a better life in America."

ARIEL: I heard that one too.

JESSICA: We all did, but please, that can't be the real reason for *all* our birth parents.

HALEY: *Lucky*. People say I'm lucky to have been adopted. People tell my parents they're lucky they got me. But am I lucky to have lost my birth parents and my birth culture? Yes, I'm fortunate to have been adopted by nice people, but was that luck?

JESSICA: Damn! You are smart!

TIFFANY: Mother and Father are lawyers. They always gave me *way too much* information.

DR. ROSEN: Like what, Tiffany?

TIFFANY: You know, because we've talked about it before.

DR. ROSEN: But maybe you can share it with the others.

TIFFANY: Stuff like I needed to know from a superyoung age about China's history of euthanasia—

HEIDI: They kill *all* the girls there.

JESSICA: I thought it was only me who got that talk.

ARIEL: My mom used to say I had a morbid curiosity about euthanasia. Come on! I used to cry myself to sleep just thinking about it. Well, sleep . . . I guess I don't mean that literally—

JESSICA: For the longest time I thought my parents were saying *youth in Asia*.

HALEY: I heard it that way too! Last year, in fifth grade, I got in trouble when I wrote something about it in my spelling homework. My teacher called my mom, who nearly had a cow. I said, "*Youth in Asia* or *euthanasia*, what difference does it make? Getting thrown in a river, left in the open to be eaten by wild animals, or dumped over a cliff? In the end you're still D-E-A-D."

JESSICA: I don't get it, Doc. Why *haven't* her parents sent her back?

HALEY: That's not funny.

DR. ROSEN: Maybe we can let Tiffany finish her thought.

TIFFANY: Mother and Father also told me that my birth parents had to give me away because of the One Child policy. People there want a boy instead of a girl for their one child. So there's *that*. But sometimes a woman gets pregnant more than once. Maybe that happened to my birth mom. If the authorities had found out, they would have fined her up to six times her family's annual income! I've heard that! And then *forced* her to have an abortion. They even force women to have late-term abortions. My parents are big into right-to-life stuff, so they say I never would have been born, as in "Just think about it, Tiffany. If your parents had been caught, the Chinese authorities would never have let you come to term." As you can imagine, I couldn't sleep much either. Still don't . . .

HEIDI: The One Child thing scares me.

DR. ROSEN: How so?

HEIDI: It makes me feel precious but in a weird way. I mean, I wasn't precious enough for my birth parents to keep, but sometimes I feel like I'm too precious to my mom and dad. I'm *their* one child.

ARIEL: Heidi's got that right. Every year for as long as I can remember, my parents have hired a professional photographer to come and take pictures of me. Their excuse is they want a pretty image to use for our Christmas card.

HEIDI: Same here.

HALEY: At my house too.

TIFFANY: Probably all of our houses.

JESSICA: Yeah, so?

DR. ROSEN: A lot of families send out Christmas cards featuring their kids. What makes yours different?

HEIDI: They take pictures in my room—at my computer or painting.

ARIEL: We do ours in the library, and I'm reading a book or something. Once I was playing violin.

HALEY: Ours are usually outside. I'm always the only *thing* in the photo—no Mom, no Dad, no Whiskers, not even much of the house or garden.

JESSICA: Get it yet, Doc? These are pictures of us as treasured and adored daughters. *The* object and focus of all attention and love. The *object,* okay? It makes me want to barf. Hey, everyone, did he tell you about my bulimia? Anyone else have that? Or anorexia? I hate to say it, Tiffany, but you're a bit cadavery—

TIFFANY: I am not!

ARIEL: The thing that really used to make me go *ick* was the way my mom would brush my hair, straighten my collar, pull on my hem, and—

JESSICA: Like they're never *not* touching me—

ARIEL: I'd spend the afternoon smiling this way, smiling that way, looking into the distance, gazing downward. Pose, pose, pose. On the one hand, our birth parents in China couldn't get rid of us fast enough. On the other hand, we're the biggest gift to our adoptive parents. Sometimes I try to imagine what their lives would have been like if they *hadn't* gotten me. It's so weird, don't you think? In China, we were considered worthless. I mean, really worthless. Here we're super-precious, like Heidi said. But you could also say our moms and dads got cheated by getting the runts—the throwaways, anyway—of the litter.

JESSICA: At least we weren't thrown in a well or whatever.

DR. ROSEN: Could we talk a little more about parents?

JESSICA: It's your group. We have to do what you tell us to do whether we want to or not.

DR. ROSEN: I wouldn't phrase it that way. I want each of you to benefit from our sessions.

JESSICA: Don't forget, Doc, my parents are physicians. I know what's what. You're going to use us for—

Dr. Rosen: Jessica, maybe we can talk about your need to constantly challenge me another time, but this session is for everyone. Can we get back to my question? Ariel, would you like to tell us a little about your mom and dad?

Ariel: My mom makes me batshit crazy. Sorry. Can I say that in here? Yes? Good. I love her, but she's such a *mom*. She wears things that are totally embarrassing.

Tiffany: Mothers can't help it. That's just the way they are.

Ariel: That's *very* understanding of you, Tiffany, but have you heard your mom talking on the phone to her friends about you? The other night she called me a hormonal monster. Even when she says nice things—*I love you* and that kind of stuff—a part of me still feels like she's lying. One time I totally lost it. I yelled at her, "I wish I was in China with my real mom!" She got so mad, she yelled right back at me. "Yeah? Well go ahead! Try to find her! See if she'll take you back!" Later she came to my room, crying like you wouldn't believe, and apologized. Soooo many times. I'm like, okay, Mom! God!

Dr. Rosen: Lots of young people say things like that. *I wish you weren't my mom* or *I wish I had a different dad*. Maybe even your mom said something like that to *her* mom or dad when she was younger.

Ariel: Maybe. So?

Dr. Rosen: What do you think she was feeling when she came to apologize?

Ariel: I felt real bad—

Dr. Rosen: I hear that, but what do you think *she* was feeling?

Tiffany: Maybe she was upset because she'd said something so inappropriate to you. *Inappropriate*. I get that word a lot from my parents.

Jessica: She should have felt guilty for acting like the worst mom ever.

Ariel: Yeah, maybe. But maybe she was right in what she said. I mean, could I ever find my birth mother? No. So who else do I have but my mom and dad?

Haley: My mom and dad always say that the parents here and the baby girls they adopt have happy endings and "the holes in all their hearts are filled with love." But what happens to the birth parents? I think about that when I can't sleep. Were my birth parents left with holes in their hearts or did they just forget about me?

ARIEL: I wonder what it would be like to *be* a biological child. Or white. When I was younger I couldn't grasp the idea that a pregnant woman would keep her baby. If I ever have a baby, I hope she'll look like me, even if I marry someone white or whatever.

HALEY: People will come to the hospital and say, "Oh, she looks just like you."

ARIEL: No one has ever told me I looked like someone in my family before. When I become a mom, I'll never have to answer questions from strangers about where I got her, if she belongs to me, or—

HALEY: If she's from Mongolia.

ARIEL: And she'll never have to answer questions about who her *real* parents are.

JESSICA: Oh, my God. I hate that! I mean, screw them. What's real anyway? Isn't it just what we're stuck with?

TIFFANY: I'll be a great mom. For sure my baby will look like me. She won't be in rags and have ants all over her face, like when my parents got me. She'll be my only blood relative that I know, and I'll love her forever and ever.

DR. ROSEN: Don't you think your mom and dad will love you forever and ever?

TIFFANY: Of course they will. But I don't know if I can explain this. I love them and they love me, but it's like Ariel said. It bothers me that I don't look even a little bit like them. They both have blond hair! Everyone in their families has blond hair. We spend a lot of time visiting relatives—and there are a ton of them—in Indiana. Once, at Thanksgiving dinner, when I was, like, six, I asked, "Why am I the only one here with a *tan*?" Uncle Jack answered, "You're our little yellow one."

JESSICA: You've got to be kidding! Jesus Christ! That seriously sucks.

HALEY: You must have been really hurt. It would have hurt me.

TIFFANY: But you haven't heard the worst part. That label—yeah, another label—stuck. Now the Indiana relatives call me Our Little Yellow One. Mother and Father have asked them about a billion times to knock it off. Forget it. They think it's cute. But the thing is, I'm not just tan in Indiana. All my parents' friends are white. Nearly everyone in our church is white. I hate it. I stick out like a sore thumb. It's really hard because it makes me feel like I'm *not* a part of them.

ARIEL: I'd love to go to China to find my birth mother.

JESSICA: Don't bother. There are like a bazillion people over there.

DR. ROSEN: Ariel, you said you wanted to find your mother. What about your father?

ARIEL: Yeah, I've always wondered about both my birth parents. Who are they? Where did they meet? Do I have a brother or sister? Grandparents? Aunts, uncles, cousins? Why did my mother give me away? Does she think about me? Has she ever looked for me?

DR. ROSEN: I notice that you shifted again to just your birth mother. Why do you think that is?

JESSICA: I'll answer that one. It's not hard, Doc. We grew inside our mothers, and they threw us away.

ARIEL: If I went to China, I'd want to look for my mother, even though I know it's hopeless. That upsets me a lot.

JESSICA: You're alone in the world like the rest of us.

HEIDI: But now we have each other!

JESSICA: Have each other? I don't even know you! You and the other one—the brainiac—are starting seventh grade in the fall. Am I right? Those are the suckiest years *ever*.

TIFFANY: Yeah, mean girls.

ARIEL: It's *still* really bad for me, and I'm in tenth grade. We have a ton of Asian kids at my school. Who's studying in the library instead of hanging with friends during lunch? Who's getting the best grades? Who's skipping parties and other social activities to do an extracurricular? Who's going to get into the *best* university? We aren't competing against all the kids to get into college. We're only competing against the other

Asian kids, because we have to check that particular box on our college apps.

TIFFANY: At least our last names aren't Chinese. A girl in my school—Chinese, born here, with immigrant parents—asked if she could change her last name to Smith or something like that so she *would* stand out. I thought that was pretty funny. San Marino High is mostly Asian now. I'm Asian, but I'm in the minority, because the nonadopted Asian kids don't consider me one of them because I grew up with white people. To them, I'm basically white. Those kids are really judgmental.

JESSICA: And what about the white kids? They think I earn my grades easily *because* of my race. They don't know how hard I work.

HALEY: I came home with an A- on a history test, and my mom went all crazy. She's like, "If you want to get into a good university program you have to work harder." "And if I don't?" "Then you'll end up like . . ." Well, it isn't anyone you would know. Anyway, I said, "Mom, I'm in the sixth grade. I got an A-. That's all. I promise to do better next time."

DR. ROSEN: It sounds like you all are talking about two different things. Academic pressure—

JESSICA: It's more like expectation, like I said before. We look Chinese so we should be completely obsessed and working our asses off like those kids with Chinese parents.

DR. ROSEN: I stand corrected, Jessica. My other point has to do with social pressure.

JESSICA: Like, who has richer parents?

TIFFANY: It used to be the old-money Pasadena girls, but now it's the children of millionaires and billionaires from China.

JESSICA: Who gets a car right when they turn sixteen? And what model is it?

TIFFANY: A BMW or a Volvo or a Nissan?

ARIEL: I got a car when I turned sixteen—

HEIDI: Really? What kind—

JESSICA: Who has the best house?

TIFFANY: A mansion on Oak Knoll. One of those big brick ones. Old money.

JESSICA: Let me guess. That's where you live, Haley.

HALEY: Nearby on Hummingbird Lane. My dad inherited—

DR. ROSEN: Let's try to stay focused on the social implications. The effect all that has on you—

TIFFANY: Okay. So are you in a house where a bunch of Chinese immigrants are still living out of plastic bags or in one of the gaudy castles the Chinese billionaires have purchased? You mean like that?

DR. ROSEN: Hmmm . . .

TIFFANY: Father says the poor immigrant Chinese are feeding off our American hospitality, while the rich are probably a bunch of criminals—like Chinese mafia or something.

JESSICA: What a bunch of narrow-minded bullshit.

TIFFANY: I didn't say *I* believed that—

HALEY: My mom and dad say that, rich or poor, those people worked really hard to get here. Everyone wants the American Dream, just like my birth mother wanted for me. That's why she gave me away.

DR. ROSEN: I'm hearing everything you girls are saying, but can we think about social pressure in a more personal way? Jessica, earlier you cautioned Haley and Heidi about what's coming for them. What did you mean by that?

JESSICA: Oh, you know, the usual. It's all about who's popular. Like, what girl is the most stylish? And that changes *all the time*. Did you come from Hong Kong, Shanghai, or Singapore? Those girls? Wow! Rich *and* mean! Or did you move here from West Hills, Chino, or, like, the real boonies?

TIFFANY: And, who's getting invited to house parties? Who's being left out?

ARIEL: Who's hooking up? Jessica, you might know a little about that one.

HALEY: I have a friend named Jade. The kids in school now call her Jaded.

ARIEL: That's harsh! And you're still just a kid.

HALEY: I heard my mom tell my dad that Jade earned her nickname the old-fashioned way, whatever that means.

JESSICA: Blow jobs.

ARIEL: Geez, Jessica. Can you lighten up a little? Even *I* don't need to hear—

TIFFANY: For the Chinese girls in my school, no question is more important than the *color* of their skin. Who has a complexion as pale as the moon? One girl, a Red Princess and the great-granddaughter of someone who walked side by side with Mao on the Long March—Okay, we get it. You're a big deal!—wins that prize hands down. I know lots of girls whose mothers take them to doctors for treatments to lighten their skin.

HALEY: Lighten their skin? How do they do that?

TIFFANY: And all the American-born and Chinese-born girls make fun of us adopted Chinese girls, because darker skin marks us as the daughters of peasants.

HALEY: My skin is darker, but I also look different than the other girls—not Chinese enough, they say.

DR. ROSEN: So we're talking about perception . . .

HALEY: It makes me so mad. I guess that's why my mom and dad sent me here.

HEIDI: Dr. Rosen, aren't those stereotypes, though?

JESSICA: Oh, God, not another brainiac. How old are you again?

DR. ROSEN: What do you mean, Heidi?

HEIDI: Well, Chinese used to be seen as low, right? Working on the railroad, in laundries, and stuff like that. Now they're seen as smart and wealthy. I mean, isn't there the stereotype of the model minority? I read an article for school that said people like us—not you, Dr. Rosen—are now labeled as inquisitive, persistent, and ambitious. With ingenuity, fortitude, and cleverness.

JESSICA: Jesus, kid, you won't even have to take that stupid SAT prep course. You've already got all the big words down cold.

HEIDI: All I'm saying is that there's no underestimating how cruel girls can be to each other. I've been reading about it, because I'm scared of . . . Oh, Dr. Rosen, I don't know if I should say this.

DR. ROSEN: Please go ahead. I want you to think of this as a safe place.

HEIDI: I'm afraid of girls like . . . well . . . like Jessica. Is that why my parents sent me here? To toughen me up? I can be tough. Really I can. Or is there another reason, Dr. Rosen? You'd tell me, wouldn't you?

DR. ROSEN: Each of you is here for her own reason. What I feel comfortable sharing with all of you is that each of your parents wants you to be happy. Now . . . We've talked about a lot of different things today, but I'd like to circle back to a couple of themes that have emerged.

HALEY: Like none of us can sleep.

DR. ROSEN: I'm happy you picked up on that, Haley.

HALEY: I've always crept around the house in the middle of the night, which is how I've heard my parents arguing about work, about this one woman who's Dad's client, and what to do about me.

ARIEL: For me, it's stress, obviously. At school and at home. It seems like my whole life I've spent the hours from two to six in the morning awake—staring at the muted TV screen, obsessively doing my homework, and trying to learn to knit to "do something productive," as my dad said. He bought me knitting lessons for one of my birthdays! Knitting lessons! And Jessica isn't the only one who drinks. I sneak gulps from the wine left over at dinner. My parents are so stupid, they've never even noticed. I've smoked weed in the backyard. I had another doctor before you, Dr. Rosen, who prescribed me Ambien.

HALEY: I just can't sleep. My mom says it's because I'm still on China time.

JESSICA: Hardy-har-har!

DR. ROSEN: What happens when it's time for you to sleep?

HALEY: Sometimes when I turn off the light, I feel myself start to wake up. I'm flying out the window and across the ocean to my orphanage in China. I see rows and rows of cots and Chinese ladies, like the waitresses at Empress Pavilion who push the dim sum carts, walking up and down. I imagine the moment when I was loaded onto a bus or a truck and brought to the hotel. I bet I was scared. I bet I was crying already. Mom and Dad say it was like *plop, plop, plop* as each baby was dropped into a new mother's arms. Did I go to the right mom and dad? Is there something wrong with me, and that's why I look different from the other babies given out that day, different from the other girls in Families with Children from China, different from my friends at school? Then I have to turn the light back on.

ARIEL: Dr. Rosen, I don't get this. I know a lot of girls from Heritage Camp for Adoptive Families who don't have a single problem. They're all happy. Or they look that way to me.

HALEY: She's right, you know. I've known the girls in FCC since we were babies. They don't let the stupid things people say get to them. I remember this one girl. We were, like, eight years old. A stranger asked her if she was a foreign exchange student. That kind of thing really bugs me, but you know what she answered? "Most exchange students are not eight years old!"

ARIEL: Have you ever been asked why you don't speak English with a Chinese accent? I have.

HEIDI: I hate when people ask if I know English or if I've adjusted to America yet. Come on!

TIFFANY: In our church, we have a group that's special for girls like us—adopted, but from Russia and Romania and places like that. We had a meeting where we were supposed to learn how to respond to jerks who ask things like "When did you know you were adopted?" Most people picture a scene where the parents sit you down and you "find out who you are." I didn't need that meeting to know how to answer, because all I had to do was look in the mirror. When people ask me that question, I always say, "When did you find out you *weren't* adopted? How do you know your mother *is* your birth mother?"

ARIEL: That seems a bit snarky. I'm just saying.

HALEY: You could try something like "The phenotypic differences between my parents and myself were always evident. I can only guess at how it would feel to be a biological child or be born white to match my parents."

TIFFANY: Phenotypic differences?

HALEY: I did a project for my school's science fair on that. I won—

DR. ROSEN: I hate to interrupt, Haley. Do you mind? Jessica, you've been unusually quiet. Would you like to share what's going on with you?

JESSICA: I've been thinking about what Heidi said earlier about me. Does everyone here think I'm a bully or mean or—

HALEY: You act tough, but I bet you're as scared as the rest of us.

JESSICA: I'm not scared. Of what?

DR. ROSEN: I'm going to step in here. I know from listening today that you girls don't like labels. I don't particularly like labels either, but my profession—like most professions—uses them. So let's take a moment to consider one that's being applied to Chinese adoptees like the five of you.

JESSICA: Great. Just what I need. Another label. What are *you* going to call me?

DR. ROSEN: Does the phrase *grateful-but-angry* have resonance for anyone? You can be grateful you have your mom and dad, because they love you and they've given you good lives with all kinds of privilege.

JESSICA: Some more than others—

DR. ROSEN: So the grateful part seems pretty obvious. And, as Ariel pointed out, there are many adoptees who are perfectly happy—

TIFFANY: *Most* of them, I bet.

JESSICA: That's probably because they weren't born with brains—

DR. ROSEN: But, often, adoption is about loss: loss of your original family, loss of culture and nationality, and, of course, loss of a way of life that might have been. This is where the angry part comes in. Just today you've shared lots of variations on anger and why you might be angry. My profession narrows it down to this: anger that your birth parents abandoned you. So the label is *grateful-but-angry,* but in our private sessions you've heard me talk about anger in a different way. Haley, do you remember what I said?

HALEY: You said anger can be a cover for something deeper.

DR. ROSEN: Do you want to share what that was for you?

HALEY: Sadness. Really bad sadness, because somewhere out there I had a mother and a father who didn't love me enough to keep me. They gave me away. They got rid of me. For their one child they didn't want *me*. I've never had a way to grieve for that. I mean, how can I be around Mom and Dad, who I love a ton, and cry for my birth mom and dad because I don't know them or have them in my life? At the same time, why wasn't I good enough for my mom and dad in China? Now I have to work really hard—and not just with my classes—to be someone they would have been proud of, if they'd known me. And for Mom and Dad to be proud of now.

JESSICA: You mean I'm sad because my birth mother cared so little about me that she left me in front of a train station . . . By myself . . . In the middle of the night . . . In winter . . . That she didn't even want to know me . . .

TIFFANY: Who *wouldn't* be sad when you put it like that?

JESSICA: I'm not sad. I'm pissed.

ARIEL: Youth in Asia.

JESSICA: Fuck this. God damn it.

HALEY: I'm sorry I made you cry.

JESSICA: That's okay. I think that's what we're supposed to do in here. And by the way, Haley, don't pay any attention to what I said earlier. You're probably gonna do a lot of the stuff I do—the drinking and all—but take it from me on the true down low. Keep up with your homework, don't forget to do some extracurriculars, and don't get caught. Okay? Don't. Get. Caught. And, Heidi, I'll try to be nicer to kids like you. It's just kinda hard for me.

DR. ROSEN: All right, girls. I'm afraid our time is up. This was a good first session. Can I count on all of you to come again next week?

BREATHE, BREATHE, BREATHE

Jin, his mother, Tea Master Sun, Deh-ja, and I return to Spring Well Village at the beginning of March 2008, just before the start of tea-picking season. My mother-in-law, who has not one good memory of life in the countryside, makes quite an impression on A-ma and the sisters-in-law when she volunteers to haul water on her first morning. Mrs. Chang will do anything to be with her son and the child growing inside me. I'm six months pregnant and my baby—*Let it be a son*—rolls and kicks and jabs. He stretches against my lungs, pushes a foot on the inside of my rib cage, and leans on my bladder. A-ma makes sure I eat her special soups with pig's feet, dates, and peanuts to nourish him and me. As for Deh-ja . . .

I was prepared to pay the fee to the headman, village elders, nima, and ruma for whatever sacrifices and ceremonies might have been required—as Ci-teh did for her brother—to allow Deh-ja back in the village. Although the birth of her human rejects was brought up by the ruma during the clash with Ci-teh, not a soul—by that, I mean everyone but A-ma, and she won't say a word, knowing how Deh-ja cares for me—recognizes her. She had been married into Spring Well Village for barely a year when her twins were born, twenty years have passed, and her life has been very hard. She looks older than A-ma and stranger than anyone people have seen on their televisions with her new dentures. If we lived entirely by the old ways, what I am doing would be a violation of Akha

Law. But if her human rejects had been born today, they wouldn't have met their sorrowful ends and she and Ci-do wouldn't have been banished. Deh-ja and I aren't taking any chances, though. We will keep her identity a secret. Fortunately, Deh-ja is a common name, and Ci-do and his new family are on a trip.

The ruma and nima announce the day to begin picking. Early on that morning, when it's still dark, I'm asked to say a few words. What is stranger—that half the village stands before me or that this worthless girl has overcome her past? And the risks are great for all of us. What we're doing has to work or else Ci-teh will take over. I begin with what Tea Master Sun taught me.

"*If you don't love tea, you can't make good tea,*" I recite. "Our tea trees are gifts from God. We can see the Akha Way in them. If you have cloned terrace bushes, one gets sick, and they all get sick. Same with pollarded trees, which are so weakened by the brutality of constant trimming. But when we find a wild tea tree, we know certain things. It has been strong enough to survive and grow on its own. It has its own separate and unique genetic makeup. If one tree gets sick, others surrounding it are unaffected. We Akha understand this, because we have a taboo against close relatives marrying. This is why we Recite the Lineage."

People murmur their agreement, understanding what's beneath my words. Purity, not counterfeits.

"As we pick today, let's remember our progress can only be slow—one bud set at a time. If we find perfect leaves, the tea we make will be the best. Together we'll share the Akha Way with the outside world."

When I step off the platform, Teacher Zhang approaches. "May I help?" he asks. I hand him a basket, and he joins us as we walk up the mountain guided by the last of the moonlight. The sun comes out and still we work, breaking only to have tea and eat rice balls. Once our baskets are full, we return to the village, where Tea Master Sun oversees laying out the leaves for their first rest.

The next day is even longer. We pick leaves and lay them out for their sunbath. Then we spend hours tossing six-kilo batches of yesterday's rested leaves over woks to kill the green. After fourteen hours, we sit outside together—families with families—eating meals prepared by those daughters-in-law who've remained in the village to care for the children too old to breast-feed and too young to help.

On the third morning, who should arrive? Mr. Huang and his son.

"I'm on spring break," Xian-rong announces, peeling out of the SUV. He's as skinny as ever and a little pale, the last probably from the ride through the turns, bumps, and ruts of the mountain.

"And I'm looking—"

I hold up a hand to stop Mr. Huang from uttering another word. "Don't say it!"

"To help," Mr. Huang finishes with a grin. He wears a straw hat, a rumpled shirt unbuttoned halfway down his chest, khaki pants that he's rolled up to his knees to keep cool, and plastic sandals.

Tea Master Sun rushes forward to shake hands. "Old friend! Young friend! So good to see two such expert tasters."

The men exchange cigarettes—not that any of them smoke—as a gesture of friendship and cordiality. Mr. Huang is as disconcerting to me as he's always been and I'll always be uncomfortable around him, but if Tea Master Sun trusts him, then maybe I should try to trust him a little bit. As for the boy, A-ma has already pulled him inside and is probably serving him one of her special brews before they go picking, continuing the friendship they've had since he and his father first came to our village.

The rest of us pick up baskets, sling them over our shoulders, and begin the long hike up the mountain to the tea trees.

The next eight days are our busiest, as we pick the first flush of leaves and process them. Once this is finished, Mr. Huang and Xian-rong prepare to return to Hong Kong. The boy looks better than when he arrived—less pale, and with a little weight from First Sister-in-law's good cooking. And of course Mr. Huang asks about my hidden grove, and I complete our customary ritual by refusing to show it to him. Some things will never change.

I pass on to my a-ba, my brothers, and other men in the village what I learned at the tea college. My plan—as was Mr. Huang's all those years ago—involves separating our leaves into two batches: one for *maocha,* the semiprocessed tea that people will be able to drink as is or let age naturally, the other artificially fermented. For now, we convert the two largest drying sheds in Spring Well into fermentation rooms. The semiprocessed tea is built up into piles a half meter high. We sprinkle them with water, cover them with burlap, and let the natural heat of decomposition begin to do its work. I know all is going well when bees begin to hover outside, so attracted are they to the sweet and warm scent. There's no evidence of mold or the sour odor of rot. Instead, the piles smell of earth and life, ripe apples and pollen. These two sets of tea will later be steamed, pressed into cakes, set outside on trays for another round of drying, and finally wrapped in our new Spring Well Village wrappers made of the finest rice paper.

Every evening, Tea Master Sun brews and pours tea for us. A-ma, A-ba, Mrs. Chang, Teacher Zhang (who is made to laugh in a way no one has seen before by my mother-in-law), and my brothers gather around the table along with Jin and me. We test the astringency of each batch of tea every three days to see how it's progressing. These are happy times with my family, even though the sisters-in-law must remain apart, as custom dictates.

My favorite moments, though, are those spent with the women in my family, doing a task that I always considered the most monotonous—sorting every single leaf into different grades. Yellow or defective leaves can be made into a low-grade tea for retired teachers, factory workers, and farmers in other provinces that we'll sell for forty yuan a kilo. The best leaves—and there are so few—are put aside for special batches I'll be making. And then there are all the leaves in between that will eventually find a proper purpose and the right buyers. Sitting around baskets outside my house, we women sort—a leaf, a leaf, a leaf. I learn who's in love—visiting the Flower Room, stealing love in the forest, getting married. I hear about petty squabbles. I'm told all the stories I missed during the years I was away.

And I get to see how much life has changed for young girls like my three nieces, who tell me about a new government campaign aimed at ethnic minority girls like them to achieve "independence, self-strengthening, intelligence, and dexterity." They're supposed to do things like learn to weave handbags with symbols showing their unique culture, but I don't see how that will help them become village cadres, go to college, or start their own small businesses. But when First Sister-in-law's daughter recites popular slogans, *"Give birth to fewer babies, plant more trees,"* and *"If you give birth to extra children, your family will be ruined,"* I understand that all three of them are thinking about and planning their lives in ways I clearly didn't at their age.

As for A-ma, she presides over us in the same way she always did—with a stern but fair hand. She's particularly tough on Deh-ja, who's adept at tea sorting but has far more important responsibilities ahead of her.

"My daughter will need to eat beneficial foods when her baby comes out," A-ma says, speaking to Deh-ja as though she's a servant. "Every new a-ma needs liver to replenish her lost blood, green papaya to help bring in the milk, and pig kidneys to alleviate her aches and pains. She needs food that will cause warming—ginger, chicken, and pumpkin. You will make sure the new a-ma eats this way for three cycles, thirty-six days and not one day less!"

Deh-ja is illiterate, so she recites recipes to herself as she sorts tea. As for me, I have a different idea of what will happen when my baby is ready to fall to the earth.

Although our days are long and it isn't monsoon season, I ask A-ma to help me make a proper Akha cap for my baby. Soon enough, all the women and girls in the household want to participate. Tonight, we sit together, a variety show on television blaring a pop song—"Fifty-five Minorities; One Dream"—in the background. The Olympics are coming and the campaign—to find fifty-five sets of twins—has inspired pride throughout the country. My three nieces giggle as they peer at my laptop screen, checking websites that post photos featuring "The Most Beautiful Girls of the 55 Ethnic Minorities" and peruse polls asking, "Which of the 55 ethnic minorities has the most beautiful and marriageable girls?" while my sisters-in-law try to remind me of skills I haven't used in years.

Third Sister-in-law still does the best handiwork, and she's as sharp with her lessons as ever, moving from gentle to cross in seconds, depending on how well I'm doing. "Needlework shows a woman's diligence and virtue," she reminds me. "You'll want to add coins, dried red chili peppers, and animal teeth to your baby's cap to drive away evil spirits. A well-protected baby should wear at least ten kilos of silver." (Which is not going to happen, but I don't tell her that.) "And don't forget to add some tiny mirrors," she recommends. "Spirits hate to see their own reflections." But when it comes to my embroidery? *Waaa!* I'm supposed to incorporate a frog, rabbit, monkey, and cat to show that my baby will be as smart, fast, vibrant, and vigilant as those animals. "My eyes sting to see such ugly work," she scolds. "You would let your baby be seen in that? Everyone will know his a-ma doesn't love him."

As I pull out my stitches, the other two sisters-in-law try to distract Third Sister-in-law from her ongoing criticisms by discussing the way the baby is lying within my body.

"The baby sleeps on Wife-of-Jin's right side," First Sister-in-law observes. "Surely it's a boy."

"No, no, no," Second Sister-in-law objects. "The baby rests on the left side. Sadly, it's a girl."

Third Sister-in-law can be easily swayed and her opinion can shift, depending on her mood. One night, my baby is a boy. The next night, she's convinced it's a girl. Tonight, though, she shrewdly asks A-ma, "What do you think?"

A-ma answers, "Anyone can see Girl is going to give her husband a son."

Later, when Jin and I are alone, I tell him the news, but his reaction is as expected. "Boy or girl," he insists, "I'll be happy. A healthy baby. That's all we want, isn't it?"

With each passing day, I love him a little more. My family admires him too, because, even though he's a member of the Han majority and I've married outside our tribe, he's respectful of our traditions.

Hard work, mutual respect, and a united goal are the threads that now bind Jin, my baby, my family, the people of my village, and me together.

After consultations with the headman, ruma, and nima, an auspicious date is selected for the annual rebuilding of Spring Well Village's spirit gate, which includes carving new protective figures of a man and a woman with their giant sex organs, as well as a dog and birds, all made from wood selected by the ruma for the strength of the trees' souls. The top male of each household participates, and A-ba takes Jin along as the head of the household in which I live. We women stay behind, as is required, but the ruma's voice carries to us through the trees.

"Let our spirit gate divert all bad things and make them go around the village," he trumpets. "Let our spirit gate chase away the hawk and the tiger. Let it bar seizures and leprosy. Wicked spirits, vampires, and werewolves, see how our male has the strength of iron between his legs to drive you in another direction! Gods, see how fat we've made our female figure. She'll make sure lots of babies will be born in Spring Well in the coming year." Last, he addresses the carved figures directly. "Powerful man, powerful woman, let all goodness and purity enter. Dog, bite all robbers and those who would wish us harm. Birds, allow riches to come in but not corrupt us."

The men are done by noon. We celebrate by sacrificing a pig, so the entire village—whether they are of Ci-teh's faction or mine—can share a banquet. Only on the next morning are we women allowed to visit the new gate.

But this will not be our only security measure. Jin and I drive to Laobanzhang to see what the people there are now doing to protect the authenticity of their teas. The headman shows us guard gates and tells us that three years of future harvests will be confiscated if someone is found selling counterfeits. So, in addition to our traditional spirit gate, the men of Spring Well install an electronic gate with a sentry post so that every vehicle that arrives can be inspected to make sure that passengers are not carrying in "outside tea" and every vehicle leaving is inspected to make sure that no outside tea has been fraudulently wrapped with our label. Every cake we process is also packaged with a newly required protection ticket, proving where it came from and what it is.

After two months, all the tea has been processed. Tea Master Sun returns home. I hire Teacher Zhang to run the business and oversee things when I'm away. He promises to write to Mrs. Chang. Jin, his mother, Deh-ja, and I must go back to Guangzhou so my husband can resume his business without the inconvenience of distance, I can test if the teas we've made are as good as I think they are in my new shop, which I'll open upon my arrival, and Deh-ja and my mother-in-law can fight over who can fret over me more.

Following what has become an unspoken tradition, A-ma and I visit my grove on my last day on Nannuo Mountain. As A-ma picks among the parasites on the mother tree to make her remedies, she has me scrape the yellow threads from the bark into a tiny container. When we're done, we wander through the grove and I confess to her my wish.

"I'd like to come home to have my baby," I say. "I want you to deliver it."

She doesn't take a moment to consider. "I must say no."

"Because it's taboo?" I ask. "You brought Yan-yeh into the world."

"It's not that. I'm honored that you've asked me, but all outside people go to a hospital or clinic to have their babies."

"I'm not an outside person—"

"I don't want you to go to just *any* hospital. I've discussed it with your husband, and he's promised to take you to America to have my grandson."

"What about the taboo of not visiting another village or else I might have a miscarriage there?"

"You've already traveled a lot with the baby inside you."

"But Spring Well is my childhood home, and I want you to deliver—"

"Girl, you need to have your baby in America for two reasons. First, so you'll be near Yan-yeh. Maybe in her heart she'll learn she has a brother. And second, to give your son American citizenship. Anyone who can afford it, does it. Even *I* know that."

"Will you come with us?"

The silver charms and coins on A-ma's headdress tinkle and twitter as she shakes her head. "I need to stay here in case someone gets sick. And a baby is due to arrive soon in Shelter Shadow Village. I could never let that bride go through delivery with just her mother-in-law to help her."

Later, A-ma gives me things to take to the American hospital in case they don't have proper medications: monkey callus for the doctor to rub on my back if the labor settles there, pangolin shell to massage my stomach to help contract my womb after the birth, the filings off a bear's paw in case I bleed badly, and a special weed to put between my legs after the delivery to heal up my "end."

"If your baby gets an eye infection, squeeze a little of your breast milk into his eye," she advises. "Do they have malaria over there? You already know the treatment, but I made a weak poultice for a newborn, just in case."

The opening of my new shop goes splendidly well. Within days, my three tea men are back too. It's wonderful to see them again, and they banter with me about the size of my belly and which of *their* names I will choose to name *my* baby. (Sweetly funny.) Obviously this wasn't the best time to start a new business, but so many people are relying on me and tea picking and selling follows its own schedule. So, just two weeks after saying goodbye to A-ma in our grove, I leave the care of my shop in the hands of my mother-in-law. The next day, Jin, Deh-ja, and I take a flight to California.

One week later, on the morning of May 15 in the Western calendar, I go into labor. When we arrive at Huntington Hospital in Pasadena, Jin fills out the paperwork and I'm wheeled to a labor room. Deh-ja promised A-ma not to leave my side, but within minutes she's out in the hallway arguing with Jin, who promised *me* not to leave my side. "If a husband sees his wife give birth, he may die from it!" I hear Deh-ja squealing like an irate sow. My husband's voice comes through the walls low, calm, and insistent. In the end, they both stay with me. I'm glad for their company and support, but this is so far from Akha tradition that together we vow never to tell A-ma.

The hospital staff is patient with us, but how can anyone argue with Jin and win? "If my wife says she needs to drink hot water to help the baby come out," he tells the nurse, "then get her some hot water." "If after the birth my wife needs to have a shell rubbed on her abdomen," he tells the doctor, "then this is what will happen." But when Deh-ja lays out a piece of indigo cloth on the side table and places a knife, some string, and an egg on it, Jin pulls out his wallet and tries to palm money into the doctor's hand.

"I'm just trying to see to your wife, sir," the doctor says stiffly. "That kind of thing is not necessary."

The contractions become more intense. Jin keeps saying, "Breathe, breathe, breathe," because it's something he's seen in movies. I love him, but in the worst moments I rely on Deh-ja. She helps me into a squatting position. I feel very high on the bed. The doctor and nurses try to crowd in, but she elbows them out of the way.

"Remember what your a-ma said about the fish," Deh-ja reminds me. "Just let your son slip out."

One more push and *wherp*.

"Will you please let me see the baby?" the doctor begs. "I'd like to clear his airway."

"Is it a boy?" I ask.

Jin answers, a big smile on his face. "Yes, it's a boy."

I edge away from the baby and ease myself back onto the mattress with my legs on either side of him. He's covered with slime, of course, but he's got a full head of black hair, his skin is pink and full of life, and between his legs are the three swollen things that will make me a grandmother one day. Deh-ja's lips move as she silently counts: Ten toes, ten fingers, two arms . . .

"Will someone tell this woman to move?" the doctor demands.

Deh-ja doesn't speak English, and Jin doesn't know what must happen next.

"In a minute. Please," I manage. "*A baby is not truly born until it has cried three times.*"

The doctor sighs and backs off a step.

With each of my baby's strong wails, Deh-ja speaks the ritual words: *"The first cry is for blessing. The second cry is for the soul. The third cry is for his life span."*

Then she motions for the doctor and nurse to come forward. He clips the umbilical cord and allows Jin to tie the string we brought below the clip. Then snip. A push and the friend-living-with-child comes out in an easy whoosh. Deh-ja hands me the heart-forget egg to eat, but already I'm forgetting the pains of childbirth. I feel tired but euphoric. The doctor takes my son to another table, where he and one of the nurses check his Apgar score. He's perfect.

When I'm allowed to bring him to my breast, I whisper into his face. "The four great spirits are the sun, moon, sky, and earth, but you also must learn about the lesser spirits who guide the wind, lightning, waterfalls, lakes, and springs. Everything on earth has a soul, even a single rice kernel."

Jin punches in the number for A-ba's new cellphone and hands it to Deh-ja, who makes the announcement in Akha: "The family will have game to eat now," meaning I've given birth to a son. A-ba's hollers come all the way through the phone to my bed.

In the middle of the night, Jin goes down the hall to watch as our baby is circumcised by Dr. Katz, a pediatrician recommended to us because he sees lots of Chinese children. Two mornings later, we're ready to be discharged, but we can't leave the hospital until we've given a woman on staff a name to write on my baby's birth certificate.

"Paul William Chang will be his American name," Jin announces.

Baby Paul—wearing the cap I made—is tucked into his car seat, and we go home. Deh-ja follows us upstairs and into Jin's and my room. He pulls back the covers and props up the pillows so I can rest on the bed with the baby. Deh-ja clucks and frets. But when Jin climbs on the bed next to me so we can gaze into our baby's face together, she starts darting from one side of the room to the other in agitation.

"What's wrong, Deh-ja?" Jin asks.

She refuses to look at Jin and sends her words to me in rapid Akha so he can't possibly follow. "The rules say that a husband

and wife may not sleep on the same mat together for ten cycles—one hundred and twenty days—because if you get pregnant again and another baby is born within a year, it will be considered . . ."

She's so distraught she can't finish the sentence. Remembering the taboo, I'm filled with sorrow for her. A baby born within a year of an older brother or sister is considered a twin.

"Deh-ja, come." I pat the mattress, and she sits down reluctantly. "I understand your worry, but I'm not going to sleep apart from Jin."

"What about the intercourse?" she whispers.

"I just had a baby!"

"Men are forbidden from trying to attempt the intercourse at this time for the reason you know and to give the wife time to recover in her parts," she persists, "but a man is a man and ten cycles lasts a very long time . . ."

I smile. "Don't worry. Jin and I will be fine."

She finally relents . . . up to a point. She goes out for a walk and comes back with lengths of ivy ripped from Rosie's yard. "I can't find magic vine, so this will have to do." She drapes the leafy strings on our front door and on the door to the nursery to bar baby-attacking spirits. After this, she shyly returns to my room. She pulls out from under her tunic a clear plastic bag with something red and squishy with a long eel-like thing floating inside.

"I took the friend-living-with-child when the man at the hospital wasn't looking," she practically crows.

"You stole my placenta?" I ask, which causes Jin to look up. My husband, who's been brave throughout, goes as white as sand when she flops it carelessly on the bedside table.

"I'm going to bury it under the house, beneath where you keep the family altar. Your son can't be separated from it! And don't worry. I'll take all the responsibility for watering it twice daily until it shrivels to nothing."

Later she comes back covered in cobwebs and dirt from the crawl space.

The next morning, we do our best to perform an Akha naming ceremony. I should have bought a rooster and raised it for Jin to sacrifice. (Deh-ja has pestered me endlessly about this.) Instead,

Jin goes to a butcher shop in Monterey Park, watches a chicken get killed and cleaned, and brings it home. After Deh-ja cooks the meal, she dips three strings in each dish, then ties them around Jin's, the baby's, and my wrists so we'll never be separated for long. Then she picks up my son and recites, "Get big! Be strong! Don't cry! May your crops be good and your animals healthy!"

The name Jin has only one syllable, so we name our baby Jin-ba.

"I hope he'll be the first in a long line," Jin says.

My feelings about Akha superstitions have wavered from the time I was a little girl and they're part of what drove me to ask for Teacher Zhang's help so many years ago, but if even one of Deh-ja's precautions will make Paul safe, then I'll never object. And I'll teach him the right traditions, like never crossing his legs near adults, and when thunder comes, dumplings must be made. I'll whisper in his ear that spirits are not too smart, and all the ways to fool them. I'll tell him that earthquakes are caused when a dragon living underground pulls at roots and shakes them and that lunar eclipses are caused by a spirit dog eating the moon. I'll tell him stories about A-ma Mata, the mother of humans and spirits, and how she divided the world. And, of course, I'll teach him to Recite the Lineage, even if it's only for my family and not his father's.

Two months later, Jin, Deh-ja, and I eat dinner in front of the television so we can watch the opening ceremonies of the Olympics taking place in Beijing. I rub a little food from our meal on Paul's lips to let him know we're eating, but really we're all distracted, mesmerized by the pageant our homeland is mounting for the world. The parade of twins from China's fifty-five ethnic minorities looks to be made up mostly of Han majority people dressed to look like minorities. Nevertheless, Deh-ja cries at the spectacle. Jin says that the most beautiful of all China's women are Akha, but what else can he say? And I contentedly hold my son.

The next few months in Arcadia are the happiest of my life. Jin's an ambitious and busy father. I've helped my village, and my new shop in the Fangcun Tea Market is doing moderately well, giving me hope that the value of Pu'er will return. I'm thirty years old. I love my son more than my own life. I'll do *anything* for him. So, personally, I've bounced back once again. But during this same time, world economies have been faltering. Now they take a deep dive. By the end of the year, property values in the United States and China have fallen into a chasm. All across the globe, people close their purses and fold up their wallets. Everyone is so scared that they stop buying toys, air conditioners, flat-screen televisions, and all manner of goods that would be shipped in cardboard. We're unsure if Jin's company will make it through this difficult period. But as Mrs. Chang reminds us on the phone one afternoon, "You and Jin are fortunate to have a son in the era of the One Child policy." That is what gives Jin the strength to fight for his business, and me the determination to help him as he has helped me.

PART V

THE TEA GIRL OF HUMMINGBIRD LANE

2012–2016

Assignment: In AP English, we've been focusing on writing essays in preparation for the college applications you'll be writing next year. Now I'd like you to take a different approach by exploring your imaginations with a short story. (No groans, please.) Writers are often told to write what they know. Take something that happened to you and reimagine it as a piece of fiction. You may write in the first or third person. You may also change the names, if you feel that will give you more freedom. (Submissions will be read *only* by me.) Please remember that for your college apps, everyone does a sport, aspires to be a doctor, or writes about their parents' immigrant experience to America. You can't get in with these clichéd topics on your applications. Be creative, expand your minds, and let's see if you can come up with something that will be translatable to a college essay designed to make you stand out. Due October 13, 2012.

The Disappointment
by
Haley Davis

On a dark night in March, Adam and Alice Bowen sat their daughter, Amy, down for a talk. Was it going to be another lecture about not raiding the liquor cabinet? Or concerned inquiries about what was happening in therapy? Or would it be the same old "How was school today? How did you do on your AP Chemistry test? Did you finish your homework?" Were they going to tell her they were separating? (Which, honestly, wouldn't have surprised Amy one bit.) Maybe her dad had been diagnosed with cancer or needed open-heart surgery? (This would have terrified Amy but wouldn't have surprised her either, because her dad was already pretty old when she was adopted.) Instead, when Adam began, "This summer . . ." Amy's hopes flew through the roof. Were they finally going to relent and let her go to Europe with her friends, by themselves? "We're taking you to China. We want you to discover your roots." That was about the last thing in the world Amy wanted or would have asked for. Really. Because who wanted to go on a family vacation at her age? But what can you do? *Fight against it. That's what.*

"I'm not going on one of those stupid heritage tours," she said.

Once upon a time, she would have loved to have gone to China. She'd wanted to get information about the object she'd been found with. Most babies abandoned in China were left with a special gift from their birth mothers: a locket, a good-luck charm, a hand-knit sweater or hand-sewn quilt, maybe even a little Chinese money. Amy knew this because she'd seen those things in pictures: some new mom and dad posing with their baby and holding up her little gift like it was a soccer trophy. Amy's memento from her birth mother, however, was a little unusual: a round cake of tea, decorated with meaningless symbols, and weighing about a pound. When Amy was little, she used to take it out every night and stare at it. It had to mean something, but what?

Then there'd been this incident in the second grade when she'd done a project and told everyone in the entire school—and their parents—that she was the first person in her family to come to America. It was the truth, but she'd caused her adoptive parents pain, which hadn't been her intention, at all. Amy had gotten really scared. *Would they send her away?* She still struggled with her identity, and she sometimes searched the Internet to see if she could find anything about her birth mother or the tea cake. In secret, because she'd never forgotten the repercussions of the second-grade episode. She didn't want to hurt her parents again, but they just weren't getting it. After all, what did they think she'd get out of a trip to China now? She wouldn't find her roots, she wouldn't get any answers about the tea cake or her identity, and—here was the kicker—the trip would make her feel worse. She already ached with loss over her birth mother.

Traveling to China would be no help. Besides, practically all the girls she knew who'd been adopted had already gone there with Roots & Shoots Heritage Tours, a company that specialized in expeditions for families with adoptees, so a trip like this wouldn't make her special or anything. She was merely part of a big wave that had brought thousands of girls like her to these shores. *Pretty weird. Pretty sad. And no big deal.*

"Have we *ever* taken you on a tour—anywhere?" Alice asked. "We don't do tours. You know that."

"But—"

"This might be the last time we all travel together," Adam said, and again Amy flashed that something might be wrong with him. "After you graduate, you'll probably want to go on a trip with your friends." *Damn straight.* "And after that, you'll likely be spending your vacations in a lab somewhere, or out in the field, or helping some scientist change the way we view the world, like your mom—"

"Oh, Adam—"

It went on like that—some stupid lovefest—but Amy didn't put up much of a fuss, because what if this *was* the last vacation they all took together? Still, did it have to be China? Why not go back to the South of France or do something new, like hike the Outback? And, of course, once the itinerary came in, Amy saw how her parents were shaping the trip to be a heritage tour, even if it wasn't called a Heritage Tour, because their last stop before flying home would be Yunnan province, where she was born.

The Bowen family left LAX at night. They were all half dead by the time they landed in Beijing thirteen hours later. They went through passport control and customs. Then they pushed through a set of double doors and *oh my God!* Always Amy had felt like the one Chinese face in a sea of white faces. Now here were a bazillion people who looked like her, and it was her parents who stood out.

They spotted a young woman holding a card with the Bowen name printed on it. She introduced herself as their Beijing guide, and her English was pretty pathetic. She wore a wrinkled skirt, a little white blouse, and scuffed shoes. A supercheap plastic purse hung off her shoulder. She led the way through the writhing throng with her arm extended to clear a path for the mismatched threesome. Amy was seventeen, but she clung to her mother like you wouldn't believe.

They went through another set of doors, and it was like stepping into an oven. Truly. Like you got a baking sheet all ready with cookie dough and your mom was going to let you slide it into the oven, but when you did, all you could think about was Hansel and Gretel and the way the witch wanted to cook them. People pushed and shoved as they loaded their suitcases, beat-up cardboard boxes, and these satchel things made out of some kind of plastic woven material in red, white, and blue into trunks, the underbellies of buses, even onto the roofs of cars. They shouted. They noisily sucked junk from their noses, coughed, and spit on the ground. It was beyond gross. And the smell? Too much garlic—like Amy had landed in a gigantic mouth with really bad breath. Add to that too much sweat and too much cigarette smoke wafting off people's clothes. *Nasty.*

"Honey," Alice said, "you're cutting off my circulation."

Amy loosened her grip on mother's hand, but not by much.

They piled into a minivan. The guide sat up front with the driver, who didn't say a single word. The traffic? It was crazy! And it was the middle of the night! They crept past apartment buildings—gray, with dim fluorescent lights illuminating a room here and there. It took Amy a while to figure out what was hanging out all the windows: bamboo sticks draped with laundry.

They arrived at the hotel, and it was ginormous! And superfancy. Adam handed over their passports and his credit card. A uniformed boy put their luggage on a cart and escorted the family to connecting rooms. Alice and Adam were excited, talking nonstop about all the things they were going to do.

Suddenly Alice stopped midsentence to stare at her daughter. "Do you have to sneer?" she asked. "We're doing this trip for you!" Later, after she got in bed, Amy heard her mother say, "Teenagers!" A part of Amy wanted her dead.

When Amy woke the next morning, she was disoriented, because her mom was *still* talking about everything she and Adam had planned, except now she was wearing shorts, a T-shirt, and a Dodgers baseball cap. Amy was so embarrassed, she wanted to pull the covers back over her head, but that wasn't on the itinerary. An hour later—showered, fed, and sunscreen slathered on every exposed piece of skin—they left the hotel. The air outside was disgusting. By the time Amy got to the minivan, her arms were totally wet. No one could sweat that fast, but there was so much moisture in the air that it was like someone had sprayed her with hot water. And it was only nine in the morning.

They walked across one blisteringly hot square or courtyard after another: The Temple of Heaven. Tiananmen Square. The Forbidden City. The sun glared down. Adam asked the guide how hot it was. She answered, "The government gives people the day off if it goes over forty degrees centigrade." He asked, "So, again, how hot is it today?" She gazed across the square like she wasn't with the Bowens. "I heard it was going to be forty-four degrees centigrade and eighty percent humidity." Adam whistled; Alice sighed. Amy took the trouble to make the calculation to Fahrenheit. *111 degrees!*

Adam bought bottles of water. The Bowens drank and sweat, drank and sweat some more. Adam took Amy's picture about a thousand times. She saw more people from around the world in the first hour than she had in her entire life. And then there were the Chinese. They were *everywhere*.

Since the weather was so gross, Amy ended up changing her clothes three times every day. Even her bra and panties. The Bowens visited more tourist spots: the Summer Palace, the Great Wall of China, the tomb soldiers in Xian, the Bund in

Shanghai. China was strange, though. It didn't have much connection to what she'd learned about it in Families with Children from China or even from going to her friends Jasmine's and Jade's houses. It was big, polluted, and crowded. If Amy had once daydreamed about meeting her birth mother, she now understood it would be impossible to find her—one woman out of the proverbial 1.3 billion people.

Finally, they flew to Kunming in Yunnan, where it was much cooler. They stayed at another fancy hotel, which prompted Adam to ask Alice, "Can you believe how much everything's changed since the last time we were here? You've got to hand it to Deng Xiaoping. *To get rich is glorious . . .*"

When they were out with their new guide, Amy heard sounds that were vaguely familiar, yet had no meaning. She saw people with skin like hers—darker—who turned out to be members of hill tribes. Sometimes people nodded to her on the street or pointed at her, but what did *that* mean? Did they recognize her in some way or did they simply think she looked peculiar with her white parents? A couple of times, people came up to her and spoke to her in Chinese. "I don't speak Chinese," Amy always answered, in English. Then those same people would turn to her parents and ask, in perfect English, "Is she your tour guide?" But how could Amy have possibly been their tour guide?

The Bowens spent the next two days hiking up mountains to take in this or that scenic spot. Amy's opinion? One view was just like another, even if these had a temple or a big statue on them. Still, something about the air and the panoramas got to her—like she had something in her eye, or pollen up her nose, or a memory she could sense but couldn't capture. Then one day, during one of their sightseeing hikes, she was standing and looking at yet another view. The pattern of the hills, a stream running through them, a path winding up through the terraces . . .

"Mom! Look!"

"What is it, honey?"

"Do you see it?" She pointed, buzzing with excitement. "It's just like my tea cake!"

"What do you mean?" Alice asked.

"We've always looked at the *V*'s as *V*'s, like simple bird drawings. But don't you see? They're the canyons between the mountains! The wavy lines are terraces. The design that meanders"—she traced what she could remember from the tea cake in the air with her index finger—"is a river or creek or something like that. The design on my tea cake is a map!"

"Oh my God!" Adam exclaimed. "You're right!"

But Alice, ever practical, asked, "But a map to what?"

"To where I was born!" Amy was so energized by her discovery that she was practically jumping up and down. "So I can meet my birth family!"

Adam and Alice exchanged glances. Amy thought, *Don't ruin this for me*. Her father looped an arm over her shoulder, pulled her close, and stared at the view with her.

"It is a map. And it's amazing you figured that out. Truly amazing. But, honey— "

"Remember how there's that design in the middle of the tea cake?" Amy interrupted. "I've always thought it looked like a tree, but it's got to be my real mom."

Alice edged away.

"Your mom is your real mom," Adam said softly.

"I didn't mean it that way." Amy didn't either. "But think about it! *X* marks the spot! It's got to be her."

"Maybe you're right." He still had that gentle tone, trying to manage his wife, who was all upset that Amy didn't consider Alice to be her real mother, and his daughter, who was as excited as she'd ever been. "But with any map you need a starting point. The *V*'s—the canyons and mountains—could be anywhere. We don't even know which direction is north."

What felt like a bomb going off obliterated Amy's elation. Her father was right, and it was a huge disappointment. But then she realized . . . *I always thought my birth mom was try-*

ing to send me a message. I was right. Goose bumps rippled along her arms.

"I'm sorry, honey," Alice said, extending her hand.

Amy took it, because she didn't want to hurt her mother's feelings any more than she already had when what she felt inside was a buoyant thrill. Her birth mom was real to her in a way she'd never been before.

That night Amy dreamed about her birth mother and the map. In the morning, she tiptoed into the adjoining room and stood at the foot of the bed, waiting for one of her parents to wake up. Alice's eyes flickered open first, and she startled when she saw her daughter staring down at her.

"What is it? Are you okay?"

"My real mom . . . I mean my birth mom, wants me to find her."

Adam blinked awake. "What's going on?"

"Let's put up a flyer," Amy announced. "Like for a lost dog."

"Where would you put it?" Alice asked, doubtful.

"On telephone poles. In restaurants. Like what people do at home. Please."

"What do you think, Adam?" Alice asked.

He sat all the way up and propped some pillows behind his back. He had the same grave look on his face as he'd had yesterday when he told Amy she needed a starting point for the map.

"We picked you up in Kunming, but you aren't from here," he said. "You were brought from another orphanage."

"I know, but what if she's visiting?" Amy wasn't going to let this go. "*We*'re visiting. What if *she*'s visiting too? What if she *moved* here? What if she's outside *right this minute*?"

"What if," Alice echoed, shaking her head sadly.

"Please," Amy begged.

"If we do this, we don't want you to have false hope," Adam said.

"We don't want you to be disappointed," Alice added. "You have to consider the odds."

Amy went back to her room, opened her laptop, and signed in to the hotel's Internet service. Numbers came easily to her so she expected to find a quick set of figures to noodle with. Except true numbers didn't exist. The first 61 adoptees came to the U.S. in 1991. That number continued to rise—to close to 63,000 between 1991and 2005. After that, the stats were harder to find, with a steady decline in adoptions from China. But if there were something like 100,000 Chinese adoptees, and approximately 650,000,000 females in China, then Amy had a one in 6,500 chance in finding her mother. The chances got a lot better if you considered only women in their childbearing years.

"If the numbers on the Internet are accurate," Alice said after Amy presented her findings.

Amy pulled up a story she'd once found and bookmarked on the laptop's screen. "Look at this, Mom. Here's an article about someone who found her mother! It says here that twenty families have been reunited!"

"How?" Alice asked as her husband picked up the laptop and began reading.

"She was on a trip like this with her parents. They were walking down the street when a total stranger came up and said, 'You look like my sister's daughter.' And guess what. That woman turned out to be the girl's aunt!"

"That's a one-in-a-million occurrence."

Amy leaned over her dad, hit a few keys, and pulled up a different story. "Then what about this one? Another family was on a trip, just like ours. Her family made a flyer to post. The first place they went in was a café. They asked if they could hang the flyer. The couple who ran the café looked at the flyer and burst into tears. It was their daughter! Now the two families spend every Christmas together."

"Those sound like made-up stories," Alice said. "There's all sorts of nonsense on the Internet."

Adam looked up from the laptop. "Actually, honey, what Amy's telling you is from an article in *The Boston Globe*. The first one was in *The New York Times*."

"But what are the odds?" Alice asked, repeating her earlier concern. "I don't want Amy to be disappointed."

"I promise not to be disappointed," Amy said.

"Mom's right, you know," Adam said.

"Please, Dad, please," Amy pled, turning all her focus on her father, because he rarely said no to her. "Will you let me do it? Please?"

But Alice gave in first. "There's no harm in trying. Get some paper from the desk. Let's figure out what you want to say."

They spent the next hour working together, narrowing down the details and keeping the English simple:

> My name is Amy Bowen. I was born on or about November 24, 1995. I am looking for my biological family. I was found in a cardboard box. I was wrapped in a blue blanket. There was a cake of tea in the box with me. I am short. My skin is dark compared to most Chinese.
>
> In case you want to know more about me, I am good at science and math. I like to ski and ride horses. I also like to hang out with friends. I am very nice. I hope you would like to meet me.
>
> To contact me, please e-mail my father at ABowen@ABArbor.com.

After breakfast, they went to the business center. They hadn't brought the photo of Amy taken when she was first found or any of those that Alice and Adam took the day they got her. All they had was the fourth-grade school picture from Alice's wallet and Amy's current passport photo. She positioned them on the piece of paper with the note and pushed the button to make copies. Then they walked around the neighborhood where they were staying and tacked up the notices. By the time they were done, Amy knew that nothing would come of her plan: maybe her birth mother didn't read English, maybe she didn't have a computer to send an e-mail, maybe she didn't know what a computer or e-mail were. And so many people lived here. What kind of coincidence could there be in the world for Amy's birth mother to be walking down this particular street, see a picture of Amy in her school uniform, and think, *Oh, there's my baby!*

Amy was very disappointed, and she felt herself spiraling into sadness. Her mom and dad worried about her, because she had a history of anxiety and depression. Her dad tried to distract her with jokes. Her mom offered to take her shopping for souvenirs to give to her friends. But Amy had a serious case of the blues. On the last night of the trip, Alice knocked on the door that connected the two rooms.

"May I come in?" she asked, opening the door a couple of inches.

"Sure, Mom."

Alice sat on Amy's bed. "I'm sorry this didn't work out. I'm sorry we brought you here. I'm—"

"Don't worry about it."

"Oh, honey, I wish I could make you understand . . ."

The way Alice's voice trailed off forced Amy to ask, "Understand what?"

"How your dad and I felt when we got you. What you meant to us then. What you mean to us now. In the months leading up to the phone call that told us we could come and get you, I did everything I could to understand Chinese culture. I went on a walking tour of Chinatown, I devoured Amy Tan's books, I watched Chinese movies. And we had all the practical stuff to do too. Our finances were critiqued and notarized; we were interviewed and authenticated. We traveled with six other family units. Three couples were married, two were gay, and there was a single woman with her mom. The way you cried—"

"I've seen the photo album," Amy said. In those pictures, you could see the family-unit people weeping and laughing. All the babies were crying too, but her mouth had been a giant gaping hole, her eyes were squished shut, her legs and arms—her whole body actually—were as stiff as a board, and her cheeks were bright red because she was screaming her head off. "I cried, and I didn't sleep."

"The other babies cried, but you howled," Alice agreed. "You howled *and* you wouldn't sleep. I'm sure you understand the objective cause-and-effect reasons for that."

"Objective cause-and-effect reasons? Can you for once speak to me from your heart and not like a scientist?"

"I'm trying." Alice sighed. "I know I can be frustrating sometimes, but I only want the very, very, very best for you. I wish for you to feel smart and invincible."

To Amy's ears, her mother's wishes sounded more like pressure to *do* more and *achieve* more, but she didn't say that.

"You see," Alice continued, "your crying was only natural. You were older than the other babies. You'd never seen a white person before. We don't think you'd been picked up or held very much. You needed a lot of love. We gave you the love and you stopped crying, but, honey sweet, we're still waiting for you to sleep."

Ha, ha, ha, and blah, blah, blah.

"I know. Stupid humor. I'm sorry."

"Would you please stop saying you're sorry?"

"What I'm trying to tell you is that I've always wondered if you were crying because you missed your birth mother. I've thought about her every day since we got you. I couldn't have a baby myself, so I've wondered if she was afraid when you were born. Was she in a hospital? Was she alone? Was your birth father at her side?"

"I've wondered the same things too," Amy admitted.

"Not a day has gone by when I haven't wondered if I hurt you more than helped you by wresting you away from your homeland and your culture. Even when you were a baby, I wondered when you would start to resent me for that. Maybe even hate me."

"I don't hate you, Mom."

"The first night your dad and I had you, we piled pillows on the extra double bed in our room to make a protective nest for you. Your dad fell asleep, but I stayed awake all night. I wept when you grabbed my finger and held it tight. Your birth mother gave me the greatest gift of my life—a beautiful, talented, and kind daughter. Every day I take a moment to thank her for that. Your first smile, your first tooth, your first day of preschool, your first *everything*—I thought of her and thanked her. And she is with you always. Your birth father too. They're in your tears. They're in your laugh. They're in you in ways you'll never be able to count. And their love is what sent you to me."

Tears began to well in Alice's eyes, and Amy felt herself being swept into her mother's ocean of love.

"From the first moment I saw you all the way to today and for as long as I live, I know that you are the daughter who was meant for me. I can never be a replacement for your birth mother, but I've done—and will continue to do—everything I can to complete what should have been her journey. I love you, and I'll always love you."

Amy held on to those words like they were a lifesaver.

Evaluation

Haley,

While you completely ignored my admonition not to write about the immigrant experience, I congratulate you for coming at it from a unique angle. There's much you can work with here as you begin to think about your college app, but bear in mind that there will be other young women across the country who may write similar essays about their own adoption experiences. A few nitpicking points: Amy, Alice & Adam feels a bit cloying to me. (Do they really all need to start with an *A*?) Watch your language usage & remember that a thesaurus isn't always your friend. And of course you'd never want to use *bazillion* or *ginormous* on a college app, but I'm sure you know that.

I'm quite conflicted about the ending. As your teacher, I

would have hated to see you fall back on the Shakespearean trope of coincidence. As a mom, I really wanted your main character to find her birth mother.

For a math-science girl, you did an excellent job. Now take the nonfiction elements and run with them, making sure you keep the emotional resonance of your fictional narrative.

CHERRY BLOSSOMS IN SPRING

"A-ma! A-ma!"

My son's screams pull Jin and me out of sleep.

"It's all right," I say, patting my husband's arm. "I'll go."

I pad barefoot down the darkened hallway to Paul's room, where he sits up in his bed, shaking, his hands clutching his duvet, tears streaming down his face. Dr. Katz, our pediatrician, calls what Paul gets night terrors. They've worsened the past two weeks, which the doctor says is completely normal. "Usually children are scared when they start first grade. They're with all the big kids now. But in second grade, a lot of kids are scared about space aliens. Maybe that's what's happening here." The ruma, nima, and A-ma would see things differently. They'd say Jin-ba is being stalked by bad spirits. Deh-ja has taken precautions, but stringing ivy around his room hasn't seemed to help. In fact, it may have made things worse, because the kids who've come over on playdates see it as *tu,* whether they're white or Han majority.

"Paul, look at me," I say gently as I sit on the edge of the bed. "Do you see me?"

The saddest thing about his night terrors is that he's not asleep but he's not awake either. He looks at me but sees something beyond or through me. His eyes are wide. He trembles. He screams again. "A-ma!"

I hold my hands out to him and rub my thumbs against the tips of my fingers in the traditional Akha gesture to bring him to me. He climbs onto my lap, but I won't know he's fully conscious until he calls me Mom. Rarely is he lucid enough to tell me what his dreams are about apart from "monsters." Tonight, though, he tells me a little of what he remembers.

"I got lost in the forest. The trees looked cracked and broken. I didn't hear any birds. It was quiet and hot. So much sweat was running down my legs I thought I'd peed my pants."

I tighten my arms around him. He's had a few bed-wetting episodes lately. If he'd been raised in Spring Well, the liquid would have just spilled down between the slats of the bamboo floor. Here, Dr. Katz calls it "something we need to be concerned about."

"Then the rains came," Paul sputters. "Monsoon, like you've told me about. I felt like I was drowning. Drowning in the forest is a terrible death, isn't that what you said, Mom?"

Mom. Good.

"You aren't going to drown in a monsoon. You live in Arcadia. We're in a drought— "

"But, Mom— "

"*Shhh*. Close your eyes. I'm right here."

I hum to him until I feel his breath deepen. I don't need A-ma to help me interpret my son's dream. He's scared about school. I understand that. But he's also picked up on some of my anxieties. I need to be more careful when I'm talking on the phone to my brothers, and I need to be extra-vigilant in my conversations with Jin. Over the last couple of years, the dry seasons in the tea mountains have lasted longer, while the monsoons have become more intense. Our tea leaf bud sets are bursting early, and the ten-day picking season has been prolonged. Worse, the new weather pattern is stunting growth—just as Paul saw in his dream. I can taste the change in the leaves, but I'm not a scientist and I don't know what it means. Still, I worry, and that worry has invaded my son's sleeping hours.

Nothing is worse than seeing your child suffer. Every morning I ask about his dreams. Did a tree fall? Was there a fire, a dog on a roof, or a broken egg? Instead of these questions calming him and helping him understand his place in the world, he's become even more scared and his dreams more tormented. I feel terrible about it, and I honestly don't know what to do.

I slip out of bed at sunrise, heat water for tea, and roll rice balls in crushed peanuts for Paul's lunch. Jin wanders in, kisses me, sits down, and opens the paper.

"May I have a peanut butter and jelly sandwich instead?" Paul begs when he comes to the kitchen and sees what I've prepared. "Just today. Just this once."

As if I would ever do such a thing.

Into my silence, he says, "Auntie Deh-ja would make one for me."

Deh-ja would too—she spoils him to the extreme—but she's in Yunnan for a month visiting her natal family, as she now does every year.

"Mom," my son persists, "why is what I want different than a ball of rice with peanuts on the outside? White outside, brown inside. Brown outside, white inside. Same thing!"

"Is that what the Han majority children eat?" I ask, because if they aren't eating Chinese food in school, maybe Paul shouldn't either.

"Oh, Mom! Everyone brings Chinese food from home."

"Then—"

"Addison likes peanut butter and jelly—"

"Addison." I taste the three syllables on my tongue. I glance at Jin, who looks up from his copy of the *Chinese Daily News*. *Addison? What kind of name is that?*

I drive car pool in the mornings, so Paul and I pick up two other kids on the way to school. Music plays on the radio. The kids sing along. I pull up to the curb for the car pool drop-offs and hit the button to unlock the doors. Paul's the last to get out. He lingers by the door as he puts on his backpack.

"Is this Addison white or Han majority?" I ask.

But he just waves, slams the door, and runs to a group of boys I recognize—all born here, all Han majority. I can't stay to watch him enter the building—too many cars and minivans behind me—but I feel a tug on my heart. We may not have strings tied around our wrists any longer, but I'll always be connected to my son.

Driving home, I have time to reflect. I'm thirty-seven, in the summer of my life. My husband is successful. He's kept his cardboard business, but that's not his real focus these days. During the darkest days of the recession, when stocks kept tumbling and real estate prices crashed, he began buying houses at the bottom of the market, which he fixed up and sold to men like himself who wanted a foothold in America and a safe place to park their money. When our son turned five, Jin underwent yet another transformation. He was finally able to put away the ghost of his father. "Paul is the same age I was when I betrayed my father," he told me. "I now understand that he would have loved me no matter what I'd done, as I'll always love my son."

With the burdens of a lifetime lifted from Jin's shoulders, he started building housing tracts in Walnut, Riverside, Irvine, and Las Vegas—for Han majority people—featuring wok kitchens and following *feng shui* construction practices. Still not content, he opened real estate offices in the lobbies of the Hilton and the Crowne Plaza—the top San Gabriel Valley hotels for Chinese tourists—and hired "jumper consultants" to provide information on mortgages and schools, help people through the U.S. EB-5 visa process, and sell properties ranging from modest houses for speculation to luxurious mansions starting at $10 million for sons and daughters attending USC or Occidental.

I've found success as well. Since 2008, the price for good tea has steadily risen. Then this year, boom! Pu'er's value skyrocketed again. My company is large—with offices in the San Gabriel Valley and Guangzhou. We sell raw, processed, and aged Pu'er from inexpensive to extremely rare and expensive blends that are given as gifts to the most powerful leaders in China. I have plenty of capital, and I do my own sourcing. I have arrangements with nearly every village on Nannuo Mountain. Farmers come to me each year, hearing I pay fairly and reliably, to tell me they've discovered ancient tea trees or abandoned tea gardens high, high up on the mountain. I tell them their tea must come from trees at least three hundred years old, and the farmers themselves need to drink from the leaves first to make sure the trees aren't so wild that they'll make people ill. My three brothers check every batch. And, if a farmer ever attempts to sneak poor-quality leaves into what he sells me, we'll never do business again.

I even have a fermenting factory in Menghai. The main room is as large as an American football field. Piles of tea—each twelve by thirty feet and a foot deep—cover the entire floor, each weighing five tons and each at a different stage of fermentation. The whole complex is surrounded by a high wall topped with barbed wire. I receive many requests for tours from international connoisseurs, dealers, and scientists. I turn them all away, saying, "If you want to learn about our ancient tea trees, come to Nannuo Mountain." Every tea I make is artisanal: no pesticides, no mechanization. All that can carry on without my presence—except for tea-picking season, when Paul and I return to the mountains to supervise picking, processing, and fermenting—because I have the help and trust of my family.

My three nieces who were all born in the same year are now nineteen years old. The government has a message for them: "Your duty to the nation is to have a child of high quality," but not one of them has married. They dismiss those busybodies who tell them that soon they'll be as yellowed pearls—too old to be fully loved. They still have eight years before they're officially labeled *shengnu*—leftover women—so they laugh at the television shows that show women desperately trying to get a man at any cost: *The Price of Being a Shengnu, Go, Go, Shengnu,* and *Even Shengnu Get Crazy*. They tease each other about the "twelve products to help *shengnu* forget about loneliness," and give those items as birthday gifts to keep the joke going: a garlic peeler, rainbow-colored linens, and single-serving teapots.

First Sister-in-law's daughter works for me in my shop in the Fangcun Tea Market. Second Sister-in-law's daughter has remained in the village but travels all through the mountains on her motorcycle to make sure the farmers who sell to us are picking the very best leaves. Third Sister-in-law's daughter lives in the San Gabriel Valley and handles my Internet sales. When and if my nieces decide they want to go-work-eat with a husband, they'll have plenty of men to choose from, for there are 30 million more young males seeking mates in China than there are prospective brides. But how to convince them? "I do what I want to do," First Sister-in-law's daughter told me the last time I saw her. "I go where I want to go." Be that as it may, I know for a fact that my mother-in-law now sits on her bench in Martyrs' Memorial Gardens when she's in Guangzhou or wanders San Gabriel Square—what we sometimes laughingly call the Great Mall of China—when she's visiting us to look for eligible (wealthy and handsome) husbands for my nieces. Let them try to get out of that!

Ci-teh and I still avoid each other, but I hear a lot about her, as I'm sure she hears about me. She converted much of the land she subleased to coffee, as she vowed she would seven years ago. Yunnan has even become a tourist attraction for Han majority coffee enthusiasts, and it's said that by the end of the year more than a million people in our province will be working in the coffee industry, since we provide over 95 percent of China's coffee production. As an added benefit, growing coffee has become a way for our government and those of our neighbors—like Laos—to replace opium poppy crops. Ci-teh sells Yunnan coffee to Starbucks for use in its Asian outlets and helped Nestlé found a coffee institute in Pu'er City, while I acted as the go-between who assisted the town of Libourne in France, home of the Pomerol and Saint-Emilion vineyards, in signing a marketing and trade agreement with Pu'er City to cross-promote their wine and our tea because both share polyphenols, which are reported to be so good for health.

I pull into the garage and find a note from Jin saying that he won't be home until late afternoon. Sitting at the kitchen counter, I open my laptop and scan through my e-mails, looking for one in particular. During my last trip from the airport in Jinghong to Menghai, I saw among the many billboards that now line the roadway one that had been purchased by an individual family. It showed an infant's face blown up so big it was blurry. The type, however, was completely clear:

> I was found outside the post office in Jinghong on May 21, 1994. My American name is Bethany Price. If you are my mother, please contact me.

The birth date and clothes were wrong, and even as a newborn, she looked more Dai than Akha to me, but seeing the billboard inspired me to send an e-mail to the girl. Could this Bethany have passed through the Social Welfare Institute in Kunming as my daughter did? Might her parents have met the parents of my Yan-yeh? Does Bethany know other girls adopted from Xishuangbanna prefecture?

Today, again, no return message.

Nor do I have any inquiries from the messages I've left on various websites. A year ago, after finding posts written by adopted girls looking for their mothers, or, more infrequently, mothers like me, looking for their daughters, I wrote my own:

> Yunnan birth mother searching for daughter left at Menghai Social Welfare Institute. She was given to new parents by Kunming Social Welfare Institute. My baby was born on November 24, 1995, in the Western calendar. I named her Yan-yeh. I put her in a box. She was found by street cleaners. I hid to make sure they delivered her to safety. I now have a seven-year-old son. I would love to find my missing daughter. You have a brother and a mother who love you very much.

I didn't mention the tea cake. In a murder investigation, as I've learned from American television shows, you always hold out the most important evidence. Would someone take the bait? But the few e-mails I've received ask the same basic question: Are you my mother? I respond with: Were you found with anything in your swaddling?

We're trying to grasp fish with our bare hands.

I've never forgotten what A-ma said to me before I left Nannuo Mountain to give birth to my son. She wanted me to have him in America in hopes that my daughter might intuit she had a brother. I know Yan-yeh is out there. I have the photo and footprint from the Social Welfare Institute. (I'll forever be grateful that she was cared for by the good matrons there and not a baby who was stolen or confiscated from her parents. Even the Chinese government estimates that between 30,000 and 60,000 children "go missing" each year to be trafficked illegally and exported like so many factory products. I ache for the mothers in China and the mothers here who must always wonder . . .) Nevertheless, shouldn't there be more clues and traces of Yan-yeh? So I search the Internet when Jin is in meetings, at night when I can't sleep, and on Wednesday afternoons during Paul's soccer practice.

I've stumbled across several sites advertising "orphanage reunion tours," where girls (and their families) can see the cribs they slept in and meet the people who once watched over them. Could my daughter have gone to China with Our Chinese Daughters' Foundation or Roots & Shoots Heritage Tours? Even if she did, would a tour operator take a girl and her family to a town as small as Menghai? Wouldn't they show people like my Yan-yeh the larger Social Welfare Institute in Kunming, where she was picked up? Mightn't she (or her parents) want to look at her file? But all the files were destroyed in the fire. Still, once a week, I go to the tour websites and examine the photos of white parents or single white mothers traveling with their Chinese daughters. The girls seem totally American with their flip-flops, shorts, and Hello Kitty T-shirts. Would Yan-yeh look like me? Like San-pa? Like my a-ma? Or his a-ma? But I haven't seen a girl with Akha characteristics or who resembles anyone of our blood.

On a Facebook page sponsored by an international group of Chinese adoptees, I saw photos of babies from the day they were found and the day they were delivered to their new parents. One infant was dressed in a dirty snowsuit with a purple knit hat. Her cheeks were chaffed with heat rash. Another—sound asleep—wore a blouse with a flouncy polka-dot collar. Yet another, perhaps eighteen months old, wore a diaper that hung down to her striped kneesocks, which, in turn, ended in red plastic sandals. I found photos of babies in ethnic minority caps, hats, and scarves, but none of them showed Akha handiwork. My heart filled with hope the day I discovered a website looking for DNA material to match mothers with daughters. I sent in mine but never got a response.

I've gone to the Los Angeles chapter of Families with Children from China to teach a cultural class about tea. (The group, I've been told, is a shadow of its former self. The people who now run things—all volunteers—are new. Plus, apparently, they never kept great records to begin with.) I've also developed tea-tasting programs at the Huntington Library for adults and kids. And on the weekends, I visit garage sales to look for old tea cakes, because what if my daughter—or her parents—decided the tea cake I left with her wasn't worth keeping?

None of these activities has yet brought me luck.

I check my watch. It's 10:00, and business e-mail is arriving, but I decide to scan the human interest articles first—in China *and* America, in newspapers, and on a few blogs I've come to admire and trust—to look for pieces about adopted Chinese girls who've found their mothers or parents or siblings. These stories keep me optimistic and make me wonder if my daughter is searching for me too.

If my daughter were ever to post an inquiry, where would she do it?

If my daughter were ever to buy a billboard, where would it be?

If my daughter were ever to try to learn about her tea cake, where would she take it?

It's said that great sorrow is no more than a reflection of one's capacity for great joy. I see it from the opposite direction. I'm happy, but there's an empty space inside me that will never stop suffering from the loss of Yan-yeh. After all these years, it's a companion rather like the friend-living-with-child. It's nourished me and forced me to breathe when it would have been so easy to give up. Suffering has brought clarity into my life. Maybe the things that have happened to me are punishment for what I did in a previous life, maybe they were fate or destiny, and maybe they're all just part of a natural cycle—like the short but spectacular lives of cherry blossoms in spring or leaves falling away in autumn.

I will never give up searching for Yan-yeh, but now, at 11:00, I force myself to move on to business.

E-mail between Haley Davis and Professor Annabeth Ho, re: Stanford Senior Thesis. First week of October 2015

Professor Ho,

I so appreciate your agreeing to be my adviser next year for my senior thesis. When I visited during your office hours last week, you asked to see a draft of my research proposal. This is the first pass:

The Impact of Climate Change on Sensory and Medicinal Attributes of Tea (*Camellia sinensis*) Grown from Tea Trees in the Tropical Regions of China

This thesis will have two areas of study: 1. How are compounds that create the taste, smell, and look of tea—a combination of amino acids, catechins, theobromine, methylxanthine, and free sugars—being influenced by global climate change? 2. High levels of biodiversity in the tropical forest lead to a rich food chain, which helps to minimize insect and parasite infestations. Specifically, the compounds previously listed make up defensive agents against pathogens, predators, and oxidative stress that have arisen among tea trees growing in their biodiverse—and increasingly threatened—habitat. In numerous studies, these natural protections have also been shown to be beneficial to *Homo sapiens*. Of these, catechins—a group of polyphenolic flavan-3-ol monomers and their gallate derivatives—are considered to be the primary health-giving compounds in tea. The most important of these is epigallocatechin-3-gallate, which is the most bioactive and which has entered the domain of "well-being culture." With the intensified monsoons brought about by climate change, many of these antioxidant compounds are decreasing by as much as 50 percent, while other compounds are increasing. Therefore, how are tea trees' natural protections being affected by global climate change and what will the consequences be on the health benefits of the tea leaf? Materials and methods include farmer surveys, interviews, and the gathering and testing of tea leaves.

Thank you for your time, and I hope to hear your thoughts at your earliest convenience,

Haley Davis

Haley,

This looks very ambitious, but what else can I expect from a student with *two* majors, Biology and Earth Sciences? You must be aiming not just to graduate with honors, as all those who choose to write a senior thesis will achieve, or even to graduate "with distinction" (assuming your GPA is high enough, which I'm sure it will be), but with the Firestone Award for social and natural science.

Before we get into the meat of your thesis, I have a few practical questions:

1. I'd like to know your personal interest in such an arcane subject. Don't get me wrong. The winners of the Firestone Award seem to specialize in arcana, which the committee appreciates. It will behoove you to flesh out that aspect.
2. I assume you plan to go to Yunnan. Are you applying for a fellowship or some other type of funding? Would you consider an internship with a larger academic study already under way? My concern is how you'll get to these farms, where you'll stay, and how you'll communicate. On behalf of the university, I can say we don't want you to do anything that will put you in danger or outside your comfort zone.
3. This looks like a multiyear study. Do you plan to carry on with your research in graduate school?
4. Regarding the "health benefits" to which you refer: We know that green tea has high levels of polyphenols. These antioxidants fight free radicals, which many scientists

believe contribute to the aging process, including damage to DNA, some types of cancer, cardiovascular disease, etc. But apart from the University of Maryland Medical Center's study, can you point to *proven* health claims? I'm not interested in marketing, anecdotal evidence, or supposition about tea that isn't backed by fact or reason. I want to see legitimate documentation on this before you move forward.

5. I presume one reason you approached me to be your adviser is that I'm Chinese. As such, I hope you'll consider adding a third area to your thesis even though it's not within the "hard science" realm: How do we reconcile the poetry and philosophy of tea with the practicalities of growing and processing the product? I grew up hearing ancient beliefs about tea from my immigrant parents: *Every hour spent drinking tea is a distillation of all the tea hours that have ever been spent;* and *Truly you can find the universal through the particular of tea*. Personally, I see a real disconnect between a sentiment like *Tea is the cup of humanity* and the hardscrabble life of tea farmers. If you can incorporate these humanistic aspects in your materials and methods, I believe the awards committee will take notice, and your thesis will rise above others.

I hope I haven't overwhelmed you.

Professor Annabeth Ho

Professor Ho,

Thank you for your thoughtful and thought-provoking questions. I realize now I should have given you a little more background. Let me try to do that, as well as answer your queries.

Last summer, I went to the World Tea Expo, which happened to be in Southern California, where I'm from. I sampled teas from Thailand, Vietnam, India, Sri Lanka, Ghana, Uganda—seemingly everywhere. A whole section of the expo was devoted to the teas of Yunnan, especially to Pu'er, which is extremely rare in China, and even rarer in the world. People at the expo were gambling that tea will be the next big thing here in the United States, where sales of loose, bagged, and ready-to-drink teas have steadily risen over the last two decades. This year, the estimated wholesale value of the U.S. tea industry is $11.5 billion. The clincher, it seems to me, is Starbucks's purchase of Teavana in 2012. It also doesn't take a genius to notice the similarities between tea and wine connoisseurs; they both talk about vintage, harvest seasons, varietals, geographic source, the effects of light, soil, weather, and, of course, age on taste. Even the language to describe flavor is similar: "acidic, followed by notes of orchid and plum."

At the expo, I also met a whole set of people I never expected to see: scientists and doctors. Yunnan is known as a Global Biodiversity Hotspot. The province is said to have "as much flowering plant diversity as the rest of the Northern Hemisphere combined," which gives it a lushness found nowhere else in the world. The province makes up only 4 percent of China's landmass, yet it's home to more than half its mammal and bird species as well as twenty-five of China's fifty-five ethnic minorities. All this got me thinking about global warming and its effect on the quality and intensity of light, which, in turn, will change the final product—whether wine or tea. Plants with medicinal qualities are coming out of the Amazon rainforest. Couldn't something come out of the tropical forests of Yunnan? And just as in the Amazon, the tea mountains of Yunnan are being encroached on by development and pollution, particularly air pollution, which I know is of particular interest to you.

Lastly, at the fair I met a man named Sean Wong. I showed him a tea cake that I have. He encouraged me to take it—what he called "an ideal specimen"—to the place of origin, as so many connoisseurs and collectors do. This was not the first time someone has suggested this to me. He said I could travel with him. I'm jumping at the opportunity.

I hope that's a help,

Haley

Haley,

I need you to dig deeper and answer my *very specific questions*. I'm here to challenge you. I hope you understand that. And please don't take this the wrong way, but I also need to inquire about your relationship with the person who invited you to travel with him. What do you know about him? Is he actually going to help you with your research? What is his motive to take a young woman to such a remote area? I'm sure you understand where I'm going with this, and it makes me very uncomfortable even to bring it up.

You have a promising academic career ahead of you. With that comes great opportunities and responsibilities. I suspect you'll be offended when you read this, but if I ultimately agree to be your adviser, I have a duty to know you'll be safe—on behalf of your parents, the university, and my own peace of mind.

Professor Annabeth Ho

Professor Ho,

To answer your questions:

1. My interest in this subject is very much tied to my upbringing. My father is an arborist. As a child, I rode along as he worked, managing orchards and visiting sick trees. He showed me how to mix compounds to feed or spray them for different needs. He once told me, "You're learning at my side," and I was, because I listened to every word he said and I absorbed them into my body like the trees absorbed their medicines and nutrients. Thanks to my father, I've had a front-row seat to observe the devastating effects of California's drought on our trees, which, in their weakened state, have been preyed upon by pests and parasites. Unlike most Stanford students and, indeed, most scientists, I've witnessed the suffocating deaths of count-

less trees brought about by what we can only conclude is global climate change. My mother, Constance Davis, is a biologist. Perhaps you've heard of her? I'm a product of both of them, and that's where my interest in my thesis topic comes from.

2. Yes, I plan to go to Yunnan. I don't need outside funding. My family will provide it. I'll take my first trip over spring break, which corresponds to Yunnan's tea-picking season. I agree that joining another study would be opportune. Tufts Institute of the Environment in cooperation with the Ethnobiology Department of the Chinese Ministry of Education and sponsored by the National Science Foundation is currently doing a multidisciplinary study (the team includes a chemical ecologist, cultural anthropologist, soil and crop scientist, agricultural economist, and others) on the effects of extreme climate events on terrace tea and wild tea crop yields in Yunnan. I've been in contact with the study's leader, Dr. Joan Barry, and she's agreed to my participation in the project—much of which I can do on my laptop in my dorm room and by analyzing tea samples in the lab here on campus. The current plan is for me to travel in the tea mountains for a week by myself to enlist informants and gather tea samples for my project. Then I'll join the Tufts team for the second week. Dr. Barry says she looks forward to seeing the results of my research.
3. Yes, I see this as a multiyear study, which I hope to pursue whether I'm accepted into Stanford's graduate program or I go to one of the East Coast universities already recruiting me. For now, though, I'd like to begin my research in the way I outlined in my earlier e-mail.
4. As for your question about the health benefits of tea, let me just say that there are currently two hundred studies being undertaken around the world addressing this topic. Believe me, I'm going into this with my eyes wide open and with all the skepticism and rigor Western science should bring to the table.

5. Point One: The fact that I asked you to be my adviser has nothing to do with your race. I thought—and continue to believe—that your work on the effects of air particulates on children living in the Yangtze delta was a good match. Point Two: I appreciate your suggestion that I incorporate Chinese poetry and philosophy into my thesis. In fact, I've already done a little research and think it might be more inclusive—and provocative—to include some popular American thoughts about tea as well. For example, a recent issue of *Bon Appétit* devoted space—I believe for the first time—to tea. In it, American culinary pioneer Alice Waters credited Pu'er for helping to lower her cholesterol by 100 points and get her "off coffee." It's not poetry, obviously, but if someone like Alice Waters says something like that so publicly, especially if it's in a food magazine and not a scientific journal, won't that drive interest in tea in general and Pu'er in particular? And won't that, in turn, make the issue of the effects of climate change on tea trees even more pressing?

In closing, I need to address your concerns about my traveling companion. While no one can fully understand another person's motives, I doubt he has any romantic interest in me. (I assume that's what you were suggesting. If not, I'm hugely embarrassed.) He's a tea nerd. I hadn't known such a thing existed, but it does. I feel lucky to have connected with an expert in the field who can address so many of your logistical concerns.

I hope you will still consider being my adviser.

Sincerely,
Haley Davis

Dear Haley,

Of course, I know your mother. Everyone in our field knows your mother for the quality and importance of her work. We've been attempting to recruit her for our Biology

Department for years. She's always said she didn't want to uproot her family. I should have put two and two together. It's my own ignorance that didn't allow me to match your name and your talents to her face. I apologize.

I apologize as well for my part in the other misunderstanding. I will gladly be your adviser. Come to my office hours next Tuesday for further discussion. Among other things, I'd like to know, given your last e-mail, if you'll be looking at tea in general or just this Pu'er that you mentioned. I see some real benefits in narrowing from a panoramic and encyclopedic view to going in depth on one varietal.

Until Tuesday,
Professor Annabeth Ho

Dear Professor Ho,

Yay! My mother will be so excited when I tell her. I am very much looking forward to working with you.

Haley

AS UNCONTROLLABLE AS THE WIND

"Are you stalking me?" I ask. "No matter where I go, there you are."

"Ah, Tina." Mr. Huang gives me an ingratiating smile. "Maybe we're meant to know each other. Have you ever thought about that?"

No.

"I call you by your American name," he says. "When will you start calling me by mine? John."

Never.

We're on the terrace of the teahouse in the Chinese scholar's garden at the Huntington Library. It's early February, and we're here to celebrate the forthcoming Year of the Monkey and to help raise funds for the final phase of the Chinese garden. Heaters warm the terrace, Chinese lanterns hanging in trees along the lakeside cast a ruby glow, champagne and appetizers are passed. Anyone who's anyone in the Chinese American community in Los Angeles is here: East West Bank's Dominic Ng and his wife; Panda Express's Peggy and Andrew Cherng; and the toy mogul Woo brothers. Some speak in Mandarin, but most use English so as not to be rude to the old-money Pasadena couples who've been supporting the Huntington for decades.

"Is Xian-rong enjoying his new home?" I inquire, trying to be polite. Jin's company sold Mr. Huang and his son houses—mansions, really—in San Marino and Pasadena, respectively.

He shrugs. "It's good to have him close by. The economy is slowing in China. We can make more money with my cranes here. You'll be seeing us much more now."

I smile, but he's known me so long that he has to realize it's not sincere.

"I'll be going to the tea mountains in the spring for tea picking," he goes on, unfazed. "May I visit?"

"You're always welcome in Spring Well Village," I answer. "I'll never forget how you and Xian-rong helped me when the bubble burst."

"This year, will you take me to your hidden—"

"I'm not too old to be still learning new English words. Incorrigible. Do you know that one?"

He drops all pretense of casual conversation. "Have you heard that the Pu'er Tea College now has a study base with a GPS system that can locate every tea tree over a thousand years old on Yunnan's twenty-six tea mountains?"

A knot instantly forms in my stomach. I swallow to push it down.

"They want to protect China's most precious gifts," he continues. "Once recorded, they can watch to make sure no one cuts down a tree to pick its leaves easily or carve graffiti in its bark. From high in the sky, they can see through mists, fog, and clouds to the outlines of mountains, boulders, and hollows."

Attempting to keep my expression as bland as possible, I let my eyes float over the crowd. Where is Jin? I need him.

"The Pu'er Tea College is not the only institution or person to have GPS." Mr. Huang intrudes on my silence. "Did you know I have access to it? Do you know what that means? For twenty-one years I've been searching—"

"No!" Unable to stop myself, I turn away. Moving through the mingling couples, I escape onto one of the little paths that wends around the lake.

"Li-yan, wait!" he calls, switching to my Akha name.

I try to compose myself.

"There's so much you don't know," he says when he reaches me.

"I don't want to hear it."

"You've never trusted me, but you need to start now."

"Why? So you can wheedle and pry your way into my life?"

"That's entirely unfair," he responds, heated and defensive. "Somehow you blame me for things that happened to you when you were young, but *I* don't know what they were or what I did that was so terrible. Couldn't you think of it another way? Maybe my visits to Nannuo Mountain helped pave the way for your success—"

"You taught us about Pu'er, but you've had nothing to do with what I've made of my life."

"Really? Then how do you think you got into the tea college? You know that Tea Master Sun and I are acquainted, but did you know the two of us have been friends for a long time? Why else would he accept you into *two* programs, when not a single other person from a hill tribe was admitted to either?"

"Then I thank you for changing my life," I say.

I start to leave, but he gently takes hold of my arm. "Have you ever wondered who your secret partner was in the Midnight Blossom Teashop?"

"Green Jade . . ." A hand goes to my mouth in surprise. "Was that you?"

"One of my companies, yes. I was your partner." He pauses to let the unbelievable news sink in. "And I came here tonight to warn you about the study base's plans."

"I don't understand. Why would you do any of those things?"

"I needed to repay your family." His voice fades and he gazes across the lake. The red reflections from the lanterns ripple across the surface. I wait. Finally, he goes on. "Your mother saved my son's life."

"What are you talking about?" My question comes out sharper than I intended, but I can't help feeling he's trying to put something over on me.

"You've never asked about my wife," he says.

This is so. How odd.

He pulls out his wallet and shows me a photo of a pretty young woman holding a baby in her arms.

"I loved her very much," he says. "She got breast cancer right after Xian-rong was born. She didn't live to see his first birthday."

"I'm sorry."

"To lose a wife is terrible, and I'll always miss her. But nothing prepared me for the anguish I felt when Xian-rong was diagnosed with bone cancer. He was three."

I'm speechless, trying to reconcile this information with my memories of our first encounter. The sound of the old PLA jeep grinding its way through the forest, the initial unsettling sight of Mr. Huang in his strange clothes, and the little bald boy in what I now know was a Bart Simpson T-shirt, skipping up the path from the spirit gate to the main part of the village as if he knew exactly where he was going. Everything about those moments was alien and frightening. How was I to know Xian-rong was sick?

"He'd had chemo and radiation therapies," Mr. Huang says, addressing my doubt. "We'd tried alternative treatments. I won't go into every detail, but some friends in Hong Kong told me about the medicinal qualities of Pu'er. I had to find the purest and most potent. Once I got to the tea mountains, I asked everywhere for the name of the best village doctor—"

"But you came to us because you were a connoisseur—"

"I wasn't a connoisseur, but I had a dying son and had to become one very quickly."

"You said you were a collector," I insist. "You came to make Pu'er. We made it. You took it away . . ."

"I made Pu'er, and I took it away, true. I sold most of it, which is not what a collector would do."

Were we so gullible that we believed everything he said back then? Of course, we were. Even so, I must look like I need more convincing.

"How can I best prove it to you? Ah, so easy. I could have been the one to make Truly Simple Elegant. Mr. Lü and I each had what we needed to make an iconic tea, but I wasn't on Nannuo for that. I came to Spring Well for your mother. She was the person everyone mentioned. If there was a cure for my son, then she would have it."

I replay those weeks in my mind. Xian-rong's exuberance never lasted very long, and he must have been bald from his treatments. And despite A-ma's continued distrust of Mr. Huang, she'd always shown a particular fondness for the boy, letting him stay with her in the women's side of the house in the afternoons when he was tired. And there was Mr. Huang's behavior, which at the time had seemed so strange: how easy he was to bargain with, how he'd said, "I need this," how much he was willing to pay for the mother tree's leaves during his second visit. Through it all, I'd been so absorbed with thoughts of San-pa—and uninformed about the outside world—that I hadn't searched beyond the surface of his words.

"Your mother's tea healed my boy."

"You don't truly believe that."

"But I do believe it, and I want to prove it. I've been funding Pu'er studies around the world, and we're discovering all kinds of benefits. But there's something about the tea from your grove that's different."

"So you're asking for my tea for your personal gain?"

"No!" He puffs his chest, insulted. "Don't you see, Li-yan? We have to protect the trees. If *I* can find your grove, how long before the study base or some unscrupulous dealer does? The camphor trees won't hide your special trees forever."

Which tells me he really does know the location of the grove. Maybe he's been there already . . .

"The two special tea cakes we made . . ." His voice drifts off again. "They had yellow threads which grew and spread—"

"I remember you telling me this before. A-ma always relied on those for her toughest cases." *And they're in Yan-yeh's tea cake . . .*

"Those threads are what's so powerful. For years, I've scoured the mountains, looking for other sources, but haven't found one. They're only in your grove, and they're what saved Xian-rong when he had a recurrence in 2007."

I remember Mr. Huang coming to my shop in the tea market and telling me that he'd been to my village and wondering why no one, not even A-ma, had mentioned it.

"And A-ma treated him again?" I ask.

He nods. "I told Xian-rong the tea would help settle his stomach postchemo. And, since he loved your mom and Nannuo Mountain, he never asked questions and was content to obey. He's been cancer-free ever since."

"Then let it go and be grateful."

"Li-yan," he pleads, "my son has recovered twice from cancer. My wife died from it. Did they have a genetic predisposition or was it just bad luck? How can I know what will happen to my grandchildren and great-grandchildren?"

"Xian-rong isn't even married yet," I respond, trying for a light tone, "and you never like the girls he goes out with anyway."

But this isn't the time for levity.

"One day he'll find the right girl." Mr. Huang leans in. "Then what? You Recite the Lineage? What about my lineage? What about Xian-rong's? You've known him for twenty-one years. What if he or his son or daughter gets sick? Your mother might be gone. You and I might not be here either. There would be no way to protect my family's security and longevity. You've never trusted me, but you should start now. I'm a man who loves his son very deeply. What would you do for your son?"

I don't tell Jin about my conversation with Mr. Huang. I don't call A-ma to discuss what he said either. I hold all the information inside me, trying to process it. Out of everything he said, one question lingers: *What would you do for your son?* I find myself watching Paul when he draws his bow across his violin strings, when he kicks the ball during soccer practice, when he wakes screaming in the night. We Akha think so much about our ancestors and the spirit world in which they reside, but our sons and daughters in the world of the living prolong our lines in the direction of the future. They will be the next ancestors. They should be protected, but at what cost? By the time Paul and I leave for China the following month, I know what must happen. I hope my conviction will be enough to sway A-ma.

On our way to Spring Well, we make a quick stop at the Social Welfare Institute to deliver clothes, toys, books, and other necessities. Paul always likes these visits, and even though he's only eight he likes to make things for the kids—like puppets made from lunch bags—but this time he'd asked if we could bring three laptops. "They could play games. They could even learn to read a little. When they're older, if they aren't adopted, they could do their homework . . . Mom, please!" Before we left home, I'd told Jin that our son is destined for a great university, because he's already building his community service record. My husband had laughed and kissed the top of my head.

And then it's on to Nannuo Mountain. Tea-picking season is always so busy that A-ma and I usually don't visit my grove until I'm just about to return home. Not this time. Directly upon our arrival in Spring Well, I ask her to come with me to my hidden grove. My a-ma has reached seventy-eight years on this earth. She's lived on Nannuo Mountain her entire life—breathing clean air, eating fresh food, and walking these mountains to care for tea trees and people alike. She's strong, and I lag behind as she strides up mountain trails that grow progressively narrow until the last one seems to disappear. She waits for me at the boulder, and together we shimmy around it.

What is another year to the mother and sister trees? In the twenty-eight years I've known of their existence, they seem unchanged. Once I had thought of the grove as a place of pain, suffering, and death. Now I'm honored to have it as my legacy. But it may be so much more than that. I go straight to the mother tree and caress its bark. Yellow powder comes off on my palms, which I hold out for A-ma to see.

"Do you know what this is?" I ask.

"It's a gift brought here by our nomadic mothers as they journeyed—"

"Mr. Huang thinks it's something more."

Hearing his name, she scowls, turns her back to me, and walks to the edge of the cliff. I keep my yellowed hands before me as I come to her side. Together we stare out over the mountains.

"He says the yellow threads cured Xian-rong," I say.

She looks at me out of the corner of her eye, deliberately avoiding my hands. "The boy was dying when he first came to us. Anyone could see that. I did what I could. I gave him tea from the mother tree and many other remedies."

"And I made two cakes of tea solely from the mother tree, which Mr. Huang took for his son."

"I only knew about the one." I wait for further recriminations. Instead, she says, "Then you helped him too. Not everyone recovers on our mountain, as you know. He was lucky."

"What if he gets sick again?" I ask.

"Each year when he visits, I look at him. He's healthy. If someday he comes to me sick, I'll do what I can for him as I do for every person on Nannuo Mountain."

"What about when you become an ancestor? What if one of Xian-rong's children gets sick?"

"You can—"

I don't let her finish. "I can deliver a baby and help a girl with a pimple. Beyond that? You're the last woman in our line with your skills. And we don't know *why* Xian-rong got better when many others don't." I give A-ma time to absorb what I'm saying. Then, "And there's one more thing."

I'll never stop respecting my a-ma. She's farmed, harvested vegetables and threshed rice, raised and slaughtered animals, cooked for an entire household, spun thread, woven cloth, made clothes, and embroidered them. She's walked every trail on our mountain. She's attended births and cared for the weak, ill, and dying. I love her, and having to explain the idea of satellites and GPS to her hurts me deeply. They are as far-fetched to her as electricity, telephones, and television once were to me, and she looks horrified as I come to my frightening conclusion.

"People are *looking* for this place. Mr. Huang *already* knows where it is."

"But no man can see it," A-ma says, her insistence carrying the weight of generations. "I'll never let that stranger—"

"Don't you see? It might not be him." A choke of understanding grabs my throat as I finally accept what he told me that night at the party. "It *won't* be him. He *warned* us. Consider what that means. The inevitability of what's coming . . . As uncontrollable as the wind—"

"No man can come here." It's agonizing for me to hear her fear and sadness. "They'll die as your grandfather died."

This is brutally tragic and terrifying for me too, but I come back at her with the type of reasoning I know she'll understand. "What happened to Grandfather was fate. It could have happened anywhere."

"But we *must* keep this place a secret."

I raise my palms so she can't avoid seeing them. "Isn't it time we learn what *this* is? Where it came from originally and if there's more out there? How, and if, it works? If it can be re-created? If it can help—"

"But the women in our line—"

"Yes, the women in our line, including you and me, are linked by these yellow threads. You and the generations before you protected the mother and sister trees from wars, caravans, and nomads that passed across Nannuo Mountain over many centuries. But now people—maybe callous men, maybe evil women, maybe deceitful dealers, maybe ruthless scientists—are going to come here with their GPS whether we want them to or not. Maybe our line has been protecting the mother tree for this moment."

"I'll always help the boy," A-ma says, despairing.

"If you can treat him, then why not those on the next mountain? Would you turn away someone who came to you from Yiwu or Laobanzhang sick himself, with an ailing wife, or a feverish child in his arms? Of course you wouldn't. If you say yes to someone from the next mountain, then what about people from other parts of China?"

A-ma begins to weep. I've cornered her with undeniable facts. Suddenly she looks like a broken, frail, old woman. I've done that to her.

"Who can we trust to take it out?" she mumbles, her voice trembling. "What's going to happen to the trees once others know about them?"

I take her in my arms and hold her tight. I don't know the answers.

A PILGRIMAGE TO THE PLACE OF ORIGIN

We linger at the entrance to the TSA security line. Mom looks elegant in a pair of cream-colored trousers and a peach cashmere sweater. Dad's wearing shorts and a Lakers T-shirt. I'm in skinny jeans and a hoodie. My hair's pulled back in a ponytail. In my carry-on, I've got my tea cake, laptop, books, and other necessities for the flight.

"I want to meet him," Dad says for about the fiftieth time.

How many variations of a response can I come up with? He'll get here. Maybe he's inside already. Even if he doesn't show up—which he will—I'll be fine. This time I try out "I'm sure he's coming."

Dad gives me a look, and Mom says, "Now, Dan, stop worrying. Think of the places *I've* gone for research—"

"I don't like that either, and you aren't my little girl—"

"She'll be twenty-one—"

"In the fall. I know. But—"

"Look, you two, I'd better get through security," I say. "I don't want to miss my flight."

Dad sighs. "Are you really going to fly off to China with some random Chinese man none of us have met?"

"Oh, Dad, you're such a dad! And I love you for it."

He gives me a weak smile, but truly, why didn't I introduce everyone when I had the chance? Because I wanted to do this on my own. Prove I was capable. Impress Mom and Dad with my independence. Et cetera.

Mom hugs me and whispers in my ear. "I love you. Be careful. We'd prefer if you'd call, but if you can't, promise to send an e-mail or text every day so we know you're safe." When I start to pull away, she draws me even closer. "I've known worry before—those terrible nights when you nearly died and your bad spell in high school—but this is a whole new level. So don't make me wrong. Your dad would never forgive me, and I'd never forgive myself."

"There's nothing to worry about," I whisper back. "I'll be fine." Which is about as far from the truth as I can get, because, despite my brave words, I'm scared half out of my pants. *Where is he? How am I supposed to do this trip by myself?*

I go through more or less the same routine with my dad. I join the line and pull out my passport, but Mom and Dad don't leave. Even after I pass through security and start up the elevator to the gates, I see them standing where I left them. One last round of waves and smiles, and then I'm on my own.

When I get to the gate, the first- and business-class passengers have already boarded through a special door. The cattle—of which I'm a part—are funneled down a separate Jetway, so I don't get to see if Sean's already seated. My parents' volunteering—if that's the right word—to buy me a coach ticket for the flight from L.A. to Guangzhou was just one of the many ways they tried to dissuade me from this trip. They have enough miles to have gotten me a seat in business, and it wouldn't have cost them a dime. By the time they accepted the fact that I was going no matter what, and they offered to pay to boot me up to business—"It's the least we can do"—I had to act above it all, as in "Oh, Mom, Dad, thank you so much for offering, but I want to seem like everyone else." And now I'm squished in with a bunch of strangers, going on an adventure to the "middle of nowhere," as Sean and the people on the Tufts team have repeatedly described it.

At least I'm on the aisle.

The plane taxis to the runway. The pilot revs the engines, and we barrel along until we lift off, passing over the sandy beach and above the ocean. The plane banks to the right—north. My hands grip the armrests as we hit a few bumps.

I wouldn't be here now if I hadn't met Sean. A year ago, on a whim really, I'd gone to the tea expo at the Long Beach Convention Center. On the first day, I attended a seminar on using the unique flavors of different teas to make artisanal cocktails. "It's the coming trend!" It was the expo's most popular event, and I came out of the meeting room more than a little tipsy from sampling Earl Grey–infused whiskey, vodka with hibiscus tea ice cubes, and drinks with names like Tea-tini (with vodka, lavender, rosemary, and chamomile), Sen-cha Flip (with gin, Japanese green tea, and frothed egg whites), and Liber-tea (made with Wild Turkey, honey, tea, and basil). "If I weren't going to Stanford," I'd commented to one of the other attendees, "I could open a bar and serve all kinds of drinks using tea, dry ice, spherification, foams, and infusions. Chemistry another way!" The woman didn't even crack a smile. Those tea people take themselves *very* seriously.

Next I'd gone to a panel on the science of tea. I don't know what I was expecting, but it wasn't a rundown of studies going on around the world looking at the purported health benefits of something I'm interested in for personal reasons but don't drink myself, except for boba milk tea that I buy in the San Gabriel Valley, which is all about the tapioca balls anyway . . . and now, maybe cocktails. Or that even in a seminar like that one, they were going to serve tea. These scientists from Tufts University, the Tea Research Institute, and a place called the Antioxidants Research Laboratory (whatever that is) started in with all this data about a particular kind of tea called Pu'er that reportedly can help with diabetes, lower blood pressure, prolong longevity, and produce palliative outcomes for everything from altitude sickness to gout to symptoms of HIV/AIDS. Talk about a buzzkill! I thought, *Some people will believe anything*. I hate people who prey on the weak or sick, giving them false hope when they should be relying on medicine and science. So I was doing a whole pat-myself-on-the-back thing—I'm going to Stanford for *real* science—when they start showing slides like I'm in a chemistry or biology class.

Randomized Double-blind,
Placebo-controlled Clinical Trials (RCT)
Effects of Tea on Body Weight, Energy Metabolism, and Recovery from Stress

Beverage formulated with green tea catechins, caffeine, and calcium: increased 24-hour resting energy expenditure (REE) by 106 kcal (4.6%) in 31 young, lean individuals.

In 12-week RCT, with green tea extract (GTE, 750 mg) containing 141 mg catechins to 60 sedentary and overweight (BMI:27.7) individuals: increase in REE and decrease in body weight, despite no change in food intake.

In 6-week RCT with black tea, 76 males divided into two groups. Half receive caffeinated beverage made from tea; half receive caffeinated placebo. Both groups presented with challenging tasks, with cortisol, blood pressure, blood platelet, and self-rated stress levels measured pre- and post-. 50 minutes after completion of tasks, cortisol levels drop 47% in tea group compared to 27% given placebo.

Suddenly, I felt on much firmer ground. They showed slides with chemical percentages, dosages, and study methodology for different age-groups, sexes, and countries in studies that covered glucose tolerance, cardiovascular disease, bone density, cognitive function, neurodegenerative disease, and, of course, various types of cancer. Outcomes ranged from "compelling" to "equivocal at best." Not exactly ringing endorsements, but I was intrigued and I sure couldn't blame it on the second sample of Sen-cha Flip I'd drunk earlier. At the end of the presentation, I asked for cards from all the participants, one of whom was Dr. Barry, who later agreed to let me work on her study.

Feeling a bit giddy, I walked down the aisles of the show and it was much like any expo, with a whole range of vendors—from the English tea-cozy ladies to Kenyan tea-plantation promoters, from Japanese women in kimonos doing a formal tea ceremony to Portland hipsters with flower-based products. I stopped for a moment to watch a man—Chinese, handsome, and five or so years older than I am—pouring tea for a group of people, letting the liquid slosh over the rims of the cups. It was truly messy and completely unlike the elegance in the Japanese booth. The man caught me observing him and called, "Join us." When I hesitated, he beckoned me with what had to be a Chinese proverb. "Every passing moment is the passing of life; every moment of life is life itself." Who says that to a random stranger? It certainly wasn't a line I'd heard before, so I entered the booth and sat down. He introduced himself as Sean Wong.

"Here," he said, pouring tea from a glass pitcher into a white porcelain cup, "I want you to sample my Pu'er." The first sip of liquid blossomed in my mouth—bitterness bubbled away by sweetness. He watched my reaction, smiled more to himself than to me, and then proceeded to brew several more vintages of Pu'er, each one better than the last. One tea had such strong *huigan*—what he described as the overwhelming effect that this tea has on breath and opening the chest—that for a moment the world went dizzy. "That's because you're drinking history," he explained.

His laugh made my heart race. And honestly, I could barely take my eyes off him. His cheekbones were sharp, his eyes seemed wary, his hair shone like lacquer. He was friendly and obviously some type of tea connoisseur. The careless way he poured the valuable teas, letting them overflow their little cups to show abundance, was oddly entrancing. Why he'd set up a stall at the expo wasn't and still isn't clear, but I'd gone to high school with plenty of girls like him and now I was surrounded by his ilk—guys and girls—at Stanford, who are part of the People's Republic of China's wealthy and international jet-setting elite.

I don't know what made me do it, but I mentioned my tea cake. Bragging, I guess. Or wanting to prolong my time with him. He was immediately intrigued.

"They say that the most valuable tea will be found right here in Southern California," he said. "It would have come with a sojourner a hundred years ago, been given as a gift, or received as payment for something."

"How valuable?" I asked.

"Last year a cake of Pu'er, weighing three hundred and ninety grams—a little under a pound—sold at auction for one point two million Hong Kong dollars. That's about one hundred and fifty thousand U.S."

"My tea cake can't be worth anything like that," I said.

"How do you know?"

The next day, I brought my tea cake to see if he or someone else could tell me about it. People offered exorbitant sums to buy it, but Sean had the most tempting offer: "Just as a person is searching for tea, the tea is searching for the person. Come with me to China for a week. We'll make a pilgrimage to your tea cake's place of origin. Put yourself in my hands. I'll take care of everything."

A pilgrimage to the place of origin . . .

"I'll be going anyway," he added. "You may as well take advantage of me. My expertise, I mean."

Okay, so I wasn't completely forthright with Professor Ho, my parents, or even myself. Sure, I'm totally into the project I got Professor Ho to advise me on. I've also got the Tufts project on my laptop, and I've looked at plenty of tea samples for Dr. Barry in the lab, which will help create a baseline for my research. When I'm in China, I'll meet farmers and collect my own tea samples. I'm going to win that Stanford award! But there was—*is*—something about Sean, besides having an on-the-ground guide who speaks the language, that made me say yes to his offer.

I went back to Stanford, and we communicated by e-mail. We met at his house once when I was home for winter break to go over plans for the trip. I'd figured he was rich, so I wasn't surprised by the address in Pasadena practically around the corner from Hummingbird Lane. It turned out to be a little more than a "house," however. It was a grand old mansion built back in the day by some mucky-muck. I figured it must have cost $15 million, give or take, which means that Sean isn't just rich, he's superrich. The grounds and the house looked beautiful and well maintained from the outside; inside, it had been gutted down to the studs. We wended our way through the construction to the old housekeeping quarters. The rooms were cozy and warm. One thing could have led to another, but he was all business, and so was I. And we need to keep it that way. We have separate rooms booked for every stop. I have the e-mails to prove it. Besides, nothing can happen if he isn't on this plane . . .

As soon as the seat belt sign is turned off, I walk toward the front of the plane. When I reach the curtain that divides coach from business, I pass through, trying to look like I belong. Most of the people are Chinese. About half of them are drinking champagne. A flight attendant asks, "Is this your cabin?" Busted.

Back at my seat, I pull out my laptop and try to work. I've gathered a lot of material about where I'm going and want to see if there are differences in how the various hill tribes use tea in rituals and folk medicines, as well as how they process it for drinking. Down the rabbit hole . . .

About an hour later, a man's voice says, "You should have told me you're interested in Yunnan's ethnic minorities."

It's Sean. He perches an elbow on the seat in front of me, with his hand languidly hanging just inches from my face. He looks unbelievably elegant, which is not a word I've ever used about a guy.

"I thought you might have missed the flight." I try to keep my voice even, but I'm not sure it works because I'm so relieved he's on the plane I can barely think.

His mouth comes up at the corners. Not a smile. Not a smirk. I have no idea what's in his mind.

"I know some Dai, Bulang, and Akha farmers," he says. "Everyone writes about the Dai, because there are so many of them and they have their own written language." The hand that droops off the seat in front of me shoos away the idea as unworthy. He seems to run through the list in his mind, checking off each tribe one by one. Then, "You might be interested in the Akha, because their culture is very similar to that of the Cree. The culture is animistic. Every living thing has a spirit."

"I've read about them and the whole Cree thing. Downside: the

Akha get to have a bad rep similar to that of Native Americans. They don't save their money, they drink, they take drugs— "

His eyes flash. "It's easy to fall for stereotypes." (Ouch. I wasn't saying *I* believed those things.) "In the West, you think the individual is supreme, but the Akha see themselves as one link in the long chain of life, adjacent to all the other links of people and cultures, all carrying a collective wave toward the beach to throw a newborn up to safety."

I feel myself bridling. "Interesting that you'd bring up newborns. If everything has a soul, then what's up with that stuff about twins?"

"That ended a while ago," he says, looking a little annoyed now. "They had a cultural belief for, to them, commonsense reasons, which they followed for millennia. Who are you to condemn their culture?"

Before I have a chance to clarify or defend myself, he taps the seat a couple of times—*done here*—and glides back down the aisle, disappearing behind the curtain that divides the plane.

"Well, that sucked," the girl next to me comments.

He's waiting for me when I get off the plane in Guangzhou. I've had plenty of hours to formulate a proper answer to his question: just because a group has a cultural belief, whether it's foot binding in China or female genital cutting in Africa, doesn't mean that we, as human beings, should sanction the practice. But he seems to have forgotten our misunderstanding or whatever that was. We go through the border formalities, pick up our bags, pass back through security for domestic flights, and board the plane for Kunming. Again we aren't seated together, nor are we together on the last flight, to Jinghong.

After three back-to-back flights over many hours and time changes, I'm so punchy with exhaustion that I notice little about the airport other than it's small, drab, and dimly lit. Outside, a driver meets us to take us to Yiwu, the ancient collection center for the Six Great Tea Mountains, starting point of the Tea Horse Road, home of the queen of Pu'er, and our base for the next four nights. It's about a six-hour drive, I've read, with bumpy hairpin turns. This, after all the flights and layovers. I take a Dramamine, roll my hoodie into a pillow, and rest my head. On his side of the backseat, Sean immediately nods off, but as tired as I am I can't fall asleep. *China!* And I'm heading to "the middle of nowhere."

This is a far different trip than the one I took with my parents. I quickly need to become accustomed to squat toilets, using toilet paper for napkins, and seeing people spit their chicken and fish bones right on the floor. For breakfast—and jet-lagged as hell—we go to an outdoor stand and order chili-flavored soup noodles being cooked over a brazier. We sit on plastic kiddie chairs around a low kiddie-size table—which is plain weird—that looks like it's never once been wiped down. A dog chews on a bone at my feet. I don't see a single white face, but there are others who are clearly marked as foreign to Yiwu: Chinese men dressed in spiffy trousers, starched shirts, and polished loafers.

"Tea traders," Sean whispers. "Watch how they act with each other. It's like the Gold Rush out here. I've found my lode, and I'm not going to tell you where it is. They're checking us out too—to see how prosperous we are and determine if we'll drive up the price of tea this year."

When our noodles arrive, I follow Sean's example and pour steaming tea over my chopsticks and other tableware, then toss the dirty liquid on the ground. The alternative would be the trots or worse. Every pandemic in the history of the world has come from China.

The tea traders leave as quickly as they came. Sean calls farmers and dealers on WeChat, an instant messaging system that allows him to speak into his phone instead of typing complicated Chinese characters, giving me an update after each: "I told them to expect us at four o'clock." Or "They said drop by tomorrow. I've never brought a woman with me. They're eager to meet you." We're just about to leave when a man who introduces himself as a new dealer sits down next to us, unzips an overnight bag to show us bundled wads of hundred-yuan notes, and asks where he should go to find good tea. Sean sends him to a family-owned tea-processing factory up the road. As we walk away, I ask, "Should I see it too?"

"I'm going to take you somewhere better and more authentic tomorrow. Today, let me show you around the town."

From what's left of it, I imagine Yiwu must have once been very beautiful, but the main street is just a strip of clunky concrete enterprises all coated in dust and dirt from the old houses being torn down and from the cheap and ugly buildings going up. We walk part of the Tea Horse Road, which, disappointingly, doesn't look like much: just a four-foot-wide cobblestone path that snakes through the old part of town and then heads down a hill. On our way back to the main drag, we pass along quiet lanes, where a few traditional buildings made of unfired clay bricks and upturned eaves still stand, chickens peck at the ground, and flowers drip over walls. Before every house, women—the younger ones in jeans and T-shirts, the old ladies in traditional clothes, and all of them wearing scarves or headdresses—sort tea a leaf at a time. This is what Yiwu must have looked like before prosperity hit, and it's much more quaint and charming, giving the feel of ageless China.

The next day, our plan is to go to Laobanzhang, the home of the king of Pu'er. We're driven over an impossible one-lane dirt road. We pass villages made up of between ten and fifty houses. I glimpse a few handmade wooden gates that look a lot like the entrance to our ranch in Colorado: two posts and a beam. Our gate has our brand carved on a wooden disk and mounted on the beam. Here, the embellishments on each gate are, let's just say, out there, with carvings of a man and a woman with outsize genitals verging on the pornographic. It's odd to reconcile the primitiveness of these figures with a country that's now an economic superpower. The cultural disconnect is magnified when the driver is forced to stop the car, because a tangle of minivans has blocked the route. Japanese tourists take each other's photos posing against tea trees that cling to the hillside—here, *in the middle of nowhere*. We get out of the car and chat with them for a bit in English. We're surrounded by mountains blanketed in gray haze, and I mentally try to match them to the markings on my tea cake, to no avail.

The tourists—so strange to see them out here—get back in

their vans. Sean waves the various drivers through the contortions required to clear the road. Finally, we're able to get back in the car. Our driver takes us to a prosperous grower's house, modern and clean, with several outbuildings for processing tea. In the courtyard, about two dozen women sit around big flat baskets sorting tea. The owner, a Mr. Piu, introduces me to the group as an American scientist, and they show me every step of the tea-making process. I even get to try killing the green and kneading. Around noon, several cars arrive, bringing buyers from around the world. We sit in a pavilion on, of course, little plastic kiddie chairs around a low table and taste tea worth one thousand dollars (!) for a two-ounce cup. I don't speak Chinese, but they all speak English.

When a dealer from Taiwan asks about my project, I tell them a little about it, ending with "Almost everywhere I look I see another opportunity for scientific study. For example, what effect will pollution have on the tea industry?"

"We have no smog here," Mr. Piu scoffs.

"Really? Then what's that stuff in the air?" I ask, pointing to the haze that lies between the hills. "I grew up in Los Angeles. I know what smog looks like. What you're seeing could have drifted here from a thousand miles away. But I'm wondering too if the slash-and-burn agricultural practices of the ethnic minorities are now catching up to them in this era of climate change."

The others nod politely, but I'm not sure they agree with me.

"How can the exact age of an antique cake of Pu'er be known?" I continue. "Is there something in it that could actually promote longevity? Is Pu'er a medicinal tonic, a drinkable antique, or merely a beverage?"

"What about social issues?" Sean asks me. "Could tea be seen as a symbol of worth: a commodity that represents change in value for women, and for China, on the world stage?"

At the word *women,* the others exchange glances like we're all a bunch of teenagers instead of an international group of travelers outside a farmer's house miles from anything resembling what I think of as civilization. But they pull themselves together quickly, because everyone seems to have an opinion about where I should go, what I should see, and whom I should meet. Soon most of them have pulled out their cellphones and are making even more connections for Sean and me on WeChat. I'm going to have plenty of subjects for my project by the time I meet up with the Tufts team.

After we've sampled about a dozen teas, lunch is served at an adjacent (child-size, again!) table: stir-fried cabbage, tomato and scrambled egg, beef with slivered ginger, and some type of crunchy root. Once the meal is finished, we move back to the tea table. Just as everyone's getting settled, Sean says, "Haley, why don't you show them your tea cake? Maybe someone here will recognize the wrapper." I pull it out of my bag and lay it on the table. People are polite enough not to touch it, but they stand to get better views, craning their necks, pointing, and discussing.

"It must be from a lost tea company," Mr. Piu guesses.

"Or a lost family," the dealer from Taiwan offers.

"Or from a long-abandoned garden high in the mountains," someone's girlfriend suggests.

"How old is it?" Mr. Piu asks.

"I don't know," I answer.

"Tea cakes made before the fifties had no wrappers," someone says. "So that's a clue—"

"But it's clearly much older than that," the dealer from Taiwan interrupts. "It looks to be hundreds of years old."

Somehow it's gratifying that the tea cake is as mysterious to them as it's always been to me.

"Have you tasted it?" Mr. Piu asks.

The idea seems shocking to me. "I've never opened it," I admit.

"Let's do it now," Mr. Piu says, reaching for the cake. "Let's taste it."

Quick as a snake, Sean clamps his hand over our host's wrist. "It's for Haley to decide when and if she wishes to open it."

An awkward silence falls over the little group.

"He never brings a girl to visit," Mr. Piu jokes, trying to defuse the tension. "Now look how proprietary he is!"

The others laugh. Sean releases his grip. More tea is poured.

A few hours later, Sean and I pile into the car. My bag is filled with tea samples and tea gifts given by our host, who says, "So you'll always remember our day together."

When we get back to Yiwu, we walk down the dusty street to a restaurant with smears of I-don't-know-what on the plate-glass windows. Sean orders soup and a simple assortment of vegetable dishes. Everything has been so go-go-go that we haven't had much of a chance to talk about anything beyond travel logistics and tea, but now he asks if this is my first time to China.

"Do I look that out of place?" I ask.

He raises his eyebrows. *Yes.*

"It's my second trip," I say. "I was seventeen the first time I came. I'm adopted, and my parents brought me on a heritage tour to find my roots."

"And did you find them?" he asks coolly, showing no surprise about my background.

"My roots? Nope. But that's all right." I feel compelled to explain. "I have a loving family. I grew up in a beautiful home. I'm getting a great education and following my dreams—"

"Which is why you're here with me."

Yikes. An awkward silence. I force myself to forge ahead.

"A few years ago, someone told me about a concept called the grateful-but-angry Chinese adoptee. Yes, I've been grateful. And yes, I've been angry. It was hard for me to separate what I *should* be grateful for and what I was *actually* grateful for. I guess that's why I decided it should be grateful *and* angry, not *but* angry. That was a long time ago. Now what I feel is something more like survivor's guilt. Do you know what I mean?"

"Perhaps I do," he answers with a hint of sadness, but I don't feel comfortable probing into *his* background.

"I could have ended up in a sucky life," I yammer on. "Instead I got a fabulous life. A lot of girls like me feel we need to account for ourselves in a bigger way than people who just come home from the hospital, no questions asked." I will myself to stop talking. But then, "Maybe this is more than you want to know."

"I want to know everything about you."

I guess I set him up for that, but it's such a dopey line, I can't even drum up a comeback. Even he looks embarrassed. Is he going to talk about himself for a while? I'm not that lucky.

"Do you see yourself as Chinese or American?"

"One hundred percent American and one hundred percent Chinese," I answer. "I'm not half and half. I'm fully both. I'll forever wear my Chinese-ness on my face, but these days when I look in the mirror I don't see how mismatched I am in my birth family or that I don't feel Chinese enough. I just see me."

My comment startles me. I struggled so long with who I was. Have I actually come to a place of acceptance?

"You're a new kind of global citizen," he says. "You can be a bridge between two cultures and two countries."

"That's going a little far, don't you think?"

"Not really. And it's not just about you, is it? You and your cohort are products of the One Child policy, which is now over, right? I've heard that over four hundred million births were prevented, but all of you are in a special category. Your perspective—and those of other women like you—is unique. It's larger than any of you as individuals. In a way, you do have immense responsibility—"

"I used to resent that. But it has given me a sense of purpose—"

"The power of international Chinese adoptees all around the world could be a force to be reckoned with!"

Now for sure he's teasing me. I give him a half smile, and we return to our meal.

Later, he walks me all the way to my hotel room. My dad would undoubtedly be relieved to know that another night goes by without any "funny business."

On the third morning, we visit a villa so remote that there isn't another house in view, with a vista that reminds me a lot of Topanga Canyon back home. The living room is floored in white marble, a gigantic flat-screen TV blares from a cabinet the size of Nebraska, and a fortune in tea packed in oversize bags is stacked against the walls. Our hostess asks us to stay for lunch. "We'll kill a chicken," she says, and the next thing I hear is a chicken's neck being snapped just inches from my ear. I taste whatever's put in my bowl—including anteater and bear paw—out of politeness. I show her my tea cake, but she doesn't have any ideas about it.

From here, we stop in to meet several farmers. Wherever we

go, three things happen. First, as soon as we arrive water is heated, leaves rinsed, and tea steeped. We meet those who treat it as something treasured, but more often than not, we're across from a farmer or his son who chain-smokes. Ashes and cigarette butts overflow ashtrays, even though we're tasting something that relies on aroma and flavor. One man even uses his electric razor while we're sipping his tea. People tell me incredible stories of poverty, hardship, sacrifice, and overnight wealth. Farmers proudly point out their running water, televisions, and motor scooters.

Second, I show people my tea cake. Everyone has a theory about it, but no one can tell me definitively what it is or where it came from. And third, folks are kind to me, but they rib Sean mercilessly. He laughs. He blushes. He ducks his head and runs his hands through his hair, chagrined but pleased. He then translates everything, or I think he does, because why else would he tell me things like "They say your hair looks like silk," "They wonder if you're an ethnic minority and how many children you can have in America," and "They want you to know that you'll always be safe and happy with me."

As we drive from place to place, he sits on his side of the backseat and I stay on mine, but the roads are bumpy with lots of curves, and the laws of physics . . . So there's *that,* but otherwise we don't do any of the obvious things like walking so close together that our fingers touch or staring too long into each other's eyes when he says something like "In drinking the best tea, you and I are having a conversation with the wind and the rain that the ancient Daoists had above the mountain clouds. Through the tea liquor, across streams, and under moon shadows we can understand that the separation between Man and Nature is not real." I mean, *come on.* Who wouldn't want to sleep with a guy who talks like that? But he doesn't make a move, and I mostly keep my eyes on the scenery. I've had casual hookups and even a few short relationships, but this feels different. I can wait, but the anticipation only fuels my desire.

Our fourth day is spent entirely in the car, as we're driven down from Yiwu to Menghai and then up Nannuo Mountain, which he tells me has the largest number of ancient tea tree groves. We check in to a rustic inn. The main building has a kitchen, tea shop, and small tea-processing area on the ground floor. The family lives upstairs. Guests stay in bungalows built in the traditional style—bamboo and thatch on stilts—that edge a canyon. Mine is outfitted with a bed, period. There's no electricity, and the toilet and shower are in a separate building to be shared by everyone here. Sean and I eat outside by candlelight. The proprietor's mother makes a simple meal from ingredients grown on the property—a soup flavored with fresh mint, string beans sautéed with chili, greens with slivered chilies, and scrambled egg and tomato—which we eat seated at the ubiquitous tiny chairs and table. After dinner, fiery homemade liquor is brought out, and the proprietor performs Dai drinking songs for the handful of guests. Last, he asks us to join in a call-and-response Akha love song that was recently made into a hit on a talent show on Chinese television.

Sean translates as the other male guests sing to the women: "The flowers bloom at their peaks, waiting for the butterflies to come—"

Then the women sing to the men: "The honeycombs wait for the bees to make honey—"

Then back to the men: "A beautiful flower calls to her love—"

We're both able to join the chorus. "Alloo sae, ah-ee-ah-ee-o, ah-ee-ah-ee-o."

After the festivities, we're handed oil lamps. Sean guides me to my bungalow. He leans in, barely brushing his lips against mine. He pulls back to gauge my reaction. The air feels so heavy between us I can barely breathe. He puts a hand on the small of my back and pulls me to him. Our kiss is like nothing I've ever experienced. In another minute, we're in my little room. The oil lamps flicker. He slowly undresses me. "You're beautiful," he says. Nothing in my life has prepared me for what I feel when we make love.

Afterward, I lie in his arms. Something extraordinary is happening, but is it too fast? He edges up onto an elbow so he can stare into my eyes. I don't know how, but I feel as though he knows me completely, and somehow I know him. And then he says the most remarkable thing.

"I've loved you from the moment you walked into my booth at the tea expo. I've brought you to the place I love most in the world. Wouldn't it be incredible if we could spend our lives traveling the world, drinking tea, and reading the great poets?"

The realities of our lives escape me for a moment. We make love again, and it's even more exquisite. When he falls asleep, I let my breathing follow his.

The next morning begins as it usually does—with Sean on WeChat, contacting the people we're going to see—but with every second heightened by blissful joy. Then we get in the car and set off. After an hour, we're driven onto a narrow unpaved stretch you could barely call a road. We reach a gate watched by a couple of men. They recognize Sean immediately and wave us through, but we don't go far before we reach another gate. It's decorated like some of the others I've glimpsed off the side of the main road—with a man with a gigantic penis and a woman with bulging breasts.

"We need to walk the rest of the way," Sean says.

The driver parks the car. Sean and I pass through the gate—he warns me not to touch the posts—and proceed along a path. The wind rustles through the trees, cicadas whine, birds trill. The moist tropical air feels warm and soothing on my skin. The first thing I see when we reach the village are some barefoot children washing dishes in a pig trough. In the end, though, it's much like the other villages we've visited. Everyone is involved in tea processing. People are bringing in baskets of tea leaves and spreading them on raised platforms to wilt, killing the green in outdoor woks over wood fires, kneading, steaming, or doing the twist on the heavy round stones that will press the tea into cakes.

We reach a house where a group of women sit around flat baskets, sorting tea. One of them is quite old and wearing full ethnic minority clothing. A little boy, eight or nine, sits next to her.

"Xian-rong! Mom said you were coming!" The boy squeals in English without a trace of an accent as he runs to Sean and jumps into his arms.

The old woman rises. "Xian-rong."

I look at Sean quizzically. "They know me by Huang Xianrong, my Mandarin name," he explains. "And this is Paul."

"Jin-ba when I'm here with Grandma!" the boy says cheerily.

"He lives in Arcadia," Sean goes on.

"Then we're practically neighbors," I say. What a trip.

The old woman, who's introduced as So-sa, doesn't speak English, but she seems happy to see Sean. She pulls us to another table under a bamboo and thatch pavilion, where one of her granddaughters, whose name I don't catch, pours tea.

"I really want you to meet Tina," Sean says to me, "because she might have some ideas about your tea cake. While we're waiting for her to arrive, why don't you show it to So-sa? You never know . . ."

When I pull it out of my bag and lay it on the table, the old woman gasps and then scurries away as though she's seen a ghost. The boy from Arcadia laughs. "Grandma . . . She's so superstitious . . ."

The woman lingers at the edge of the main house, peeking out at us, wiping her eyes, then disappearing again. Sean looks at me and shrugs. The granddaughter pours more tea, but the whole thing is weird.

"Is she crying? Maybe we should go," I say, rising.

Before Sean can respond, the old woman sidles back to us and angrily addresses him.

"She thinks my father has sent us," he translates, but he sounds as confused as I feel.

"Your father?"

"My father and this family have a long history together."

She gestures up the mountain and rattles off a stream of sentences directed at me.

"She wants you to go with her," he translates, obviously editing. "She says the two of you must go alone."

"What does she want?" I ask nervously. It's one thing to be in a remote village with Sean, but it's quite another to go off with some crazy old bat.

"She says no men are allowed," Sean answers, but his voice goes up at the end as if in question. "You'll be fine." His words are hardly reassuring.

"I don't want to go anywhere—"

Then the old woman snatches my tea cake and runs away! Without thinking, I take off after her, but she's a lot stronger than she looks. She's sure-footed as she dashes up the narrow mountain path. I'm a lot younger, but I'm not a farmer and I'm not accustomed to the altitude. I have to grab on to the limbs of trees and scraggly weeds to keep from falling. Higher and higher we go. I should have turned back after five minutes, but now it's too late because now I truly *am* in the middle of nowhere. In the forest. Picking my way through a spidery network of pathways. Monkeys screeching. Birds calling alarms. A half hour, an hour, longer. I can't lose sight of the old woman, because if I do, not only will my tea cake be gone but I'll be hopelessly lost. My lungs burn, my thighs ache, and all I can think about are my mom and dad, how much I love them, and how broken they'll be if I don't come home.

The old woman stops in a small clearing, finally allowing me to catch up. I'm gasping for breath, but she's fine. She gives me a steady look, takes my upper arm with a firm hand, and turns me toward the view. She holds up the tea cake and then points to the mountains. Instantly I see it—the *V*'s, the terraces, the stream. The realization makes my knees buckle. Is the old woman my mother? She can't possibly be.

She practically drags me up the hill. We're climbing and climbing. The whole time she's jabbering something that sounds like *a-ma-a-ma-a-ma*, stopping occasionally to point at her belly and then up the mountain. Pretty soon the path disappears entirely. Up ahead I see a boulder—the squiggly circle I know so well. No one could find this place without the map, because it's so well hidden. The old woman tucks my tea cake inside her tunic. Like a crab she edges around the boulder with me right behind her. I'm shaking badly, but I make it to the other side.

Camphor trees centuries old create a canopy above us, sheltering several tea trees. The old woman pulls out the tea cake, but I don't need her to point out the tree that's been the symbol I've dreamed and wondered about my entire life. Up in the boughs a woman picks leaves, which confirms my impression that this grove, while hidden, is both well cared for and private, as though only these two have ever been here. I start to feel something. Memories. Although I can't possibly have a single memory of this place. Then, from deep within me, a profound sense of love radiating out to everything around me complemented by reciprocal waves of love coming at me, enveloping me. All that seems impossible too. I'm both perplexed and overwhelmed.

Finally, the woman in the tree notices us. Her eyes widen. Then she becomes so still it's as if her heart has stopped beating and her muscles have frozen. At last she begins to move, slowly climbing down, stepping gracefully from limb to limb. When she reaches the ground, she looks from the old woman to me. A moment of confusion. Then recognition. I know her too, because I've seen traces of her in my face in the mirror.

My mother. My a-ma.

ACKNOWLEDGMENTS

The Tea Girl of Hummingbird Lane begins with a dream and the Akha aphorism *No coincidence, no story*. The same could be said for the writing of this novel. I was on vacation and woke up one morning with half a title in my head: The Something-Something of Hummingbird Lane. I didn't know what the "something" would be until it came to me at an event hosted by Susan McBeth of Adventures by the Book, where I spoke. She had arranged to have Kenneth Cohen do a Chinese tea ceremony and tasting, featuring Pu'er, before my presentation. By the end of the day not only did I have a title but I knew what the historic background for the new novel would be.

As I began planning a trip to Xishuangbanna for spring tea-picking season, Chui Tsang, then president of Santa Monica College, asked my husband what I was working on. When Chui heard it had something to do with tea, he asked, "Could it be Pu'er?" It just so happened that the previous week Chui and his wife, Echo, had been to a Chinese banquet where they were seated next to Wanyu (Elaine) Luo, who is the largest Pu'er importer into the United States. The following week, Angelina Shih drove Echo and me out to Hacienda Heights to meet Elaine at the home of one of her friends. That woman, Linda Louie, owns Bana Tea Company, which deals primarily in Pu'er. (I advise all interested readers to visit her website: www.banateacompany.com.) We spent the afternoon sampling different types of Pu'er, including one that was fifty years old. Elaine reminisced about growing up in the tea mountains and how she came to want to preserve and promote the traditional methods of making and drinking this rare tea, while Linda spoke eloquently about the history, culture, and world of connoisseurship that has developed around this leaf.

At the end of the afternoon, I asked Linda if I could e-mail her for advice about whom I should meet and where I should go on my trip. She said—and remember, we had known each other for only a couple of hours—"Why don't you come with me on my next buying trip?" which happened to coincide exactly with the dates I had already scheduled. So off we went, first to Guangzhou, where we visited the Fangcun Tea Market, and then to Yunnan to Jinghong, Menghai, Nannuo, and Yiwu, with side adventures to Luoshuidong and other villages. To all these people who helped set the story in motion, I am deeply grateful. To Linda, in particular, I must add further thanks for being my guide at the World Tea Expo (twice!), introducing me to so many incredible people who helped to make the novel immeasurably better (including Angie Lee, owner of 1001 Plateaus Tea), her hours of translation, and training my palate. Linda is a dynamic and tireless advocate for Pu'er, and I'm now very lucky to call her my friend.

Traveling with Linda and me were Jeni Dodd of Jeni's Tea and her partner, Buddha Tamang, owner of the Himalayan Bardu Valley Tea estate, a plantation in Nepal. What adventures we had! Many thanks to: Li Lin for his cautious driving; Tea Master Chan (Vesper) Guo Yi for his enthusiasm, knowledge, and taking us through his massive tea-fermenting warehouse; Mr. Liu for inviting us to a tea pavilion high on a mountain, where we sampled many teas, looked through drying sheds, and learned about the GPS systems now monitoring the oldest tea trees; Chen Xinge, the host of Fujin Ji guesthouse on Nannuo Mountain, for teaching us how to press and wrap tea cakes and decorate the rice paper wrappers, as well as for his beautiful singing of Akha love songs; his girlfriend, mother, and daughter for making sure we were properly fed and giving us much tea to taste and gossip to mull over; Ah-bu, a young Akha woman, for sharing not only her story but also those she'd collected from elders over the years; Wu Yan Fei, Ah-bu's sister-in-law, for walking us up steep hillsides to visit ancient tea trees and showing us the village's swing. This family also taught me how to kill the green and knead leaves. (Hard work!)

In Yiwu, we met Zheng Bi Nung, the owner of a thriving tea factory, where close to thirty women were sorting tea a leaf at a time. He gave us lunch (which included one of many chickens whose necks would be snapped for us) and recounted the story of Lü Li Zhen and his quest to make Truly Simple Elegant. We visited Yu Xiu Fen, an extraordinary tea grower and businesswoman, whose teas are given as gifts to people in the highest levels of the Chinese government. We spoke with farmers—in their homes, by the sides of roads, and on remote hilltops—as well as other tea merchants and connoisseurs. To all of them, thank you so very much for your knowledge and expertise, as well as your willingness to share the inspiring, yet often difficult or sad, details of your personal lives. Thank you to Ginny Boyce, travel agent extraordinaire, for getting me to the tea mountains and back again.

I'd like to acknowledge the following authors for their insights into the history, culture, and etiquette of tea: John Blofeld (*The Chinese Art of Tea*), Beatrice Hohenegger (*Liquid Jade;* and editor of and contributor to *Steeped in History: The Art of Tea,* along with contributors Steven D. Owyoung and John E. Wills, Jr.), Lu Yü (*The Classic of Tea*), Alan Macfarlane and Iris Macfarlane (*Green Gold: The Empire of Tea*), Victor H. Mair and Erling Hoh (*The True History of Tea*), and Jinghong Zhang (*Puer Tea: Ancient Caravans and Urban Chic*). In 2008, *The Art of Tea* published a special issue on Pu'er with articles on different tea mountains, the tea crisis, and international pricing by Bao Zhuo, Chen Zheng Wei, Chen Zhi Tong, Aaron Fisher, Heidi Kyser, Guang-Chung Lee, Li Jun, Luo Ying Yin, Yang Kai, Ye Huanzhi, Zeng Zhixian, and Zhou Yu. Christina Larson's article, "Rich Man, Pu'er Man," for ChinaFile explored issues of authenticity and pricing, while Mark Jenkins's piece for *National Geographic* gave me interesting details about the Tea Horse Road.

One day, out of the blue, I received an e-mail from Arris Han, asking to interview me, as a Chinese American, about my personal interest in tea for a project she was working on. We then pursued a lively correspondence, talking all things tea. Online, I found interesting articles about Yunnan's tea plantations, *huigan,* and cultivation, posted by the UNESCO World Heritage Centre, Bev Byrnes, and Peter Peverelli. The May 15, 2015, issue of *Bon Appétit* explored the booming interest in tea in the United States. At the World Tea Expo, I attended a tasting hosted by the Hunan Tea Company, where I learned about yellow-hair tea. Then it was on to seminars on the chemical mysteries of Pu'er (presented by Kevin Gascoyne), the social history of tea (presented by Bruce Richardson and Jane Pettigrew), and mixology (presented by Abigail St. Clair).

The scientific writings of Jeffrey B. Blumberg, Bradley W. Bolling, and Chung-yen Oliver Chen greatly contributed to those sections of the novel devoted to the purported health aspects of tea. Dr. Selena Ahmed, an ethnobiologist, has been gracious and helpful. I've heard her speak several times and was fortunate to attend her lecture at the Natural History Museum in Los Angeles, which included taste tests of cocktails using tea and other plant-based bitters and infusions. She and photographer Michael Freeman traveled the entire length of the Tea Horse Road and produced a stunning book called, not surprisingly, *Tea Horse Road*. The abstract for the multidisciplinary and multisponsored study on the effects of global climate change on ancient tea trees of Yunnan, of which Dr. Ahmed is a part, is the clear inspiration for Haley's work. I thank Dr. Ahmed for her brilliant mind, her dedication, and for answering my countless questions.

I am hugely indebted to the writings of Paul W. Lewis, who served as a missionary to the Akha with the American Baptist Foreign Mission Society in Burma from 1947 to 1966, and then went to northern Thailand in 1968 to continue his study of the Akha as an anthropologist. His *Ethnographic Notes on the Akhas of Burma* and *Hani Cultural Themes* (written with Bai Bibo) were invaluable resources. The writings of Deleu Choopoh and Marianne Naess ("Deuleu: A Life-History of an Akha Woman" in *Development or Domestication? Indigenous Peoples of Southeast Asia*), Thomas S. Mullaney (*Coming to Terms with the Nation*), Chih-yu Shih (*Negotiating Ethnicity in China*), and Zhang Weiwen and Zeng Qingnan (*In Search of China's Minorities*) further developed my understanding of the Akha. If you're interested in learning more about the Akha's culture, I can recommend the following websites: the Akha Heritage Foundation (with special thanks to Matthew McDaniel, whose article on Akha beliefs, lifestyle, and their concept of seeing themselves as one link in the long chain of life I used almost verbatim), Akha Minority—Facts and Details, Ethnic China, Virtual Hilltribe Museum, and The Peoples of the World: Akha.

Many years ago, I met Xinran, who has collected hundreds of stories from women in China. I am a huge admirer of her work, and I'm honored that she's helped me on various projects over the years. Her book, *Message from an Unknown Chinese Mother*, is powerful and heartbreaking, and a must-read for families with children adopted from China. Articles by Barbara Demick and Laura Fitzpatrick provided information on Chinese babies who've been stolen from their families for illegal adoption and other aspects of the dark side of the One Child policy. Shifting to the American experience, I'd like to acknowledge Kay Bratt for *Silent Tears: A Journey of Hope in a Chinese Orphanage*, and Jenny Bowen, founder of the Half the Sky Foundation, for *Wish You Happy Forever*. After I finished writing the novel, someone recommended that I watch *Somewhere Between*, a powerful documentary about teenage adoptees, one of whom goes to China and finds her birth mother. I would like to recommend it to all of you as well.

Early in my career, I was invited to speak around the country at various chapters of Families with Children from China. To the many moms in that organization and to all the moms of adoptees I know personally, my heartfelt thanks. For special mention, I'd like to acknowledge Martha Groves, who shared with me not only her own story but those of many others during our interviews and e-mails. The articles she's written for the *Los Angeles Times* were particularly insightful. Over the years, I've also met several young women who were adopted from China, but for this novel I wanted to reach out more broadly across the country to find those willing to share their experiences with me. I'd like to give enormous thanks to Charlotte Cotter and Kathryn Holz, both adoptees and board members of China's Children International, for the hours they spent answering my questions. For nearly a decade now, I've had an e-mail correspondence with Terrence May, who lives in Colorado. He and his adopted daughter, Lianne May, shared with me very different perspectives from different periods in their lives. Lillian Poon wrote to me about her experience as a Chinese American adoptee, while Juli Fraga's *New York Times* article about being an adoptee who has now given birth to a daughter gave me additional insights. To be clear, the character of Haley is not representative of *all* Chinese adoptees. Haley is her own person with her own set of problems. That said, many of the things that she feels and the words she speaks (as well as those shared in the group therapy session) come from young women traveling on the interesting road of Chinese adoption. Haley's story wouldn't be what it is without their help.

I spend a lot of time in the San Gabriel Valley, but I relied on friends and family with specialized knowledge to help me with details. I ate my way from block to block with foodies Holly Hawkins, Sandy Law, and Angelina Shih. My cousin, Mara Leong-Nichols, gave me the lowdown on what it would have been like for Haley growing up in Pasadena. Nick Mook, truly the tree whisperer of Southern California, advised me on the drought and the parasites attacking our weakened trees. The writings of Andrew Khouri, Tim Logan, E. Scott Reckard, Frank Shyong, and Claire Spiegel helped me capture the details of the Chinese influence on Southern California real estate and the issues affecting Asian American high school students.

Every detail matters to me, and I try to be as accurate as possible. (All mistakes are my own.) I learned a lot from the works of the following writers and scholars: Denise Eliot (on the stresses on Asian American teenagers), Mei-yin Lee and Dr. Florian Knothe (on ethnic minority textiles), Allen T. Cheng (on the queen of cardboard), and Leta Hong Fincher, Don Lee, Mary Kay Magistad, and Julie Makinen (on the phenomenon of "leftover women"). In *Women, Gender and Rural Development in China,* I found an interesting piece on the Care for Girls Campaign by Lisa Eklund and another on reproduction and real property in rural China by Laurel Bossen.

I've now written at length about all the people who inspired me with their wisdom, grace, and expertise—whether in person or through their writings—but I hope you'll allow me a few more lines to thank the people who helped send the novel into the world: my agent, Sandy Dijkstra, and the others who work in her office, were loyal and passionate; Susan Moldow appeared as a fairy godmother; Nan Graham warmly welcomed me to Scribner; Kathryn Belden, my new editor, brought a keen eye and a kind heart to the page; and everyone else at Scribner impressed me with their hard work, exquisite aesthetics, and enthusiasm. Thank you to Bob Loomis for holding my hand and never letting go. At home, I wouldn't be able to do the things I do if not for the help of Nicole Bruno, Maria Lemus, and, on occasion, Stephanie Donan. My sister, Clara Sturak, has my back, and I follow her editorial suggestions without question. My mother, Carolyn See, passed away as I was polishing the final draft of the manuscript. I feel fortunate that I was able to read most of the novel to her. I will miss her love and support. None of this would matter to me if not for my sons, Alexander and Christopher; daughter-in-law, Elizabeth; grandson, Henry; and husband, Richard Kendall. My deepest gratitude goes to you for the strength, inspiration, love, and teasing you send my way every day.

ABOUT THE AUTHOR

Lisa See is the author of the *New York Times* bestselling novels *Snow Flower and the Secret Fan, Peony in Love, Shanghai Girls, China Dolls,* and *Dreams of Joy,* which debuted at #1. Ms. See is also the author of the *New York Times* bestseller *On Gold Mountain,* which tells the story of her Chinese American family's settlement in Los Angeles. Ms. See was honored as National Woman of the Year by the Organization of Chinese American Women in 2001 and was the recipient of the Chinese American Museum's Historymakers Award in fall 2003.

A SCRIBNER READING GROUP GUIDE

The Tea Girl of Hummingbird Lane

Lisa See

This reading group guide for The Tea Girl of Hummingbird Lane *includes discussion questions, ideas for enhancing your book club, and a conversation with Lisa See. The suggested questions are intended to help your reading group find new and interesting angles and topics for your discussion. We hope that these ideas, along with Lisa See's own responses to questions about the novel, will enrich your conversation and increase your enjoyment of the book.*

Topics and Questions for Discussion

1. Discuss the significance of the epigraph. The *Book of Songs* is the oldest extant collection of Chinese poetry, written between the seventh and eleventh centuries B.C. What kind of resonance does it have today?
2. *The Tea Girl of Hummingbird Lane* begins with an Akha aphorism, *No coincidence, no story.* What are the major coincidences in the story? Are they believable? How important are they in influencing your reaction to the novel as a whole?
3. Perhaps the most shocking moment in the novel comes with the birth of the twins and what happens to them. A-ma explains that "only animals, demons, and spirits give birth to litters. If a sow gives birth to one piglet, then both must be killed at once. If a dog gives birth to one puppy, then they too must be killed immediately" (pages 27–28). The traditions surrounding twins are very harsh, to say the least, but were you able to understand what happens to them within the context of Akha culture? How does this moment change Li-yan's view of Akha Law, and what are the consequences? Are there any aspects of the Akha culture that you admire?
4. What is Li-yan's first reaction when she sees her land? Why does A-ma believe the tea garden is so important? Why does A-ma believe that the trees are sacred? What is the significance of the mother tree?
5. San-pa and Li-yan's relationship ends tragically and causes them both great pain. Is what happens between them fate, or is it bad luck? In your opinion, does their community's negativity about their union shape the outcome of their marriage? Does his death change your feelings about him?
6. Can the experience Li-yan's village has with selling Pu'er be thought of as a microcosm for globalization? Why or why not? Are all the changes to the village positive? Given

all we hear about China being a global economic superpower, were you surprised that the novel starts in 1988?

7. As a midwife, A-ma occupies a position of relative power on the mountain, although as "first among women" (page 4), she still comes after every man. Can such a traditional role for women be truly empowering? In the context of their society, what are the limits and expanse of A-ma's power?
8. This novel uses a number of devices to tell Haley's story, including letters, a transcript of a therapy session, and homework assignments. It isn't until the final chapter, however, that you hear Haley in her own pure voice and see the world entirely from her point of view. Did this style of storytelling enrich your experience of the narrative? Did it make you more curious about Haley?
9. In the chapter transcribing a group therapy session for Chinese American adoptees, which Haley attends, many of the patients have mixed feelings about their adoptive and birth parents. Were you surprised by their anger? Did reading this novel affect your feelings about transnational adoption?
10. The three most significant mother-daughter relationships in the novel are those between A-ma and Li-yan, Constance and Haley, and Li-yan and Haley. The connection between Li-yan and Haley, although arguably the emotional center of the novel, exists despite the absence of a relationship: though the two women think a great deal about each other, they do not meet until the very end of the story. How does this relationship in absence compare to the real-life relationships between A-ma and Li-yan and Constance and Haley?
11. What are the formal and informal ways in which Li-yan is educated? How are they different from the ways other members of her family were educated? What role does Teacher Zhang play in Li-yan's life and how does it change over the years? How important is education in Haley's life?

12. When she meets Jin, Li-yan is more experienced and much older than she was when she fell in love with San-pa. How are the two men different? What do you think Li-yan learns from her first marriage?
13. Almost everyone in the novel has a secret: Li-yan, A-ma, San-pa, Mr. Huang, Deh-ja, Ci-teh, Teacher Zhang, Mrs. Chang, and Jin. How do those secrets impact each character? How are those secrets revealed and what are the results, particularly for Li-yan and Ci-teh's relationship? The only person who doesn't have a secret of major significance is Haley. What does that say about her?
14. When Li-yan returns to her village to confront Ci-teh, the ruma tells the women that Li-yan is still Akha even though she has a new home and lifestyle. How do questions of identity, especially as they relate to Li-yan's status as an ethnic minority, play into the events of the novel? How does Li-yan's identity shift? Do her nicknames, especially her American nickname, inform this shift?
15. By the time Li-yan and Haley meet, each has been searching for the other for many years. However, Haley already has a family and an adoptive mother. Is there room for Haley to have two mothers? Do you think Li-yan and Haley will relate to each other as mother and child? Or will their relationship be something different? What do you suppose Haley and Li-yan will talk about first?

Enhance Your Book Club

1. Sample Pu'er as a group. How does it compare to your experience of other kinds of tea?
2. If you have access to one, visit your local Chinese history or art museum.
3. Consider reading Lisa See's *Snow Flower and the Secret Fan*, which follows a lifelong friendship between two women, members of the Yao ethnic minority, in nineteenth-century China.
4. Lisa's website, www.LisaSee.com, features more information for book clubs and readers about *The Tea Girl of Hummingbird Lane* and Lisa's other books. Visit "Step Inside *The Tea Girl of Hummingbird Lane*" to learn more about tea, the Akha, and adoption—through video, photographs, and articles. Enjoy video interviews with Lisa and visit Yunnan through the photographs she took on her research trip. You can also find out how to have your own tea-tasting book club.

A Conversation with Lisa See

What was your inspiration for the novel?

I'd been thinking about writing about China's One Child policy and transnational adoption for something like twenty years, but I hadn't been able to figure out *my* way into the story. One day, I was walking to the movies with my husband and I saw up ahead of us an older white couple with their adopted Chinese teenage daughter between them. Her hair was up in a ponytail, and, as it swung back and forth, I had a vision of her as a fox spirit. In Chinese tradition, fox spirits can be naughty and mischievous. They're always doing things like sneaking into a scholar's study late at night, while he's preparing for the imperial exams, and then having sex with him. See what I mean about naughty and mischievous? But in a fox spirit's best moments, she has the ability to bring great love and to help create families. So, when I saw that fox tail swinging back and forth, I thought, yes, this girl is like a fox spirit in the sense that through her presence she'd brought great love and helped create a family. That was the moment when I knew what my next novel would be. It turned out, though, that the Akha ethnic minority doesn't have fox spirits in their culture. That was a big disappointment! Everywhere I went, I kept asking Akha people if they had some type of spirit that had a long tail, but no. In the end, I could only carry the inspiration of that fox spirit in my heart.

What's your writing routine like? Is it the same for every novel?

There's typically something I've been thinking about for a long time, like adoption from China, the "beautiful girls" of the 1930s I wrote about in *Shanghai Girls*, or the lovesick maidens that I wrote about in *Peony in Love.* Sometimes, I don't know my personal way into a story, but then an image or a moment opens up everything for me. Once that happens, I become obsessed.

I usually start with a seven- to ten-page outline. I know the characters, the emotions, and the time period. Then I begin to do the research. Without question, research is my favorite part of the process. I never know what I'm going to find. There are days when I'm hidden in the UCLA Research Library and I'll come across something and think, Oh, I've got to use *that!* What this means is that the research helps build the plot.

My characters are living in a real world and in real time. But writing characters who are living in history also means they're stuck with that history. With *The Tea Girl of Hummingbird Lane*, I couldn't move the 2008 Beijing Olympics, the global recession, the bursting of the Pu'er tea bubble, or when electricity first made it to the tea mountains. I look at these things as signposts. I may not know what will happen to the characters day-to-day, but they're always moving toward the next real-life signpost.

You went to China to do research. During the course of that research, did anything you learned change the course of the narrative? What was the most memorable moment from your travels?

About a billion things changed the course of the narrative! It's an absolute must to go to the places I'm writing about. I want to see, hear, smell, taste, and feel everything. Many writers tell me they don't do this. They want the Miami or Timbuktu of their imaginations. But for me, stepping off a plane and smelling coal smoke, eating a Dai-ethnic-minority meal that features different kinds of moss and algae, or "killing the green" and coming away with sore arms because it's such hard work are not things that should come out of a book, nor are they things I should just make up because I want the Yunnan of my imagination. I want the real Yunnan! And I want to give that to readers. So, truly, every single thing that happens on one of my research trips changes the narrative, but I'll tell you about one in particular.

Before I went to China, I looked at all twenty-six ethnic minorities who live in Yunnan. Some of them I could easily dismiss. Maybe they lived by a lake and not in the tea mountains. Maybe they didn't have a tea culture. Anyway, by the time I left for China, I'd narrowed my list down to five ethnic minorities. I was particularly interested in the Dai people. In fact, I was 99 percent sure that I'd be writing about the Dai. Then I met an Akha family. The daughter reminded me a lot of myself in the sense that she loved to ask questions and loved to tell stories. We were in what felt like the middle of nowhere, sitting under a makeshift pavilion, drinking her family's exquisite teas as she told stories about her mother and grandmother. She'd also collected stories from the elders in her village and on her side of Nannuo Mountain. Her own personal story was pretty amazing too, and in many ways it became part of Li-yan's life story. By the time lunchtime rolled around on that first day, I knew I'd be writing about the Akha, which meant all that other research went right out the window.

If you want to know more about the trip, I have photos on my website. Just go to the "Step Inside *The Tea Girl of Hummingbird Lane*" section of my website.

In some ways, *The Tea Girl of Hummingbird Lane* reads like a historical novel, and many readers were surprised that it opens in 1988. Do the Akha still follow their traditions? I was particularly shocked by the characters' treatment of "human rejects."

Readers tell me all the time that they keep flipping back to the start of Part I, which states the story begins in 1988. They can't believe that people didn't have electricity or still lived in such a harsh environment then. We're lucky to live where and when we do, but life is still hard for great numbers of people around the globe. Every day another 250,000 people move out of extreme poverty, 285,000 get access to clean drinking water, and 300,000 get electricity—all for the first time.

The Akha still follow many of their traditions, but those have also changed or been modified over time. The traditions associated with engagement and weddings used to transpire over many weeks, but people don't have time for that now. The various wedding traditions are still followed, but each part is much shorter. The Akha also still celebrate the Swing Festival and build the village gate each year.

As I wrote in the novel, the Akha in China no longer practice twin infanticide. I know that this scene is shocking, and it was very hard for me to write. If I may, I'd like to try to put the practice into perspective. There are cultures around the world that have revered and celebrated the birth of twins, while other cultures have killed twins or killed one of the twins to bring the world back into what they consider alignment with nature. (The idea that a woman shouldn't give birth to litters is in no way unique to the Akha culture.) But again, I'd like to remind my readers that we live in a unique time and place compared to most of the world's population.

For centuries, having twins was considered to be very dangerous for the mother. This was a physical as well as an economic issue. First, would the mother survive? Second, would she be able to care for two infants? Often, the stronger baby was chosen to survive. In the case of fraternal twins, if there was a girl and a boy, that usually meant that the boy got to live.

I was talking to a book club on Skype one day, and a member of the group, a woman from Eastern Europe, told us that when she got pregnant with twins, her mother pinned charms on her clothes to protect her and the babies from the evil eye. She wasn't allowed out of the house for her entire pregnancy, because carrying twins was seen as an embarrassment and shameful. In her culture, twins were also considered a source of sorrow and pain, since many of them were born too early to survive outside the womb. Even in this country, it's only been in the last twenty or thirty years that prenatal and preemie care has improved so much that survival rates for mothers and babies have risen dramatically.

International adoption is a central theme of the novel. How did you capture the complex feelings of international adoptees?

I started with the empathy I feel for their issues of identity. In many ways, we share a mirror image of the experience. Most girls who've been adopted from China are the only Chinese faces in their families, and they experience American culture and traditions exclusively. I have red hair and freckles, but I grew up in a very large Chinese-American family in which I had one of the few white faces. So how do we identify ourselves? The people around us are our mirror. They tell us who we are. But it's more than that. When I was a kid, I wasn't just surrounded by my Chinese relatives. I also played in Chinatown, ate Chinese food, and went to Chinese weddings, funerals, and one-month birthday parties. As a result, I've often wondered where I fit in. Am I American, Chinese American, or just a mutt? Many of the young women I interviewed have asked themselves a variation of that question: Am I Chinese, American, Chinese American, or something else?

I was also really struck by the label of the grateful-but-angry adoptee. I talked to moms, dads, and young women about it. Over time, I came to the same conclusion that Haley does in the novel. That it's less about being grateful-but-angry than it is about being grateful-and-sad. This was summed up for me by one young woman who said, "I know I'm the most precious person in my family, but I wasn't precious enough for my birth family to keep me as their one child."

How did you approach the group therapy chapter? Did it involve research?

We have a lot of friends who adopted girls from China, and some of my Chinese relatives adopted daughters from China, but I also wanted to find young women around the country who would share their experiences with me. Some of them I met quite randomly. When I was in Florida to give a talk, the woman seated next to me at the luncheon mentioned that her niece was adopted from China. Another time I was in New York to give a presentation at a museum. When two young women came through the line to get their books signed, they happened to mention that they'd been adopted from China. Whenever something like that happened, I'd ask if I could send them some questions. I had a list of about a dozen of them. Some were very specific and easy to answer: Were you sick when you arrived in the U.S.? But other questions were more like topics. I wanted their thoughts about the grateful-but-angry adoptee label, if they felt connected at all to China, and if they or their parents had ever been the target of racist or unthinking comments. ("How much did she cost?") What I got back were letters thirty to fifty pages long. These young women completely opened their hearts and shared their experiences with me. I'll be forever grateful to them for that.

And I'm happy to say that we've stayed in contact with each other. Last summer, I received photos from one young woman's graduation from Yale. I heard from a family I'd interviewed that their daughter called after reading the group therapy chapter to say that I'd used a couple things she'd told me. They'd never known she felt that way. They had such a great conversation that she ended up sharing the answers she'd written to me with them. That, in turn, opened an even deeper series of conversations. I feel very honored to have been a part of that. But I'd have to say that the most amazing thing happened when I was waiting in the green room about to give my very first talk about the novel when I received an e-mail from one of the young women I'd interviewed. She'd just found her birth family in China! Interviewing and getting to know these young women, who are so thoughtful and open about their lives, has been one of the most rewarding experiences of my entire writing career.

Did writing the novel change your relationship with tea?

Yep! I've become a total tea snob! I've always been a tea drinker, but now I only drink Pu'er. I drink raw Pu'er in the morning, because the fresh, grassy taste feels so bright and cheerful. As the day wears on, I switch over to ripe Pu'er—one that's been aged over many years and has a mellow taste. Think of the forest floor or antique wood. Sometimes after dinner, I'll make small cups for my husband and me of a very special Pu'er that was made from the leaves of a single one-thousand-year-old tree.

I really liked the character of Deh-ja. Can you tell us a little about her journey?

I'm so glad you asked about Deh-ja. I love her! So you'll never guess what happened. After she was banished, I thought that was the end of her character. Years later, when Li-yan was walking to Thailand, who did she bump into? Deh-ja! That totally surprised me, but it made me very happy to see her again. Then, many years after that, when Li-yan and Jin were on the steps of the Social Welfare Institute in Menghai, who was there? Deh-ja! Again! I was even more surprised. She wasn't in my plot outline, and yet she kept elbowing her way into the story. As Li-yan says to her, the fact that they kept bumping into each other in the most unlikely places had to mean something. For Li-yan, that meant taking Deh-ja home with her. For me, it meant Deh-ja *needed* to be in the story. And for Deh-ja, it meant that her persistence had won.

Can you talk a bit about the reunion between Li-yan and Haley? Why did you choose to end the novel that way, and would you ever consider writing a sequel?

This is probably the number one question I get from readers, and I love it, because I get to give an answer that I hope shows a bit about my creative process and how I think about creativity. My editor and I talked a lot about the ending. Should there be, at the very least, another chapter? But as we talked about it, we kept coming back to the question of what would happen in real life? Haley would say, "Hi." Li-yan would say, "Hi." Then Haley would say, "I think I'm your daughter," and Li-yan would say, "I think I'm your mother." Then what? In real life, they'd talk about what had happened to each of them over the past twenty years. But readers already know all that. I couldn't write forward for the next twenty years or even the next year, because *The Tea Girl of Hummingbird Lane* ends in 2016. (Maybe I'll write a sequel in twenty years. . . .)

For that reason, I decided to end the book where I did. Not only that, I wound up cutting about ten pages from the last chapter. But there are hints of what could or should happen. In my original draft, Sean/Xian-rong proposed to Haley, she said yes, and they planned what would happen next for them. That seemed too tied up in a bow to me, plus Haley is still quite young and I would hate for her to abandon her education or her ambitions in any way. (Not that Sean would let her do that. He's not that kind of guy.) But I can tell you for sure that they will live happily ever after. We also have a hint of what will happen with the mother tree and the hidden grove. In the scene where A-ma and Li-yan are in the grove, A-ma asks who's going to help them. Don't you think that Haley, who's just about to climb the mountain, will be that person?

But for me there was an even bigger reason to leave things a bit open-ended. We tend to think of reading as a passive activity: you sit and read someone else's words. But I think reading is an incredibly creative process. I may have written the scene, characters, and plot, but readers are the ones who paint the pictures in their heads. And anyone who's in a book club knows that each person reads and interprets stories, characters, and motives differently. When we read, we're drawing on our childhoods, on our feelings about our mothers and fathers, sisters and brothers—on your own experience if you were an only child, what your education was like, where you grew up, what kind of work you do, and if you were having a good or bad week when you read the novel. You're painting pictures in your head that are influenced by the writer, but each picture is unique and yours alone. I love that!

When I get e-mail from readers about this topic, I typically write a shorter version of this explanation, ending with asking what they think should happen next. I've received some amazing e-mails from people who've come up with incredible ideas, with things I never imagined. One woman even wrote a ten-page single-spaced letter with what she thought could happen next. She had enough ideas for two sequels! It's things like that which make me feel like I was right about ending the novel the way I did. Read! Be creative! Imagine!

The significance of mother-daughter relationships is a thread throughout your work. How do you think that theme is further developed in this novel? Why do you continue to return to it?

The Chinese written character for "mother love" is composed of two elements: one part means *love*, the other part means *pain*. I've been on a personal journey as I've explored "mother love"—not just the written character but the emotions—over the years. My thoughts have evolved as I've been influenced by where I am in my life as a woman, mother, and daughter.

When I first wrote about "mother love" in *Snow Flower and the Secret Fan*, I thought I understood it completely. A daughter would look at her mother—the person who was binding her feet in the name of love—and think *love* and *pain*. But when I began working on *Peony in Love*, my point of view changed completely. It wasn't about how a daughter looks at her mother; it's about how a mother looks at her children. I thought about my own experiences as a young mother. When Alexander was about two months old, he got one of those terrible ear infections. He was so sick. I remember walking around the house in the middle of the night with him whimpering on my shoulder and thinking to myself, *If only I can get through tonight.* I didn't know that in just a few years he was going to learn to drive! Now that's real terror! Waiting up for a teenager to come home—man, oh, man—*love* and *pain.* And mother love doesn't end just because our kids grow up, go to college, get jobs, get married, and have children of their own. That's when real life fully starts happening to them. Sometimes very bad or sad things happen to them. But what can we, as mothers, do at that point? We can't prop our kids on our shoulders to comfort them. All we can do is take their pain and carry it in our hearts. That's a mother's love.

Now I've evolved yet again. As I'm sure you noticed, *The Tea Girl of Hummingbird Lane* is filled with mothers and daughters. There's Li-yan and her mother, Li-yan and her daughter, Haley and her adoptive mother, Constance and her mother. There's also Jin's mother, and the two Akha mothers—Deh-ja and Ci-teh—all of whom are central to the plot. I clearly had mothers on the brain.

One of the things that's mystifying and magical to me is how writing can be a reflection of what's happening in my life, even if I don't necessarily understand it at the time. I was twelve days from turning in the final draft of the novel when my mom was diagnosed with cancer. She died ten days later. Then I was busy putting together the memorial, dismantling her life, and dealing with my own grief. It wasn't until a couple of months later, when I was looking at page proofs, that I saw that this novel is also very much about mother love, even though it isn't spelled out as such. In this case, it's about separation and loss. The separation between Li-yan and Haley. The separation between A-ma and Li-yan. The separation between Deh-ja and her babies. The feelings of separation that Constance often feels when it comes to her own mother as well as to Haley. Even though my mother didn't yet have her diagnosis when I was writing the novel, I think that somewhere deep inside I knew what was coming, and all that came out on the page. Mother love—*love* and *pain.*